PRAISE FOR STEPHANIE BARRON'S
BEING A JANE AUSTEN MYSTERY

Jane and the Madness of Lord Byron

"The incomparable Stephanie Barron spins an irresistible tale as she ventures once more into the glittering world of the Regency. Featuring Lord Byron at his maddest, baddest, and most dangerous to know, Barron's latest has Jane Austen crossing swords with England's most notorious poet in mesmerizing style. From its deftly crafted mystery to its pitch-perfect Regency tone, this book is a delight." —Deanna Raybourn

"Take two literary titans, one Prince Regent, a dead debutante, and nineteenth-century Brighton . . . and you have the perfect set-up for sleuthing. Another fabulous adventure with Jane Austen!" —Lauren Willig

"Superb . . . Barron's ability to capture Austen's tone helps make this series one of the more literary and enjoyable of the pseudo-Austen oeuvre." —*Publishers Weekly* (starred)

"[The] writing is so joyous and clever and entertaining that it might have been written by the great Austen herself."
  —*The Denver Post*

Jane and the Barque of Frailty

"Barron does an admirable job not only with the [Jane Austen] mysteries, but also in mimicking Austen's style."
  —*The Tampa Tribune*

"Satisfying right to the last revelation . . . Like Regency great Georgette Heyer, the author excels at both period detail and modern verve. Aping Austen's cool, precise and very famous voice is a hard trick to pull off, but Barron manages it with aplomb." —*Publishers Weekly*

"Charming, literate and unequaled in its dissection of Regency-era social injustices." —*Kirkus Reviews*

Jane and His Lordship's Legacy

"Considered by some as the best of the 'neo-Austens,' Barron gets high marks for authenticity and wit." —*Booklist*

Jane and the Ghosts of Netley

"The latest installment in Stephanie Barron's charming series . . . [is] a first-rate historical mystery. Barron writes a lively adventure that puts warm flesh on historical bones. The nice thing is she does so in a literary style that would not put Jane Austen's nose out of joint."
—*The New York Times Book Review*

"A wonderfully intricate plot full of espionage and intrigue . . . The Austen voice, both humorous and fanciful, with shades of *Northanger Abbey*, rings true as always. Once again Barron shows why she leads the pack of neo–Jane Austens."
—*Publishers Weekly* (starred review)

Jane and the Prisoner of Wool House

"There's plenty to enjoy in the crime-solving side of Jane. . . . [She] is as worthy a detective as Columbo."   —*USA Today*

"A carefully written, thoroughly researched novel . . . An enjoyable, authentic portrayal of this classic author, a strong setting and a thoroughly enjoyable plot will convert new readers to the series as well as satisfy longtime fans."   —*The Mystery Reader*

Jane and the Stillroom Maid

"Barron does a wonderful job of evoking the great British estates and the woes of spinsters living in that era . . . often echoing the rhythms of the Austen novels with uncanny ease."
     —*Entertainment Weekly*

"This work bears all the wonderful trademarks of the earlier titles, including period detail, measured but often sardonic wit, and authenticity."   —*Library Journal*

Jane and the Genius of the Place

"This is perhaps the best 'Jane' yet. The plot moves smoothly and quickly to its denouement. Barron's mysteries also educate the reader, in a painless fashion, about the political, social and cultural concerns of Austen's time. Jane [is] a subtle but determined sleuth."   —*Chicago Tribune*

"Barron tells the tale in Jane's leisurely voice, skillfully re-creating the tone and temper of the time without a hint of an anachronism."   —*The Plain Dealer*

THE JANE AUSTEN MYSTERIES
BY STEPHANIE BARRON

Jane and the Canterbury Tale

Jane and the Canterbury Tale

BEING A JANE AUSTEN MYSTERY

STEPHANIE BARRON

BANTAM BOOKS TRADE PAPERBACKS
NEW YORK

A Bantam Books Trade Paperback Original

Copyright © 2011 by Stephanie Barron

All rights reserved.

Published in the United States by Bantam Books, an imprint of The Random House Publishing Group, a division of Random House, Inc., New York.

Bantam Books and the rooster colophon are registered trademarks of Random House, Inc.

Grateful acknowledgment is given to reprint from THE CANTERRBURY TALES by Geoffrey Chaucer, translated by Burton Raffel. Translation and notes copyright © 2008 by Burton Raffel. Used by permission of Modern Library, a division of Random House, Inc.

Library of Congress Cataloging-in-Publication Data
Barron, Stephanie.
Jane and the Canterbury tale : being a Jane Austen mystery / Stephanie Barron.
p. cm.
ISBN 978-0-553-38671-4
eBook ISBN 978-0-345-53035-6
1. Austen, Jane, 1775–1817—Fiction.   2. Women novelists—Fiction.
3. England—Fiction.   I. Title.
PS3563.A8357J329 2011
813'.54—dc22   2011000501

Printed in the United States of America

www.bantamdell.com

246897531

Book design by Caroline Cunningham

Jane and the Canterbury Tale

CHAPTER ONE

Marriages Made in Heaven

"... either you or I will win
My lady, and if it's you, rejoicing in
Her love when I am dead, why then you'll have her."

GEOFFREY CHAUCER, "THE KNIGHT'S TALE"

WEDNESDAY, 20 OCTOBER 1813
GODMERSHAM PARK, KENT

"AH, MISS AUSTEN," CRIED MR. RICHARD TYLDEN AS HE offered me a glass of claret this evening—most welcome, as the day had been exceedingly wet, and the crush of persons in the ballroom at Chilham Castle so great as to entirely prevent me approaching the fire—"It has been an age since we met! And yet you appear to greater advantage than ever, if I may permit myself to offer so bold a compliment. That gown is excessively becoming. A shade *exactly* suited to a lady of your colouring."

As the gown was new, and a source of inordinate pride—the very kick of fashion and purchased at breathless expence only six months before in Brighton—I blushed like a school-girl. "You flatter me, Mr. Tylden."

"Indeed I do not!" he insisted, and raised his glass in salute. "To marriages made in Heaven," he intoned, "and acquaintance renewed, after far too long a lapse."

I had no intention of flirting with the poor man, who is already long since married and devoted to his country church; but I condescended to beam at him before taking a sip of wine. I could not help but be pleased with my situation—having come into Kent with my brother Edward's entire family party in September, I had endured a headlong whirl of gaiety ever since, and tho' excessively fatiguing, the change from the quieter pleasures of the Hampshire countryside had undoubtedly done me good. I might revisit all those treasured scenes of happier days, when Edward's beloved Elizabeth reigned at his beautiful Godmersham Park; serve as counselor to my niece Fanny, who was caught in all the toils of young womanhood; and appear as boon companion to the affected and rather silly spinster charged with the governance of Edward's madcap younger daughters. In the midst of which, naturally, I snatched the odd hour to jot my immortal phrases into the little books I sew up from bits of foolscap. They have a distinct advantage, in being no larger than the span of a pocket in a lady's gown—into which mine are frequently slipped, when an unwanted visitor shatters the solitude of Edward's great library.

There is nothing like a sojourn in the environs of Canterbury, indeed, for the refreshment and further education of a novelist—albeit a secret one, like myself. Everyone is rich here, and each has his peculiar story to tell. I think I could spend my whole life in Kent, collecting my characters and assembling my comic situations; and as I am presently at work on the story of a wealthy and indulged young lady by the name of Emma Woodhouse, who orders the existence of everybody about her exactly to her liking, much as my niece Fanny does—I could not be better placed. A wedding-party at

Chilham Castle, for example, with all the elegance of Edward's Kentish neighbours, must provide endless food for the writer's imagination. Add to its recommendations, that it is the *perfect* occasion for the parading of my beloved wine-coloured silk—and you will understand a little of my inner exultation.

No matter if Mr. Tylden were sparse of hair and stooped of shoulder; I knew myself to be in excellent looks, and must be gratified that someone, and a *male* someone at that, had admired my prize on its first wearing.

"It has been some time since you were come into Kent, I think?" Mr. Tylden persisted.

"Four years, at least."

"So long! I shall have to dispute the question of hospitality with your esteemed brother, Miss Austen—I certainly shall! I wonder you know your nieces and nephews again, after so long a lapse!"

"But you forget, sir—my brother has lately been staying with all his family on his Hampshire estate, in the village where I myself reside, so that our intercourse has been a matter of daily occurrence."

"Just so. Nearly half the year they were gone to Chawton, and a refurbishment of Godmersham Park undertaken, I collect, during Mr. Knight's absence. We were excessively glad to have the whole party back again."

I frowned a little at the use of Edward's adoptive name, tho' it is hardly the first time I have heard it since coming into Kent. My brother must leave off the name of Austen, now that his patroness, our distant cousin Mrs. Knight, has passed from this world. In acceding to his full inheritance, Edward and all his progeny must be Knights forevermore; the Will so stipulates it. Mr. Tylden has accepted the change with more aplomb than myself; he did not stumble over his address, as I am forever doing, when some Kentish neighbour hails Edward unawares.

"And there are the fortunate couple now," Mr. Tylden observed, setting down his glass with a benevolent look, as befit a man who had united Captain Andrew MacCallister with Adelaide Fiske. The two had just entered the ballroom, followed by our host, Mr. James Wildman, the bride's cousin; and were receiving congratulations from every side.

"And you truly regard theirs as a marriage made in Heaven?" I enquired idly.

"Who could not? So much gallantry on the gentleman's side, and so much beauty on the lady's!"

These observations were certainly apt; and if nothing more than gallantry and beauty were required for conjugal happiness, the MacCallisters bid fair to enjoy a halcyon future. The Captain is a man of thirty, battle-hardened and a coming fellow—attached to the Marquis of Wellington's staff, no less. Some six years his junior, Adelaide Fiske is just that sort of tall, raven-haired beauty possessed of speaking dark eyes, that must turn every head upon entering a room. She possesses the carriage of a duchess and a figure that should make a courtesan wild with envy—tho' I may not utter that judgement aloud in *present* company; only my brother Henry should know how to appreciate it, and he is in London at present. Adelaide Fiske's life to date, however—but it would be as well to dwell as little as possible on the lady's sad career. The history of Adelaide's first marriage and widowhood are all to be forgot, now that she is once more a bride; and I should do well to heed Mr. Tylden's better angels, in wishing the pair nothing but good fortune—and leaving off the name *Fiske* for the *MacCallister* she has vowed to cherish until death.

It is unbecoming in a spinster to dwell upon the ominous at a wedding feast; it smacks of disappointment.

"Ah, they are to dance!" Mr. Tylden cried in appreciation. "Only look how well they appear together!"

And it was true, of course. MacCallister swept his wife into the daring strains of a waltz, his dress uniform a blaze of colour against her pale blue gown. His hair might be of a fiery carrot hue and his features nothing out of the ordinary way, but his shoulders were good; and his countenance was suffused with adoration as he gazed at his wife, so that it seemed almost indecent to observe them. *Here* was the true article: love deep and encompassing, not the pale social convention that too-often passes for it. I read triumph in the soldier's look, and guessed he had worked long to win his prize. In the lady's countenance there was greater reserve; she had long ago learnt to meet the publick eye with composure. Scandal is a hard school for young ladies gently bred.

"Your niece has also taken the floor," Mr. Tylden observed. "We must regard the waltz as *approved* in Kent henceforth, Miss Austen, if Miss Knight consents to dance it."

Miss *Knight,* indeed. And there was my own dear Fanny, who at the advanced age of twenty had been feverishly practicing the steps of the new dance with her brother the whole of the week past. Her countenance was becomingly flushed, and her grey eyes sparkled as she turned about the ballroom in her oyster silk—we had purchased the stuff for the gown in London together a few weeks since, and she was sublimely conscious of having *two* flounces to her hem and a bodice cut alarmingly low.

Her partner was a gentleman I did not recognise; his arm encircled Fanny's waist in a shockingly intimate manner I must attribute to the waltz. He was tailored to swooning point in a black coat and cream satin breeches, his dark locks windswept à la Brutus, and his cravat a miracle of complexity. Far from affecting the Dandy, however, he proclaimed the sporting Corinthian with every inch of his muscular frame. It was his eyes that must chiefly draw attention, however—

brooding black eyes that fixed upon Fanny's with a smouldering look. She had excited a dangerous emotion in the young man's breast, I judged—one it should be as well, perhaps, to discourage before it caused general comment. Intrigued, I taxed Mr. Tylden for the gentleman's name.

"That is Julian Thane," he informed me stiffly. "A very wild young man, from all I hear. Sent down from Oxford in his second year, for crimes as yet unnamed."

"The bride's brother?" Adelaide Fiske had been a Thane before her *first* marriage; and this young buck had his sister's dark looks and self-possessed air. Julian Thane was the sort of man to throw all the girls of Canterbury into strong hysterics, indeed, if I knew anything of Fanny's acquaintance. Rakes were in short supply in Kent at any season.

From the indignant looks that followed Mr. Thane from nearly every young man in the neighbourhood, I concluded with some amusement that the interloper should be treated with coldness henceforth; he had poached in other men's preserves.

Grouped near the French doors letting out onto the balcony were three such Kentish fellows: John Plumptre, a serious young man of Oxford, with intellectual pretensions and a tendency to disapprove of frivolity; George Finch-Hatton, the blond god whom all the local girls apostrophized as *Jupiter,* whenever his planet swung across their firmament; and James Wildman, son and heir of our host, the most gentleman-like member of the set. I had known them boy and man, in company with my own nephews, as the most attractive and indolent passel of gilded youth as might be met with—friends from birth, companions by schooling and inclination, and united this evening in their disapprobation of my niece's choice.

Fanny could not have done better than to have accepted Julian Thane for the waltz; she must be in hot request for the remainder of the evening—provided Thane consented to part with her. He looked much as a lion might, that had felled a gazelle; and he was supremely indifferent to the rancour of his friends.

"Young Thane is heir to Wold Hall, in Leicestershire," Tylden supplied, "tho' he inherited little enough but debt when his father went off—the old gentleman being as deep a gambler as ever lived. All the Thanes are sadly ramshackle, tho' it does not do to say so on this happy occasion— Ah, Mr. Knight! Is not this an excellent ball? Are we not blessed in the amiability of our friends?"

"Good evening, Tylden," my brother Edward answered. "I have come to claim my sister for the waltz. She appears too handsome, indeed, to stand stupidly by with the rest of the chaperons. Dance with me, Jane?"

I had watched Fanny often enough in recent days to have an idea of the steps, tho' I had never attempted the waltz myself. I might have demurred, indeed—but here was Edward, a man of consequence in the neighbourhood, still handsome at six-and-forty, and from his lost expression, acutely lonely amidst the general revels. As I allowed him to lead me to the floor, I wondered for the thousandth time why my brother had not chosen some *one*, among the eligible ladies of his acquaintance, to marry. Five years had passed away since the death of his beloved Elizabeth, and still he mourned her. It was not for me to trespass on such private ground, with officious suggestions of *companionship* and *suitable matches*. I could only consent to partner him about the ballroom, when wretchedness pressed too hard upon him.

"What do you think of that fellow commandeering Fanny?" he demanded, as he led me to the floor. "Is he an insufferable bounder, or a callow youth not yet up to snuff? I cannot like the steadiness of his hands, Jane—the sensation of grasping a lady's waist ought to be novel enough to make him tremble with embarrassment, whereas *that* jackanapes is as cool as a cucumber! One would think he spent every evening with his fingers tangled in a lady's bodice!"

"Perhaps he does," I said with amusement. "But you need never fear for Fanny; she is the soul of propriety. Confess, Edward—Mr. Thane is excessively handsome, and Fanny is enjoying herself hugely! I have not seen such an elegant fellow—or such brilliant indifference to publick opinion—since . . ." I paused, having been about to utter the words *Lord Harold died,* but supplied instead, ". . . my time in Brighton."

"Ah, so now Julian Thane's the equal of Lord Byron, is he? My cup runneth over." Edward glanced darkly at the pirouetting pair. "Poor Fanny is aflame with blushes!"

"Edward," I chided, "she is merely flushed with the exercise! You refine too much upon a trifle—the waltz is everywhere accepted at private parties now, and Fanny looks very well as she turns about the room. How her mother should have delighted in it! Such a picture as she makes!"

I had long thought privately that Fanny was too little seen, too little known, beyond the circle of her intimate acquaintance in Kent. She ought to have had a true London Season, with a hired house and vouchers for Almack's—but such an establishment was not to Edward's taste. It was unfortunate that one of her mother's relations did not take Fanny under her wing, and chaperon her about the Marriage Mart, for Elizabeth had been of baronet's blood, and her family might claim the notice of the Great—but I could not raise the subject without being assured that Fanny was perfectly content with her lot. Of course she was! It was not in her nature to find fault with circumstance. Fanny was apt to be grave and sober, when she ought to have been dreaming and frivolous; and for my part, I rejoiced to see her spinning about the room as tho' her feet had grown wings. Little danger that so circumspect a child should let a man of Julian Thane's stamp run away with her.

Edward's eyes followed his daughter as he clasped my hand and waist. "She looks nothing like Elizabeth, you know. Too much Austen in her for *real* beauty. But she'll do. By God, she'll do. My Lizzy would be content, I think. I haven't failed them all entirely, Jane, have I?"

"Impossible, dearest."

But when he dragged his gaze from Fanny, I saw that the lost look had not entirely left my brother's eyes. And I feared that it would remain with him forever.

Perhaps, I thought, as my feet found the music, there really *were* such things, once, as marriages made in Heaven.

IT WAS NEARLY MIDNIGHT WHEN CAPTAIN MACCALLISTER besought the attention of our entire party, to offer a short speech of thanks. He was supported by his hosts, Mr. and Mrs. James Wildman—he an elderly man victimised by gout, and she a handsome woman of easy manners, much given to company and gossip. It could be no surprize that the Wildmans had insisted upon throwing a ball in their cousin's honour; they were forever looking for an excuse to welcome half the neighbourhood at their board.

"I am no Kentishman," MacCallister commenced, "but from the kindness shewn me in recent weeks, could imagine myself an intimate of the neighbourhood from birth; and my gratitude is boundless. When duty and honour call me far from home, when the heat of battle rages about me and my thoughts revert to blessed days of happiness, Chilham shall hold no small corner in my heart. Indeed, it shall stand as the place I owe the greatest joy any man may claim."

At this, he took the hand of Adelaide, and raised it to his lips with such an expression of mingled pride and humility that I wonder she was not overcome. "To the lady," he cried, "who has made me the happiest of men, in consenting to be my wife—may she live long in beauty!"

"Hear, hear," murmured the attendant company, and it seemed to me a sigh ran lightly about the room, as tho' a faint breeze had passed over it.

I sipped at my champagne, and found my eyes drawn to the figure of a woman. Still handsome despite her advancing years, she stood a little removed from the family party of Wildmans and Thanes; a stately lady enough, with a strong aquiline nose and hair the colour of iron, whose shoulders were wrapped tightly in a costly Paisley shawl. She was a stranger to me. And yet there was something tantalisingly familiar in her looks—a haughtiness that suggested she cared for nobody.

"Edward," I whispered. "Who is that lady, to the rear of Captain MacCallister? She looks capable of commanding an army—indeed, I should not be surprized to learn she was the soldier's mother!"

"There you would be out, Jane—for she is the mother of the bride."

"Of course!" I said with sudden comprehension, tho' the lady looked nothing like Adelaide. "She puts me more in mind of her son, Julian Thane—the one who was waltzing with Fanny."

"Waltzing," Edward said testily, "*and* claiming the *next two dances,* until that excellent John Plumptre was forced to intervene—which is most particular and unbecoming behaviour in Thane, do not you think? That young buck has the air of a hound who will not be turned from the hunt, once he has caught the scent—"

"And so you have taken a strong dislike to him," I rejoined. "You have nothing to fear in Fanny's good sense, and surely she could do with a bit of flattering attention, Edward. She is twenty, after all."

Very well, I will confess that I cherish a certain *anxiety* regarding Fanny—who so ably filled the post of mother to her ten younger brothers and sisters, as to be almost spinster-like in the very bloom of her youth. My anxiety is that she will end her days like my sister, Cassandra, or God forbid, like *me*: Content enough, to be sure, and freed of all the cares attendant upon marriage and children—but lingering, and dwindling, on the fringe of a world she once claimed as her birthright. I could not bear for Fanny to be merely everyone's *aunt*. And her apprenticeship in that order was already marked: She had been so busy preparing the boys for Winchester, and compelling the girls to see the London dentist, and ordering the cook which joints were for the table, and which for the kitchen, and overseeing the stillroom, and ensuring that her father's every comfort was met, so that he might be observed to feel the loss of his cherished wife as little as possible—that the poor child was quite worn out. Fanny had been forced to the management of a great household at too young an age, and it was a wonder she did not choose the sanctuary of a convent, over the gaieties of a ball.

Further debate was suspended, however, for the bride had chosen to speak.

Adelaide's voice was clear and deep, with a musical timbre, and her white hand seemed almost translucent as she lifted her glass.

"To my gallant husband, Captain Andrew MacCallister— may God preserve him from harm as he serves King and Country, and return him to *this* loving heart, which has such cause to know his unexampled worth."

We drank to this, and had only just drained our glasses dry, when a singular interruption occurred.

A footman belonging to the Castle made his way through the throng, bearing a curious item on a silver tray. It was a small silken pouch of a warm rosy colour, intricately embroidered in gold threads, and knotted with tassels. The servant's object was clearly Adelaide MacCallister, and as she watched him approach, her lips curved in a smile as tho' she was expecting a childish treat. If the peculiarity of the purse being delivered in the midst of a ball were not enough to silence the assembled guests, the bride's response certainly was.

"Is this your doing, Andrew?" she demanded as the footman bowed, and presented his prize.

But her husband laughingly declined all knowledge of the gift.

"Very well," she cried. "Whom must I thank for this beautiful reticule? Some one of our guests? Or—*Julian!* Have you made over to me all your unscrupulous winnings, from playing at lottery tickets with our dashing cousins?"

There was a ripple of amusement from the onlookers, but no Julian Thane appeared to answer his sister; he must be absent from the ballroom.

"How came this here?" the bride asked as she took up the silken pouch.

"I received it of a stranger at the front door, ma'am," the footman said.

Mrs. MacCallister's eager fingers stilled, and to my surprize, I saw the colour slowly ebb from her cheeks.

"A gift to the bride on the occasion of her wedding, the man said."

"Man? What sort of man?"

"A common enough fellow, ma'am. He did not give his name—and I neglected to ask it, perceiving him to be merely the bearer of another's gift."

She nodded faintly, and took the thing from the tray—but with an expression of such dread on her countenance now that I felt an answering chill trace its finger along my spine.

"My darling," Captain MacCallister murmured. "Are you unwell?"

"Nothing I regard." She loosed the strings of the pouch with deft fingers, and tipped the contents into her palm.

If I had expected a pile of rubies, I was fated to disappointment. The pouch contained nothing but a quantity of dark brown beans, rather like coffee only twice as large; several slipped from Adelaide MacCallister's fingers, and scattered on the ballroom floor.

A murmur of conjecture rose from the assembled guests, and I glanced at my brother Edward, curious to know what he made of the anonymous gift; his eyes were narrowed, but his countenance betrayed only a vague puzzlement. I imagine all of the observers felt the same.

Swiftly, the bride tipped the brown pods back into the embroidered pouch and knotted the tassels with fingers that seemed almost nerveless. Then she turned with a brilliant smile and called, "Pray let us have music! The night is young, and we must dance!"

"My darling—" Captain MacCallister attempted, but she held up one hand in mute refusal. As the guests turned in search of partners and the strains of a violin rose around us once more, I observed Adelaide MacCallister make her way haltingly from the ballroom, her husband staring after her in confusion.

The bride had not entirely quitted the place, however, before her formidable mother intercepted her. I may have imagined it—my eyesight is *not* what it was in earlier days, alas—but I would swear that Mrs. Thane slipped the offending pouch from her daughter's hand.

CHAPTER TWO

The Shooting-Party

Jealous folk have always been dangerous people—
Or at least that's what they want their wives believing.

GEOFFREY CHAUCER, "THE STEWARD'S TALE"

THURSDAY, 21 OCTOBER 1813

IT WAS NEARLY TWO O'CLOCK IN THE MORNING WHEN THE carriage drew up before the doors of Godmersham Park, and I confess I retired immediately, regretting that the fire in the Yellow Room's grate had turned entirely to ash. The Yellow is generally my bedchamber, or Cassandra's, when we are come to stay with Edward in Kent—and a very comfortable room it is, only not in the dead of night, when the buttercup hue of the silk hangings are entirely devoid of warmth, and the autumn draughts are hurrying along the Great House's corridors like so many unquiet souls.

Fanny's maid was sitting up in expectation of her, but having accepted of the sleepy girl's services only long enough to know my tedious length of buttons was undone, I stepped out of my wine-coloured silk and straight into bed. My endurance for such endless amusements dwindles with each passing year; I have not endeavoured to make a study of insomnia, or cultivated the practice of judicious napping upon the sopha each afternoon, that I might hope to shine in Society.

In this I must be a sad disappointment to Fanny, whose spirits remained so elevated throughout our brief carriage ride home—Chilham being but a few miles from Edward's estate—that in her mind it might have been only eight o'clock, and the whole evening before us.

I did not neglect to twit her on the immensity of *one* of her conquests.

"Mr. Thane?" She spoke airily, with an insouciance I failed to credit for an instant. "He is very *elegant*, to be sure, but I could not be entirely easy in his company, Aunt. He lacks . . . conversation."

"Conversation?" her father repeated, indignantly. "Manners and all sense of propriety are what he lacks, my girl—and don't you mistake!"

Fanny opened her eyes very wide; I detected a hint of a smile about the corners of her mouth, but could not be certain of this; the glow of a carriage's side-lamps will make of every shadow a genii.

"Papa!" she exclaimed. "Do not tell me you were *put out* by Mr. Thane's air of town bronze?"

"Town bronze! Is that what you call it?"

"Oh, not *I*," Fanny assured Edward innocently. "It was Mr. Tylden who described him thus. The clergyman, you know. He informed Mrs. Wildman that Mr. Thane displayed the very best sort of *ton*."

"—For a sadly ramshackle family," I murmured almost inaudibly. It seemed Mr. Tylden suited his praise to his auditors.

"I thought Mr. Thane excessively handsome," piped up Harriot Moore, from the corner of the conveyance, where she was quite crushed against the bulk of her husband.

"But as personal perfection invariably masks a host of

worldly faults," returned George Moore coolly, "we cannot suppose Mr. Thane possesses even one amiable quality."

I have neglected to mention the Moores until this moment, which would sadly discomfit *one* of them. Mr. Moore is a tiresome creature in his early forties, the son of the late Archbishop of Canterbury, and tho' commendable for the gravity of his thoughts and the depth of his understanding—neither of which I should attempt to deny—he is sadly wanting in a *sense of humour*. Mr. Moore is rather too apt to stand upon ceremony, and consider what is his due in matters of precedence, and the deference that ought to be shewn to the son of so august a prelate—a prince of the Church. As he is unlikely to attain those heights his father once commanded, despite taking Holy Orders, I must suppose that an insistence upon precedence and deference are all that are left him. But I cannot abide a clergyman who must harp upon the grim vicissitudes of human existence, and neglect to revel in its absurdities. For what else do we live, if not to make sport of our neighbours, and be laughed at by them in turn?

Harriot Moore is a very different creature than her husband, sweet-natured and loving and a trifle simple-minded, tho' generally prized as being the youngest sister of Edward's cherished Elizabeth. She is Mr. Moore's second attachment, and a full ten years her husband's junior. Harriot makes it her business to be as much in company at Godmersham as Mr. Moore will allow. On the present occasion, the pair have been staying with us nearly a week, with the object of attending the wedding at Chilham, for both Harriot and George Moore have long been on excellent terms with the Wildman family.

"I was sadly disappointed in Mr. Tylden's sermon," he declared, turning the conversation adroitly from Julian Thane and his disputed degree of polish. "I thought it dwelt *too much* upon the temporal, and *too little* upon the sacred aspects of matrimony. Had I been offered the duty of uniting such an ill-sorted pair as that soldier and Mrs. Fiske, I should have known where my conscience lay—I should have abjured them sternly to cast off the enticements of the Fashionable World, and prepare rather for the inevitable *end* of their earthly toils."

"But is not that your funeral text, dearest?" Harriot enquired with pardonable bewilderment.

"You do not, then, regard an excess of gallantry and beauty as the perfect foundation for conjugal bliss?" I demanded, with a mental wink at Mr. Tylden.

"Both have brought Mrs. Fiske—I should say Mrs. *MacCallister*—nothing but grief in the past," Moore replied.

"You are acquainted with the lady, I apprehend."

He shrugged. "Only a little, and quite long ago."

"Pshaw!" cried Harriot gaily. "You were *in love* with her, George, before she consented to have Fiske! And the merest *child* Adelaide must have been, too—no more than seventeen, and you a widower in your thirties! I am sure I shock you, Jane," she confided, leaning a little across her husband, "but I ran a very poor second to Adelaide Fiske, when Mr. Moore looked about him for another wife. I was six-and-twenty, you know, and long since on the shelf."

Mr. Moore stared coldly before him, unmoved by his wife's raillery. "Your penchant for levity betrays you, my dear."

Throughout this interesting exchange, Fanny might have been deaf and mute. An odd little smile still hovered at the corners of her mouth, but she was not attending to the Moores' debate; she had learnt long ago to ignore her Aunt Harriot's tedious partner in life, and quite often her aunt as well. Fanny is enough of an Austen to refuse to suffer fools gladly; but in the present instance, I suspected her thoughts were more pleasurably engaged.

So, too, did my brother Edward.

"Jackanapes," he muttered—a reference that *must* be for Mr. Thane and his town bronze—and subsided against the carriage's squabs.

I LINGERED IN MY BED UNTIL TEN O'CLOCK, WHEN A SCRATCH-ing at the door proclaimed my coffee was arrived. The fire had been lit several hours before, but I had slept on regard-less, being aware that Fanny would certainly not be stirring. One rarely appeared downstairs before noon, the morning after a ball.

Yesterday's rain was in abeyance, but the skies remained persistently grey, and a renewal of showers could not be far off. It would be a day for sitting close to the library fire, in one of Edward's comfortable armchairs, and attempting yet again to absorb the interesting narrative of *Self-Control,* by Mary Brunton. I say, *yet again,* because try as I might I cannot like the novel. It is an excellently-meant, elegantly-written work, without anything of nature or probability in it. However, it shall serve very well for my purpose—which is to hide my own little scrapbook of jottings, as I doze by the fire.

The gentlemen would already be gone out with the beaters—a scheme for shooting had been renewed last evening at the ball, between the Chilham party and my nephews, young Ed-ward and George, who were wild for sport. If only, I thought with gloom, Mr. Moore could be prevailed upon to join them. But there was no one less inclined to manly pursuits than that taciturn individual; he preferred to invade the li-brary, and glower over a massive tome, entirely cutting up my enjoyment of the place.

I glanced again through the window, and considered of the cool perfection of Edward's Doric Temple; of the damp earth and autumnal flutterings in meadow and grove; of the scent of smoke and leaf-mould on the air. There had been so few days without rain since our coming into Kent, so few solitary rambles suited to contemplation. I set down my cup and threw back the bedclothes. If I were to enjoy any kind of exercise out-of-doors this morning, it was imperative that I bestir myself.

I HAD BEEN RAMBLING FOR SOME BLISSFUL THREE-QUARTERS of an hour, and was just considering a return to the house and the recruitment of breakfast, when a breathless voice called my name.

"Aunt Jane! Aunt *Jane*!"

Wonder of wonders, it was Fanny who approached, pelting at a girlish lope through the wet grasses from the direction of Bentigh, and the old stone bridge over the Stour.[1] I was astonished to find my niece awake, much less abroad, and concluded that she had spent a wretched night—there was *that* in her looks that warned of disquiet.

"My dearest girl," I said as I perceived her disheveled aspect and flushed countenance, "your petticoat is six inches deep in mud!" And it was hardly her second-best petticoat, as one might expect for a wet morning's exercise; she had obviously dressed with care, in another of the elegant gowns and the green pelisse ordered in London a few weeks since. *And* she had put on her new bonnet, with the sprig of cherries drooping rakishly over one eye. I suspected an attempt to Fascinate an Unknown. Could she have consented to meet Julian Thane clandestinely in the Park at the crack of dawn?

"Never mind my petticoat," she said impatiently. "I do not

---

[1] Bentigh was an avenue of limes and yews. It led toward the old Norman church of St. Lawrence, where the Knight family worshipped. —*Editor's note.*

regard a little mud. I have been out following Edward and George—they are shooting this morning, you know, and all the gentlemen from Chilham have joined them. Mr. Plumptre and Mr. Wildman and the rest, with their dogs. But oh, Aunt—"

"Does Mr. Thane shoot as well?" I asked, with an eye to that bonnet.

Fanny made a dismissive movement with one gloved hand. "Worse luck, he does not. And I particularly wished to see— But, Aunt Jane, you *must* attend! There has been a man found in our meadow."

"A man?"

She grasped my elbow as tho' I might require support.

"He is lying on the old Pilgrim's Way. Quite dead."

The Pilgrim's Way ran, as it had since Chaucer's time, along the Downs to the north of Godmersham, and divided Edward's land from that of his neighbour, the same Mr. Wildman of Chilham Castle; indeed, it ran straight towards St. Mary's Church in the little village of Chilham, where Mr. Tylden had united the MacCallisters only last evening. In other words—it ran *behind* Edward's house, whereas Fanny had come from the direction of the lane in front, which ran just beyond the river—quite the opposite end of Edward's acres.

"I do not understand you," I protested. "The Pilgrim's Way is on high ground to the north!"

"Yes, yes," she said hurriedly, "but you must know there is a side-path, often used by those who know of our church, that runs from the Downs, skirts the house, and comes out into the lane. I do not think it is above a mile from the *true* Pilgrim's Way; and Papa does not mind those who employ the bridge for the purpose of visiting St. Lawrence's, for Mamma's grave is there, and he likes to think of more than just ourselves visiting the church. When I was little, Mamma used to say that grass never grew on the Pilgrim's side-path, because so many pious feet had trod it."

I suspected grass never grew there from a dearth of sunlight, but forebore to utter so acid a remark. "I see. And now there is a man lying there?"

"Indeed," my niece hurried on, "and I suppose he might be a pilgrim in earnest, from the look of him."

"Not one of our neighbours, then, thank Heaven?"

She shook her head. "A tradesman, I should judge, in a stout travelling cloak, with a leather satchel lying a little off the path, beside a walking stick. He must have dropped them as he fell."

I turned resolutely towards the river and the ancient Pilgrim's Way. "How did he die, Fanny?"

"Shot through the heart, John Plumptre says."

I stopped short and stared at her in dismay. I will confess that I had been perfectly content to think nothing of corpses and death during my visit to Kent; it was not the sort of country for melancholy. Weddings suited the general animation of the neighbourhood far better.

"Bessy, Mr. Plumptre's spaniel, set up a baying over the body—"

Fanny's voice wavered as she offered this inconsequential information; in all her haste to report the news she had forgot, for a little, to be tender-hearted. "Oh Aunt—I think Mr. Plumptre is afraid that one of *us* killed him! *Quite by mistake,* of course—having aimed for a pheasant."

Fanny, I could see, feared this, too: That one of her brothers or friends had taken an innocent pilgrim's life as carelessly as he might a bird's.

"I must go in search of my father," she said more steadily. "You will forgive me, Aunt—he must be informed."

"Of course."

Among his various duties and honours as a man of consequence in Canterbury, Edward counted the office of First Magistrate. A surgeon being now useless, my brother was the next person who ought to be summoned.

Fanny was off again at a run for the house, her hand pressed against her stays, which must be cruelly impeding her lungs. Edward would still be closeted with his valet, unaware of the signal burden about to befall him. There would be the coroner to rouse, the jury to empanel. An inquest held in some publick house in Canterbury. An attempt to ascertain the unfortunate man's identity, and convey the dreadful news to his relicts—

And one of our own young men to console, for having murdered a man all unwittingly. I sent up a hurried prayer that *which* fowling piece had fired the fatal shot, should *never* be ascertained—and kicked savagely at a pebble as I mounted the old stone bridge.

The River Stour chuckled below, but the happy dream that had been my sojourn in Kent was suddenly all to pieces.

CHAPTER THREE

The Unexpected Hessians

. . . Fortune had once
Been his friend, for a time, and then his foe.
No man can ever expect her favor to last. . . .

GEOFFREY CHAUCER, "THE MONK'S TALE"

21 OCTOBER 1813, CONT.

THE GENTLEMEN LOUNGED IN AN UNEASY GROUP, RESTRAIN-
ing their dogs, near the publick footpath. The beaters—two
fellows employed by Edward's gamekeeper—sat cross-legged
in the dirt near a pair of canvas bags whose humped shapes
suggested the hunting had already been well advanced when
the fatal accident occurred. The spaniels' tongues were lolling
cheerfully from their mouths, as tho' a human corpse were
not so very different, after all, from one with feathers; they
leaned happily against the legs of their masters, who were un-
wontedly silent when they ought to have been chaffing each
other.

The corpse itself was sprawled across the Pilgrim's Way, an
inert figure clad in browns and greens that must have been in-

distinguishable from the autumnal verdure; small wonder neither beater nor hunter had noticed the fellow. The man's utter stillness, coupled with the blood-stained earth all around him, had thrown a pall over the shooting-party.

The scene might have been an engraving by Cruikshank: *Mishap of a Sporting Nature, Or, the Wrong Bird Bagged.*

There was John Plumptre, his serious dark eyes holding an expression of trouble and a faint line of apprehension on his brow; glorious Jupiter Finch-Hatton, whose posture as he leaned against an oak suggested a fashionable malaise I suspected he was far from feeling; James Wildman, who started forward upon perceiving me, as tho' determined to offer a lady every civility regardless of chaotic circumstance; and my own nephews George and Edward. Their frank looks of dread recalled countless episodes of schoolboy mischief gone terribly awry: arms broken whilst tree-climbing, window panes smashed with cricket balls poorly batted, and dolls' heads severed by makeshift guillotines. They were blenching at the prospect of their father's inevitable lecture, on the thoughtlessness of young men wild for sport.

"Aunt Jane," Edward said nervously—he is but nineteen, tho' he affects an attitude of someone far more up to snuff, as must be expected of The Heir—"You have met with Fanny, I conclude."

"Yes, Edward, I have. She is gone for your father. May I see the poor fellow?"

"Do you truly wish—that is to say, I should have thought—a spectacle *not* for the frailer sex—" This, from Mr. Wildman, who being the eldest at five-and-twenty, appeared to regard himself as the minder of his fellows.

I smiled at him rather as one of his old governesses might. "Pray do not make yourself anxious, Mr. Wildman. I am quite accustomed to death. My father was a clergyman, you know."

"Ah," he said, and looked slightly mortified.

I walked resolutely towards the corpse, the gentlemen heeling their dogs a discreet distance from my skirts, and made as if to kneel down beside the Deceased. I was forestalled by John Plumptre, who flung his shooting coat—a high-collared affair of drab that just brushed his ankles as he strode through the fields—down upon the ground. "The blood," he said briefly. "It has soaked into the earth."

I nodded my thanks, and knelt carefully on the coat.

My heart was pounding, however much courage I may have affected for the reassurance of the young gentlemen— for tho' I have looked on Death before, I never meet Him without the profoundest sensibility. I closed my eyes an instant, drew a steadying breath, and forced myself to study the unfortunate creature whose mortal remains lay before me. I owed the dead man that much—to note what I could of the way he had died—for the five sporting fellows ranged about were so discomfited and mortified by the terrible event, they seemed determined to take no notice of the corpse at all. Perhaps then it might be swallowed up by the forgiving turf, and all should be right as rain in their world. But no—*this* was no apparition conjured by an excessive indulgence in claret the previous night; this was real, and the bucks of the neighbourhood should be forced to grapple with it, if I had my way. Death should never be so incidental as the bagging of a pheasant. I leaned over the man, consumed by an immense feeling of pity.

He lay on his back with arms flung wide and one leg bent beneath the other, hazel eyes staring sightlessly at the canopy of bare tree branches overhead. The wound in his chest had oozed a good deal, but was darkened and quiet now. He was in his middle forties, I should judge, and had apparently lived a life much out-of-doors, from the weathered condition of his skin, which was quite tanned for October. Not much of this could be seen, however, for he was bearded—a factor that must suggest the labouring class; a gentleman might sport a moustache, but rarely whiskers. The fellow's clothes bore out the assumption, for they were of worsteds and nankeen, nothing out of the ordinary way. The boots, however, raised a question in my mind. For tho' they were caked with mud and had seen hard use, they appeared to have been cut by an excellent cobbler from an expensive hide, in a stile I should only describe as *Hessians*.

I frowned. What business had a labourer wearing a gentleman's boots? Even admitting that they might be purchased at second- or third-hand, what folly urged their display on a wearisome journey by foot? Our man gave every appearance of having walked to the place of his death—a satchel and stout stick rested nearby.

A pilgrim, Fanny had said. One token alone suggested the activity: a large silver cross hung round the corpse's neck on a solid silver chain. Something about its shape, or perhaps the irregularity of its design, brought to mind the amber cross my brother Charles had purchased for me in Malta—and the thought rose unbidden that our corpse had travelled in distant lands, perhaps by sea. This was foolishness, of course— anything might be purchased in London, after all, regardless of which village the man claimed as home. Perhaps his satchel would tell us something of his identity—

I had half-risen from my knees in order to rifle the corpse's belongings, when the canter of hooves announced my brother's approach. Of course Edward would saddle a horse—he might even have been on the point of riding out for pleasure, as was his custom each morning, when Fanny burst upon his scene big with news.

He dismounted rather heavily, and tossed the reins of his hack to young Edward without a word. He was frowning as he observed my crouching position by the body.

"Are you on the point of swooning, Jane? Have none of these blockheads supported you?"

"Indeed I am not!" I retorted indignantly. "Only puzzled exceedingly by what I find. Or rather—not *puzzled,* exactly, for the matter is clear enough."

He raised his brows quizzically as he dropped down beside me, his fingers feeling for an absent pulse in the corpse's neck. "Quite cold," he observed grimly.

"That is not all," I murmured in an undertone. "I must tell you, Edward, that for several reasons I am *most uneasy* in my mind."

"Were you to be otherwise in the presence of a dead man, Jane, I should be severely shocked." He tossed one cutting phrase over his shoulder at the knot of sporting men standing respectfully behind: "Which of you young fools cut off this man's life?"

There was a painful silence.

My nephew George cleared his throat noisily, a sure sign of panic.

"To be frank, sir," began James Wildman—

"—We haven't the slightest notion," interrupted Jupiter Finch-Hatton. He thrust himself away from his languid pose against the oak and dusted his gloved fingers with an air of distaste. "We'd just flushed the nicest little covey of pheasant a man could wish to find. All our guns were raised; most of 'em fired. Impossible to know which dropped the feller. Oughtn't to have been there. Trespass on a private manor. *Preserves.* Damned impudence, my opinion. Got his just desserts."

"Thank you, Finch-Hatton. When I want your *opinion* I shall certainly ask for it," my brother rejoined brusquely. "James, what was your party's position when the last shots were fired?"

Mr. Wildman appeared relieved; this was a question he

could answer. He whirled around and pointed in the direction from which I had come, but well to the right of the Lime Walk. "Quite a way off—thirty yards, I should think."

"Forty," corrected John Plumptre. "And the beaters were driving towards us, of course, when the pheasant went up. As Finch-Hatton says—a beautiful little covey, and we got most of them, sir. We'd no notion that any of the shot went awry until the dogs—"

"Quite," Edward said abruptly. "And when you came up with him, was he already expired? Did he speak?"

"Not a word, sir. I knew as soon as I glimpsed his face that life was extinct."

My brother was hardly attending to Plumptre, I thought, his gaze being fixed on the corpse and his countenance teeming with speculation. Edward had seen all that I had, and formed what I should guess were similar conclusions; but it would be best to discuss such matters in private.

"Observe the satchel," I murmured. "How it sits off the path, near the walking stick. As tho' both were *placed*, not fallen, there."

"Have you searched his things?"

"Not yet."

Edward assisted me to rise, then lifted Plumptre's coat and tossed it in a careless bundle towards the young man. "Thank'ee. You'll find, I believe, that it's not much stained."

Edward glanced coolly at the reddened ground, nodded once, and strode to the spot where the satchel lay.

The strap that had secured it was torn open and some of the contents had spilled out onto the ground. Edward collected these, examined them briefly, and then slipped them back into the leather sack. "A knife in a sheath," he said, "a crudely drawn plan of the Pilgrim's Way from Boughton Lees to Canterbury, showing our side-path to St. Lawrence Church; a flask of Blue Ruin against the rain; a heel of brown bread; and a Bible. Perhaps he *was* a pilgrim, after all."

"Is there no name written in the Bible? No family history of births and deaths?" I asked.

Edward shook his head. "And odder still, Jane—there's not so much as a farthing on the fellow. Unless he wore his purse next to his skin."

I glanced at the corpse, which still stared Heavenward, oblivious to our deliberations. I did not like the thought of searching for a wallet within his coat; it was stiff with blood. "Perhaps," I suggested, "being intent upon a holy journey, he came as a mendicant—and relied upon the succour of strangers."

"You do not believe that," my brother said quietly, "and neither do I."

He began to pace delicately along the edge of the path, scanning the ground. "A welter of footprints, worse luck— we cannot know if they were made by this fellow, or our own pack of young sportsmen. But here, Jane—" he crouched abruptly, his gloved finger probing the dead bracken some ten yards from the corpse—"a pair of horses were tethered to this tree. The hoofprints are just visible in the soft ground."

"A *pair*?" I repeated.

Edward glanced up at me, his blue eyes hard and bright. "Perhaps our pilgrim owned a horse, once. Edward!" he called to his son, "take Rob Roy and ride for Dr. Bredloe at Farnham. If he's not at home, find out where he is. Do not be satisfied until he returns to Godmersham with you."

"Very good, sir," my nephew said stoutly, and swung himself into his father's saddle.

"What am I to do, Father?" George asked breathlessly.

"You—and the rest of these young reprobates—may make yourselves useful, and carry this unfortunate man up to the house. We shall invade Mrs. Driver's scullery, I think, tho' she may well give notice on the strength of it." He wheeled on the beaters, who had been chewing idly on pieces of straw as tho' we were engaged in nothing more than a delightful picnic excursion. "You there, Monk, collect the bags, and Jack, you take the gentlemen's guns. On no account should they be cleaned; leave them in the gun room just as they are, until I have had an opportunity to examine them."

"And the dogs, sir?" Monk objected.

Edward glanced at me. "The dogs will follow Miss Austen, I think. She has a way with them."

This was an outrageous lie, but I did not regard it. "Dr. Bredloe is also the coroner?" I asked, as I hurried to keep pace with my brother, who was striding ahead of the shooting-party as it struggled to bear its ghastly burden. The leg that had been bent under the corpse in falling, had already stiffened in that position. I was on the point of alerting Edward to this curious fact when he stopped me with a word.

"Bredloe is a man who knows how to keep his mouth shut. I think that is of vital importance, Jane, do not you?"

FOR A WONDER, THE PACK OF SPANIELS DANCED AT MY heels all the way back to the house.

CHAPTER FOUR

The Pilgrim's Tale

"For I dissolve all promises and vows,
All grants you think I've made, all guarantees.
You fool, don't you know that love is free,
And I would love her whether you weren't or were?"

GEOFFREY CHAUCER, "THE KNIGHT'S TALE"

21 OCTOBER 1813, CONT.

~

"MY DEAR MISS AUSTEN!" CRIED MISS CLEWES, WHO WAS hovering near the stairs with a square of linen clutched in one bony hand as I entered the Great Hall, "I was never more shocked! When our excellent Fanny *told* me what dreadful events had occurred in the Park, and of the *death* of that poor innocent at the hands of our gentlemen—a pilgrim, no less, intent upon an errand of expiation for his soul—I declare I suffered *palpitations*! Poor Lizzy and Marianne administered my vinaigrette, tho' I am sure they were *equally* overcome, poor lambs! I should be lying down upon my bed this *instant*, were it not that my sense of duty required me to remain up-right, and offer what assistance a frail woman may, in a household o'erwhelmed by tragedy!"

Miss Clewes is a recent addition to Godmersham, having been engaged by Fanny as governess for her little sisters only a few months ago. In this capacity, Miss Clewes follows a succession of unfortunates, both old and young, who have attempted to earn their bread by imposing order in Edward's chaotic nursery in the years since Elizabeth's death. I do not dislike Miss Clewes; indeed, I pity any woman whose circumstances are so sadly left that she must secure a respectable position in a genteel household—for governessing is in general an unhappy lot. I know full well that without the excessive generosity of my brothers, my sister, Cassandra, and I might well have been forced to a similar servitude—existing in that wretched limbo between serving hall and drawing-room, never comfortable in either sphere and despised as imposters by both. Instead, we two have been sustained by the funds contributed yearly by our excellent brothers—and by Chawton Cottage itself, which Edward was so good as to make over to our use. Tho' we possess no carriage and set up no stable, tho' we scheme and contrive to dress in a respectable ape of fashion, we four women—for I count my mother and my fellow lodger Mary Lloyd in this—are blessedly fortunate. The luxury of being free from want has allowed me to indulge the frivolity of writing. That I have been able to command a minor independence, from the monies secured by the sale of my novels, is but an added comfort. Miss Clewes was never so lucky.

Some awareness of the similarity, and quelling difference, in our circumstances encouraged me to answer her cheerfully now, when I might have lashed out with impatience. Miss Clewes is too prone to die-away airs for my taste; and tho' not unintelligent, her volubility cannot serve to recommend her sense. A silly but well-intentioned creature without a particle of harm in her—that is Miss Clewes. Or so I was thinking, until she uttered the fatal sentence that must banish all charity.

"Naturally, I went *straight* to our excellent Mr. Moore, that he might offer a prayer for the repose of the dead," she assured me, with evident satisfaction. "I thought it an office of the *first* importance, and was gratified to discover that my failing energies were equal to *so much*, at least."

"You had better have sent him on an errand to Canterbury!" I sighed in exasperation. "Mr. Moore is *exactly* the person I should wish as far from the scullery as possible, at this present. He is sure to read us a sermon on the sad consequences of the encouragement of *sport* as a pursuit for young gentlemen, with illustrative anecdotes of his own excellent rearing under the late Archbishop. Dear Lord, I *must* attempt to keep him out of Edward's way—"

Miss Clewes was immediately wounded. "My dear Miss Austen," she cried, wringing her handkerchief—"I had no notion you would be *displeased* by a consideration of Christian charity—and must beg you will *forgive* my *presumption,* if such it was—but indeed, Mr. Moore's views on the rearing of young people are highly worthy. On countless occasions he has condescended to advise me on the curbing of dear Lizzy's temper, and the encouragement of Marianne in the use of the backboard—"

I did not linger to learn further what Mr. Moore thought necessary to the education of young ladies. Instead, I hastened in the direction of the housekeeper Mrs. Driver's preserve: the warren of rooms below-stairs that comprehend the kitchens, serving hall, housekeeper's and butler's sitting rooms, pantries, stillroom, and scullery.

This last was a clean but chilly room equipped with two deep wash basins, a draining board, and a trestle table of scrubbed pine. The dead pilgrim had been laid carefully on the latter, to the evident disapproval of Mrs. Driver and the scullery maid, a girl of perhaps seventeen, who stared in bewildered horror at this invasion of her realm. A large stack of breakfast dishes had been hurriedly removed to the draining board, and steam still rose from the wash basins; the girl's raw, red hands twisted nervously in her apron.

"Get along with you," Mrs. Driver said crossly, "gawping like a heathen at a poor, Christian man wot's met his Maker—" and she urged the maid out into the passage.

I eased through the doorway, which was almost entirely blocked by the worthy Mr. Moore, who appeared disinclined to breach the scullery itself and perform the duty for which he had been despatched. Perhaps it was the mingled odours of dirty dishes, hot iron tubs, and aging corpse that discouraged him—a faint expression of distaste was writ on his harsh features. Or perhaps he abhorred a crush—the small room was rather crowded with my brother Edward, his son George, Mr. Finch-Hatton, John Plumptre, and James Wildman—who, having laid their burden on the trestle table, appeared uncertain what further was required of them.

"George," Edward said, "take these fellows upstairs where they may wash, and then recruit the general strength with tankards of ale all around. Mrs. Driver shall see to a nuncheon, presently."

"That is very good of you, sir," Wildman said hesitantly, "but I wonder whether we might relieve your mind by taking ourselves off—and returning to Chilham directly."

Edward's blue eyes met the younger man's indifferently. "You may certainly do so—once the coroner has seen this man and heard your recital from your own lips. Until those duties have been discharged, I must beg you to remain under this roof, James."

Wildman glanced at Finch-Hatton, who shrugged slightly.

"Naturally we shall remain," John Plumptre said stiffly. "I should not *dream* of leaving you with such a tangle on your hands, Mr. Knight, having been a party to the cause of it. That should be a shirking of responsibility no gentleman worthy of the name would entertain. We shall be grateful for the nuncheon, but our first object must be to ascertain whether Miss Knight is entirely recovered from her shock of this morning—which, in the event, must have been considerable."

"Oh, Fanny's all right," Finch-Hatton drawled. "I'd go bail she'd stand buff against anything—capital little body, Fanny! But if we *must* stay here, we might have a neatish game of billiards, by the by. You don't object to ale in the billiard room, sir, surely?"

"Not unless you're prone to spill it," Edward returned brusquely. "Mrs. Driver has enough mess on her hands this morning."

Finch-Hatton had been lounging in the doorway again—it seemed the only possible attitude that young man could adopt. Now he thrust himself away from it with such an air of insouciance that the dead stranger might have been so much trussed game. What *was* it about Jupiter that drove all the young ladies of the neighbourhood to tears of ecstasy whenever he came in their way? The blond hair, unruly over the chiseled brow? The full lips, given to the most sardonic of twists? The powerful figure of a sportsman? —Or exactly this attitude of immense boredom towards the world and everyone in it? I suppose it might be considered *something,* for a young lady to excite so weary a fellow's notice; but for my part, the conquest seemed not worth the prize.

"George." Edward nodded peremptorily in the direction of the door, and the gentlemen trouped out of the scullery without another word.

"Young Finch-Hatton is growing positively insolent," Mr. Moore observed. His nostrils were compressed as tho' *insolence* bore as strong an odour as the stables. "I wonder his papa does not check him. But, then, as I suppose it is *possible* he will be called an earl one day—perhaps the cultivation of arrogance is permissible."

"An earl?" I repeated. Fanny had said nothing of this; Mr.

Finch-Hatton's prospects had thus far entailed nothing more than the inheritance of Eastwell Park, a rather ugly modern house some seven miles distant.

Mr. Moore shrugged. "It is unlikely, of course—but Finch-Hatton stands to inherit the title if the present Earl of Win-chilsea fails to produce an heir. His cousin's estate is so entailed.[1] You may imagine how this increases his appeal among the damsels of the neighbourhood. My excellent wife has condescended to remark upon it."

"Enough of Jupiter," Edward said. "You have heard something of our sad mishap, I collect?"

"And of its cause," Mr. Moore replied heavily. "On how many occasions have I observed the total want of care and reverence so essential to the employment of firearms, among the youth of our acquaintance! I suppose we must give thanks that it was not one of our *own* young gentlemen who suffered the fatal tragedy; but that any should be compelled to offer up his life, in the cause of another man's *mere sport*—"

There it was, the inevitable stricture—but Edward cut off his old friend with one raised hand. "This fellow did not die of a fowling piece," he said quietly. "Step closer, and observe the wound."

As I expected, Edward had seen all that I had seen: the stiffness of the limbs, unnatural in one only lately killed; the way the blood had seeped entirely into the ground in the hours before the body was discovered by Bessy the spaniel, so that Mr. Plumptre's coat was not even stained when we knelt upon it; the deathly cold of the unfortunate man's skin; the coagulation of fluids around the wound; and the wound

[1] Mr. Moore proves prescient here. George Finch-Hatton (1791–1858), the Jupiter of this account, did indeed succeed his cousin as 10th Earl of Win-chilsea in 1826. He has gone down in history for having fought a duel with the Duke of Wellington, who was then Prime Minister, over Catholic Eman-cipation in 1829. Jupiter opposed it. —*Editor's note.*

itself—which was formed of a single, neat hole in the left breast, undoubtedly through the heart.

"There are even the marks of powder on the man's coat," I observed distantly, "as tho' his assailant stood quite near him when the pistol was fired. A sort of Judas kiss, in fact."

"Pistol?" Mr. Moore glanced at me in consternation; I must presume that ladies were not permitted to display a broader knowledge of the world than was seemly, when in the presence of the late Archbishop's son. "Are you suggesting he was already *dead* when those young fools fired upon him?"

"They did not fire upon him," Edward declared. "They fired upon a covey of pheasant—and bagged five birds. I shall make a thorough examination of the fowling pieces, and await Dr. Bredloe's expert opinion, naturally—but I should think this man has been dead for hours. Would not you agree, Jane?"

"Entirely. I should be interested to learn the doctor's opinion as to the approximate hour of death, however—the night air in autumn is chill, but the ground still retains some warmth; that variance must affect the degree of stiffening we have observed."

"Good God!" Mr. Moore exclaimed, with all the outrage of a man confounded by a female's brazen disregard for decorum; "are you actually *suggesting* that this man was . . . was . . ."

"Murdered? I am, sir."

The clergyman shot me one appalled glance, then strode quickly towards the body.

There was a brief silence, punctuated by Mr. Moore's shallow breathing; Edward raised one amused eyebrow in my direction, and shrugged slightly. Then the clergyman said, in a voice quite raw with suppressed emotion, "You have summoned Bredloe? He is even now making for Godmersham?"

"I hope so, indeed."

Mr. Moore swung around and stared at Edward, his pallor ghastly. "Idiot! You had better have thrown the corpse in the Stour, and allowed some other to find it!"

"What wild talking is this?" Edward exclaimed, astonished.

"You do *understand* that this is no pilgrim lying dead in your house? You *apprehend* the disaster that is about to break about all our heads?"

I stared at my brother in bewilderment, and read an equal incomprehension in his countenance.

"What can you possibly mean, sir?" I attempted.

Mr. Moore swept his hands wide in a gesture of despair; out of habit, perhaps, they formed a benediction over the dead man's chest. "You see before you the corpse of a prodigal son returned—and at how *ill* an hour. I do not know what may be said to Adelaide. Or how the intelligence is to be conveyed to her. When she learns—"

"You would refer to Mrs. MacCallister?" I asked.

"I would." But Mr. Moore was not attending to me; his gaze was all for Edward—the First Magistrate of Canterbury. "This man is none other than Curzon Fiske, whom his wife believed dead long since."

"—And on the strength of that belief," my brother said slowly, "was yesterday married to another."

We were none of us required to utter the hateful word *bigamy* aloud; it jangled unspoken in all our minds.

CHAPTER FIVE

A Pact of Silence

Success—as clerics say, all things have their time—

GEOFFREY CHAUCER, "THE MERCHANT'S TALE"

21 OCTOBER 1813, CONT.

"BY ALL THAT'S HOLY," EDWARD SAID SOFTLY AS HE STUD-
ied the corpse's features, "you have the right of it, Moore.
Curzon Fiske! The beard and whiskers deceived me—not to
mention the humble mode of dress and the excessive tanning
of the skin, which should not be unnatural in one only lately
returned from the Indies. I should never have known him,
however, but for your better knowledge of the man."

Mr. Moore visibly recoiled. "We were acquainted well
enough when we were boys, to be sure," he said. "I do not
think there is more than a twelvemonth's difference in our
ages, indeed, and our fathers were friends of long standing.
But in later years, our ways lay much apart."

"—Once Fiske won the hand of Adelaide Thane, you
would mean." My brother met the clergyman's gaze with a
level look. There had been just that suggestion in Harriot

Moore's teazing last night—that her husband had once cherished a *tendre* for the young lady who had married Curzon Fiske.

Mr. Moore frowned. "The entire nature of Fiske's pursuits—his whole manner of living—was repugnant to me, as well you know, Edward! I could not regard his stile of living, or his choice of acquaintance, with approbation. It has been long and long since we two had anything but reproaches to offer one another; and tho' I was grieved indeed to learn of Curzon's death, I will freely own I thought it a happy release from a life that had grown burdensome—to more than just himself."

"You had no notion he survived the fever that was reported to have killed him?" my brother asked mildly.

"None whatsoever! Do you sincerely believe I should have *countenanced* Mrs. Fiske's marriage yesterday to Captain MacCallister, had I doubted the veracity of those reports?"

"I do not."

"Very well." Mr. Moore looked slightly relieved. "Then I suppose it is for us, now, to determine what is to be done."

My brother knit his brows. "I propose to await Dr. Bredloe, as I have stated already. There must be an inquest, and it is for the coroner to decide when and where that shall be conducted. Once Bredloe has seen enough of the remains, I propose to remove Mr. Fiske to a more suitable location in Canterbury—whichever publick house Bredloe chuses for the empanelment of his jury."

"But there is Mrs. MacCallister to consider," I interjected. "Surely she must be told?"

"On no account would I have us commit such needless folly!" Mr. Moore's words burst from his mouth with a ferocity I had never witnessed in him—and he was a man whose ill-temper was notorious. "No possible good may be served by cutting up that unfortunate woman's peace; she is happy in her present union; let her remain so! It should be the final insult her late husband might deliver, to destroy Mrs. MacCallister's reputation—having already destroyed so much."

"You forget yourself, Moore," Edward said bluntly. "The man was foully murdered. Would you deny even Curzon Fiske his measure of English justice?"

"I would deny such a man *anything* he had so palpably failed to earn," Mr. Moore returned with heat.

"Gentlemen!" I cried. "I beg of you—a quarrel between yourselves cannot hope to serve our ends. Pray consider what you are about."

Edward smiled grimly, and Mr. Moore bowed—more in respect of a lady, than of any sense I might have uttered.

"There is but one honourable course of action before us," the clergyman insisted. "Convey to that unhappy pair the intelligence of Fiske's discovery if you *must*—but preserve an absolute silence regarding the *nature* and *time* of his death. The man was murdered, so you say—but we cannot possibly apprehend the circumstances; he might have done away with himself, after all; and the principal point, as I see it, is that Fiske *is no more*—as he was believed, long since, not to be!"

"But—" Edward objected.

"That Fiske is *dead*," Mr. Moore blundered on, "preserves the respectability of his wife's late marriage; and I cannot see that canvassing the exact *hour* or *agent* of that death will achieve any greater purpose! The blackguard may have died two days ago, as easily as half an hour since; and therefore, no discussion of the subject ought to be allowed further than this room. Will you both swear to that?"

He glared defiantly first at my brother, and then at me, as tho' suspecting I should be the sort of woman determined to spoil sport. I could not find it in my heart to disappoint him.

"But surely the *time* of Mr. Fiske's murder must tell us a

good deal about the *identity* of the one who killed him?" I observed, with all apparent innocence. "It appears to me a vital point. When he was merely a faceless pilgrim, anyone might have done the deed; a mere footpad or chance miscreant. But as a gentleman formerly well-known in the neighbourhood—one returned from distant climes at almost the very hour of his wife's marriage to another!—Fiske becomes a sinister presence, one of peculiar interest. The very elements of scandal you would suppress, Mr. Moore, are exactly those that must be probed, if the murderer is to be named."

"Trust a woman to entirely misapprehend the facts," he retorted impatiently.

"I would argue that my sister has grasped them more clearly than yourself, Moore," Edward said, with a speaking look for me. "Captain and Mrs. MacCallister were to set out from Chilham Castle on their wedding trip this very morning, were they not? A tour of Cornwall, I collect, where the Captain possesses some acquaintance?"

"He has the loan of a country house in the neighbourhood of Penzance," Mr. Moore supplied. He ran his fingers through his greying locks distractedly. "But they intended to reach no further than London today, and were to spend an interval in Town, I believe. All the more reason to hold the inquest quietly in their absence."

"You cannot be *serious,* Moore," Edward retorted in exasperation. "It will not fadge, and you know it. I am First Magistrate for this neighbourhood; I regard my charge as a sacred one; I should never shut my eyes to certain truths, merely because they invite scandal for one or another of my acquaintance. Curzon Fiske was once a respectable member of Kentish society—and you would hush up his death as tho' he were a convict, shot while escaping from Newgate! You must be mad to think I should agree to such terms, merely from considerations of Mrs. MacCallister's reputation! If she married MacCallister while Fiske yet lived, she undoubtedly did so in error—and the ill may be immediately remedied, with a quiet service performed this very evening at Chilham. You must see the sense of that—and I am persuaded you will regret your scheme, once your mind has grown cool."

"And *I* am persuaded that *you* will long regret this morning's work, Edward, when events have destroyed much more than Curzon Fiske!" The clergyman struggled for mastery of his temper; appeared on the point of speaking further; then wheeled and strode in fury from the room.

My brother and I stared at one another in consternation.

"Well, well." Edward sighed. "I cannot think that marrying George Moore was the *wisest* thing poor Harriot has ever done."

"We must not judge him by this morning's events."

"I beg your pardon, Jane, but I judge the fellow on a *host* of events, witnessed over a period of some years," my brother retorted bitterly. He paused in contemplation a moment, and I was reminded of nothing so much as my late father, when wrestling with a spiritual question of no small doctrinal importance. I had never thought Edward very like dear Papa before—Henry has more of my father's humour in him; but there is as much Religion, I must suppose, in the conduct of Law as there is in the salvation of men's souls.

Edward's eyes met mine. "Tho' I hate to do it, I suppose I must send an Express after the MacCallisters, Jane—and tear them from their happy dream as soon as may be."

"Ought not the message to come from Mr. James Wildman's hand?" I suggested gently. "He is, after all, Mrs. MacCallister's cousin. Better that he should break the unhappy truth, than that she should learn it from a complete stranger."

"You have the right of it, Jane, as always," Edward said gratefully. "I shall roust Wildman from the billiard room straight away, and set him down with pen and paper."

"I wonder that Mr. Wildman himself did not recognise Curzon Fiske," I said thoughtfully. "For surely he must have known him well, in better days."

"Nobody thinks to recognise a dead man," my brother said simply, and quitted the room.

There was a bustle above-stairs; I suspected the coroner was arrived. And so, with one last glance for the silent figure laid out on the trestle table, I closed the scullery door behind me and ascended to the Great Hall.

CHAPTER SIX

The Uses of Gossip

"Now let the woman speak her tale this day.
You act as if you're drinking too much ale."

GEOFFREY CHAUCER, "THE WIFE OF BATH'S PROLOGUE"

21 OCTOBER 1813, CONT.

DR. HAMISH BREDLOE IS A SCOTSMAN, WHO LEARNT HIS profession in Edinburgh—a very knowledgeable centre of learning, I believe, in matters of natural philosophy. Having established an excellent practice as a physician in London some decades since, he had lately retired to the wealthy environs of Canterbury, and had been burdened with the office of coroner at his own request. At a time in life when a man might be expected to cultivate peace, and bask in the glow of honours accumulated through long years' acquaintance with the Great, Dr. Bredloe had discovered a restlessness and boredom that might soon have killed him, had he not devoted his energies to the determination of Manners of Death, and the inveighing against Misadventure, Malice Aforethought, and Person or Persons Unknown. An interest in the sordid and the low may not have won him numerous invitations to dine among the great houses of Kent; but it had rendered him invaluable to gentlemen like Edward—who were charged with the maintenance of justice, and took that charge in all seriousness. Edward regarded Dr. Bredloe as a man possessed of the keenest understanding, and one whose good opinion he would not lightly foreswear. Hence his utter abhorrence of Mr. Moore's proposals, regarding a conspiracy of silence; Edward should never attempt to suborn the coroner, as he must undoubtedly have done had he acceded to the clergyman's scheme.

Mr. Moore was not to be discovered above-stairs, and had perhaps sought reflection in his wife's company, or in guiding his young son through a lesson in Greek, as I had observed he was wont to do when the desire for mastery was firmly upon him. Edward was able, therefore, to conduct Dr. Bredloe to the body at once—explaining, as he did so, the curious circumstance of the gentleman's identity.

Beyond curtseying at Dr. Bredloe's observance, and bridling a little under his sharp glance, I did not hover in the coroner's vicinity. He would undoubtedly wish to disrobe the corpse, and there could be no cause for my observance of such an examination; I was content to learn the doctor's conclusions once he had regained Edward's book room, and was established over a glass of Madeira.

In the meantime, I sought out my niece Fanny.

I found her standing distractedly in the little saloon at the rear of the house, arranging a posy of late summer flowers that *must* have come from a succession-house, for none of Godmersham's blooms had survived the relentless chill rains.

"Aren't they lovely, Aunt?" she murmured, her cheeks aflame. "Mr. Thane has been so kind as to send them from Chilham. He knows nothing of our sad business here—reflects only on the gaieties of last evening, poor fellow! What a shock it shall be to him, when he hears!"

Mr. Thane, offering a tribute of flowers to a lady, the morning after a ball. The Regency Buck was up to every trick, and should never be backwards in any attention—my dear Fanny's head was certain to be turned. She could not leave off admiring her flowers, though a nuncheon had been thoughtfully laid out upon a sideboard: sliced apples, a large cheese, cold ham and tongue, and a platter of sausages with the special mustard for which Mrs. Driver is famous.

Of the gentlemen, my nephew George, Jupiter Finch-Hatton, and Mr. Lushington—I had forgot to mention Mr. Lushington, but shall explain him presently—were to be seen; the rest of the shooting-party, Fanny informed me, were hanging over Mr. James Wildman as he attempted to craft his delicate missive to his cousin Adelaide.

"Tho' ten to one they are merely disturbing his train of thought, and causing him to blot his copy," Finch-Hatton observed with a yawn. "I declined to make another of such a great passel of boobies."

"Mr. Plumptre might be of signal assistance," Fanny retorted, her eyes flashing, "for he is a very *learned* young man, I believe, and devotes considerable hours to questions of philosophy."

"—Sure to drive poor Mrs. MacCallister into strong hysterics, then," Finch-Hatton rejoined, "and make a vile situation entirely desperate. Plumptre was never such a dead bore when he was living in Kent—I declare that Oxford has much to answer for, when unexceptionable young men are turned prosy and prudish, and all from reading too much in books. Ought to be outlawed, in my opinion."

Mr. Lushington burst out in laughter at this sally, and speared a sausage with a convenient knife. "Good God, George," he said—meaning Mr. Finch-Hatton, not my young nephew; there are no less than four Georges at Godmersham at present. "A few more books might render your conversation bearable—to me as well as to the ladies. Any more of it,

I warn you, and I'll pack you off to Oxford myself—tho' you *are* several years past your scholarly prime."

Mr. Stephen Rumbold Lushington is an excellent man, all smiling, wide teeth, and good address; he is our Member of Parliament for Canterbury, and is, I daresay, ambitious and insincere—your short men often are—but he speaks so well of Milton, when he has a volume of the master in his hands, that I am a little in love with him, despite his being a year younger than myself and already married these fifteen years at least. And why is Mr. Lushington staying the night at God-mersham, one may ask? Because in this house there is a constant succession of small events; somebody is always going or coming. The world entire walks in and out of my brother Edward's doors and heartily consents to remain for dinner. Mr. Lushington, besides being our MP, is also Manager of the Lodge Hounds; he came to talk of fox hunting with young Edward, and shall be leaving us one day or another. I shall make good use of him before he goes, however, for I mean to get a frank for my letter to Cassandra—if ever I find a moment to sit down and write it.[1]

"Is it true, Aunt, that the dead pilgrim is really Curzon Fiske?" George demanded breathlessly. He was, after all, but seventeen—and tho' much inclined to ape Jupiter's affectations, and in awe of Mr. Lushington, he could not mask avidity with studied indifference.

"So it would seem. Your father, I am sure, shall tell you all about it."

"Dashed smoky affair," Mr. Lushington remarked briskly.

---

[1] Members of Parliament and peers were permitted to affix their signatures or seals to letters, allowing them to be delivered free of charge—a practice known as "franking." Otherwise, Cassandra would have paid the fee for Jane's letter, according to its weight, upon receiving it from the post. —*Editor's note.*

"But Mr. Knight shall sort it all out for the rest of us, I am sure."

"Were you at all acquainted with Mr. Fiske in former years, sir?" I asked.

He appeared to hesitate, tho' perhaps he was merely digesting his sausage. "I suppose I knew him a little, but very long ago, I'm afraid. You could have knocked me over with a feather when I learnt he had been found but a stone's throw from this door—and dead yet *again*!"

"Poor Mrs. MacCallister," murmured Fanny in my ear. "To think that she was married to the Captain in all innocence—and that the union is now thrown under a cloud! How unkind is Fate! I have been turning it over in my mind all morning—and am so troubled in spirit I declare I have not been able to swallow a mouthful! Every feeling revolts at the sight of *food*, when such tragedy oppresses the soul!"

"Then I am certain I possess not the slightest sensibility at all," I told her mildly, "for I have never sat down to breakfast—and am utterly famished! I shall certainly carve myself a slice of ham, and perhaps some cheese, and if Mrs. Driver can discover one of Cook's apple tarts hiding in the larder, I may be so bold as to request a slice, with a strong pot of tea. If events continue as they have begun, my dear Fanny, we are all of us likely to miss dinner, as well—so pray force yourself to whatever you find least disgusting, lest you faint dead away upon a sopha."

"The sausages are excellent," Mr. Lushington observed.

"Made of pheasant," Jupiter Finch-Hatton added with a roguish look, "tho' *not* the ones we bagged this morning."

"*Pheasant,*" Fanny whispered with revulsion, the circumstances of Mr. Fiske's discovery no doubt rising in her mind. "How can you speak so, Mr. Finch-Hatton, when a man lies dead but one floor below?"

"Now, don't go all *missish* on me, Fanny." He pierced a

slice of apple with an idle fork, and offered it to her with a bow. "Man's been dead for years, after all—or as good as."

"But only consider of the anxieties that must attend this dreadful news among all those who remain at Chilham Castle," she returned in a trembling accent. "Mrs. Thane, for instance, and . . . and . . . young Mr. Thane, both of whom must feel so *deeply* for Mrs. MacCallister in the present case—do you not think, Aunt, that it is our duty to accompany Mr. Wildman when he returns home, to condole with all his relations? We might be able to assure them, from our hearts, that every proper observance is being accorded to the unfortunate Mr. Fiske's remains."

As I wished very much to observe the effect of the unfortunate Mr. Fiske's *second* death upon those most nearly related to him, I was on the point of adopting Fanny's scheme; but I required rather more of the late gentleman's history first.

"My dear girl," I suggested, "you are looking decidedly unwell. Let us send the gentlemen back to their billiards, until such time as the coroner is able to hear their story of the morning's events—while you and I repair to your boudoir. We might have our tea and apple tart brought up at once, and consume them there in peace."

"I assure you, I could not swallow a mouthful!"

"Fanny, I should like to have a word with you in private."

As one of my speaking looks attended these words, her indignant expression faded. "Very well, Aunt. I do admit to wanting my tea." She ignored Mr. Finch-Hatton's speared apple, sweeping by that cosseted gentleman with a scornful look that quite astonished him. "George, do pray challenge Mr. Finch-Hatton and Mr. Lushington to a game—and mind," she added in a lowered tone as she passed her brother, "that you trounce Jupiter soundly."

"Now," I said once we were settled by a brisk fire in the

comfortable sitting room Edward had made over for his eldest daughter's comfort, and which had been freshened with paint and hung with gaily-flowered paper during her absence that summer, "tell me everything you know of Curzon Fiske and Adelaide Thane."

Fanny's generally placid countenance was suffused in an instant with a wary aspect. "I did not take you for a common gossip, Aunt Jane."

"Nonsense! You have been in receipt of my letters your whole life—and they are never filled with anything else! Very amusing, too, I daresay you find them. Do not be a hypocrite, Fanny. I cannot admire Jupiter Finch-Hatton, but I confess in this we are in agreement—*missishness* does not suit you."

My niece flushed. "It is because of such creatures as Finch-Hatton and the rest that I was determined never to canvass all that old business—when Mrs. MacCallister is so happy, and so blessed, in her *present* choice. If you knew the avid looks and whispered slander that have followed her, even in the weeks preceding her wedding-party . . . I should never willingly add to so vile a chorus."

"And I commend you for it. But do consider, you pea-goose, how strident the chorus shall become when the lady—or her husband—or perhaps, even, her brother—is taken up by your excellent father for *murder*."

"What?" Fanny reared up from the sopha in dismay, and whirled upon me like a tigress. "You cannot mean it! None of the Thanes—and neither of the MacCallisters—was of the shooting-party this morning! You might as well accuse my brother Edward, or Jupiter himself!"

"I might, had Mr. Fiske been shot by a fowling piece in the middle of a crowd of beaters and dogs—but he was not, Fanny. He was murdered in cold blood in the dead of night, probably by a duelling pistol at close range. Or so I suspect the excellent Dr. Bredloe shall soon inform us."

I took a sip of tea to allow her time to clamber down from her high horse. "I observed the black marks of powder discharged upon the man's coat. He was certainly standing within inches of the person who killed him, and his belongings were tidily stowed to one side of the path—which suggests that he both knew his murderer, and was expecting to meet that person exactly where we found his body at about eleven o'clock this morning."

"Good Lord," Fanny said faintly, and sank back down upon the sopha.

"I am not an intimate of Kentish society, as you know." Cook's apple tart, I discovered, was unequal to the one my friend Martha Lloyd was in the habit of making, but was commendable nonetheless. "I have not been among you, indeed, in some four years. Adelaide Fiske, neé Thane, was an utter stranger to me before she proceeded down the aisle of Mr. Tylden's church—and her first husband I do not recollect ever having met at all. I have heard some of the gossip you mention, of course—your young friends Sophia Deedes and her sisters were at it, hammer and tongs, even during last night's ball—but I should far prefer a more sober history, delivered by *yourself*."

"But you cannot truly believe it possible that someone we know—someone, perhaps, that I even danced with—could be capable of shedding an innocent man's blood?"

Ah. The shadow of Julian Thane's compelling countenance had slipped between us.

"I think it unlikely in the extreme that Mr. Fiske was killed by a stranger to himself," I told my niece. "Beyond that, I may speculate nothing. Only consider, Fanny, how odd it is that he should appear in the neighbourhood of Chilham, on the very night of his wife's second marriage . . . an event that he could have thrown into chaos."

"—Had he known of it," she pointed out. "We cannot be

certain he was even aware of the festivities at Chilham. Had he been, should he not have exerted himself to halt so bigamous a proceeding? Aunt Jane! Can you believe it possible that *any* gentleman should behave otherwise? No, no! You throw everything that is *right* and *good* into disorder, and by so doing, force all the parties concerned to behave in the most awkward and extraordinary fashion! Surely there is a more rational, and simpler, explanation?"

Poor Fanny. She had much to learn of the world, if she believed that all about her were *right* and *good,* and the reverse extraordinary. But I said only, "Murder has the effect of twisting awry what once appeared to be order. I cannot begin to conjecture what occurred in Mr. Fiske's case—who might be embroiled, and whom we may place entirely in the clear—until I know more of the man and his history."

Fanny drew breath, and studied my countenance for the space of several heartbeats. "You are a formidable lady, are you not, Aunt Jane?" she asked wistfully. "When I was a child, I was used to think you were like a good faerie—always dropping out of the sky with your delightful stories, and the dolls-clothes you embroidered so neatly; playing at cricket regardless of the stains the lawn left on your dress, and teaching the little ones to toss spillikins. It is only now I am grown older—and have been privileged to read your novels, and apprehend the subtlety of your observations—that I know how cold a reason you command."

"I shall chuse to take that as a compliment." I set down my tea, which was growing tepid despite the warmth of the fire. "Cold reason may be a useful tool, Fanny, in your father's pursuit of justice; for make no mistake, he *shall* pursue it, whichever one of his neighbours he must force into a noose. As he said only this morning, Curzon Fiske was a Kentishman, and deserves his measure of English law—no matter how depraved his past life may have been, or how justly his murderer regarded the taking of such a life. You may help me, or no; but in helping me, you may save one of your friends from all the calamity of an unjust accusation."

"Or tie a rope around his neck," she said grimly. "This is serious speaking, indeed. Very well—I shall tell you what I know, but let it be understood, Aunt Jane, that I was a child when Adelaide Thane consented to be Fiske's bride, and but seventeen when that gentleman fled England. He is so much older than the fellows of our set—I daresay he was almost *elderly*, nearly Papa's age!—that I was never acquainted with him myself. Much of what I have learnt, therefore, has been taught at second-hand. Partial as the intelligence may be, however, I shall make you a gift of it."

CHAPTER SEVEN

The Curious History of Curzon Fiske

You slender wives, though much too feeble for battle,
Be fierce, like tigers roaming far-off India—

GEOFFREY CHAUCER, "THE CLERIC'S TALE"

21 OCTOBER 1813, CONT.

CURZON FISKE, FANNY ASSURED ME AS WE SETTLED IN FOR a comfortable coze, was born of highly respectable parents— his father the second son of a viscount, and his mother the daughter of an earl. The family lived in stile in Chartham, Kent, some four miles distant from Godmersham. Fanny was well acquainted with another Chartham family, the Faggs, whose father held the parish living there; and it was in part from the intelligence gleaned by the clergyman's numerous daughters—all of whom were acknowledged to be lamentably plain, and thus prone to gossip from a persistent desire for Notice—that she was in possession of so many of the whisperings that surrounded Curzon Fiske.

He had been reared, it was said, with considerable indulgence, being privy to the wilder habits of his noble cousins;
and tho' sent away to Eton at the age of ten, where his
schoolboy days were edified by the example of one George
Moore, a year his senior, he declined further instruction at the
higher centres of learning, spurning both Oxford and Cambridge. The death of his excellent father while Fiske was as
yet in his minority, threw his estate into the hands of trustees
until he should achieve the age of one-and-twenty. Having
done so in due course, he came into a respectable compe-
tence, without having inherited a fortune. This, according to
Fanny, he contrived to dissipate in the swiftest possible fashion, through a determined exploration of the more notorious
gaming hells the Metropolis might offer; an unbridled fond-
ness for coats by Weston and boots by Hoby; and a predilec-
tion for the maintenance of a string of racehorses that
invariably failed to place.

If Fiske's former neighbours in Kent suspected that his
funds were equally at the disposal of a string of High-Flying
Cyprians, those frivolous members of the Muslin Company,
whose petulant favours must be won with excessive outlays
of cash on carriages, jewels, and snug little residences in Rich-
mond—such exploits had never come to Fanny's ears. Or perhaps she thought her elderly Aunt Jane should be *shocked* to
learn such things from her innocent niece's lips. Regardless,
no mention was made of Mr. Fiske's amorous proclivities—
until the advent of Adelaide Thane.

It was evident to all, Fanny cautioned, that by the age of
four-and-thirty Curzon Fiske had achieved so remarkable a
degree of dissipation that he was no longer acknowledged by
most of his old friends in Kent. There were genial clubmen
abiding in Town—rakes, for the most part, or Pinks of the
Ton, Slap Up to the Echo, who continued to regard Mr. Fiske
as a Knowing One, and the best of good fellows—but re-

spectable mammas, with daughters to push off on the Marriage Mart, shepherded their charges in the opposite direction when Curzon Fiske hove into view. For the pockets of Mr. Fiske were entirely to let, and he was well-known to be hanging out for a rich wife.

By six-and-thirty, he had been forced to sell his patrimony in Kent—the comfortable manor at Chartham—and send his aging mother and unmarried sisters into lodgings in a dismal quarter of Bath. By seven-and-thirty, he had been refused by no less than nine young ladies of unimpeachable virtue and moderate wealth. At eight-and-thirty, he espied Adelaide Thane moving through the figures of the quadrille at Almack's on the arm of his old friend, George Moore, whose first wife had lately died—and was lost.

She was, at the time, but seventeen years old. She betrayed already, however, the regal bearing and dark beauty that would ripen, in time, to the depth of elegance I had admired so completely last evening. Fiske stared at her as she went down the dance, and determined to wrest her attentions from Moore.

Miss Thane was no heiress. Her father had been a gamester, well-known to Fiske from numerous encounters across the punting tables. She was exactly the sort of woman he ought *not* to pursue, much less marry—and so of course Fiske was compelled to achieve both. In wooing Adelaide Thane, he pitted himself against one of his oldest friends; George Moore was frank in admitting his object was to gain the lady's hand, and the rivalry added spice to Fiske's conquest. He set himself to be all that was charming; devoted himself to Miss Thane and her mother—who was wise enough to recognise a wastrel when she met one, having lived her life in a gamester's pocket—and succeeded in encouraging that wary female to ride tyrant over her daughter, threatening the young lady with incarceration in her bedchamber and bread-and-water for a week, if Adelaide chose to encourage such an ineligible *parti*.

Naturally, when Fiske was forced to flee London for relief from his creditors, the impressionable Miss Thane was ready to throw her future into his hands, and elope to Paris. The triumph was achieved one windy midnight, with a headlong flight to Dover and a perilous crossing prolonged by foul weather for some twenty hours, the prospective bride prostrate with seasickness for the duration.

"How long ago was this?" I interjected.

"The year Six, I believe," Fanny replied, "for it was *then* that Mr. Moore took Aunt Harriot as his wife."

"—Seeking consolation in the arms of propriety and baronet's blood, having been worsted in the fight for Beauty."

"I should not describe Aunt Harriot as *ill-favoured,* exactly," Fanny said doubtfully, "tho' it is certain she cannot shine when compared to Adelaide Fiske, and she possesses only a moderate understanding. Dear Mamma was still with us in the year Six—and tho' I was *not* in request as a bridesmaid, I recollect taking some enjoyment in Aunt Harriot's wedding. The only peculiar aspect of the ceremony was that the parish clerk at Wrotham, where Aunt was married, held Mr. Moore in such profound dislike that he ensured the funeral hymn was sung instead of the usual Nuptial Psalm."

"Dear, dear. But to return to Curzon Fiske, and his harum-scarum bride—"

"Miss Thane would, as I have said, been seventeen at the time of her elopement to the Continent. I do not know how the couple contrived to live, tho' it is *rumoured* that Mr. Fiske set up a gaming establishment in one of the lesser towns—Lyons, perhaps, or Liège—I am forever confusing the two—and that his beautiful young wife condescended to *deal faro* at one of the tables."

Fanny's intelligence from this point forward was a patchwork of conjecture and fable. Nevertheless a vivid portrait emerged, of the two reckless citizens of the world making their glittering way across the Continent, regardless of Napoleon's armies or the sudden falls of governments. They were spotted in Warsaw, as guests of a count; they took lodgings in St. Petersburg, and entertained the Tsar; they counted prelates in Rome and renegades in Sicily among their favoured intimates. Whenever they fled a locale the pair were sure to leave debts behind them; but curiously, Curzon Fiske seemed increasingly well-to-do. His wife went in jewels and the latest modes, which set off Adelaide's figure and looks to perfection; his way of living was invariably of the first stare; and the baggage train that followed from province to province was a marvel of conspicuous display. By the time he returned to England—

"Returned?" I queried. "He faced down his creditors in this country, at last?"

"He must have done. Else Adelaide Fiske could not have been welcomed into the bosom of Chilham Castle by Old Mr. Wildman, as she undoubtedly was, three years after her headlong elopement."

And so, in the year 1809, Curzon Fiske returned triumphant to the land of his rearing, with the object of devoting his accumulated wealth to the purchase of an estate in Kent. He had matured in his travels on the Continent, it was said, and thrown off his rackety ways in an effort to please his wife; his intention now was to re-establish his good name—and Adelaide's—in Society. He descended upon Canterbury's August race-meeting, and renewed acquaintance among the Plumptres and Finch-Hattons and Wildmans and Austens (they were not yet Knights); was much seen at Chilham Castle—and looked gravely into a number of houses said to be available for hire. One was leased at last at considerable expence, and staffed with servants from London; Mrs.

Fiske left her cards on visiting days, and formed one of the party at the local Assemblies; and the Fiskes were pronounced by all in Kent as a delightful couple, handsome in the extreme.

Little more than a twelvemonth passed away, however, before Curzon Fiske was off again—bound for India this time, and *without* the beautiful Adelaide.

"She had borne enough, I suppose, and wished to remain in her settled life," I mused. "Mr. Fiske was obliged to flee his creditors, I presume?"

Fanny wrinkled her nose. "If it were *only* that . . . I *have heard* that tho' he arrived in Kent with a considerable fortune—as much as thirty thousand pounds, it has been said—he squandered it in the old way, gambling being a sort of fever with him. But there was *some other reason* why he could not stay—why Mrs. Fiske, as she then was, remained behind—and the breath of scandal is never far from the story. I simply do not have an inkling as to what occurred on that dreadful night, Aunt, when he disappeared—"

"You make it sound like a horrid novel, my dear," I retorted, amused.

"But it was! A sudden removal from the Fiskes' home, and an abrupt arrival at Chilham, on the bitterest of January nights, when the wind and snow howled. The duns were at the Fiskes' very door, they said, and the lease on their house in receivers' hands. Of course Old Mr. Wildman took them in, tho' James has said his father could not like it; and what should Curzon Fiske do, but set to drinking claret at a furious rate, and challenging all the gentlemen present to whist for pound points—when everyone knew he had barely a shilling to his name!"

"You were not of the party at Chilham on that occasion, I collect? What year would it have been—1810?"

"I was not present," Fanny admitted in a grudging tone,

"and neither were my brothers, being as yet schoolboys at Winchester—but Jupiter Finch-Hatton knows what occurred, and it was from him I had some part of the story."

"Very well. What does Jupiter say happened next?"

Fanny leaned towards me with a conspirator's air. "The gentlemen—Jupiter and James and Mr. Plumptre, who was then but eighteen—agreed to play at whist with Curzon Fiske. Jupiter insists it was in an effort to bring some peace to Mrs. Fiske—Mrs. MacCallister, I should say—because her aspect was so wild and distraught, and her husband would do little to comfort her."

"And?"

"And . . . I do not know what happened *next*," Fanny admitted, with a flattened expression. "Only that Jupiter turned owlish and cagey, and quite *knowing* beyond what anyone might bear, so that I was out of reason cross, and lost all patience with him."

I sighed.

"When a person who has been frank turns to evasions and hints," Fanny insisted with asperity, "there is nothing to be done but to ignore him. Anything more would be to reward quite tiresome behaviour."

"Undoubtedly. And yet you say that Curzon Fiske left Chilham. And without his wife."

"There was some sort of row that night, I think," Fanny offered with a pretty knitting of her brows, "all the gentlemen having dipped quite deep into the claret. Perhaps the quarrel regarded the winnings, or pound points."

Or perhaps, I thought, *it was to do with Adelaide. For certainly Curzon Fiske did not take her with him, when he fled England for the last time.*

"In any case," Fanny persisted, "Mr. Fiske was gone from Chilham by morning, leaving a note he was bound for India; and Mrs. Fiske was abandoned to the charity of her cousins."

"Poor woman! And she only one-and-twenty!"

Fanny shrugged. "She thoroughly enjoyed her career as an Adventuress well enough while it lasted, so one cannot entirely pity her—but I believe the Wildmans treated her with considerable kindness. They even repaired the broken relations that had obtained between Adelaide and her mother, so that Mrs. Fiske was received once more into Mrs. Thane's house. Her fine clothes and jewels and other belongings were seized by her husband's creditors; but she lived so quietly and respectably, and the Wildmans backed her so nobly, that her reputation was restored, in time."

"Three years since," I mused, "and she had no word of Curzon Fiske?"

"Not until the report of his death was received," Fanny concurred. "We learnt the news of James Wildman, when he rode over one pleasant afternoon in April last year—some eighteen months ago, now. A fever, it was said, contracted while Fiske was in the service of the Honourable East India Company—and the body had been buried in Ceylon."

"And so Mrs. Fiske was released of her onerous wedding vows, put on her mourning-clothes, and after a decent interval, was permitted to re-enter Society."

"Where, at the age of four-and-twenty, she was so happy as to make the acquaintance of one Captain Andrew Mac-Callister," Fanny concluded.

Andrew MacCallister. How much did he know, I wondered, of his wife's storied past? Or the nature of her first attachment? And what would be his astonishment, upon learning that Curzon Fiske—so far from having released Adelaide to her happy future—had thrown his dark shadow over her vows, and made of her a bigamist?

CHAPTER EIGHT

The Tamarind Seed

You must have seen, and more than once, one face
In a crowd, so white, so pale, you knew at the sight
This man was walking to death, and could not escape. . . .

GEOFFREY CHAUCER, "THE MAN OF LAW'S TALE"

21 OCTOBER 1813, CONT.

"JANE," MY BROTHER EDWARD CALLED FROM THE GREAT
Hall as Fanny and I prepared to descend the stairs, "Dr. Bredloe has finished his examination of the corpse, and is partak-
ing of refreshment in the drawing-room. I should be grateful
if you would join us there."

"I am sure Mr. Wildman has finished writing what must be
conveyed to Captain and Mrs. MacCallister," I murmured to
Fanny, "however little he may have relished the task; and
there is the Express to be despatched in pursuit of the pair.
Pray inform Mr. Wildman, therefore, that he is not to stay for
us; we might better pay our respects to his family tomorrow,
when the unhappy couple is returned to Chilham Castle."

An interval of reflection had convinced me of the usefulness of observing Adelaide MacCallister in the bosom of her family—and therefore, to visit that family prior to the lady's return could afford me little interest. The day was already so advanced as to make the sacrifice of a carriage ride to our neighbours insignificant; my time should be better devoted to my brother and the coroner.

"I know very well that you and Papa mean to *conspire,*" Fanny said archly, "and that I am wanted in the drawing-room not at all—" But she went on her errand without further demur.

Dr. Bredloe was a little man, with sandy hair that I guessed had once been as red as Andrew MacCallister's. The doctor was a neat figure in his black coat and clubbed queue, the very picture of professional wisdom. He set down his glass of Madeira at my appearance and sprang up from his perch on the drawing-room settee, which was still covered in the elegant damask Elizabeth had chosen long ago. If I wondered at Edward's conveying the coroner to such an apartment, rather than the more masculine comforts of the library, the conviction that the prosy clergyman Mr. Moore might be in possession of the latter explained our sudden formality.

"Miss Austen, I presume?"

"Dr. Bredloe." I curtseyed. "My brother, I find, reposes the utmost confidence in your judgement. How fortunate that you were not otherwise engaged this morning, when need summoned you!"

He bowed and offered me a chair, which I immediately took. The coroner then seated himself once more on the slippery surface of the settee. Edward stood by the fire, one boot resting on the fender, his blue eyes surveying us inscrutably.

"Your brother," Dr. Bredloe observed, "reposes a curious confidence in *you,* Miss Austen—dating, I collect, from your conduct during an affair of murder that occurred prior to my coming into Kent."

I glanced at Edward; if he had indeed related some part of

the activities of Jupiter Finch-Hatton's mysterious uncle, and the brutal murder of a young woman at the Canterbury race-meeting some years ago, he had decided unequivocally to take both Dr. Bredloe and myself into the confidence of the Law.[1]

Excessively wise of Edward, was it not?

"I cannot say that I agree with Mr. Knight's decision to disclose what we have discovered in the past hour, before I have empanelled my jury," Dr. Bredloe continued, with a beetling of his brow, "but my opinion is neither here nor there—Mr. Knight stands before us as First Magistrate for Canterbury. He assures me that you are familiar with the procedures of an inquest, and have in fact appeared before a Coroner's Panel yourself in the past?"

"On more than one occasion, I confess." I dropped my eyes demurely to my folded hands; it cannot be becoming to betray too intimate a knowledge of murder.

"Excellent. Then I would beg that you examine the items laid out on the Pembroke table, just over there."

With a glance of enquiry for Edward, I rose and crossed to the table, where a motley assembly of effects was displayed.

These included a blood-stained leather wallet, much worn, and a quantity of banknotes—what my young nephews should call a "roll of soft." It was a remarkably *large* roll of soft, indeed, such as should open Edward's and George's eyes—and that it had been allowed to remain in Curzon Fiske's possession once his life was snuffed out, confirmed my suspicions that no mere footpad had despatched the dubious pilgrim.

Set beside this was a square of paper, with the words *St. Lawrence Church* writ upon it in black ink that had bled and faded from the damp; worse still, the paper itself was turned rusty red in places from what I felt sure was Fiske's blood.

[1] Jane is referring to events previously related in the volume of her detective adventures entitled *Jane and the Genius of the Place*. —Editor's note.

He had been shot, after all, in the chest—and this note must have been secured within his coat. Some other markings there were on the paper—a figure that might have been the hour of an appointed meeting, or perhaps the initials of Fiske's correspondent—but these were so obscured by the crimson stains as to be unintelligible. It was the final item, however—which sat innocently enough on the Pembroke table—that caused my breath to catch in my throat. I lifted it delicately between my thumb and forefinger: a single, dark brown bean. It had the texture of wood and the lightness of a thrush's feather.

"Edward," I said. "Do you recognise this?"

"Not well enough to name the thing—but I may say that it appears to be similar to the beans secured in the silken pouch, received by Adelaide MacCallister last night at the ball," he returned calmly.

"Eh?" Dr. Bredloe enquired. "What's that you say?"

Edward offered a succinct account of the wedding celebrations at Chilham Castle, the appearance of the footman, and the curious gift he had offered the bride.

"And you observed that the pouch's contents discomposed her?" Dr. Bredloe asked keenly.

"I thought her close to swooning," I admitted.

"—As tho' she knew what the offering foretold," the coroner suggested. "The return of an unwanted husband from the dead. Aye, it's a nasty business altogether—a bride turned bigamist on her wedding day; a brave young officer foresworn through no dishonourable intent of his own; and a man murdered, to set all to rights."

"We cannot surmise so much, until we have spoken to the parties concerned," I protested, and held aloft the bean. "Where exactly was this discovered, sir?"

"In the depths of Curzon Fiske's breast pocket," Dr. Bredloe replied. "It was tucked into that piece of paper you may observe on the table."

—The bloodied paper, with the words *St. Lawrence Church* penned upon it. Death had made an assignation with Curzon Fiske, and sent the bean as surety.

It was possible that Fiske himself had delivered the silken pouch to the door of Chilham Castle. *A common enough fellow,* the footman had described him; and so, indeed, Fiske had appeared in his deceptive pilgrim's clothes. Were the beans a talisman between Adelaide MacCallister and the man who had abandoned her? —A message she had interpreted immediately upon opening the embroidered pouch, and spilling out its contents? Had Fiske waited in the Castle's shadows until all the wedding guests departed, and received as reward a folded missive, with a few words scrawled hurriedly upon it, and a bean returned as a token of faith?

One would have to compare the writing on the note to Adelaide MacCallister's hand—or perhaps, I thought more feverishly still, *her new husband's . . . .*

I apprehended that Dr. Bredloe was still speaking.

". . . a plant common to the Subcontinent and its surrounding regions, extending even as far as China, I believe, of which the fruit offers both medicinal and dietary advantages."

"I beg your pardon?"

"The *tamarind,*" he said testily. "That is a tamarind seed, Miss Austen—the tree's fruit, which is quite large and bitter in its unripe stages, contains numerous seeds of that kind. Natives of India use the tamarind in sauces and chutneys. The seeds, when dried, may serve as counters in children's games, or for more mature forms of gambling."

"Gambling." I considered the proclivities of Curzon Fiske. "Might this seed be considered in the nature of a warning— and its acceptance from the bearer, an assumption of *risk*?"

Dr. Bredloe smiled. "How the ladies do rush to invention! I should never undertake to conjecture the *meaning* of the tamarind seed; it may be enough to say that like the unfortunate Mr. Fiske, it travelled from India to England."

"And thus connoted the Exotic's return," Edward mused. "I collect that you are familiar with that part of the world, Bredloe?"

"Through the realm of literature only," the doctor answered wistfully. "I should dearly love to see a tiger, however, before I die—and an elephant! Only conceive of such an animal, like a house moving on four legs! My first passion, Mr. Knight, is natural philosophy—and indeed I hoped to form a part of Sir Joseph Banks's scientific expedition to Botany Bay in my youth, for the collection of specimens unknown to Europe; but personal affairs intervened, and in the end I never embarked. The expedition sailed without me; and so it has been, ever since."

"There is still time to wander, surely?" Edward smiled.

"Before I die? I confess I cherish that hope. But so long as present duties call—I must be content with species known to England, for a little while longer."

"—And all the varied forms of evil to be found among them," I murmured. "Tell me, Dr. Bredloe, do you know what sort of gun killed Mr. Fiske, and how long he might have lain on the side-path from the Pilgrim's Way?"

"As to the latter point—" The coroner shrugged. "It was a chill night and a wet one. You observed, no doubt, the stiffening of the corpse. We men of science refer to the phenomenon as *rigor mortis*—and it has not yet begun to pass off, in Mr. Fiske's case. In the relative warmth of the scullery, however, we may expect it soon to do so. The wound had ceased to bleed long hours before I examined Mr. Fiske; and if pressed, I should say that life had been extinct some hours. You may attest to the time of the corpse's discovery?"

Again, the coroner scrutinised me keenly.

"I was walking towards Temple Grove near eleven o'clock

when Miss Knight came upon me with the news. I suspect the discovery was made mere moments earlier."

"Then let us put the murderous event in the vicinity of midnight," Dr. Bredloe said with satisfaction. "A more exact time must be impossible, solely from the evidence at hand."

"And the gun?" Edward pressed.

"I could not recover the ball that tore through the fellow's heart." The coroner looked all his regret. "It exited by way of his back, and is no doubt lying somewhere on the ground or among the trees hard by St. Lawrence's."

"We shall certainly attempt to recover it," Edward said thoughtfully. "There are men enough about this place to go over the ground with necessary thoroughness."

"I would beg, sir, that you refrain from employing any of the young gentlemen who formed the shooting-party, or even your beaters, in the task." Dr. Bredloe bowed to my brother, by way of softening the sting of his words. "It would look exceedingly odd to the empanelled jury—which, as you know, are generally simple fellows enough—if one of those who discovered the Deceased was *also* so unlucky as to find the ball that killed him. I have known a surfeit of knowledge to hang a man."

"Would you have it whispered I used my position—my authority in the Law—to shield my sons and their acquaintance?" Edward demanded stiffly.

"Not at all, sir! But neither would I have it said you failed to keep a proper distance, when murder was done so near to your own estate. Summon the constables from Canterbury to conduct your search, man, for God's sake!"

Edward appeared to unbend at these words; the sense of them must be apparent, even to one sitting high upon the horse of Dignity. "Very well," he said. "What are the constables to seek?"

"A flattened ball of lead," Dr. Bredloe said, "and perhaps some bits of burnt wadding—such as should be discharged from a duelling pistol. If we were to find even the pistol itself—! But we cannot hope for so much good fortune. It was certainly a single ball that killed Mr. Fiske, however—the hole in the chest is very neat, indeed—and the gun was fired at close range."

"The scorch marks upon his jacket," I murmured.

"Precisely." The coroner turned his gaze upon me. "Which tell us *what*, Miss Austen?"

"That Curzon Fiske did not fear his killer. So much we have already surmised, however, from the suggestion of an assignation, provided by the tamarind seed and the slip of paper. One matter still puzzles me, however, Dr. Bredloe."

"And that is?"

"Why Curzon Fiske did not *stop* his wife from marrying Captain Andrew MacCallister yesterday! Only consider: He returns to England with funds in his coat pocket, and so far from revealing his survival to his anxious family—adopts a subterfuge, and lies in wait on the Pilgrim's Way while Adelaide vows to love and cherish another. What possible motive can have dictated his extraordinary behaviour?"

"The same conjectures have troubled me these several hours, Jane," my brother admitted. "If, as we suspect, it was *Fiske* who caused that silken pouch to be presented on a tray, then he intended to frighten Adelaide badly."

"In which object, he succeeded." I glanced swiftly at Edward. "A man who waits for his wife to commit bigamy, so that he might inform her of his secret knowledge, does so from a desire for power."

"Ah." Dr. Bredloe sighed, with what seemed to be satisfaction. It was the sound I have heard my nephews make, when coming to the end of a difficult mathematical proof. "You would suggest *blackmail*, Miss Austen?"

"I would." I set the tamarind seed back upon the Pembroke table. "What a very nasty person Mr. Fiske begins to seem!"

CHAPTER NINE

The Devil in Dancing

*You see? he was saying, here's the proof you can find
That women were the ruin of all mankind.*

GEOFFREY CHAUCER, "THE WIFE OF BATH'S PROLOGUE"

21 OCTOBER 1813, CONT.

"MR. WILDMAN BEGGED THAT I WOULD SAY ALL THAT IS proper, Papa, in gratitude for the morning's shooting," Fanny offered with creditable calm, "and added that he hoped you would excuse the press of anxiety, which made it impossible for him to suspend his errand to Chilham any longer."

"He is gone, then?"

"And George Finch-Hatton with him."

"Good. I could do without Finch-Hatton's lounging in such a crisis; if a corpse cannot hope to excite the fellow to honest activity, nothing may."

"And yet," sighed Harriot Moore, who was engaged in knotting a fringe as she sat with Fanny in the saloon, "young Mr. Finch-Hatton is so *excessively handsome*. And you must see, Edward, that all that lounging is essential to his *charm*."

We had discovered the ladies in this elegant little sitting room at the rear of the house, overlooking the faded garden, where they were safe from the depredations of Fanny's brothers and the younger children, of whom Harriot's son now formed a part; he was relegated with Lizzy and Marianne to Miss Clewes's preserve of schoolroom and nursery. Of the billiard-playing gentlemen there was no sign; perhaps that party had broken up when Mr. Wildman quitted the house.

Fanny flushed at Harriot's words, but her look was all for Edward. "I believe you do Mr. Finch-Hatton an injustice, Father! I found his air of calm good sense quite *refreshing* a few hours since, when my brothers could offer only *ghoulish* remarks, and others I shall not name must be insufferably prosy!"

It is a thing with Fanny to call Edward *Papa* when she is on easy terms with him, and *Father* when outraged. I suspect she is not entirely immune to Jupiter, no matter how tiresome he may appear to a woman of eight-and-thirty like myself—he is so very tall, after all, and so very blond, and so very langourous in his gaze as his eyes survey one from bodice to hip. All the young ladies cannot help but be out of their senses about him.

And then there was Harriot, I reflected—not so very young, but just as susceptible.

"Nonsense," Edward said briskly. "It is impossible to do Finch-Hatton an injustice—that would be according him far more worth than any man should allow. The fellow ought to buy a pair of colours in a fighting regiment, and *lounge* about the Continent under Wellington's eye. To have a horse shot out from under him would be the making of him. Have all the young men left us, Fanny?"

"Mr. Plumptre did not think it proper to depart before speaking with Dr. Bredloe. You *had said,* if you will recall, that the coroner must wish to question all the shooting-party."

"Now *there*," Harriot interjected with the voice of approval, "is a young man I *thoroughly* esteem. Such cogent reflections! Such solid respectability! So much sense in every word and expression! I am certain Mr. Plumptre is a great comfort to his mother. I am certain a young woman could go a *long way,* Fanny, without meeting a more worthy man—or one so deserving of every tender consideration."

"Worthy," Fanny repeated in a hollow voice.

"Indeed," Harriot concluded mistily, "he puts me in mind of my own dear Mr. Moore, in the first days of our courtship."

It must be a fatal allusion; Fanny cast up her eyes towards Heaven.

"Trust Plumptre to follow my instructions to the letter." Edward sighed. "Shall I find him in the library, engrossed in a book of sermons?"

"I believe he is debating theology there, with Mr. Moore," Fanny supplied, with admirable command of countenance.

"Of course he is. I shall spare you the interview, my dear— but pray inform Cook we will have another to dinner. Bredloe has had the sense to decline the honour; he wished to make arrangements in Canterbury regarding the unfortunate Mr. Fiske. But we must feed Plumptre, I suppose."

As it was probable no dinner would be served without the speedy removal of the corpse from the scullery, I silently blessed Dr. Bredloe, and carried Fanny upstairs to change her dress for the evening—her boudoir having the advantage of being as *far* from the intellects in the library, and the wits in the saloon, as Godmersham could offer.

"AND WHO, PRAY, HAS BEEN SO UNWISE TODAY AS TO BE *insufferably prosy* within range of your hearing?" I demanded.

"I am sure that John Plumptre is an excellent young man," Fanny began as I stirred up the fire. She was curled on the sopha before the blaze, her slippers discarded and her feet tucked under her. It is so much the fashion for young ladies to go about half-naked, that she is in a perpetual state of goose-flesh; and as I glanced at her, she shivered. If the idea occurred that a corpse in the house was the source of her discomfort, rather than the chill weather, I did not voice it, but threw another log upon the fire and drew the curtains against the swift autumn dark.

"An excellent young man," I echoed, "and not unattractive, with his expressive dark eyes and sober look. However—"

"However, when a gentleman of one's acquaintance will read one a lecture on the *impropriety of the waltz,* despite having solicited one's hand for the very same dance in the course of the evening—"

"Oh, dear. You refused him, I collect?"

"I was already engaged to waltz with Mr. Thane." Fanny's chin rose. "Had Mr. Plumptre been rather more *beforehand* with the world—"

"Or simply with you—"

"Exactly. But to suggest that I *disgraced* myself, Aunt—merely because I showed a relative stranger the same sort of disinterested favour I might have bestowed upon John Plumptre, had he solicited my hand *prior* to Mr. Thane, instead of standing about in that stupid way, conversing with his companions, as tho' all one intended at a ball was to *talk*—"

"Mr. Thane, I suspect, is the real difficulty, and not merely for John Plumptre."

Fanny threw me a look brimful of laughter. "It is excessively diverting, is it not, how Mr. Thane has ruffled all the male plumage? Even Jupiter, I swear, was thrown off his stride by the Corinthian's air and address."

"Jupiter does not *stride,*" I scolded. "He swings into orbit, far above the scene, and suspends all animation until required to answer for himself."

" *'Pon my soul,'* " Fanny growled in a creditable imitation of Mr. Finch-Hatton's utterance. " *'Ought to be horse-whipped. My opinion, course.'* "

"Confess, Fanny—you should be bored to tears with an excess of Finch-Hatton's society!"

"Naturally"—she sighed—"but I shall never say nay to standing up with him in a ballroom. There is every possibility he will be an earl one day, you know. Besides, he holds so much weight with the other gentlemen that any lady Jupiter deigns to solicit for a dance is in request the entire evening thereafter."

"Whereas Mr. Plumptre—"

"—Achieves the reverse. He is excessively *worthy,* I am sure," Fanny persisted in a voice of loathing, "and no doubt brilliant in his understanding—but so *tedious* in his opinions, Aunt! He is like an old woman, tho' he cannot be more than one-and-twenty! To condescend to *scold* me on my conduct at the Chilham ball—and to say that the waltz is an *activity unbecoming in a lady,* one no *true Christian* should countenance, when I am perfectly aware he was longing to dance with me all the while—"

"And so, being denied that pleasure, he must regard you as a Work of Satan—set down to tempt him from the path of virtue. It is his youth, I think, that betrays him," I said thoughtfully.

Tho' I would not declare as much to Fanny in her present attitude, I do admire John Plumptre, as one whose mind and character are unimpeachably elevated—and I have guessed a little at the ardent nature of his feelings for my niece. Poor man! That a quiet, unassuming fellow with a strong intellect and noble feelings, who possesses neither moist palms, a gangling frame, nor an unfortunate wetness about the mouth, as so many youths appear to do, should nonetheless be supplanted by his more dashing acquaintance—is the way of the world, I am afraid. Plumptre has every advantage behind him, and if his chief fault is to utter platitudes in moments of pique, a few Seasons should cure him of the evil. "Both Wildman and Finch-Hatton are several years Mr. Plumptre's senior, are they not?"

"They must be full five-and-twenty, I believe, and the closer friends of the trio," Fanny replied. "Plumptre is rather like our George, you know—always desperate to be included among the older boys, and affecting a greater maturity so as not to be caught out."

Our George was but seventeen years of age; he is a stripling beside the Wildmans and Plumptres of the world. "George must have been awed, indeed, to be among this morning's shooting-party—and shall probably suffer nightmares on the strength of it. I cannot think a corpse has come in his way before this."

Careless words—and it did not require Fanny's stricken look, or choked silence, to remind me that *all* my brother's children had been forced to endure the sight of their mother, turned to lifeless clay at the tragic age of five-and-thirty, not many years since. Before I could beg forgiveness, however, Fanny rushed into speech.

"If the fact of Mr. Fiske's death disturbed Mr. Plumptre, he hardly betrayed it. If I must charge him with a fault, Aunt, it is that he lacks all *sensibility*. When confronted with murder, does he blench, and fall back? No! He must draw himself up, and assume the airs of a magistrate—and pronounce the decided opinion that one *Julian Thane* shall be found guilty of violence."

I stared at Fanny, aghast. "Plumptre never said such damning words in the presence of James Wildman! Mr. Thane is Wildman's *cousin*, after all."

"Ye-es," Fanny agreed doubtfully, "but I do not believe James *likes* Thane very well, for all that. He said that Julian was a *smoky fellow,* for all he had excellent *ton,* and that he wouldn't answer for his temper when the claret was in him."

I sank down on the sopha beside her. "Do not regard it, Fanny. Those young gentlemen will say a good deal they ought not, when thrown together with little to do, and a fresh corpse laid out in the scullery. Only conceive how unsettling for all of them, believing that one of *their guns* had despatched Curzon Fiske."

"Yes, but the knowledge—which I fear my brother Edward conveyed to them—that Mr. Fiske was in fact killed by a *single lead ball,* has relieved their minds so much, that they are ready to indict the first stranger who comes to hand." There was a fretful edge to Fanny's tone. I must credit her delicate sense of Justice—or Julian Thane's dexterity in the waltz.

"It seems," she continued with a diffidence not wholly natural, "that Mr. Thane has *been out* some once or twice."

A lady who has *been out* is considered on the Marriage Mart, and a virginal member of Society intent upon changing her status as swiftly as may be. A gentleman who has *been out,* however, is quite otherwise: for he is one who has met a rival at twenty paces on a duelling ground, with seconds to the rear and a swift carriage standing ready to convey him to the Continent, should he prove so unlucky as to kill his opponent.

"How very dashing, to be sure," I murmured. "And does Mr. Thane keep his duelling pistols by him, when he comes into Kent?"

"He certainly did not display them in the ballroom!" Fanny flashed with asperity.

CHAPTER TEN

A Dish Best Served Cold

"Watch your tongue, when a king is across the table."

GEOFFREY CHAUCER, "THE SUMMONER'S TALE"

FRIDAY, 22 OCTOBER 1813

IT WAS A SUBDUED PARTY THAT SAT DOWN TO DINNER LAST evening; and I might have passed over the interlude without comment, and proceeded directly to my account of today's events, had not Mr. Stephen Lushington, MP, obtruded himself on my notice.

I have said before that I am half in love with Mr. Lushington. He reminds me a little of my brother Henry, with his persistent good humour and air of Fashion. It cannot be an accident that both men are fourth sons—your fourth sons being left so entirely without expectation, that they must push for themselves from the moment they leave the cradle, and are, as a result, creatures of charm and insinuation their whole lives long. In this, Stephen Lushington is all that a Member of Parliament *ought* to be—so smiling, so replete with energy and fervour, and so condescending in his notice of the generality of mankind, even females who may be judged essentially worthless for their lack of vote. Mr. Lushington, one instantly perceives, is possessed of the sort of fine understanding that acknowledges the *unofficial* power of Woman in the Home—the sort of influence a Sister, or Aunt, or Daughter, or Wife, may exert upon the opinions and strength of the Voting Member. A subtlety of mind and a delicacy of expression, in the condescension of such politicians, as they cultivate the vanity and good opinion of ladies like myself, who have only to see the London papers brought round to the door, to have them read; ladies who consider themselves to be thoroughly informed on all matters of Governance and Policy, and may be trusted to voice those opinions in the firmest language imaginable—is the kind of perfection I cannot fail to enjoy. Mr. Lushington offers exactly that complex of High Art and Absurdity I find most diverting in Modern Life.

Our MP was determined to be gay this evening; and as gaiety was so decidedly out of place, given the fact that Dr. Bredloe had *not* succeeded in removing the remains of Curzon Fiske from the servants' wing, Mr. Lushington's only appreciative auditors *must* be Miss Clewes and Harriot Moore. Edward, to whom most of his sallies were directed, preserved a quelling silence, his fingers idling on the stem of a wineglass and his looks devoid of all but polite disinterest. Young Edward, Mr. Lushington's principal acquaintance in our household, was hardly more communicative. The two had formed an easy alliance over a pack of hounds, Young Edward's chief interests lying in the realm of Sport; but hunting could hardly be deemed an appropriate topic of conversation, given the unfortunate circumstances of Curzon Fiske's discovery—which left the Sporting Fellows casting unsuccessfully for a topic.

Fanny, who held the honour of hostess at the lower end of the table, was in excellent looks this evening. She had determined to meet the lowering event of *murder* by donning one of her most cunning gowns, a very daring confection of burnt-orange silk with mammeluke sleeves—introduced last Season but still novel in Kent—which were draped and fitted at three-inch intervals from shoulder to wrist with bands of bronze spangles. The neckline of this interesting mode was cut in a diamond shape, ornamented with a garnet cross; and the whole apparition suggested a Fanny cast back to the days of Juliet and her Romeo—to which she had added the fillip of short curls held by a riband about her forehead. She required only a balcony and a swain beneath it, and looked both romantickal and ravishing. I little doubted she was the object of every male eye in the room. Fanny appeared determined to ignore Mr. John Plumptre, however. He, tho' seated at her right hand, was in no state to appreciate either her dashing appearance or her degree of pique, being as yet engrossed in a convoluted discussion of Ecclesiastical Privilege with George Moore, seated opposite. Mr. Lushington and I faced one another in the middle of the table. He was resplendent in a bottle-green coat and dove-grey satin breeches. I was flanked by my nephews, and he by Harriot Moore and Miss Clewes, who had been added merely to round out the numbers; ordinarily the governess would have been dining on bread-and-milk in the nursery.

"And how have your young charges amused themselves today, Miss Clewes?" Mr. Lushington cried. He is a married man, after all, with children of his own, and may be allowed to shew an honest concern for the Infantry. "Sewing their samplers and toasting crumpets by the fire, while young George Moore torments them with charges of toy cavalry?"

"Oh, sir, I should hope that Master Moore may never teaze his cousins in the brutal way most boys find commonplace—he holds the little girls in such esteem, you know, as being able to speak a little Italian, and find such places as Ceylon on the globes."

"Ceylon!" The MP was amused. "Are Lizzy and Marianne intent upon joining the Honourable East India Company? Or have they a taste for tigers?"

"I believe the matter of Ceylon arose," Miss Clewes said in a lowered tone, "because of poor Mr. Curzon Fiske. It was in Ceylon, I believe, that he died. Or rather—where he was *thought* to have died. Oh, dear, it is all so very confusing!"

"Do you mean to say," Lushington demanded with a penetrating look, "that you spoke of the . . . *accident* . . . in the nursery?"

Miss Clewes looked conscious. She darted a nervous glance first at Edward, and then at Harriot Moore, who appeared impervious to Mr. Lushington's words, being engrossed in a halting tale my nephew George had commenced. We cannot curb George of his graceless habit of speaking across the table, tho' it is frowned upon in polite society; in a family party such as this, however, much may be ignored.

"I ought to have shielded the children from all knowledge— and well I know it!" Miss Clewes threw an appealing glance at me, as if I might defend her against the Member's attack; but I make it a rule *never* to speak across the table—when I am disinclined for a particular party's conversation.

"I fear the intelligence so cut up my peace that I was on the point of *swooning*, Mr. Lushington," Miss Clewes continued, "and once Lizzy had secured my vinaigrette, and Marianne had burnt the ostrich feathers intended for Miss Knight's new hat—"

"What?" Fanny exclaimed, from the lower end of the table. "Miss Clewes, you *didn't*!"

"I commend Marianne," John Plumptre interjected gravely. "It is something to find, in so young a child, a disregard for mere objects of vanity—and a *truly Christian* sense of duty towards a fellow creature in distress."

"Fiddle," Fanny retorted. "It was all play-acting and heroics, I am sure. The vinaigrette must have revived Miss Clewes, without the sacrifice of my feathers. They were only recently procured in London, at considerable expence!"

Plumptre's expression hardened. "I wonder very much, Miss Knight, if there is *any* pleasure you would be willing to forgo, out of consideration for another's welfare?"

Fanny flushed, torn between mortification and outrage.

"You go too far, sir," Edward said quietly from his position at the head of the table. "All of us who have reason to honour and cherish Fanny know the sacrifices she has long made, on behalf of her little brothers and sisters, since the hour of my dear wife's death; no one could so ably have filled Elizabeth's place. Fanny rates her own concerns so far beneath everyone else's; it is what one must particularly admire in her. But being a stranger to this household, no doubt you have failed to apprehend what all of us know too well to mention."

Fanny's eyes welled with tears at her father's words; and in part from a desire to turn the conversation, I said rather loudly to Miss Clewes, "You are quite recovered from your indisposition, ma'am, I hope?"

"I am a little better, thank you, Miss Austen," the governess said as she pressed one trembling hand to her heart. "I am sure that *you,* who went immediately to the *dreadful* scene, must particularly feel how *violent* death cuts up one's peace! I wonder you were not prostrate upon a sopha the remainder of the day! To *consider* of the unfortunate man lying on the Pilgrim's Way—such a *sacred* place, too—and quite dead, with none of us the wiser, but going about our business as tho' we had hearts of stone!"

"Your sentiments do you credit, Miss Clewes," George Moore said with a satiric edge to his voice, "but in the present case you may rest easy. Dying on the Pilgrim's Way is perhaps the *only* sacred note Curzon Fiske struck in his varied career. For my part, I shall not mourn him."

"George!" his wife cried reprovingly. My nephew's tale, it seemed, had failed to entirely drown out the interesting conversation.

"Forgive me for speaking plainly, Harriot," Mr. Moore returned, "but I never loved the fellow, tho' we were raised as boon companions; and if his death inspires any regret, it is that it did not come sooner—in Ceylon, as was reported! At least *one* person might then have been spared further humiliation," he added, in an undertone.

"One person," Mr. Lushington declared, "appears to have been so entirely in accord with your sentiments, Moore, that he made certain Fiske proved as dead in fact, as he was reckoned in rumour!"

The clergyman met his gaze coldly. "You go a little fast for me, Lushington. I will not yet admit another party to have been involved. Is it inconceivable that Fiske should have done away with himself?"

"Completely and utterly!" The MP pounded his fist on the table, and my wineglass teetered. "Do you honestly believe the man journeyed long months by sea, risking all to return to England, merely to despatch himself in the middle of a common footpath? Nonsense! Where is the motive? And, more to the point—where is the weapon?"

"I never understood Fiske's reasons for *living* as he did," Mr. Moore asserted. "I cannot be expected, therefore, to apprehend why he should chuse to end that life. As for the weapon—no doubt it shall be found, in time. And then we may thankfully put a period to a scoundrel's existence."

"Oh, *George*," Harriot mourned.

But Mr. Lushington would not be silenced. He shifted his chair a little so as to face Mr. Moore, and leaned towards him with a fixed smile. "I rather wonder at your confessing so violent an antipathy before the Magistrate—and at his own table, too!—while Fiske's manner of death remains uncertain. But perhaps you have sources of intelligence others do not.

Perhaps you are privy to the judgement of the coroner, before even a panel has been named. As you are comfortably united by marriage to the Law, in this instance, I suppose you may believe yourself safe from suspicion!"

This clever little speech, so vicious in its implication, was offered in a jovial spirit, as tho' Mr. Lushington meant nothing but good humour all round. His beaming looks and the droll twinkle in his eye, as he practically accused the clergyman of murder, inspired Miss Clewes to titter behind her hand, as if our Back Bencher had offered a very good joke. Harriot Moore, however, sat frozen in her place beside Mr. Lushington, unable to turn her head in either his direction or her husband's; and Edward went so far as to rise from his seat.

"Have a care what you say, Lushington." My brother's voice was as steel. "I take the responsibilities of my office with as much seriousness as you regard *yours;* and to suggest that George Moore would expect otherwise, in any dealings between ourselves, is an offence to both."

"Good Lord!" Mr. Lushington cried, and raised his broad hands in protest. "Pure badinage, Mr. Knight, I assure you! I have a lamentably idle tongue, that wags all the day long as most of your politicians' tongues will—and it has caught me in coils long before this! I beg your pardon—I should not like to give offence to *anyone* present."

George Moore, too, was on his feet; his cold grey eyes glittered with malice. "Offence! You offered much the same thing to Fiske, did you not, on the night he fled England for India? —The night, Mr. Lushington, that your *lamentably idle tongue* accused him of cheating at cards?"

CHAPTER ELEVEN

The Search Party

. . . He used to be a friend of yours,
And he was killed last night, given no notice. . . .

GEOFFREY CHAUCER, "THE PARDON PEDDLER'S TALE"

22 OCTOBER 1813, CONT.

FANNY ROSE FROM HER CHAIR ALMOST BEFORE MR. MOORE had done, and with a stiff nod of the head to her Aunt Harriot, led the ladies from the dining parlour. I should dearly have loved to remain, to hear what fascinating invective might drop from the mouths of the gentlemen present, but I should have to be content with pumping my nephews on the morrow—that is, this morning—for not even Jane may keep her chair once the decanters of Port are to be passed round.

"Miss Clewes," Harriot said faintly as we crossed the Great Hall, "I should like to see my son before I retire, if I may—would you be so good as to accompany me to the nursery?"

"I should be *delighted*," Miss Clewes answered firmly. Mr.

Moore is such an object of admiration for her, that I am sure she has taken Mr. Lushington in severe dislike. "You look excessively tired, dear Mrs. Moore; perhaps a little warm milk before the schoolroom fire? I always offer it to the children, you know, when they have said their prayers and donned their night-clothes; I warm it by the spirit lamp. I do not think I have ever known a night of disturbed rest, when once I have imbibed warm milk before bed!"

With such soothing words, and a modicum of fussing about Harriot's Paisley shawl, and an arm at her elbow to assist her up the stairs, did Miss Clewes prove herself of some worth; for she succeeded in removing the two most awkward ladies from the drawing-room, and leaving Fanny and me to speak freely.

"Do you think the men will come to blows?" Fanny enquired anxiously as we sat down before the fire and took up our required amusements—transcriptions of sheet music, in my case, and a scrap of embroidery in Fanny's. "I dread to hear the shattering of crystal, or perhaps foul language. Tho' I do not believe that my father or Uncle Moore is equal to either. I cannot speak for Mr. Lushington."

"Mr. Lushington! He shall rather *laugh* his way out of the business, I think, than resort to his fists. Moreover, you are forgetting the good sense of John Plumptre, which must divert the minds of all present," I soothed. "Plumptre is not the sort of young man to sit by and tolerate foolishness or calumny."

"No, indeed—Mr. Plumptre made his sentiments abundantly clear on that score this evening, did he not? Although his subject *then* was the inherent frivolity and . . . *selfishness* . . . of women. At least, that is how *I* interpreted what he said." Fanny gave a hard tinkle of laughter. "I am excessively glad that I never nursed a *tendre* for Mr. Plumptre. I should be sadly cast down by his opinion of me—whereas at present,

I may be thankful for my escape. A man without a particle of humour is what I cannot endure."

As I knew very well that Fanny *had* nursed a *tendre* for Plumptre—that there had been a time, before such things as waltzes with Julian Thane or badinage with Jupiter Finch-Hatton, when her countenance was wont to flush whenever Plumptre's quiet good looks made their appearance in our drawing-room, I disregarded the bitter feeling in this speech and went straight to its heart.

"Do not regard anything he chuses to hurl at your head, Fanny," I cautioned. "John Plumptre is a man very much in love, if I do not mistake."

"In love! You *heard* what he said to me, Aunt! You *heard* his poor opinion of my character!"

"I did—and knew him for a man who is suffering under the lash of jealousy. If he seems intent upon wounding you, it is from a desire to win your attention from others—however illogical his methods may seem. He is like a small boy who will not leave off tugging the curls of the little girl he adores."

Fanny turned her head aside.

"If he is not at your feet this very evening, begging forgiveness for his ill-judged words, I shall be very much surprized," I said cajolingly. "Do not be so foolish, pray, as to reward him with stony silence. Now, Fanny: What is your opinion of that last exchange between Mr. Lushington and your Uncle Moore? Had you an idea the two held each other in dislike?"

"I should not have called them *intimate friends,* perhaps, but I have perceived no hint of the discord we witnessed tonight. They have been guests in this house for two days, and have conducted themselves with nothing but propriety and cordiality."

"For my part," I said thoughtfully, "I should have thought them unacquainted before this mutual visit to Godmersham—

and yet you heard what Moore said: Mr. Lushington was present at the famous card party at Chilham Castle, on that night three years ago when Curzon Fiske fled to India."

"So, too, must Uncle Moore have been present," Fanny observed. "Else he should not have been able to repeat what Mr. Lushington then did, or said. Perhaps he and Aunt Harriot were on a visit to Chilham at the time."

She was correct, of course. Phantom faces rose in my mind, chance guests around a green-baize table, their looks years younger, their frames thinner, themselves shadowy in aspect and purpose—George Moore and Jupiter Finch-Hatton; Stephen Lushington and John Plumptre; Curzon Fiske and his host, James Wildman. A strange assortment of gentlemen—their ages, aims in life, and the means they chose to achieve them . . . utterly different. . . .

And the MP had accused Fiske of cheating. Did not such rash words generally end in a meeting at dawn, rather than voluntary exile? I supposed the outcome depended upon the spirit in which the accusation was received. —Not with gloves slapped across the face, but a craven apology?

It came to me then, with a force of conviction unbidden and unquestionable, that the murder perpetrated on the Pilgrim's Way had its root in that fateful card party—Curzon Fiske's last hand of whist as an acknowledged Englishman, in the bosom of his neighbours and acquaintance, some three years since. Dr. Bredloe might chuse to believe the affair was simple, and that once the MacCallisters were returned from their aborted honeymoon, he should find his murderer in husband or wife—but I suspected there was more behind Fiske's death than mere wedding-night violence. The quiet corpse lying cold in the scullery still wielded a malevolent power: it had pitted friend against friend only this evening. The seeds of Fiske's death were planted, I felt certain, in that company of whist players at Chilham Castle; and whatever they had said or done that wretched night still divided them. Indeed, the apparent peace achieved once Fiske was fled to India was entirely destroyed at his unexpected return—the secret that bound his fellows was sure to spill out, like water overflowing from cupped hands. *One* among our quiet neighbours had known Fiske was not dead of a fever in Ceylon; one had waited for him to reappear, like a phantasm or bogey from the grave; and one had determined that Fiske should never leave the Pilgrim's Way alive. . . .

"That poor man's death," Fanny murmured, "has unleashed a nasty spirit in this house. Do you not feel it, Aunt? We are all in discord, as tho' we breathed a bitter atmosphere. I believe I shall go up to bed early. I have no heart for embroidery tonight."

"Have you none for whatever apology John Plumptre might make?" I asked, in an attempt to rally her.

She shook her head with a faint smile, and exited the drawing-room.

I DID NOT LINGER LONG MYSELF, FOR WHEN THE GENTLE-men put in their appearance at last, and stood around the tea table when it was brought in, that I might pour out for them and preserve the *appearance* at least of a cordial country-house evening, the talk was all of hunting—it being the most neutral topic the party might hit upon. John Plumptre, as I had expected, struck the correct note, in remaining firmly upon the path of what was unobjectionable, impersonal, and incapable of giving offence; he talked with determination of hard frosts, stopped earths, thinning coverts, and sound hunters, in which he was heartily joined by my nephew Young Edward, whose unbridled enthusiasm for every form of sport is the most tiresome thing about him. Mr. Lushington, as Keeper of Hounds, might join in with impunity; and my brother the Magistrate observe all with a dispassionate eye. Mr. Moore, upon learning that his lady had already retired, buried himself in a book; and not long thereafter excused himself from the party.

Mr. Lushington surprized me excessively by bending over my hand, and offering the most fulsome compliments on the hospitality of the house, explaining that he found he must depart on the morrow—possibly before breakfast—on urgent business that could not wait. As Mr. Plumptre would also be leaving us in the morning, he, too, said all that was proper when I rose to retire—but I offered *him* more than the polite nothings I had given our MP.

"Do not be in a hurry to run away from us, Mr. Plumptre," I suggested. "We enjoy your society so much; and in a difficult hour, the presence of a friend is a solace, not a burden."

"You are very good, Miss Austen." He looked a trifle discomposed, as tho' his cravat were suddenly too tight. "But I know too well that I have hurt where I ought to have healed. I fault myself—indeed, I cannot recall my behaviour at dinner this evening without shame and reproach. I will not say more; there is nothing that may be said, in defence of my ill-judged temper."

"Which is why you ought to have breakfast with us, Mr. Plumptre," I returned with amusement, "for much may be forgiven over the morning coffee, particularly if the sun is shining, as I expect it shall be tomorrow. *Try* to enjoy a good night's sleep; and know that each new day is a chance to start life afresh. Or so I have always found it."

"Thank you. I shall." He bowed over my hand—such a boy, for all his airs and intellect; an uncertain boy with eloquent eyes, who has yet to plumb the mysteries of his own heart or anyone else's—for all he may study Philosophy.

I TOOK BREAKFAST IN MY ROOM, ON A TRAY, AS BEFITS A lady of my advanced years; fancy me, sitting up in a great bed with draperies, and a brisk fire in the hearth, and a cap on my head as I write in this journal. The breakfast-parlour shall be all the better for my absence, provided Mr. Plumptre and Fanny have the solitary use of it; as the weather is indeed much improved from yesterday, I would expect both Young Edward and George shall already be out shooting, with sandwiches in their pockets, and Edward will have ridden into Canterbury to see to the inquest—

LATER THIS MORNING

I BROKE OFF ABOVE, BECAUSE A SUDDEN SHOUT FROM THE direction of Bentigh and the Lime Walk roused me from my study—a male shout, full and rich with the satisfaction of discovery. I threw back the bedclothes, stepped to one of the Yellow Room's great windows, and peered through the glass. I could discern nothing. The consciousness, however, that the party of constables prescribed by Dr. Bredloe, as being best suited to a thorough searching of the murderous ground, must already be established on the Pilgrim's Way, urged me to throw off my wrapper, don a serviceable gown, wash my face and pin up my curls under a suitable cap for day wear, and search out my spencer. I could not allow such a fine morning for a walk to pass in indolence.

Ten minutes' brisk exercise brought me up with the search party—rough local men, by the look of them, urged to greater endeavour by a stout individual with a sash of office tied about his chest.

"Good morning, Constable," I said brightly, as tho' it were the most natural thing in the world for a lady to be nosing about a scene of murder on a bright October day. "I am Miss Austen, sister to Mr. Knight the Magistrate, you know, who lives at this place. How are your men getting on?"

"Well enough, ma'am," he returned cautiously. "Well enough. I had the honour to speak with the Magistrate myself this morning, in Canterbury."

"I am sure you were an immense source of comfort to him." I offered this flattery with a confiding air. "My brother is desirous that everything to do with this sad affair should be conducted according to the absolute letter of the Law—and to know that *you* are about the search for the spent ball must greatly relieve his mind."

"It's kind in you to say it, ma'am."

I glanced at the several fellows bent over the brush, sweeping it with their hands, which were gloved in rough workman's leather. "I daresay with such capable fellows, you might be so fortunate as to discover the duelling pistol itself! What a feat *that* should be! Quite a feather in your cap, Constable . . ."

"—Blewett, ma'am."

"Of course." I beamed at him. He unbent a little.

"You know about the pistol, Ma'am?"

"Oh, yes. I was present, you know, when Mr. Fiske was discovered—and with my brother when the body was first examined. It seems clear that a single ball despatched him, poor gentleman."

The constable glanced over his shoulder, found no one to be observing him, and said in a hoarse whisper, "Then I don't mind admitting as we've been so lucky as to find the ball—it were dug right into the trunk o' one of the chestnuts, right off the Pilgrim's Way, just about chest-high."

So Fiske had been standing, as we suspected, when he was killed.

"Which tree?" I demanded cheerfully.

Constable Blewett led me to the tree without further hesitation; I had secured my *bona fides,* from a simple complex of confidence and presumption.

"The ground is sadly trampled hereabouts," he said apologetically, "the beaters and the gentlemen as was out shooting, having milled about the place something dreadful; but the snick in the tree is clear enough."

He was correct: The ground near where Fiske had lain was a morass of footprints, none of them clearly distinguishable the one from the other; I could not even make out the imprint of my own half-boots, where I had crouched over the body yesterday. My heart sank. The constable's men had only confused matters further. But the tree to which I was directed stood some three yards from the body's position, in the opposite direction along the side-path from where Edward and I had discovered the two sets of hoof-prints. As Blewett observed, the gash in *this* tree's bark from the lead ball was breast-high. As I gazed at the furrow in the wood, the constable drew from his pocket a flattened slug of metal, and displayed it in his palm.

"There she be," he said with satisfaction. "Went in and out of the blasted—of the *unfortunate* gentleman, clean as whistling Bob's yer uncle."

I confess I stared at it, fascinated. I was once treated to some instruction in the art of duelling, by a master of the same; and the object I now regarded bore not the slightest resemblance to the lead ball thrust down a pistol's muzzle.[1] The ball's path through Curzon Fiske's body had so distorted its original shape that it appeared to be nothing more than a fragment of metal, flattened and oblong, incapable of doing harm to anybody.

"It is impossible to discern from this what sort of weapon fired it, I suppose."

"Oh, you could say right enough it were a pistol, ma'am— the weight of lead is too small for a rifle."

---

[1] Jane refers obliquely here to a period in Southampton, when her late friend Lord Harold Trowbridge taught her to fire a dueling pistol. The episode is recounted in the volume of her detective memoirs entitled *Jane and the Ghosts of Netley. —Editor's note.*

"I see."

"I'm sure as the crowner won't have no difficulty placing it as the ball what came from the pistol itself," he added with complacency.

"The pistol itself?" I repeated.

"Aye." His eyes widened, big with news. "We found it a quarter of an hour ago, sitting innocent as ye please on a headstone in St. Lawrence churchyard. 'Twas Vicar as called our notice to it; he were up early, were Vicar, and he's a keen man for seeing what didn't ought to be there. I don't wonder the Magistrate—your good brother, ma'am—failed to discover it yesterday, with all the bother over the corpse. Why a duelling pistol should be set like a present on the headstone in the churchyard—"

"Where is the pistol now, Blewett?"

He gestured with his head towards Godmersham. "Why, up to the Magistrate's, of course."

I SPED MYSELF BACK TO GODMERSHAM WITH MORE HASTE, and less appearance of casual exercise, than I had left it. I found Edward seated behind his desk in his own book room.

This is a small apartment at the rear of the house, tucked to the right of the staircase. It is an intimate sort of closet, less grand and imposing than the library, where thousands of volumes are stored, and the two fireplaces anchor either end of the vast room, with five tables and various armchairs scattered in between. Edward's book room is where the business of the estate is conducted, where he meets with his tenants and his steward, and where he retreats in time of exhaustion or sadness or trouble.

I have even known him to sit there in moments of joy, of course, when there is world enough and time to spend a few moments merely gazing out over the back garden, and considering of how fortunate a man's life may be.

Today, however, I found him smoking tobacco in a pipe—a practice so little usual with him, that the reek of it forced me backwards upon the very doorstep.

In front of him, on the desk, sat a gun: made of chased silver and burnished wood—rosewood, at a guess—with a sinuously curving butt. It was a handsome thing, probably from one of the finest craftsmen of the art. I searched my mind for the name of such an one. *Manton.* That was it! Gunsmith to the nobility. Purveyor, in former days, to one Lord Harold Trowbridge.

"Jane," Edward acknowledged, and took a draw on his pipe.

"The constables have found the pistol, I see." I endeavoured to make my voice steady and light.

"So they have. Should you like to see it?"

I approached the desk. Edward did not shift his position, nor touch the thing; he merely reclined in his chair, one leg crossed over his knee, idly smoking. His eyes were narrowed; he was staring not at me, but at some phantom in the middle distance.

It was difficult to conceive that such a beautiful object—so lovingly made, so dearly purchased, and housed, no doubt, in a velvet-lined box with its mate—should exist solely for the purpose of making a fool of its owner. For what else may a duelling pistol accomplish? I do not speak of *honour*. I heard enough of such folly from my friend the Rogue's lips to know how deep tragedy may cut at men's souls; how the notion of honour—its defence, its hasty outrage—eats at their complacency, their confidence, their whole position in the World. I have known dear friends destroyed by a chance word, when in their cups, and sent flying in terror from the only life they have known; I have heard of good men who died, all on account of that useless word—*honour*. And its agency? This bandbox trinket, bought at breathless expence, from a man who understood the engineering of death—Manton.

"You will observe the wood is damp," Edward said, "from lying out in the churchyard all night. A sad thing—such a treasure should be more nobly treated."

"Have you learnt anything from it?"

"—Who fired it, or left it to be found on the grave, you would mean?" Edward set down his pipe. I do not think I had seen his features set so harshly in many years—not since his beloved Elizabeth's death. "The pistol cannot tell us what occurred on the night of the wedding ball, to be sure. But it may scream the identity of its owner. Manton is careful to engrave his guns with the name, or initials, of the purchaser."

I stared at him wordlessly, and felt my heart begin to pound.

"This one," Edward offered, almost as an afterthought, "appears to belong to James Wildman. Do you think, Jane, that our friend and neighbour has killed a man?"

CHAPTER TWELVE

A Call of Condolence

"There are two roads, one death, the other shame.
These are your choices."

GEOFFREY CHAUCER, "THE PHYSICIAN'S TALE"

22 OCTOBER 1813, CONT.

"OF COURSE I DO NOT BELIEVE MR. WILDMAN CAPABLE of murder!" I retorted. "And I should be very much sur-prized, Edward, to learn that *you* do."

He lifted his brows. "As Mr. Knight, whose lands run alongside Chilham's, divided by the ancient Pilgrim's Way—as a friend who knows and esteems Wildman's whole family—as one who has watched young James himself grow from boy to man—I must declare it impossible. As First Magistrate, however, in possession of a gun responsible for the death of Curzon Fiske . . ."

"You must weigh the possible guilt or innocence of every person within ten miles of the Pilgrim's Way," I concluded quietly. "I quite take your point. But James Wildman—! I cannot conceive of so elderly a gentleman toiling along the

Pilgrim's Way over the Downs in the dead of night. He must be nearly seventy if he is a day, and prostrate with gout!"

Edward's brow furrowed at this. "It was young James, and not his father, that I had in mind," he said gently. "Observe the initials."

I bent over the gun. There, chased in the silver, was an intricate monogram of a large *W*, flanked with a *J* and a *B*.

"The father is James, as is his son—but the son claims as his middle name *Beckford*," my brother explained.

I wrinkled my nose at monograms. "I cannot conceive of a person less likely to provoke a quarrel, or more completely in control of his own temper, than young James Wildman. Indeed, he is the very *last* person I should expect of killing a man in a fit of rage!"

"But this was *not* a crime of passion, Jane," my brother rebuked me. "Surely you must see that. Fiske was despatched by one who appointed the hour and place of his killing; one who conducted himself with a cool calculation throughout. Young Wildman is entirely capable of a premeditated act; and I should judge he possesses enough courage to undertake even murder, if circumstances so compelled him."

"Circumstances! They should have to be quite extraordinary, for Wildman to risk so much—"

"That is understood. But Fiske's reappearance in this country—Fiske *alive* when he was thought to be dead—is extraordinary enough." Edward rose abruptly from his chair. "I must ride to Chilham Castle without delay, and enquire of James where he keeps his pistols, and the habits that attend his use of them. The inquest is set for tomorrow morning, Jane. It would be as well to be apprised of certain facts before the event, lest the wrong fellow be clapped summarily in chains."

"You would not gaol a man on mere *suspicion*, surely?"

"No." He gave me a level gaze. "But Bredloe's panel might. I am required to submit to the coroner's judgement, my dear—and that judgement, in our awkward English fashion, derives from the inquest's panel of good men and true. I should like to be able to influence the panel's conclusions—I should like them to return a judgement of Murder by Person or Persons Unknown, if I can manage it, and thereby purchase myself an interval for the conduct of our researches—but to that end I am forced to interrogate most of my neighbours in a limited amount of time."

"*Our* researches?" I demanded.

"You should be invaluable in conversing with the ladies of the household—particularly Mrs. Thane, and Mrs. MacCallister. I must assume that unhappy lady is returned from her ill-fated honeymoon. Will you ride with me, Jane?"

I DID NOT REALLY *RIDE* WITH MY BROTHER, OF COURSE. I have never been an accomplished horsewoman, but on the rare occasions I find myself mounted sidesaddle on a sweet-mouthed little mare, it is invariably at Godmersham, where the whole world is on such easy terms with Edward's stables that I should feel absurdly dowdy in refusing to ride. I do not at present possess a riding habit, however—the one Elizabeth once pressed upon me being long since outworn and outmoded—and I did not like to appear at Chilham Castle arrayed in a manner that must do my brother little credit. I proposed, therefore, that Fanny and I should take out Young Edward's tilbury, so that Fanny might practice her driving; and her father should ride beside us as escort.

In truth, Fanny requires neither instruction nor much practice in driving, being a pretty enough whip and fully inclined to drive herself about the Kentish countryside whenever opportunity offers; but the present scheme allowed my niece to indulge one of her chief delights—instructing *me* in the art—and we had not proceeded a hundred paces up the country lane in the direction of the crossroad for Chilham, before she was placing the ribbons confidently in my hands.

There is nothing to equal the sensation of holding two narrow strips of leather while, at the nether end, the mouth of a horse fights one for mastery. Clutch too tightly on the reins, and the poor animal will throw its head up, eyes rolling, as tho' one fully intended to break its neck; allow the reins to lie slack in the palm, and the beast will seize the bit between its teeth and career off down the road with every intention of overturning the vehicle and casting horse and driver both to ruin. Fanny is adept enough to drive two-in-hand, a feat I have not been so brave as to attempt; today we had but the single horse before the tilbury, and trotted along at a jaunty pace I felt myself *almost* equal to maintaining.

"You look very well, Jane!" Edward cried, "and in that new bonnet with the curled ostrich plume, quite *dashing,* indeed!"

"The road bends a little just ahead, Aunt, as you will perceive," Fanny murmured with commendable calm. "You will wish to ease back a trifle on the left rein, and guide Rowan's head around."

I accomplished this feat, my heart pounding in my mouth as the tilbury tipped slightly to one side, terrified lest the equipage lose all purchase on the bend and roll without warning. But Rowan, if the truth be known, is better able to find his way than I am to guide him—and the good horse made me appear to greater advantage than I deserved.

"I should not like to be put to the test of a truly *fresh* animal," I muttered to Fanny. "When I recollect the pair of smart goers the Countess of Swithin was wont to drive, and before a perch phaeton, too—"

"She sounds to be what George would call *top of the trees,*" Fanny observed comfortably.

"She hunts with the Quorn."

"Ah. There you are—we cannot hope for such daring in Kent.

It would not be tolerated by your Jupiter Finch-Hattons, you know. No gentleman of the neighbourhood should like to think the ladies more *Corinthian* than himself."

Some thought of the probable retort the late Lord Harold Trowbridge's niece, Desdemona, Countess Swithin, should offer this paltry complaisance brought a smile to my lips; but I did not accuse Fanny of poor-spiritedness. For one thing, I was too intent upon controlling my horse; and for another, I knew full well that the manners obtaining among countesses of the *ton* would never do for a Miss Knight of Godmersham. Fanny judged the tolerance of her society to a hairsbreadth, and should never be accused of overstepping its limits.

Such, of course, had *not* been the experience of one Adelaide Thane Fiske MacCallister—and I reflected, as I returned the ribbons to Fanny's capable hands, that therein lay a question: Had Adelaide acquired so many surnames—so many changes of station and fortune in her brief four-and-twenty years— *because* of her willingness to flout convention, or in despite of it?

Endeavour to learn what her relationship has been with James Wildman, Edward had urged in a lowered tone as he handed me up into the tilbury. *I must ask her about the tamarind seeds, of course, and what her movements were after the ball was done at Chilham that night—but you, Jane, have the whole of her life to discover.*

The whole of her life. I wished I did not feel so daunted by the task; I am accredited a subtle conversationalist, I own, and am not unperceptive regarding the motives of much of the human race—but I dislike playing the busybody, and Adelaide MacCallister had no reason to confide anything to a stranger. Her family was all about her, did she require a confessor. To urge her conversation at such a time must be repugnant to any right-thinking person's sentiments. I should be forced to contrive.

It seemed but a moment more, and we were trotting up the broad sweep that led to the Castle. Fanny pulled up her horse, and a footman ran from the hall to Rowan's head, while another stood ready to help us down. I heard Edward call carelessly as he swung from the saddle, "Is your young master at home, Twitch?" and the Wildman family's butler, a rather stout figure in black, scraped a bow.

"Mr. James is at home, sir, as is Mr. Wildman, but I must enquire whether they are receiving visitors. The household is a trifle . . . discomposed."

"I'm here as First Magistrate, Twitch," Edward said gently, "not as a neighbour paying a call. Please convey my apologies to your master and his son, and beg that they receive me on business that may not be delayed."

"And the ladies, sir?"

Edward's eyes drifted over me and Fanny.

"We had intended to pay a call upon Mrs. Wildman, but if that is inconvenient, pray do not disturb her," Fanny said impulsively. "We are quite happy to send in our cards, and drive home. It is a lovely day for an airing, after all."

I had not expected my niece to wilt before the manners of an imposing upper servant, and was momentarily exasperated with her. But I reflected that even so pert a creature as Miss Eliza Bennet should have done the same, upon arriving at Pemberley, had she been aware that Mr. Darcy was already in residence—and that perhaps some explanation might be found for Fanny's unwillingness to thrust herself into the Chilham household.

"Twitch," said a voice from the doorway, "why do you leave our visitors dawdling on the sweep, when they ought already to have been announced? Step lively, you fool!"

I glanced towards the entry, and saw a formidable figure: iron-haired, thin-lipped, her eyes dark and imperious as Cleopatra's.

"Yes, Mrs. Thane," Twitch answered woodenly, and led us into the Castle.

CHAPTER THIRTEEN

A Delicate Interrogation

This cunning world would keep me forever in fear,
Unless I worked this hard at keeping things clear.

GEOFFREY CHAUCER, "THE SHIPMAN'S TALE"

22 OCTOBER 1813, CONT.

IT IS ONLY NOW THAT WE ARE RETURNED HOME, AND I AM established in a comfortable chair before the library fire with a shawl draped over my chilled feet, that I may reflect a little on the strangeness of the atmosphere at Chilham Castle today. I have been somewhat acquainted with the household and family in past years, and have reckoned them to be a fine, high-spirited, handsome collection of people, without much seriousness in their heads or purpose in life; a family that enjoys giving pleasure to others as much as to themselves, and which has been marked out neither for great distinction nor hideous misfortune.

Mr. James Wildman amassed his wealth in trade—through the management of a vast sugar plantation in Jamaica, owned by one Mr. William Beckford. Mr. Beckford is grown infa-

mous in the Polite World, I understand, for having seduced at
a tender age the son and heir of an earl—and for being forced
to flee the country with his wife in the wake of the subsequent
scandal. To us Austens, however, he figures merely as cousin
to our own Miss Beckford of Chawton, who until this past
spring lived at the Great House with all the Middletons. How
small is the world between Hampshire and Kent, to be sure![1]

William Beckford is known far beyond England, however,
for a connoisseur, a collector of art, a musician who once
studied under no less a master than Mozart, and as the author of the horrid novel *Vathek*. It is Beckford's name that
young James Beckford Wildman claims—Beckford having
stood as the boy's godfather. We may assume the choice of
both name and patron to signify *gratitude* on Mr. Wildman
Senior's part, rather than any approbation of William Beckford's tastes or habits. The amassing of a considerable fortune must be said to sweep all prudish reserve aside—and Mr.
Wildman owed his present comfort entirely to Beckford's Jamaican plantation. He managed the Quebec Estate, as the
plantation was known, so well, in fact—and Beckford proved
so profligate in his building and furnishing of his absurd pile
at Fonthill Abbey—that Wildman was presently able to relieve his illustrious employer's straitened circumstances, by
purchasing the plantation outright; and at a very good price,
if rumour is believed.

The revenues from Jamaican sugar proved so lucrative,
that Mr. Wildman was gradually able to put enough by to
purchase Chilham Castle when his son was but four years
old. The Wildman income is thought to be in the neighbour-

[1] Jane refers here to Maria Beckford, originally of Basing Park in Hampshire, who helped rear her dead sister's children at the request of Mr. John
Middleton, her brother-in-law. The Middletons leased Chawton Great
House from Edward Austen from 1808 to 1813, and Maria Beckford visited Jane when both chanced to be in London.—*Editor's note*.

hood of *twenty thousand* a year. (If only another such Prize might be secured on the Marriage Mart for my own dear creation, Caroline Bingley! But Chilham is no Pemberley, alas.)

The Castle is far older than its present owner's claims to gentility, having been built in the early seventeenth century on the ruins of a medieval motte and bailey. Set on high ground, and facing the little village of Chilham, it is a pleasant façade in the Italian Renaissance stile, much improved in recent years by Jamaican profits. The building curves in a polygon shape, with the last link missing—establishing an inner courtyard flanked by the horseshoe of the house. All the principal rooms are to the rear, facing some twenty acres of gardens that fall away in gradual terraces below; Capability Brown had the original draughting of it, tho' later hands have struggled gamely to mar his work.

Today, however, the air of Chilham Castle verged on the tragic, with a fillip of the sinister. Even the sunshine that was wont to stream through its leaded windows had fled hurriedly to more hospitable roofs; wind sighed in the lofty eaves; and had a ghoul commenced howling in the best Gothick manner I should not have been surprised. I must impute such a change to the influence of the Thane family.

We followed Mrs. Thane into the Great Hall, where she turned abruptly at the foot of the sweeping Jacobean staircase. She was arrayed entirely in black crepe, of an outworn mode that suggested it had been purchased in respect of her late husband's passing; a mourning brooch of jet was fastened upon her bosom. Was so much magnificence meant to honour a son-in-law she had refused entirely to acknowledge while living?

"You are Mr. Knight, I collect—a near neighbour," she pronounced. "And you are Miss Knight?"

Fanny curtseyed.

"And that person is Miss . . . *Austen*, is it? The poor relation? You are Mr. Knight's spinster sister, I believe?"

Shock very nearly left me speechless. "One of them, ma'am."

"*Both* unmarried? What a sadly unprosperous family! I recollect your face from the ball, of course, and must regret that we were not then introduced; I was but briefly in attendance, as my ill-health will not permit me to indulge in protracted dissipations."

The wedding of her daughter, a protracted dissipation.

The basilisk stare turned on Fanny. "You, however, I could hardly fail to notice. *You* danced several dances with my son."

From the haughtiness of the lady's tone, we must assume she regarded Fanny's waltzing with as much disapprobation as John Plumptre—but from an entirely different cause. Mrs. Thane might have been a monarch, and Fanny an unlettered girl from a distant village, whose pretensions in seducing the prince must be ruthlessly suppressed. I bridled on my niece's behalf, but no words were necessary—for Edward stepped forward, his countenance set.

"How pleasant to animadvert on the gaieties of a few days ago," he observed, "and how sad to think they were of such short duration! I am First Magistrate of Canterbury, Mrs. Thane, and cannot help but be charged with resolving Mr. Curzon Fiske's murder. I have urgent business with Mr. Wildman and his son. Pray lead me to them."

It was an order, not a request; and Mrs. Thane's head reared back, as tho' she had been treated to an insult. "May I remind you, sir, that there is a *servant* present!" she hissed.

Edward glanced satirically at Twitch. He stood as tho' deaf, a little in advance of Mrs. Thane.

"I am sure most of the servants were aware of the tragedy long before you learnt of it, ma'am, as the local beaters were in at the discovery of the body; and I should never stand on ceremony with James Wildman's man," my brother said in an accent of considerable amusement, "for I have known him these twenty years and more. Is your master in his book room, Twitch? You need not announce me." With that, he bowed easily to Mrs. Thane, and strode off towards the rear of the house.

Twitch made no move to impede Edward; rather, he gestured towards the opposite passage—which at Chilham is known as the Circular Gallery—and said, "If you will allow me, Miss Fanny, the ladies are sitting in the drawing-room. I'm sure Mrs. Wildman will be most happy to see you."

"I shall conduct them to her," Mrs. Thane interjected. "And as you are now at leisure, Twitch—perhaps you may think on the *proper* deference becoming to a servant, and the ways in which impertinence is *generally* rewarded in better-regulated households."

With these quelling words, she strode down the passage towards the drawing-room; and after a single amazed look, Fanny and I followed her.

"Miss Knight and Miss Austen," the lady announced on the threshold; and Mrs. Wildman and her two daughters rose to greet us.

Mrs. Wildman is a good deal younger than her husband, being not yet fifty, and her daughters are nearer in age to Fanny. She was born and bred in Jamaica, where Mr. Wildman married her, and remains so persistently opposed to the English climate that she goes about swathed in shawls even in the heat of August. Her daughters are less exotic and less indolent; but I do not think I indulge in phantasy when I say that all three ladies met Mrs. Thane's appearance with an expression of dismay, one that swiftly changed to delight at discovering ourselves behind her.

"My dearest Fanny!" Mrs. Wildman exclaimed, and kissed her on both cheeks. "We did not expect this pleasure. And Miss Jane, as well! We are so grateful to all at Godmersham for what you did yesterday—for young James, particularly, who was *much distressed* at the terrible events of the morning. To go out shooting, the weather fine and the company delightful, and to find oneself presented with a corpse! —And the early conviction, too, that one's fowling piece might have been responsible! For a wonder, my son declares, with *absolute certainty,* that he never recognised Mr. Fiske at all! Tho' he knew him so well in former days. Well!" The voluble Mrs. Wildman looked with finality from myself to Fanny. "It only goes to show how terrible is the change wrought by Death!"

Or a growth of beard, a pilgrim's clothes, and the weathering sun of Ceylon, I thought.

While the others murmured pious nothings at Mrs. Wildman's inescapable truth of Nature, I reflected that however difficult I might find an approach to Adelaide MacCallister, or however formidable a watchdog her mother should prove, there was little I could not learn of the history of both from a polite show of interest in Mrs. Wildman's talk. She was a comfortably ample lady dressed in the first croak of fashion—as it is understood in Kent—with a lace cap to her dark hair, which was now streaked with silver; slightly protuberant brown eyes that widened expressively with her exclamations; and a pug dog she carried habitually on her arm, with all the appearance of having forgot it was there.

"Do come and sit down, Miss Jane, and settle yourself over there, Miss Fanny, between Charlotte and Louisa—"

We did as we were bade. It was obvious our hostess was bursting with ambition to talk over the whole affair, but Fanny hastened to say all that was proper, before the tide of speculation and outrage swept all before it.

"We felt it most necessary, ma'am, to offer our deepest sympathy at Mr. Fiske's loss, and also the sad disruption of Captain and Mrs. MacCallister's plans," she said. "We would not have dreamt of descending upon you so suddenly otherwise."

"*Impertinence,*" I heard Mrs. Thane mutter; only Louisa, the younger of the Wildman daughters, stole a glance at her—half frightened, half defiant.

"Bless your heart, Miss Fanny, for saying straight out what everyone cannot help but think," Mrs. Wildman returned impulsively. "I'm sure I never wished Curzon Fiske ill—and I've known him a good many years longer than Augusta there, having watched him grow from boy to man"—this, with a nod for Mrs. Thane—"but I don't mind saying I wish he'd passed over in Malaysia or Tahiti or whichever of those dreadful Oriental parts he ran off to, instead of sticking his spoon in the wall, as the saying goes, not a mile from our front door on the very night of the ball! And I suppose your good father *must* undertake the business?"

This was a bolt of shrewdness I had not expected.

"I fear so, ma'am," Fanny replied.

"He is even now closeted with your husband," Mrs. Thane hissed. "*I* ought to have been consulted. *I* am her mother."

Mrs. Wildman stared at her cousin in amazement. "And what has Adelaide to do with Mr. Knight the Magistrate?" she demanded. "You're not thinking it's *Adelaide* he wants to throw in gaol? Nonsense! Edward Knight has more wit than to believe a new-made bride would steal from her husband's bed on her wedding night to do murder—or that a man like MacCallister would let her!" She laughed heartily. "There, I've made all the girls blush, and sweet they look with it! You leave off trying to rule the roost, Augusta, and let the gentlemen settle the unhappy tangle!"

"Did young Mr. Wildman's Express succeed in reaching the couple?" I enquired.

"Caught up with them not far out of Maidstone," Mrs. Wildman replied eagerly. "They'd not been travelling above two hours, you know, on account of having risen late and taken their good time in quitting us. Lord, how happy the

Captain was to be whisking his bride away to London! To be sure, Town's tolerably thin of company, with Parliament adjourned and all the *ton* folk rusticating among the pheasant and grouse, but I should guess the Little Theatre is open, and the good Captain's friends at the Horse Guards would be ready enough to drink to his dear lady's health!"

"How unfortunate," I murmured, "that all his plans were thrown into disarray. The Captain was in excellent spirits, I suppose, in setting out?"

"Aye, but the look on his face when the pair of them came back again—!"

At this, there was a marked disruption. Mrs. Thane rose so precipitately from her chair that she succeeded in knocking over one of the profusion of small tables the Wildman girls had strewn about their mother's drawing-room, in an effort to make it appear more fashionable, and less like the drawing-room they had grown up in; such are the fruits of expensive educations at the finest establishments in Bath. The table fell against the harp that Charlotte was most assiduous in playing, whenever the opportunity to exhibit might present itself, and a selection of strings emitted a chance *thrum!*, not at all displeasing, which caused me to wonder *how much* instruction, indeed, was required to appear proficient on the harp.

"Enough," Mrs. Thane proclaimed in a voice that must chill the very marrow. "I will *not* have my daughter's affairs talked over in this odious and despicable way. I must beg, Mrs. Wildman, that you say nothing further to these people. Indeed, I wonder that *anyone* so wholly unconnected with ourselves should regard the subject as one for common discussion."

"Why, Mamma?" said a voice low and distinct from the doorway. "Are you afraid of what they might *say*—or *you* might *learn*?"

CHAPTER FOURTEEN

The Bride's Tale

"I think I loved him best, because in fact
His love was such a trembling high-wire act."

GEOFFREY CHAUCER, "THE WIFE OF BATH'S PROLOGUE"

22 OCTOBER 1813, CONT.

ADELAIDE FISKE MACCALLISTER, NÉE THANE, ENTERED the drawing-room with all the grace she had long claimed; but I should judge that her usual composure was lacking. She was beautifully arrayed in a morning dress of striped French twill, with a high, stiff collar and sleeves tightly buttoned at the wrist, a complex of stile and neatness not often achieved. Her countenance, however, was drawn and pale, and the expression in her eyes was bleak; her dark hair was simply arranged in a knot at the nape of her neck that in another woman should have appeared dowdy; on Adelaide, it achieved a Grecian purity.

Striding into the room behind her was her brother, Julian Thane. He was dressed for riding—but so elegantly that I must have assumed his destination to be Hyde Park, rather than his cousin's stables. A stray lock of dark hair curled romantickally over his forehead; his countenance was interestingly pale. He bowed carelessly to us all, but his eyes were fixed on his mother's forbidding looks.

"As we sow, dearest ma'am, so shall we reap," he said by way of greeting. "Is that not the bit of wisdom you are forever whispering in my ear? How apt, in the present instance! Nothing would do for you but to cut Addie dead upon her marriage—thereby ensuring that her blackguard of a husband should find little profit in mending his ways. We are justly served! The fellow is never done plaguing her, even in death!"

"Silence!" Mrs. Thane replied.

Her son's black brows snapped together and his eyes narrowed; but without another word, he dismissed the woman from his consideration and turned towards Fanny. "Miss Knight. It is truly a pleasure to meet with you again—the morning's sun doing only greater justice to your charms."

Fanny coloured, and offered the hand he was clearly seeking. He bowed over it, then looked enquiringly at me. "I regret that I am unacquainted with your . . . sister?"

Such a blatant essay at flattery! But when tempered with a raised brow and a quirk of the lips, could not fail of being charming.

"My *aunt,* Miss Austen," Fanny returned reprovingly. "May I present Mr. Thane?"

"I am very glad to meet you, sir." And so I was. For many reasons—romantic and violent—Mr. Thane could not help but be an object of interest with me. I judged him to be younger than Adelaide—perhaps only just of age.[1] How well had he known Curzon Fiske, or the sad history of his sister's marriage? Would not he have been away at school for much of it? The curious rebuke Thane had only now offered his

---

[1] Gentlemen, in Austen's day, came of age at twenty-one. —*Editor's note.*

mother suggested an intimacy with—and a repugnance for—his sister's trials. What were Thane's loyalties to Adelaide—or her new husband, Andrew MacCallister?

And would not a gentleman who had *been out* some once or twice, as Fanny put it, be more likely to challenge Fiske to a duel rather than shoot him in cold blood? There were any number of spurs to such a meeting; Thane might have accused his late brother of desertion, for example, or of an insult to a lady, and been entirely within his rights in challenging Fiske. Murder outright, however . . . I did not think it suited the gentleman.

Being too well aware of the danger of prejudice, however, I resolved to ignore the promptings of my better self, and rank Julian Thane high among my suspects.

Fanny had risen from her place and moved towards Adelaide MacCallister; she was speaking in her firm, soft voice, and I must attend.

"I hope, Mrs. MacCallister, that you do not think ill of us for descending upon Chilham Castle in this way—so hard upon the tragic discovery. The fact of my father's being charged with a duty in respect of Mr. Fiske's death, and his intention of paying a call upon Mr. Wildman, resolved my aunt and me in accompanying him; but indeed, we have outstayed our welcome, and ought to be taking leave."

"Pray, do not go on my account," she returned calmly, and seated herself in one of Mrs. Wildman's Louis XV chairs. "I know full well why your excellent father has come—and must speak with him in my turn, no doubt, whenever he commands it. Curzon was murdered; he was shot down like a dog in the night, and left to bleed out his heart; and I should be a very strange woman indeed if I did not feel the loss. I loved him to distraction once—and his was a terrible death. No matter how poor a husband, or how reprehensible a man, he did not deserve it."

"Adelaide!" Mrs. Thane was outraged. "Hold your tongue! Pray consider of the Captain!"

A faint smile twisted Mrs. MacCallister's lips. "I consider of little else, Mamma, as I am sure you know. But I *do* feel this death most acutely; and the fact that I am now united to another, with all the bonds of affection and duty that attend such a union, cannot entirely negate the love I once bore my first husband. I am happy to speak of him; indeed, I think I shall sooner lay his unhappy ghost to rest, if I *do* speak of Curzon. Were you at all acquainted with him, Miss Knight?"

Fanny shook her head.

"Nor you, Miss Austen? You were denied a singular pleasure, then." She laughed a little to herself, as tho' revolving a good joke, a smile teasing at the corners of her mouth. Had I not detected the signs of grief and worry in her countenance at her first appearance, I should have thought her free of all care. Something of this knowledge must have strayed across her mind, for she raised her eyes to mine with limpid clarity.

"I know it is very bad in me not to betray more sensibility," she confessed, "but had you only known Curzon—! He was the most high-spirited man I have ever met, the most charming . . . and the least scrupulous. I shock you—I know I shock you—but the openness with which he met each deception he practiced, and owned to his thorough vice, almost disarmed reproof! He was so *honest* in his misdealings, you see. Had I been a little older, and more aware of the cost of his folly, I should have avoided him like the Devil, tho' it must have broke my heart; as it was, I was just young enough to cast reason to the winds—and I adored him. There was a time when I should have died for him, sold myself for him, stolen for him—and regarded all as a privilege."

"Adelaide!" her mother cried. "Consider where you are!"

The lady glanced aside, as tho' in contemplation of a distant scene, lost to memory. "Such frolics as we had, and such disasters! Such extremities of passion, such quarrels, and such reconciling! I shall never feel for any man in that way again; and I declare I am relieved to own it."

"*Wretched* girl!" her mother spluttered. "Only *think* if the poor Captain should hear you!"

"Andrew?" Mrs. MacCallister laughed again; but this time, the gaiety was rueful. "Andrew understood the bad bargain he bought in me—for I told him all, myself—but I must pity him just the same. It is something, for a man to find himself foresworn on his very wedding night—I should have liked to have spared him *that* indignity, at least."

"Nonsense," her brother said languidly. "Tylden tied the knot right and tight again between you this morning. Andrew's a good'un; he'll stand buff, don't you fear it, Addie. The fellow's not the sort to stumble over rough ground; there are few men I'd rather see beside you in such a fix as this."

"Let us hope, then, that he is not dragged off to Canterbury gaol," Adelaide observed calmly.

"Good Lord!" exclaimed Mrs. Wildman with a startled look. "The very idea! And the Captain such an honourable gentleman, too! I should think he'd seen enough of death under Wellington's command without having to seek it in Kent. You mark my words, Addie—it'll be a common footpad as did for poor Mr. Fiske, and long since gone from the neighbourhood if he has a particle of sense. Fearsome times we live in, with the Regent spending all our incomes and a different army to be paid for every week— It is no wonder the footpads have grown so troublesome; they must make a living somehow as well, poor fellows."

"A footpad will hardly have discarded James's duelling pistol in St. Lawrence churchyard, Cousin Joanna," said Julian Thane.

His words, naturally, caused a sensation.

"James's pistol!" cried Charlotte Wildman incredulously.

"The one Papa ordered specially in London a few years since?"

"That's the ticket—the pistol, or one of the pair, from Manton's that James is forever showing off. He likes to clip the suits from playing cards at twenty paces, Miss Knight, when he's a trifle bosky," he confided to Fanny, "and the billiard-room wall is shot through with holes on the strength of it."

Almost despite herself, Fanny dimpled; Thane's manner was irresistible.

"I am sure Julian is mistaken," Mrs. Wildman said comfortably as she patted Charlotte's hand.

"Nothing to do with me," Julian drawled. "I had it from the Magistrate himself—when he sat me down to ask what I did the night of the ball. Told him I drank a brandy with James after the last of the guests had gone—it was that Tylden party, naturally; one can never be rid of the prosy parson. Twitch shut up the house, and we all went off to bed. Unfortunately, as I sleep alone"—this, with a telling gleam at my niece I could *not* approve—"I've nobody to support me in the assertion. No reward for the just, upon my honour! One has only to snore like a lamb until ten o'clock in the morning, to be met with an accusation of murder the next day!"

"But what *can* James's pistol have been doing in St. Lawrence churchyard, in Heaven's name?" Mrs. Wildman reverted, in a bewildered tone.

"Well may you ask, Joanna. Well may you ask." A strangely triumphant smile broke on Mrs. Thane's countenance. "I have an idea the Magistrate shall be *most pressing* on that point."

"Whatever are you about, Augusta?" Mrs. Wildman demanded. "You look positively in alt!"

"Perhaps it is a natural elevation of feeling, Joanna, at the reflection that sinners may cast no stones!"

"Sinners?" Mrs. Wildman repeated blankly.

"There shall be no more talk of Adelaide creeping from her marriage bed in the dead of night, once *James* is clapped in irons!"

Mrs. Wildman emitted a sharp scream, and flung her hands to her breast, with a look of such terror on her visage that I quite felt for the silly woman; her daughter Louisa hastened to her aid with a vinaigrette, which I must imagine was often employed for the purpose of regulating her mother's spirits. And there, too, was Thane.

"Dear Cousin Joanna, I fear you are overset," he observed with solicitude. "Pray allow me to escort you upstairs."

"Never mind playing off your airs, Julian," Louisa said crossly. "*I* shall convey Mamma."

She was supported in this by her sister; and the three Wildman ladies quitted the room in high dudgeon—and probably a measure of relief.

Fanny rose from her chair and curtseyed to the Thanes. "Indeed, you have been very kind—but Miss Austen and I must take our leave."

"Before your father's business is concluded?" Adelaide enquired. "My husband is even now in his hands, Miss Knight. I collect it is the coroner's assumption that poor Andrew somehow discovered the existence of his rival, and killed him in a passion of jealousy."

"Do sit down, Miss Knight," Julian urged. "I should never forgive myself if you were to leave us, while the issue of Andrew's fate still hung in suspense."

Fanny looked to me in bewilderment. She had not the slightest idea whether to be firm, and beg that the tilbury be brought round, or to linger at the request of the Thanes. She had no notion her father wished me to learn what I could of the interesting grouping now before us. Theirs was the strangest complex of frankness, on the one hand, and determined suppression on the other, that I had ever witnessed in a family; and I wondered whether the casual boldness of both children was the sole weapon available to combat so repressive a parent.

Mindful of Edward, I determined to adopt a similar bluntness and decide Fanny's quandary. I retained my chair, and smiled warmly at Adelaide MacCallister.

"Whatever the coroner may have suggested, my brother shall weigh against all that he observes and is told. He must pursue the obvious—and forgive me, Mrs. MacCallister, but in such a case as this, your husband *must* be possessed of the most obvious motive—but Edward is hardly a simple man, and as magistrate he is aware that murder may be a complex business."

"Indeed?" the bride said. "Then I may begin to hope."

Julian Thane emitted a short bark of laughter. "Hope! Tell me, Addie—in which direction does hope lie? Must we hope that *James* shot Curzon? Or his father, our excellent Cousin Wildman? Would you rather I had done it, perhaps? Or even . . . Mamma?"

"Julian!" hissed Mrs. Thane.

He thrust himself out of his chair and began to pace before the fire like a caged animal. Fanny, I observed, had flushed becomingly and her eyes glittered as she watched his progress; Thane's energies were palpable in the room, a current that ensnared and compelled. He was unlike any young man she had yet encountered in Kent, and knowing too much of rogues myself, I sympathised with her fascination.

"Do not be a fool, Mamma," he muttered. "If James's pistol fired the killing ball, then some *one* in this household employed it. We must all be suspect until the murderer is discovered."

"Nonsense," she said quellingly. "It is as Joanna says—a footpad did away with Fiske, and stole the gun from Chilham first."

Thane stopped his revolutions upon the hearth and stared at her in disbelief. "Good God, Mamma! Do you wilfully cultivate the credulous?"

The lady shrugged defiantly. "I do not see why my explanation should be any worse than another. Indeed, I regard it as the truth."

"Perhaps that is because you are not in possession of all the facts," I interposed quietly, before she could respond. "There is the matter of the tamarind seed, for example."

A pause followed these simple words, a pause so profound it was as tho' air and light had left the room, paralysing all within it except myself.

I glanced from one Thane to another, conscious of Fanny's confused hesitation beside me. "It *was* a silken pouch of tamarind seeds Curzon Fiske delivered to this house on the night of your wedding, was it not, Mrs. MacCallister?"

"How do you...we cannot know it was Curzon who..."

"I advise you most strongly, Adelaide, to say nothing further to this woman," Mrs. Thane spat out. Her suspension of breath had subsided; her gaunt face was livid with fury. "Despicable presumption! She is no better than her brother's spy! I must beg you to leave us at once, Miss Austen!"

Fanny rose, and with a swift bob was halfway to the door when Julian Thane reached her, and clasped her wrist.

"Don't," he said. "Don't go—yet. Your aunt interests me strangely." He shot me a look. "What are you talking of, with your tamarind seeds? I know nothing of them, tho' my sister and parent obviously do."

"Were you not present when the footman presented a gift to Mrs. MacCallister, in a silken pouch, in the midst of the ball? He had received it of a stranger—a *common enough looking fellow*, I believe he said—at the Castle's front door."

"When was this?" Thane demanded.

"During Andrew's toast," Adelaide supplied faintly.

"Ah. I *was* from the ballroom at the time—and returned only as the glasses were raised. A silken pouch, you say?"

"Inside was a collection of largish brown beans," I explained. "Or so I thought them to be. Mrs. MacCallister received them with little pleasure."

Thane crossed to Adelaide, and stared at her broodingly. "You told me nothing of this."

"I thought it irrelevant."

"Irrelevant, Addie! Fiske sends you his calling card—"

"Enough, Julian!" Mrs. Thane bellowed.

"It was only later," I persisted, "when we discovered a similar bean in Mr. Fiske's pocket, that the coroner explained to me what it was."

"Curzon had a tamarind seed in his pocket?" Adelaide repeated. "I suppose it slipped from the pouch. It *must* have been he, then, who stood at the Castle's door. Oh, Julian!" She covered her face with her hands. "Only consider of it! Standing alone and friendless in the dark, while his wife wedded another!"

"The seed did not slip from the pouch," I said.

Adelaide lifted her head from her hands and stared at me. "How can you possibly know that?"

"Because it was twisted inside the note that summoned him to his death," I explained. "A sort of token—perhaps that he might put faith in his murderer?"

Her dark eyes were wide and pitiful in her pale face, all hint of gaiety vanished; and her brother, for the moment, was deprived of speech.

Our interrogation had reached this interesting point, when Andrew MacCallister entered the room.

CHAPTER FIFTEEN

A Choice of Pistols

For he was not long home from another war:
Forgiveness for sin was what a pilgrim sought.

GEOFFREY CHAUCER, "GENERAL PROLOGUE"

22 OCTOBER 1813, CONT.

"FORGIVE ME, ADELAIDE," THE CAPTAIN SAID AS HE HESI-
tated in the doorway. "I did not know you entertained
guests."

"It is only the Magistrate's daughter, Miss Knight, and her
aunt, Miss Austen," his bride returned. "They accompanied
Mr. Knight on his business."

"I see." MacCallister's voice and expression were heavy;
gone was the joy I had read in his countenance at his wedding. His gaze drifted from Adelaide to her brother, and fixed
upon Julian Thane's face; with a flicker of his sandy eyelashes
he said abruptly, "The Magistrate wishes to see you again,
Julian—there having been a variance in our accounts. I am
sorry for it."

"Our accounts?" Colour rose in Thane's face, and to my

surprize, his eyes slid towards Fanny. "What would you mean, Andrew?"

"Merely that I told Knight the truth as I knew it—and I collect that you did not."

Thane stiffened as tho' a glove had been flung in his face. "Do you call me a liar?"

"Of course not." MacCallister walked wearily into the room and took up a position behind Adelaide's chair, his hands resting on her shoulders. She glanced up at him searchingly, but said nothing. "A liar utters falsehoods. You said nothing at all."

"I do not pretend to understand you," Thane returned, on his dignity.

"You withheld *certain facts,* Julian. I urge you to disclose them now. Mr. Knight is waiting. He holds all our fates in his hands."

There was a silence; then, without another word or look, Thane strode to the drawing-room door and quitted the room.

MacCallister sighed. "Pray present me to your acquaintance, Adelaide."

"They were about to take their leave," interjected her mother acidly.

"Tho' Mr. Knight is as yet engaged?"

"Andrew," his wife said intently, "what did you mean, just now? About Julian?"

He glanced down at her. "Present me to your acquaintance, Adelaide. I should prefer Julian to speak for himself, once he determines to do it."

I observed her delicate throat to constrict, as she swallowed her fear with effort, and returned her gaze to ourselves. "Miss Knight—Miss Austen—may I present my husband, Captain MacCallister, to your acquaintance?"

Fanny and I rose, and curtseyed as MacCallister bowed.

"You were our guests at the wedding ball, I know," he said, "but with such a crush of people—there may have been as many as two hundred in the room—I cannot pretend to have retained the names of most of my well-wishers. Let us say that we *renew* our acquaintance—and I shall undertake to greet you both with greater civility in future."

"You are very good," I said. "I do not believe there is one bridegroom in ten who may discern an individual from the mass of those at his wedding celebration!"

"And now I fear we *must* take our leave," Fanny said firmly. "If you would be so good as to summon a footman, Captain MacCallister, I will request my tilbury to be brought round."

"Hah! Drive yourself, do you?" Mrs. Thane queried. "It is of a piece with the general stile of Knight effrontery; you did *not* accompany your father at all, but brought yourselves, from a desire to gossip and feed on our troubles! Spiteful girl! I shall take care that my son wastes no more of his notice on *you*!"

Fanny flushed; her lips parted in indignation, but it was Captain MacCallister who answered his mother-in-law.

"Julian may have little enough liberty in the immediate future, once he has sworn his testimony at the inquest."

"What do you mean, Andrew?" Adelaide demanded. "What are all these hints and warnings?" She slipped from under his protective hands, and rose to face him.

He stared at her gravely. "Julian did not spend Wednesday night in blameless sleep, Addie. Nor did I. I bear responsibility for entangling your brother in this affair—and must beg your pardon."

Adelaide's looks were ghastly, her beauty a mocking skull. "Andrew—"

"I do not know the countryside hereabouts so well as Julian; he has been cantering over these Downs forever. I asked him, therefore, to ride with me down the old Pilgrim's Way that divides your cousin's estate from Mr. Knight's. There is a side-path from the Pilgrim's Way that leads to St. Lawrence churchyard. We achieved it at about half-past two on Thursday morning." The Captain's voice dropped. "We met with your late husband, Addie—and gave the blackguard all the money we could pool between us, to be gone from England by daybreak."

It should surprize no one that at these words, Adelaide MacCallister fainted.

I HAD JUST SUCCEEDED IN WRITING AN ACCOUNT OF THE morning's events, from a hope of understanding them better, when my brother Edward strode into the library and made directly for the decanters set out on a side table. He tossed back a mouthful of brandy, then topped up his glass with an absorbed expression on his countenance; tho' he did not appear to be in an ill-humour, I did not like to pelter him with questions just yet. I allowed him an interval for stirring the fire, and frowning into the flames, and swallowing another draught of his restorative drink; and once he had thrown himself into the chair opposite, I regarded him quietly, until he should chuse to speak.

Silence is a restful quality in a woman, one few women may command.

"Fanny manage the tilbury all right, without my escort?" he asked.

"Perfectly well, I assure you."

The brandy glass sat idly between his palms, half empty. He sighed, as tho' very well pleased to be in his own home again. "Rowan's a well-mannered tit; he'd never run away with the girl. I bought him from James Wildman last spring, did you know that?—one of his three-year-olds."

"You were always an excellent judge of horseflesh, Edward."

"Yes. But of *men,* Jane?" He thrust himself from the chair and tossed off the brandy, then stood with his boot on the fender and stared unblinking into the heat of the fire. "Do you know what a galling trick it was, to be welcomed as a friend into my neighbour's book room, only to demand of him where his son keeps a brace of duelling pistols, and whether one is at present missing?"

"I am sure it was painful and repugnant to you," I answered quietly, "but I am even more certain that Mr. Wildman understood it to be your duty."

"Duty!" Edward retorted with loathing. "Yes, and I suppose I must call it my duty to *hang* one of my friends before very long."

"Not that—but to find justice for Curzon Fiske, perhaps."

Edward was silent a moment.

I studied his profile and felt it safe to venture a question. "What did Mr. Wildman say, when you enquired of James's pistol?"

"He laughed, and said the guns were forever lying about—because James has a penchant for shooting at targets in the most unlikely places. When he is up in London, he may commonly be found at Manton's Shooting Gallery, culping wafers; but when in Kent, is reduced to snuffing candle-flames at thirty paces on the terrace, and has not been unknown to nick playing cards affixed to the billiard-room walls."

"So Mr. Thane intimated."

My brother glanced at me swiftly. "I forgot. While I was insulting one of my oldest friends, you were about your own researches."

"I suspect that what I learnt is merely a corollary to your intelligence. But with regard to the pistol—it appears that *anyone* in the household might have taken and employed it, if James is so careless of his weapons as his intimates claim."

"Exactly so. What an unpleasant construction we are forced to draw! —For whoever stole the gun must have known it should be recognised as James Wildman's, and must have intended, therefore, to throw suspicion of murder on the young man. The son and heir of Chilham Castle—where presumably the murderer was a *guest*, Jane. Such effrontery!"

"Decidedly bad *ton*," I soothed, "but I do not see why you should deplore a murderer's poor taste, Edward. Surely few virtues may be expected in one who would shoot a man in cold blood?"

He could not suppress a snort of laughter at this appalling truth; perhaps the brandy had succeeded in warming him.

"But tell me," I urged. "How went your interview with Captain MacCallister and Mr. Thane? For Fanny and I could not linger to learn the particulars; with Mrs. MacCallister in a faint and her mother in a fury, we had all we could do to take our leave from the Captain, and tool the horse towards home. Fanny was exceedingly anxious, Edward—I believe she admires that young gentleman more than I should have suspected from the strength of a few dances—"

"The waltz," my brother interjected gloomily. "I should never have allowed it."

"Fiddle! What did MacCallister mean, by saying that he and Thane met with Fiske and paid him a considerable sum to leave the country?"

"Mean? Surely it is readily understood? That roll of banknotes we discovered in the man's coat—nearly *five hundred pounds*, Jane!—came entirely from MacCallister and Thane; and they are agreed in having presented it to Fiske somewhere between the hours of two and three o'clock in the morning. From something the young buck said, I suspect

Thane won most of James Wildman's quarterly allowance at whist a few nights since, and turned it over to the Captain when need demanded."

"But do they admit to shooting him?"

"They deny it, when questioned separately or together. Neither will implicate the other to save himself; neither admits to having taken Wildman's pistol; and both claim to have thought themselves relieved of a damned nuisance, in having paid Fiske to disappear."

"And they swear they returned to Chilham Castle together?"

"Categorically."

"Then who killed the man?" I demanded indignantly.

"That is what I have still to discover! I must persist in making myself odious to the entire neighbourhood, particularly the Wildman family, until the affair is sorted—and I relish the business not at all."

"It seems unlikely that *some other* should have met with Fiske in exactly that spot, Edward—*and* in possession of Wildman's pistol—and killed him," I pointed out reluctantly.

My brother sighed. "I cannot pretend to always know truth when I see it, Jane, but I do not think MacCallister or Thane dissembled when they spoke to me this afternoon."

"Thane did not tell you *all,* at his first interview," I reminded him, "and I have another reason for suspecting his veracity. He pretended to know nothing of the tamarind seed, or the note establishing the hour and place of meeting. Yet if he went with MacCallister—"

"The Captain, too, knew nothing of any note in Fiske's pocket," Edward said. "When I raised the tamarind seed, he recollected his wife's receipt of the curious silk purse—but said it played no part in his errand during the wee hours. I was forced to the odious task of requiring each gentleman to provide me a sample of his penmanship—and would swear that neither resembles the fist on the scrap of paper we found."

"Then how did the Captain and Thane know where to find Curzon Fiske?"

"MacCallister's batman was the agent of their early morning gallop across the Downs." Edward turned from the fender and stood with his hands shoved into his pockets, staring at the pattern in the Turkey carpet. "He is a good enough fellow by the name of Bootle, frank and loyal to a fault. He serves the Captain as a sort of valet, or general factotum—and I gather has been with him some years. At any rate, when Bootle brought up a can of hot water at half-past midnight, when MacCallister was preparing to retire, the Captain noticed that his man's eye had been blackened in a fight. When he questioned Bootle why he had engaged in fisticuffs on the night of his master's wedding, the batman informed the Captain that he had been compelled to defend the Missus's virtue."

I raised my brows at this.

"A stranger had been loitering in the Castle's stableyard earlier in the day, asking for MacCallister's groom, and as Bootle also fulfills that function for the Captain, the summons eventually found its way to his ears. Bootle met the fellow, was charged with a missive for the Captain which he promptly forgot to deliver in all the bustle of the wedding— and resumed his usual duties. It was only when he returned to the stables that evening to see to the Captain's horses that he recalled the incident, and the note he still bore in his pocket. He offered a chance remark to one of the grooms—that the stranger puzzled him exceedingly, as having been dressed like a labourer, but possessed of the Quality's accent; and the groom said confidently that the stranger was none other than the Missus's *real husband—that Mr. Curzon, what married her first.*"

"And so the batman knocked the groom down?"

"He did. Or as Bootle should put it, he offered him a bit of the home-brewed. It is a pity we did not carry Gabriel in our train today, Jane—he might have profited from an interval in the stables, in hearing the entire story recounted in lurid detail. I doubt not it grows hourly in the retelling."

Gabriel was Edward's chief groom, and often rode up behind Fanny when she tooled the ribbons of her tilbury; but not, however, when Edward himself rode escort.

"Strange, that a Castle groom should have recognised Fiske when James Wildman did not."

"James saw only a corpse yesterday morning—and probably averted his eyes as swiftly as possible. The groom, remember, heard Fiske speak—and a voice may do much to recall a face to memory, which a beard might obscure."

I moved to the decanters myself, and poured out a glass of sherry. "What did MacCallister do then?"

"He demanded the note from Bootle, of course!"

"—Which established the meeting place on the Pilgrim's Way?"

"Exactly." Edward smiled. "MacCallister burnt the note, I am afraid—which is unfortunate. It might have proved useful at the inquest. But he did *not* wish it to fall into his wife's hands. He suspected she should recognise the fist, and suffer anxiety. His whole object appears to have been to sustain her illusion that Fiske was long since dead in Ceylon—it appears never to have been his object to disclose the truth. You may imagine the agitation with which he met Adelaide, in his marriage bed."

"—And left her, an hour or so later. Poor man! It seems a cruel way to be served on his wedding night. I imagine Fiske derived no little pleasure from thoroughly cutting up his rival's peace." I raised my eyes to my brother's. "Does Mac-Callister say that Fiske demanded payment in his missive?"

"No. Money appears to have been the Captain's own idea, one Thane seconded. From a better knowledge of Fiske, it was Thane's conviction that he would invariably stand in need of funds, and should be likely to agree to anything in return for them."

I set down my sherry glass, and met my brother's gaze squarely. "But what if Thane and MacCallister are lying, Edward? The possibility must be faced. Men who promise to vanish on the strength of five hundred pounds, are rather more likely than not to reappear once the blunt is spent—and demand a thousand pounds the next time! We are talking of blackmail, after all, for the preservation of a lady's reputation. What if our soldier and his second determined that an easier method of payment should be made? As a military man, the Captain is accustomed to cunning adversaries; he was canny enough not to take the meeting in solitude. And so brought his second—a man who knew the ground, and has a reputation for being an excellent shot."

"I must consider the whole story from that aspect, of course," Edward admitted. "I must regard it as possible truth—or a passel of lies."

We contemplated the hearth together, our thoughts roving across uncertain ground. The flames were settling after a merry burn; and in their depths I conjured a little of the possible scene: Two young men, burdened with their hideous knowledge and the desire to protect Adelaide, riding some two miles along the Pilgrim's Way in the dead of night in expectation of a dangerous man. They should have been fools to set out unarmed. And the thought occurred: Perhaps it *was* an actual Meeting, as a gentleman would understand it—a duel of honour at twenty paces, measured off by moonlight. But then I shook my head. There were the scorch marks on Fiske's coat to consider. They had not been made at twenty paces.

"Our conjectures do not hold together. Consider, Edward: MacCallister is attached to Wellington's staff; he has survived the Peninsular campaigns, where so many came to grief; surely the man owns a pistol of his own?"

Edward glanced at me. "Indeed he must. He should have no need of James Wildman's."

"Nor of placing Wildman's pistol for any to find, in the middle of St. Lawrence churchyard; that is a wanton act of effrontery I cannot believe MacCallister or Thane capable of. No—I am inclined to believe that it was money indeed, not lead balls, that MacCallister and Thane delivered that night. But if so—who sent Curzon Fiske the note wrapped around a tamarind seed?"

"Whoever killed him, I imagine." Edward reached for the brandy decanter. "A killer who hates young James Wildman enough to see him hanged."

CHAPTER SIXTEEN

Revelations of an Inquest

He had a ready summoner at hand,
No rascal craftier in this British land,
For he'd created a skilful net of spies,
Who watched for him as they roamed (procurement eyes).

GEOFFREY CHAUCER, "THE FRIAR'S TALE"

SATURDAY, 23 OCTOBER 1813

I PREVAILED UPON MY BROTHER TO ALLOW ME TO ATTEND the inquest, tho' he assured me there must be no occasion for me to give evidence. Others—my nephews among them—had first discovered the dead man, and borne him into the house; Mr. George Moore had identified the corpse as Curzon Fiske. The coroner himself had examined the body before empanelling his jury. In sum, the evidence must have been a tidy parcel, neatly disposed of—but for the testimony that should inevitably be sworn, concerning Captain MacCallister's nocturnal ride.

That Edward was uneasy in his present rôle as magistrate, I discerned from the moment of entering his equipage. What he most wished from the Coroner's Panel was indecision; a want of verdict should buy Edward time. He was determined to take care with his researches before condemning any of his acquaintance for murder—but the panel would probably be less nice, and more hasty, in their judgement. How to prevent those clear-eyed fellows from fixing too readily upon Captain MacCallister was Edward's ticklish problem.

All discourse on the subject was impeded, however, by the fact that George Moore rode with us. The quarrel with Stephen Lushington might have put the Back Bencher to flight; but it was not for Mr. George Moore, celebrated ecclesiastic, to withdraw from Godmersham. A full ten days he had fixed for his visit, and a full ten days he should remain, however unsuitable the present circumstances might prove for his entertainment. He could not regard my attendance at the inquest with approbation, and as his disgust took the form of a sober lecture on the proper place of ladies in the Divine Scheme for England and the world, I was out of all charity with him. Edward, too, seemed little inclined to support the pomposities of his old friend. He spent the better part of the eight-mile journey in gazing out the carriage window, lost in thought.

The inquest was to be at ten o'clock, in the publick room of the Little Inn, an ancient tavern that sits in Sun Street, hard by Canterbury Cathedral. The affair of Curzon Fiske's death had achieved no very great publicity in the town, the murder having occurred but lately and in the country. I was not surprized, therefore, to see faces I recognised lining the benches arranged before the coroner, magistrate, and panel. Mr. Wildman was there, and his son James Beckford, as well as their guests the MacCallisters, and Julian Thane. Mrs. Thane, to my astonishment, was absent—she must have been laid low with a stomach complaint, to have denied herself the pleasure of abusing Canterbury's worthiest citizens.

Of the few strangers, I suspected some were relations and friends of the empanelled jury, come to observe their honourable service. Adelaide MacCallister and I were the only ladies present.

George Moore consented, at least, to share my bench—tho' from the expression on his countenance, he preferred to let no one suspect we were acquainted. He nodded distantly to Adelaide, who was arrayed in unbride-like black; if she acknowledged this pious salute, or her former acquaintance with Moore, I could not say; a veil disguised her features.

Julian Thane, with his rogue's dark curl falling negligently over his brow, exerted himself enough to cross the room and greet us. I offered my hand—how often may I expect a handsome young rake to kiss it in future?—and he bent low with a grin.

"I trust you are well, Miss Austen?"

"Perfectly, I assure you."

"The atmosphere of an inquest agrees with you?"

"I am not so missish as to faint, sir, from an excessive exposure to the Law."

"Miss Knight, however, declined the pleasure."

"Miss Knight had a prior engagement—she was to ride today with Mr. John Plumptre, I believe."

Mr. John Plumptre, met with a similar intelligence regarding his fellow man, should have darkened and turned away with a glower; but Julian Thane merely pursed his lips in a silent whistle. "And I had hoped her to be an undiscovered flower, blooming in retirement. Such a sad romp as Miss Knight turns out to be! Invariably in request, throughout the neighbourhood! I shall have to challenge her to a course of jumps when I am next at leisure—there is a prime hunter in Wildman's stables ideally suited to a lady. And I have no doubt Miss Knight shall prove pluck to the backbone."

He bowed and returned to his sister. Just so does Defiance meet the threat of Damnation.

Andrew MacCallister, for his part, looked as cool and grim as tho' he rode into battle. He wore his dress uniform, of the 7th Light Dragoons, and must impress even the ignorant with his appearance of command.

There was a bustle to the rear; I turned, and observed Edward and Dr. Bredloe, who made their way up the centre aisle; and behind them came the panel of men who should decide how Curzon Fiske died.

They were an assortment of tradesmen and farmers from the surrounding environs—but whether knowledgeable or ignorant, malicious or kindly-disposed, who could say? A collection of strangers, for the most part, bound by a single duty; individuals forced to work in harness for the space of the proceeding. And I was reminded, of a sudden, of the *Canterbury Tales*—that collection of Chaucer's Pilgrims, unknown to one another until their meeting in a tavern, bound for the space of their journey by the stories they chose to tell. If one could but hear the thoughts of these twelve men, as they weighed what Dr. Bredloe and Edward might say! Of a sudden I felt anxious, as I had not felt before; the security of an Adelaide MacCallister or her Captain, even of a Julian Thane, seemed too important to hand over unconditionally to these unknowns.

Dr. Bredloe convened the proceeding in his driest manner. The panel's first duty was to view the corpse, which lay in a closet to one side of the publick room; having submitted to the task, they returned to their benches in a subdued fashion, and were allowed a moment to collect themselves. Dr. Bredloe stated that Deceased's wife, Mrs. Adelaide Fiske, had identified the corpse as her husband; he must have required her to do so, before ever the inquest began. I felt George Moore stiffen beside me; he had expected to testify to Fiske's identity, and indeed, had attended the inquest for no other purpose. Was he indignant at having his rôle usurped? Or relieved? Some profound emotion had turned him rigid. I fancied it had more to do with Adelaide, than himself; and wondered very much if he still carried a *tendre* for her, after seven years.

But my nephew Edward was recounting the discovery of the body by the party of gentlemen and their beaters; he looked very young as he stood before the coroner, conscious of his father's eyes upon him. Dr. Bredloe thanked the boy, and allowed him to stand down; then addressed the state of the corpse, the nature of the wound, and the probable manner in which it had been received. The constable next displayed the pistol, and James Beckford Wildman was called upon to identify it as his own, in a voice that trembled only slightly.

Naturally, a murmur went up at this from the assembled audience; there were some in the crowd, curious onlookers, who knew nothing of facts that all at Chilham must have mastered. Edward gazed steadily at young James, and asked him in a clear voice when he had last seen his pistol.

"I cannot say with any certainty, Your Honour. I know it to have been in my possession on Tuesday last, when I engaged in some target shooting; I later cleaned the gun, and replaced it with its companion, in its case; but as the case is left in my father's gun room, where any might find it, I cannot tell when it disappeared."

"But you did not, yourself, take the gun out for the purpose of firing it at Curzon Fiske the following night, or early Thursday morning?"

Young Wildman paled, but his chin lifted a little and his gaze did not falter. "I did not, Your Honour."

"You have heard Constable Blewett say that it was found on a tombstone in St. Lawrence churchyard?"

"I have. I do not know how it came there."

"Mr. Wildman, were you at all acquainted with Curzon Fiske?"

"He was the husband of my second cousin, and as such,

was often entertained at our home. He left the Kingdom some three years ago, however, for India, and we believed that he had died out there."

"When did you receive word of Mr. Fiske's death?"

"Some eighteen months since—in April of last year."

"And you received no subsequent word of his survival? You did not expect to find him on the Pilgrim's Way Thursday morning?"

"I did not—and indeed, Fiske was so altered, I should never have recognised him."

Dr. Bredloe intervened at this point, with a polite smile for Edward. "Tell me, Mr. Wildman—how would ye describe your relations with Mr. Fiske when he was alive, and living in England?"

For the first time, James Wildman's eyes dropped; he seemed, for an instant, uncertain what he should say. Then he shrugged slightly, and a wistful smile flickered across his lips. "I had barely achieved my majority when Curzon quitted Kent for the last time. As a boy, I thought him quite the most engaging fellow I had ever met—Top o'the Trees, a Go Amongst the Goes. He cut such a dash, you understand, that he was a great favourite with all of us when we were young."

"So you parted on terms of cordiality?"

Wildman hesitated; and almost imperceptibly, his gaze slid towards myself.

Impossible. He could have no reason for staring at *me*.

And then I understood: it was George Moore's counsel he sought.

Moore was rigid, again, beside me, and his gloved hands were clenched in his lap. Did I imagine it? Or did he shake his head ever so slightly as James Wildman studied his countenance?

"We parted on terms of complete indifference," Wildman answered woodenly.

"No quarrel?" Dr. Bredloe persisted. "No reason to hate the man, when you discovered he was back in Kent?"

"I did not discover him back in Kent. I discovered his corpse," the young man said evenly.

Dr. Bredloe studied Wildman for an uncomfortable and inscrutable instant; then released him to his father.

THERE WAS A PAUSE IN THE PROCEEDINGS AT THIS POINT, so that the jury might partake of refreshment; the panel were led into a separate parlour for this interval, while the rest of us rose and stretched our limbs.

"Pray make my apologies to Mr. Knight," George Moore said abruptly as he quitted our bench. "I have an errand that cannot wait, in the Cathedral Close. I believe I have seen enough of the deplorable business here; I shall return in an hour's time, in the hope that it shall be concluded, and that we might all return to Godmersham together."

I curtseyed to the clergyman without a word; he lifted his hat; and I was left to wonder what had so discomposed him—or what trial he believed himself to have survived.

The final wager, a voice whispered in my brain; *the fatal game of whist, on the night before Fiske fled to India three years ago.* What had been the stakes? And what the outcome? Why the charge of cheating, left unanswered? George Moore was determined, certainly, that James Wildman should give no hint of the discord that had divided Fiske from his oldest acquaintance.

Dr. Bredloe opened the parlour door, and the panel filed once more to their seats, presumably refreshed.

As the proceedings recommenced, two more strangers made their way into the Little Inn's publick room: a tall, bearded man respectably dressed, with the look of a solicitor or steward about him; and a bowlegged, shabbily-dressed fellow I recognised at once for a seaman, from long acquaintance with the type during my years of residence in South-ampton. His skin was much weathered and tanned, his grey hair was long and tied in a queue, his whiskers grizzled, and his canvas trousers stained with salt. I had occasion to re-mark upon these details, because the sailor chose to seat him-self next to me, the place having been vacated by George Moore; he nodded and grinned as he sat, displaying numer-ous gaps in a wretched mouthful of teeth.

The bearded gentleman took no seat at all, but stood near the far wall, his earnest gaze fixed on my brother. For of course, Edward had begun to speak.

Now, I thought, must come the inquest's most dangerous passage: the revelation of Captain MacCallister's summons by the dead man, and his nocturnal walk. Julian Thane, I no-ticed, was so unaffected by the prospect as to be paring his nails with a pocketknife. His sister's hand, however, was clenched tightly on MacCallister's arm; a woman of less courage should have quitted the room entirely.

But my brother surprized me.

He spoke briefly in Dr. Bredloe's ear. The coroner immedi-ately nodded and turned to the panel, with a precise account of the possessions discovered in Curzon Fiske's coat. The roll of banknotes was displayed, in the amount of nearly five hun-dred pounds; the scrap of paper with the blurred script was shewn to each man, with the proper interval required for each to attempt to read it; and finally, the tamarind seed—which Dr. Bredloe affirmed was from a plant native to India—was held aloft. The coroner explained, at Edward's prompting, that the scrap of paper had been wrapped around the seed—as tho' the tamarind were a token of good faith. The paper, he suggested, had established a meeting, for the only legible words upon it were *St. Lawrence Church*.

At which instant, my brother thanked the coroner and begged permission to call one Barnabus Twitch before the panel.

Of a sudden, there he was: the Wildmans' imperturbable butler. He was dressed as he had been the previous day, in his livery and wig; he bowed to Dr. Bredloe, and took his oath at Edward's behest.

"Your master, Mr. Wildman of Chilham Castle, gave a ball on Wednesday last," Edward observed.

"He did, sir."

"And during the festivities, a stranger appeared at the Castle door, I think?"

"That is so." Twitch inclined his head. "A manservant—Joseph by name—attended the door, as I was otherwise engaged; but being uncertain what reception the man was due, Joseph sought my advice."

"And why did he do so?" Edward asked.

Twitch blinked with the placidity of a cow. "Joseph was confused by the person's aspect and appearance. He spoke with the accent of the Quality, Your Honour, but his clothing did not suggest an elevated station."

"And this fellow was unknown to you?"

"I had never seen him before in my life."

"What was his errand at Chilham Castle?"

"He wished to present a gift to the bri—the widow of Deceased."

"Do you know what that gift was?"

"A purse of silk, as it were a kind of reticule, embroidered all about with gold threads."

"It sounds like an exotic object. Did you accept it from him?"

"I did, sir—and give it to Joseph to present to the lady."

"Do you know what the purse contained?"

Twitch smiled. "I saw it opened myself. At the time I had no word for what was in it, but I know now they was tamarind seeds."

A second murmur rose from the crowd; they were so far diverted from the matter of murder at this point, being adrift on an exotic sea, that I doubted they should ever find their way back.

"You have heard, I think, that a tamarind seed was found in Deceased's coat, wrapped inside a note that established a meeting on the Pilgrim's Way."

"Yes, Your Honour."

Edward glanced at the coroner's panel. "I put it to the men of the jury that this seed we speak of, which must be considered a rare and unusual item in England, is unlikely to have come from a *different source* than the seeds in the silken pouch."

Edward allowed the panel an instant to absorb the implications of his thought, but I wondered very much what he was about. Did he intend to condemn *Adelaide,* whose hands had opened the stranger's gift? Would he next imply that her hand had written the note, and tucked the seed inside it? I could not risk a glance in the lady's direction; I feared to see her sensibility, or her husband's indignation.

The sailor beside me was agog with interest, leaning forward intently with his elbows resting on his patched knees. He must have taken shore leave from one of the Kentish ports—Deal, perhaps, or Dover—and wandered into Canterbury with an eye for publick spectacle. As a source of entertainment, an inquest could hardly equal a Tyburn hanging; but beggars could not be choosers, after all.

Edward was speaking again; I must attend.

"Were you at all acquainted with Deceased in previous years?" he asked Twitch.

"Mr. Fiske? Aye—I've known him, to look at, these seven years or more."

"Would you kindly step into the closet with Dr. Bredloe, and inform us whether Deceased is the person who delivered the silk purse to Chilham Castle? We might then explain the seed discovered in his pocket."

Ah. Edward hoped to keep Adelaide entirely out of it.

Twitch opened his mouth as if to protest, then closed it with resignation. He was led into the compartment where Curzon Fiske lay.

The seaman rose and began to make his way towards the centre aisle; we had not succeeded in securing his interest for so much as a quarter-hour.

"That's Mr. Fiske, well enough," Twitch declared as he emerged from the closet, "tho' I'd not have known him straight off, with that beard."

"And was it he," Edward asked, with palpable satisfaction, "who rang the bell at Chilham Castle Wednesday night, and asked that the purse of tamarind seeds be presented to the lady?"

"No, Your Honour, it was not." Twitch shook his head emphatically. "But I can tell you who did."

He lifted his arm and pointed directly at my seaman, who had almost achieved the publick room's door.

CHAPTER SEVENTEEN

A Man Impossible to Move

*"That quickness of mind is given, at birth, to every
Woman: lying and weeping are birthright gifts
From God, natural weapons to help us live."*

GEOFFREY CHAUCER, "THE WIFE OF BATH'S PROLOGUE"

23 OCTOBER 1813, CONT.

SUCH A LITTLE THING, THAT POINTED FINGER; BUT IT CAUSED
the sort of chaos to which even a Royal rout should never be
equal.

"Stop that man!" Dr. Bredloe cried, at which the seaman
heaved open the publick room door, and dashed towards the
Little Inn's front entry.

I rose, but the entire throng was before me; I had an idea
of MacCallister and Thane surging through the Canterbury
bystanders, determined to seize the fellow, and being stopped
by a knot of men in the doorway; heard a great halloing from
the main body of the inn, and the crash of an overturned
bench besides. I glanced about me, and saw that Adelaide
MacCallister had not stirred from her place; her head drooped

a little beneath her bonnet and veil, the countenance obscured. I hesitated, and then crossed the aisle to where she sat.

"Are you unwell, Mrs. MacCallister?"

She turned her head, then raised her veil. "Miss Austen! What a comfort it is to see another lady in this miserable place!"

Impulsively, as it seemed, she extended her gloved hand, and I took it between both of my own. "I hope that we need not remain very much longer."

"They have not called me," she said in some agitation. "They have not called *Andrew,* or Julian. . . . The agony of waiting! How long are we required to endure it? I confess that I live in dread of the moment, however. It was almost too much to witness poor James—"

"And yet he acquitted himself admirably, did he not?"

She drew a trembling breath in an effort to calm herself; she was far more discomposed than I had ever seen her. "I cannot say whether he spoke well or ill. He certainly did not speak *frankly.* I cannot blame him for that; we are all terrified of what we do not know—of what may be hidden in those around us, the impulse to violence. You cannot know what it is like at Chilham Castle—each of us aware of James's pistol, and the use to which it was put, and wondering *who* among us employed it. . . . Every word is charged with unintended meaning, and the very air of the place is turned poisonous. Oh, God, that I had never come there, to trouble such good friends!"

I sank down on the bench beside her; she was shivering, and I placed an arm about her shoulders. "Come. You require refreshment. Shall I get you some coffee? A glass of wine, perhaps?"

She shook her head, and leaned a little towards me; I perceived that she was weeping. And then a shadow fell across us.

"Mrs. MacCallister," Edward said gently. "I am sure you

feel faint. It has been a very trying day, indeed; will you not take an airing? I should be happy to escort you outside through the side door; no one shall trouble you in that direction. We might attend your husband's return."

She glanced up, her eyes as dark as rain-washed violets; then she nodded and pulled the veil once more over her features.

When Edward returned a few moments later, he was alone.

"I set her to walking in the Cathedral Close until such time as MacCallister is able to escort her home. There is nothing for her to do here. It is a damnable business, Jane!"

My brother, the *gallant*. Not even Edward is immune to the pleasure that a pair of fine eyes, in the face of a pretty woman, may bestow.

THE CORONER'S PANEL HAD PROVED ADMIRABLY RESTRAINED during the interval, and had failed to break ranks when the rest of the room had pelted out the door in pursuit of the seaman; but the patient fellows were beginning to shift uncomfortably on their benches, as if uncertain what next should be required of them.

"I warrant you did not expect this result, when you put your questions to Twitch," I observed drily.

Edward studied the Wildmans' butler, who still stood placidly in the area reserved for witnesses, until he should be told he must do otherwise.

"*That seaman* is the fellow who caused your manservant such perplexity?" Edward demanded. "I should have thought one glance at his clothes might be enough to earn him the tradesman's entrance!"

"Ah, but then Your Honour never heard the lad speak," Twitch returned comfortably. "Fair Eton and Cambridge, he is, when he gets to jawing. May I stand down, sir?"

"By all means. I have already taken too much of your time. Have you a conveyance back to Chilham?"

"I'll stand up behind Mr. Wildman's curricle, thank you kindly, sir. I expect Mr. Wildman and Young Mr. Wildman will be making for home soon." He bowed. "I hope you catch the fellow."

As the butler quitted the room, Edward consulted his pocket watch, then turned to the panel. "Pray adjourn to the private parlour, where I shall have some ale sent in to you."

With grateful mutters and thanks, the men did as my brother suggested. Edward closed the door upon them, and glanced at me thoughtfully. "I am not sure that Twitch has not done us a very great service, Jane."

"By providing an excuse to suspend the proceedings?"

He smiled, and went off to order the ale.

He was good enough to bring me ratafia and cakes upon his return; and we sat in splendid solitude, nibbling contentedly, until the distant sounds of riot pronounced the search party returned.

It was Julian Thane who thrust open the publick room door, and Thane who dragged the seaman in by his collar. Behind him strode Captain MacCallister, with his sabre pointed at the seaman's back. After MacCallister came a flood of people, many more than had originally filled the publick room, the chase through Canterbury's streets having attracted an admiring train. There were children and beggars, flower sellers and pedlars of sacred relics from the Cathedral Close; and even one or two housewives seduced from their shopping, with paper parcels on their arms.

There was no sign of Adelaide MacCallister.

"Pray bring the fellow forward," Edward commanded.

Thane dragged the seaman before the empty benches where the panel had formerly sat, and glanced round in perplexity.

"Dr. Bredloe!" Edward called towards the rear of the room. "What do you wish? Your panel is closeted with their ale!"

The coroner sighed, and forced his way through the throng. In a matter of seconds the panel returned, several wiping their mouths on their shirtsleeves, and took up their places.

"Now, then, my lad, what is your name?" Dr. Bredloe demanded of the seaman.

The wizened old man surveyed the coroner imperiously. "I hardly think I am *your lad*, Dr. Bredloe—if indeed I have your name correctly. My own is Sir Davie Myrrh, late of Ceylon." And he performed a bow that should have graced the portals of Almack's.

THERE, HOWEVER, ENDED THE SEAMAN'S EFFORT AT CO-operation. Sir Davie refused entirely to answer any questions put to him, until, he said, he should have taken counsel of his solicitor; and being required to name that gentleman, offered the direction of an intimate of Temple Bar, London. Dr. Bredloe lifted a quizzical brow at my brother, and raised his hands as tho' incapable of further decision; and after a brief, private colloquy, coroner and magistrate appeared to be mutually satisfied. Dr. Bredloe turned his attention to his panel.

"Men of the jury," he said, "the Magistrate has requested an adjournment of this proceeding, so that the present confusion might be thoroughly penetrated. Do you agree to such an adjournment, with the inquest to be resumed at a later date, under the Magistrate's advising?"

There was an uneasy silence. One member of the panel—a man of middle years, with the stalwart looks of those who spend their days in the fields, lifted his hand hesitantly to his forelock. "Begging yer pardon, Crowner, but what about the *corpus*? Adjourn howsoever long you like, but there'll be a stink."

"Having entered into the record my examination of Deceased," Dr. Bredloe said, "and having required the panel to view Deceased's remains, there can be no bar at present to Christian burial. Proper interment need not wait on the resumption of the inquest—provided the Magistrate concurs."

The Magistrate concurred.

In addition, he ordered his constable to take Sir Davie Myrrh, late of Ceylon, into custody on the suspicion of murder; and so the seaman was led away to Canterbury gaol.

"IT IS ALTOGETHER AN IMPENETRABLE BUSINESS," GEORGE Moore observed, as our carriage rattled along the road to Godmersham. His countenance was considerably lighter than it had been on our journey out to Canterbury; either his errands in the Cathedral Close, or his estimation of the inquest, had cheered his humour. We were forced to a tête-à-tête, Edward having determined to follow his new-found oddity to Westgate, where the gaol was housed, in order to interrogate him more closely. He should not have been doing his magisterial duty otherwise; but deemed it unlikely the man should relent, and speak without his lawyer. The mystery of Sir Davie Myrrh would have, perforce, to await that fellow's arrival—an event that could not occur before Monday at the earliest.

I glanced through the carriage window; we had covered but two miles of the distance to Godmersham, and a tedious interval lay before us. Mr. Moore had drawn a small leatherbound volume from his coat, and was preparing to immerse himself in its pages; Aeschylus's *Prometheus,* I observed. I pursed my lips, unwilling for my curiosity to alienate the gentleman further, and bring down a rain of strictures upon my head—but I might never have so perfect an opportunity to question him again.

"Such matters are always impenetrable," I began, "when the parties involved are less than frank."

"You would refer to that deluded seaman, I presume."

Mr. Moore had been treated to a summary of the business from Julian Thane, having missed the episode himself.

"Yes—the seaman, naturally . . . and poor James Wildman, of course. One could perfectly discern that he did not wish to speak frankly of Curzon Fiske. I must suppose that partiality for his cousin Adelaide sealed his lips; but there is a history, there, begging to be told."

"I suspect you know little of the matter, Miss Austen, being a stranger to Kent, and most of the people in it."

It was a snub; a decided snub; Mr. Moore meant to quell my pretensions as thoroughly as tho' I had been Miss Clewes, and throwing out lures to Jupiter Finch-Hatton. But my gambit succeeded in this: the clergyman closed his book.

I regarded him coolly. "The history of Fiske's final wager will have to be canvassed, of course, however unpleasant the exercise must prove. Your calm good sense will be invaluable to my brother, Mr. Moore—for you were one of the party at Chilham Castle, were you not, when all the gentlemen played at whist for pound points, and Mr. Lushington accused the dead man of cheating?"

"The events of that night can have nothing to do with Fiske's death, Miss Austen."

"The man was *murdered*, Mr. Moore," I returned in exasperation. "A violent act does not arise in a vacuum; it requires profound emotion to spur it on—hatred, for example, or a desire for vengeance. Add to this that Fiske was killed by a pistol belonging to Chilham Castle, in the very neighbourhood he fled three years before, and the likelihood increases that the two episodes are linked."

"By one of the whist players, you would suggest. You forget, I think, that we all presumed Fiske to be dead—and were dancing at his wife's wedding when he died."

I shrugged my shoulders. "The fact of his murder proclaims that one among you knew that he was alive. Perhaps Fiske corresponded with an old acquaintance."

Mr. Moore's eyes narrowed. "Is the exchange of letters now enough to hang a man?"

"Certainly not. One would have to detect in such letters a spur to violence. Or perhaps another discovered an innocent correspondence, and was moved to murder on the strength of his secret knowledge—that Fiske lived, and was returned to Kent. This can all be merest speculation; but I am persuaded you will perceive the value to the Magistrate of a clear narrative of events: The fatal whist-party, the accusation of cheating, and Fiske's flight. That should do much to throw light on the murder, and I can think of no one better suited to supplying such a narrative than yourself, Mr. Moore. You will know how to divide emotion from fact, and offer an account untinged by personal emnity."

The sharpness of Mr. Moore's looks increased; his brows drew down, and his lips compressed.

"You flatter me, Miss Austen."

"Do I, sir?" I affected surprise. "Then my portrait of your character must be flawed in its chief points. It has been my habit to regard you as prizing a profound understanding above all else."

"That is self-evident." He drew himself up. "But what right you assume to question me regarding that abhorrent occasion—or advise me on my present course of action—I fail to apprehend."

I offered a bewildered gaze. "Have I done so? I intended merely to suggest that Edward must be distinctly indebted to your assistance. However, if you mean to persist in being *private* about the affair, Mr. Moore, I must assume that you regard it with uneasiness."

"On that question I may put your mind at rest, Miss Austen," he retorted with obvious dislike. "There is nothing in my life, I am thankful to say, that I regard with uneasiness; I am so much in the habit of interrogating my conscience, and acting according to its dictates, that I am a stranger to moral ambiguity. I would advise a thorough canvassing of *your* conscience in future as a useful aid to conduct."

"Come, come, Mr. Moore." I could not disguise the amusement in my voice; it *would* break out. "Hypocrisy is a quality in a gentleman—particularly a cleric—that I cannot endure! Three years since, you so far disregarded your conscience as to *gamble* with a hardened gamester you admit to having thoroughly disliked—and for so breathless a sum as pound points! How reckless of you, to be sure! I perceive that even the most correct of men—in Holy Orders, and with a reputation to consider—may lose his head from time to time. Some profound emotion, rather than Reason, must account for it; but the question that will invariably arise, is this: Was it *ardent love* for Adelaide MacCallister—or *profound hatred* for her husband?"

Mr. Moore was now quite white about the lips, and it was with difficulty that he controlled his temper. "Your strictures, Miss Austen, are distasteful, and unbecoming in one whose rôle in life ought to be submissive and retiring. I owe you no explanation of my conduct, and your presumption in demanding it—in speculating upon the nature and motives of actions long past, and in which you had no part—is repugnant. I decline utterly to discuss the matter further; you do not deserve such notice."

He reopened his book, and made a poor pretence of reading it; and I sighed a little at my failure as I returned to gazing out the carriage window. Such men as may be unmoved by flattery, wit, calculation, or humour are beyond the reach of my powers; and Mr. Moore was certainly one of these.

CHAPTER EIGHTEEN

Correspondence

*The worm of conscience will shudder, and somehow show
Wickedness its face, which may well be
Hidden from all the world but God and he.*

GEOFFREY CHAUCER, "THE PHYSICIAN'S TALE"

SUNDAY, 24 OCTOBER 1813

MR. SHERER, OUR EXCELLENT AND MOST REVEREND MR. Sherer of St. Lawrence Church, whose sermons so frequently envigour the flagging Christian spirit, is vicar also of Westwell—a neighbouring village in Kent—and from this multiplicity of livings, which any clergyman's wife must rejoice in, as ensuring the Sherers' worldly comfort and survival, has come a peculiar evil, in that Mr. Sherer is forced to quit his excellent vicarage here at Godmersham, and repair to Westwell for a period of *full three years*—the curate charged with supplying Mr. Sherer's duties in that place having failed to suit the parishioners so well as they should like. The complaints that have come to Mr. Sherer's ears in recent months have so alarmed that assiduous gentleman, that nothing will do but the curate must be got rid of. What the poor fellow's crimes may have been—a disinclination for sermon-making, a persistent stutter, or perhaps too glad an eye to the ladies of Westwell—I cannot tell; Mr. Sherer will not speak of them, but only look grave, while Mrs. Sherer casts up her eyes to Heaven.

"These young men, Miss Austen, ought not to consider Holy Orders, if the vocation is *not* upon them," she says, with all the vicarious complaisance of one who has married an Emissary of Providence. "Too many are simply out for *all they can get*."

"And if they are, who can blame them?" Mr. Sherer observed heavily as he quaffed my brother's sherry, tea being too dangerous an offering for the Sabbath. "The world offers such young men but poor examples of clerical life! If one were to credit the world of Fashion, we are all scoundrels and renegades! Only consider the insults to which the Divine Work of Holy Orders is subjected, among the novelists and playwrights of the stage!"

"Oh, the *stage*," Mrs. Sherer returned dismissively. She is a plump woman with protuberant blue eyes, much given to fondling the bugle beads that adorn her bodice, of which she is inordinately proud. "If you look for respect for the Cloth, my dear, among the swaggerers of Covent Garden, I despair of you! But surely there are many admirable portraits of the Clergy in works of literature? I do not speak of *novels*—"

"I beg you will not utter the word, my dear," Mr. Sherer declared, with a look of pain, and a hand pressed to his brow. "When I consider of the hectic success of that vulgar work—you know the one I would mean, that all the young ladies hereabouts are forever consulting—and the shameful picture of its clergyman, so very *worthy* a young man I thought, and feeling just as he ought about his Patroness—so quick to apologise whenever his natural feelings outstripped his good sense—"

"I think you must refer to Mr. Collins," Fanny interposed,

without a hint of betrayal in her voice. "He comes in *Pride and Prejudice*. I found him vastly amusing, myself."

Mr. Sherer shuddered, and reached for Edward's decanter.

"You read it, then?" I enquired, in a cheerful accent. "This novel you profess to despise?"

"I? Read a *novel*?"

"—For your portrait of the clergyman is as clear as life, Mr. Sherer. It cannot have been formed by merely *hearing* of Mr. Collins spoken of, among your acquaintance."

The poor vicar flushed. "I cannot say. I cannot recall. It is possible that Mrs. Sherer read me the passages aloud, in her natural indignation at the licence of the author! I declare that *any* sort of trash may be found at the booksellers today— even in so sacred a city as Canterbury! The French have much to answer for, indeed!"

What Buonaparte might have to do with the failings of Mr. Collins, I did not trouble to enquire; I have given over admiring Mr. Sherer, tho' his sermons *are* so inspired. My sympathies *now* are all for the dismissed curate.

It does seem hard that the poor young man (for a curate is invariably a young man, and invariably poor) should have all the tiresomeness of Westwell's duties, while Mr. Sherer enjoys all its tithes. Perhaps the curate experienced a little of the revolutionary fervour which is so catching in Europe and England these days, and refused any longer to be Mr. Sherer's slave; but whatever the cause, the curate is to be gone in a fortnight, and Mr. Sherer and his wife—whom I *cannot* admire—removed to Westwell, leaving another eager young man to do the Lord's and Mr. Sherer's work at Godmersham. *Our* new curate is rumoured to have a wife, who is said to be musical—which might prove beneficial to Fanny's happiness, at least.

All this we were told when the Sherers came to take tea with Fanny after the morning service—Sunday being a day of strict observance in the Godmersham household, particularly when George Moore is among its intimates. I do not think his little son was permitted to smile, much less laugh, for the whole of the morning; and when Lizzy broke out in giggles at something Marianne whispered behind her hand, Mr. Moore gave both girls so scandalised a look that they were reduced to blushes, and led immediately from the room by Miss Clewes, her lips compressed in profound disapprobation.

My brother Edward was gone from the house, on a sombre errand: Curzon Fiske was laid to rest in the churchyard at Chilham not an hour since—Mr. Tylden at St. Mary's having the honour of the funeral rites. How varied and strange has that gentleman's divine service been, in recent days! Edward, both as neighbour and magistrate, could not stay away; and in this observance he was joined by all the gentlemen of Chilham Castle, not excepting Jupiter Finch-Hatton, who has remained at Chilham to support his friend James Wildman ever since the wedding. Jupiter, I am told, comes to us for several days' visit tomorrow, ostensibly to bid farewell to Young Edward and his brother George, who set out for the autumn term at Oxford on Thursday; the Moores are to leave us on the same morning. I must therefore glean as much from George Moore as I may, before he passes entirely beyond my ken.

I am in as much disfavour with that gentleman, however, as Lizzy and Marianne—and should not have been surprized had he warned his excellent wife against me, so grievous were my improprieties of yesterday; but in this I was proved wrong, by Harriot's drawing me aside once the Sherers were bowed out the door, and begging me earnestly to accompany her in a walk about the grounds.

Fanny, who had just received a letter on a silver tray from Johncock, Edward's butler, was too engrossed to permit of her joining us; her cheeks were tinged pink, and her expression distracted. Tho' I should have liked to pry, I held the impulse in check—one cannot always be looking over the shoulder of a young woman of twenty—and accepted Harriot's invitation with pleasure. Harriot may not be possessed of the most *profound* understanding; but it is often your simpler minds that perceive the greatest truths about the gentlemen they marry.

We two set off through the back garden, and made our way towards the little temple on the hill where I was so often used to write, when Elizabeth was alive—how long ago now it seems!—and where I once sat in the stillness of a late-summer dusk, and watched the elegant figure of a black-coated Rogue climb the slope in search of me. Godmersham has become in some part a landscape populated by ghosts—for me as much as for Edward—and I suppose this is the penance exacted by time: the longer we outlive our cherished companions, the more we are haunted by them. But I shook off this note of melancholy, for Harriot was speaking—like a caged bird, she was forever warbling about something, inconsequential to all but herself.

"How damp the air is, tho' it was bright but yesterday! I must suppose we are to expect more rain. It is the most tedious aspect of autumn, is it not, Jane, that the weather should be so persistently damp? It quite lowers one's spirits."

Harriot's voice was fretful, which was *not* usual in her; and when I stole a glance at her countenance, I observed that she was looking hag-ridden, as tho' sleep, or peace of mind, had been wanting of late. Perhaps she was increasing again; that would explain both the desire for an airing and the unquiet nights.

"I am sure you have been longing for your own home these several days at least. It cannot be thought pleasant, to assist in a study of murder, while a guest of the Magistrate."

"Oh, no!" She stopped short impulsively and laid a gloved hand on my sleeve. "You are all so lively, and so kind, that it makes quite a change from our usual domestic circle. Little George, I am sure, is much the better for his playfellows in the nursery, and then, too, Miss Clewes is such a wise and careful creature! I confess I should like to lure her away from Fanny! But I never should, you know. I daresay I could not meet her wages."

She flushed as she said this, and dropped her eyes, and without comment we began walking again, the temple looming ever larger in our view.

I suspected there was some little embarrassment in the Moores' circumstances, from the fact of Harriot having worn an outmoded gown to the Chilham Castle ball; and, too, she was frequently enquiring of Fanny or me, in a naïve tone, whether various London firms supplied their goods on terms of credit, or required what she calls *ready money*. Fanny was so careless of her aunt's feelings as to once ask whether the Moores ever *dealt in the article,* meaning actual pounds and pence; and Harriot merely opened her eyes wide, and declared that everyone she knew was accustomed to having things on tick.[1] It seems the habit of her household, to run up careless bills and face the reckoning much later.

But now I wondered. Surely the son of the Archbishop of Canterbury—who held a respectable living in East Peckham, by no means his first vicarage—was supplied with an income adequate to his needs and station? Or did George Moore regard his station so highly, that his stile of living demanded greater means than he could command?

The clergyman's face rose unbidden in my mind; and

---

[1] Although Jane's letters to Cassandra during this two-month visit to Godmersham say nothing of Curzon Fiske's murder, no doubt due to Cassandra's disapproval of Jane's unseemly interest in detection, she does refer to the Moore family's circumstances by directly quoting Fanny's words on the subject. See Letter 95, dated November 5, 1813, in *Jane Austen's Letters* (New York: Oxford University Press, 1995), Deirdre Le Faye, editor. —*Editor's note.*

around it hovered James Wildman, Jupiter Finch-Hatton, and others at the green baize table—where Curzon Fiske had required his friends to play at whist for pound points. Had this been George Moore's first exposure to gaming—or was the laying of bets a confirmed vice, a passion pursued in secret, that drained his resources and brought increasing anxiety to his wife?

"Forgive me, Harriot," I murmured as she stumbled on the gravel path, and drew a halting breath. "Are you quite well?"

"I am very well, thank you, Jane. It is just that I am a trifle uneasy in my mind. I should not speak of it, perhaps—let us talk of something else. I shall be better presently, I am sure. The air does one so much good, despite the mizzle that will certainly come on! You are a great walker, I think?"

"I attempt to go round the park every day; it is the chief resource left to an indifferent rider."

"I was used to ride when I was a girl," Harriot remarked wistfully, "and loved nothing more than a tearing gallop— but it does not do to think of such things, now I am become quite an old matron. What should I do with a hack, indeed, eating its head off in the stable—the wife of a clergyman, with all the duties of a parish to attend to!"

My conviction of my companion's distress grew. Was it want of funds that had so oppressed her spirits—or want of amusement, with her grim Mr. Moore for companion? I cast about for a sensible topic—I could enquire dull nothings about her child, or comment upon her progress in knotting a fringe—but such banalities were to no purpose, when a murder had been done. Harriot was my own for the space of a half-hour, and I must violate her gentle sensibilities, and put questions that must discompose her.

"I know full well what it is to practice a parsonage's economy," I said with sympathy as I slipped my arm through hers. "You will recall that I am a clergyman's daughter—and how my father managed to raise *eight* of us, on three hundred a year—which is all the living can have provided for much of my childhood—I cannot think!"

"*Eight,*" Harriot repeated in a quavering voice. "And I myself am one of thirteen! I could not bear so many children, Jane. The shabby-gentility of such a household! The endless turning and dyeing of gowns—the redressing of last year's bonnet—and how are so many *lives* to be provided for? So many girls to be married off, when they do not possess a farthing?"

I might have been nettled at so artless a speech—being myself the portionless product of just such a shabby-genteel household, and all unmarried—but I heard the note of despair in her voice, and pitied her.

"—For a clergyman, Jane, cannot expect to leave anything much even to his eldest son—or to purchase a commission in a crack regiment for a younger one," Harriot persisted.

"Two of my brothers went to sea," I said thoughtfully, "the Navy being a profession not very particular as regards to fortune. But your cavalry regiments *do* come dear."

"And little George is so passionately devoted to the Marquis of Wellington!" Harriot said mournfully. "I am sure Mr. Moore will see his way clear to George's *education*—the value of a period at Oxford cannot be denied—but as for allowing his son to entertain any profession beyond Holy Orders . . ."

She did not bother to conclude her sentence. Little George would *not* be permitted the extravagance of a cavalry regiment.

"I am sure Mr. Moore has many pressing obligations," I said carefully.

"He must," she returned, "for we are always short of funds, and turning off the kitchen maid, and making protracted visits to the homes of friends, so as to have a saving of coal and candles. I am sure if your brother Edward were not such a patient creature we should have worn out our welcome years since! But I cannot help wondering, Jane, *why* it should be so. Mr. Moore's first wife was a daughter of the Earl of Errol, and came to him quite well dowered. I know that I was raised in only a baronet's household—and that I have not the habit of economy—but I did not go to my marriage penniless, either! But I cannot learn where the portions have gone! And that the better part of the parish tithe money should be spent in Mr. Moore's *charitable works,* rather than upon his family, is what I cannot comprehend!"

"His charitable works?" I repeated, in puzzlement. "What sort of works, Harriot?"

"A mission in the East Indies, I believe—for he is forever sending parcels there. I suspect there is *gold* in them."

"Impossible! Mr. Moore sending gold to India!"

"And receiving letters from that region in return. They require a dreadfully long period for their transport, Jane, coming as they do upon East Indiamen—at times no letters arrive for months, and then three will appear all at once!"

Good God. George Moore had been in correspondence with someone in India. Was it impossible that it should have been Curzon Fiske—and Harriot mistaking India for Ceylon? But why would Mr. Moore send parcels of gold to either place? Or to a man he professed to despise?

I was too suspicious; I chided myself for a fanciful mind. No doubt Mr. Moore engaged in legitimate business— Harriot had said the correspondence and parcels were carried by East Indiamen, as how else should they travel? I had done Mr. Moore an injustice; I had been too hasty in judgement. He indulged, merely, in a speculator's investments—attempting, perhaps, to secure that expensive future for his little son.

Or, a voice said unbidden in my mind, *had he been paying Curzon Fiske to stay out of England—and remain dead to all his relations?*

"I suppose Mr. Moore is apprenticing to become a Nabob," I said lightly. "Perhaps he has been trading in rubies, against the day that little George requires a crack regiment. His correspondence with India has been active some years, I collect?"

"He certainly did not undertake it when first we were married," Harriot returned in a troubled tone, "and indeed, we contrived to live in much greater comfort, without the worry of duns at the door! I dread to think, Jane, that it is our hopeful family that has driven Mr. Moore to speculate, if speculation it is! Certainly he did not do so before Eleanor and little Harriot were born."

And the girls had come into this world quite recently, in fact—within the past four years. Both were deemed too young to accompany their parents on this visit to Godmersham, and remained at the vicarage in East Peckham.

The correspondence had commenced within the past four years. Within, therefore, the interval of Fiske's exile.

"I have pleaded with Mr. Moore for long and long to divulge the whole," Harriot was saying in her gentle voice. "But he becomes cold and grave when I tax him for the truth. I could bear anything, Jane, no matter how dreadful—but *not* coldness!"

I thought of George Moore's rigid looks during our carriage ride home, and shivered. He was a cold-hearted fellow, indeed; but cold enough to shoot a man who had returned to Canterbury, despite the fortune paid out to keep him in the Indies? Nothing could be easier than that Moore should slip out of his bedchamber at Godmersham in the dead of night, and meet with Fiske on the old Pilgrim's path beyond the Stour. Perhaps he had already known that Fiske would be present—without recourse to notes or tamarind seeds.

"And have the Indiamen brought any letters in recent months," I enquired, "or has there lately been a period of drought?"

"I had hoped the business was entirely at an end, indeed," Harriot confided, "for there had been nothing for the longest while. But then my hopes were dashed, at no less than *two* letters arriving on the same day, but a few weeks since! Mr. Moore was much preoccupied by them, and shut himself up in his book room, so that I was seized with anxiety that the charitable work had gone awry—but then he emerged, and would say only that we must certainly go to Godmersham for a fortnight's visit, and dance at Chilham Castle. So the intelligence received cannot have been so *very* dreadful, after all, do not you think, dear Jane?"

It seemed fantastic—it *must* be so.

As fantastic as the idea of George Moore deliberately stealing his old friend James Wildman's gun—and leaving it to be discovered in St. Lawrence churchyard.

I glanced from the temple in the distant direction of Bentigh, and the side-path where the corpse had been discovered—and was so surprised as to discover two figures on horseback, cantering spiritedly along the Stour. One was certainly Fanny, in her becoming new riding habit of military cut—and the other, a whipcord figure in black and dove grey, with a high-crowned beaver on his dark locks. Julian Thane. He had succeeded in luring Fanny out-of-doors on a *Sunday,* in defiance of the funereal calm that obtained within Godmersham; and from her animated looks, his success was complete. I recollected the letter on the silver salver, and was frankly glad I had not elected to pry. Fanny deserves more adventure than she has opportunity of obtaining.

"Jane," Harriot repeated. "Are you tired?"

I turned resolutely away from the dashing pair by the riverbank. Harriot, thankfully, had not observed them. I should not like to consider of Mr. Moore's strictures that evening on the subject of *Sunday riding*. "Only a little chilled, my dear. I am wanting a good fire and my comfortable chair in the library. Shall we turn back?"

Tho' I said nothing to Harriot, I felt I must speak soon with Edward. He knew these people—this collection of genteel, comfortable, and secretive whist players—far better than I, and should more readily divine what lay hidden in their hearts. Without his privileged knowledge I merely groped through darkened halls. When the stakes were murder and the consequences death, one took care how one trod.

BUT ALL THOUGHTS OF GAMESTERS AND THEIR CHARITABLE missions were momentarily fled upon my return home. Edward had returned from Chilham, and brought a letter for me—from Adelaide MacCallister.

Chilham Castle,
24 October 1813

My dear Miss Austen,
   Words cannot express my gratitude for your kindness yesterday. I do not think I could have borne another moment in that dreadful room—and had you not intervened, and your brother condescended to escort me from the place—I must surely have been overcome. If only the matter were not merely suspended, but put behind us all! To live in the present degree of apprehension is a kind of purgatory, unlike any I have known since the first days of my late husband's flight. The friendship and concern of all at Godmersham, however, may encourage me to be equal to anything. Do I ask too much, or may I call upon you tomorrow? I confess it would be a pleasure to escape the confines of this house for a little.

Yours, etc.
Adelaide MacCallister

I studied this missive thoughtfully, perusing it several times, and was so abstracted as to remain unresponsive when my brother taxed me for an account of its contents.

"I beg your pardon," I said at length, when Edward had thrice pronounced my name. "Pray cast your eye over this note I have just received from Chilham."

He took the single sheet of hot-pressed paper, and had only to glance at the hand before his eyes narrowed.

"Jane," he said softly.

I glanced around the Great Hall; we were surrounded by little groups of Godmersham's intimates, all conversing before parting at the stairs to dress for dinner.

"Do not speak until we may be private," I murmured.

For I had seen what Edward had seen. The sloping, copperplate script of my letter was indistinguishable from that on the blood-stained scrap of paper discovered in Curzon Fiske's breast pocket.

Adelaide MacCallister, it seemed, had set the fatal hour of meeting on the Pilgrim's Way.

CHAPTER NINETEEN

A Magistrate's Duty

"O lord! The lady I love has now forsworn me,
Condemned me, innocent, to death."

GEOFFREY CHAUCER, "THE LANDOWNER'S TALE"

24 OCTOBER 1813, CONT.

~

"I HAVE BEEN A FOOL," EDWARD SAID, AS HE CLOSED THE door of his book room firmly on the world and took up his preferred position near the fire. "I procured a sample of every fellow's handwriting at Chilham Castle during our visit Friday—from the venerable Wildman and his son, to the gallant Captain and his batman—not excepting Julian Thane or the butler Twitch—and found my match nowhere. But I did not undertake to seize a piece of women's notepaper, with so much as an inventory of linen scrawled upon it—and here Mrs. MacCallister delivers herself into my hands!"

"Is a mere letter so damning?" I faltered. "And is the similarity in the script so conclusive?"

"You have the evidence of your own eyes, Jane! Would you deny that the fist is exact in every respect to that of the note discovered upon the body?"

"I cannot."

"And, too, there is the fact of the tamarind seed. It was Adelaide MacCallister who received the pouch full of them on her wedding night."

"—received it of an unknown sailor purporting to be a baronet, *not* Curzon Fiske!"

"I should dearly love to learn the connexion between those two men, for there undoubtedly is one—but Myrrh will reveal nothing until his solicitor is come." My brother began to pace before the hearth, his countenance suffused with varying emotions—anger, frustration, despair. "Do you believe it so impossible that a lady, but a few hours newly-married, should resort to violence against the shameful evidence of bigamy?"

"No, but—"

"Why defend Adelaide MacCallister, Jane, when you know her for an Adventuress of old? She possesses the sort of high courage and daring—not to mention an utter lack of principle, if her past way of life is to be credited—that should stop at nothing!"

"Indeed, you are too severe upon her, Edward," I protested. "You leap from conjecture and common gossip to an indictment of the lady's character, when in fact you know little of her life, or the sufferings she may have endured at Fiske's hands. She was the merest child when she married him, and by all accounts was forced to survive by her wits. It does not absolutely follow that she is become a murderess as well."

"I fear in this instance your tender heart betrays you," my brother retorted. "It is always the way of a woman to take another woman's part, and to believe the gentler sex incapable of the most ruthless acts—"

I opened my mouth to object, for I had known a number of murderous females in the course of my life, but Edward forestalled me.

"The return of Curzon Fiske placed in jeopardy every triumph Adelaide had strived to achieve—renewed respectability, an upright husband who cherished her, and the right to move in the highest circles through that husband's attachment to Wellington's staff. Consider what she should lose, Jane, if Fiske claimed his marital precedence!"

"She had every reason to abhor Fiske's return—but you cannot prove, Edward, that she put a bullet through the man's heart!"

"I need not prove it," he said steadily. "I need merely to place the strongest possible motive—and means—and opportunity before the Assizes, Jane, and allow Justice to run its course. To do otherwise, as First Magistrate, should be a sad dereliction of my duty."

"Edward!"

"I am in possession of unequivocal evidence." He fluttered Adelaide's letter before my eyes, every fibre of his being taut with anger. "Mrs. MacCallister set the fateful hour of Fiske's death—her own hand bears witness to it. He should not have been waiting longer on the Pilgrim's Way, once the Captain and young Thane had paid him off, unless he expected a fairer visitation that night."

There was little I could say in reply. Julian Thane's own words must rise in memory; for when I had told him of the silken pouch, he apprehended immediately that it had come to his sister on her wedding night as a summons from the Dead. *Fiske sends you his calling card,* he had exclaimed as he whirled upon Adelaide—and she had dismissed the pouch as irrelevant.

In this, she had certainly uttered a falsehood. The tamarind seeds had spoken one name aloud in her heart—and her hand alone must have twisted a seed in the note she had written to Fiske, establishing the time and place of meeting. Indeed, she had wilfully prevaricated from the moment of the corpse's discovery, and allowed others to bear the brunt of suspicion. And there remained the troubling fact of young James Wildman's pistol, discarded so innocently among the tombstones of St. Lawrence churchyard for Mr. Sherer to find. . . .

I met Edward's gaze. "If what you believe is true, Mrs. MacCallister has exposed every gentleman of her acquaintance to the gravest suspicions of murder, rather than admit to communication with her dead husband. If she is innocent of murder, however many assignations she may have kept, fear for her own safety might prompt such behaviour."

"—Or the desire to preserve her present happiness, urged her to silence a man the world already believed to be dead," my brother returned.

"We cannot know what demands he then made, or how he threatened her security, when they spoke on the Pilgrim's Way."

"We cannot know that they spoke at all!" Edward burst out. "A man impatient for his beloved wife need only clasp her at once to his heart—and receive the fatal ball."

The powder burns on Fiske's coat made Edward's phantasy all too probable.

"But do you believe that Mrs. MacCallister should then *incriminate her cousin James*—the kindest of men, and her playfellow from old?" I demanded. "Impossible!"

"I should think it preferable to hanging her brother or husband—and theirs must be the only other pistols readily available to the lady in her midnight hour of need. No, Jane—a Wildman gun would have to serve, and there were plenty lying about in the Castle gun room. I have only to learn whether the note was delivered to Fiske by Julian Thane or Adelaide's maid—assuming the latter knew where Fiske was to be found—and the thing is clear."

"Fiddle! Make her your murderer if you will, Edward, but the case will not serve once you consider the pistol! She might have restored it to the gun room in all innocence, once Fiske was dead. Nobody should have connected James's gun, in its velvet-lined box, with the murder. No—whoever killed Fiske *meant* for James to be blamed. That is the material point. Fiske's murderer *hated* young James Beckford Wildman, and wished to see him hang! Until you may tell me why Adelaide should do so, I shall not credit her guilt!"

"What you chuse to believe, my dear, is your own affair— but it cannot influence the evidence. Or the nature of my duty."

I rose and approached the hearth, where my brother stood brooding over the flames, his booted foot on the fender. "You mean to charge Adelaide MacCallister with murder?"

He glanced up at me. "I must."

"But if she may offer an *explanation* for her note's presence in Fiske's pocket—"

My brother's looks hardened. "The lady has lied to me, Jane, throughout the whole of this business. I cannot *now* credit any story she might chuse to tell. Surely you must see that!"

"I see only that I shall have to prove you wrong, Edward."

"I wish you may," he said.

And drove off to bring misery to Chilham Castle.

KNOWING WHAT I DID OF EVENTS THE ENTIRE HOUSEHOLD was as yet in ignorance of, I did not submit to dining with the Moores and Fanny and my young nephews on this last Sunday before their return to Oxford. I pled a head-ache, and retreated to my bedchamber to write to my sister Cassandra. I made little progress, however—to fill my page with amusing nothings on the exploits of the nursery set, or the design of Fanny's newest cap, or young Edward's success with the harriers, could not serve to distract me from an acute awareness of the scene that must be unfolding at Chilham even now. Perhaps I ought to have accompanied Edward—I might have been some comfort to Mrs. Wildman in her trouble at least— but I knew myself for a coward. A note of thanks to *me* had thrown a rope about Adelaide MacCallister's neck; and having delivered it to the Magistrate, I stood in the guise of traitor. The distress of all her relations should justly make them hate me.

At length I tore the letter to Cassandra in twain and tossed it on the fire. It lay smouldering atop the logs, the wood being too damp to burn cleanly; smoke billowed in gusts as it nosed its way up the chimney. The hazy scrim between my eyes and the fire seemed to mock my effort to penetrate Curzon Fiske's death; nothing about the affair stood in sharp relief. It was all a smoke of falsehood and omission, of motives obscured, tales only partially told, and passions suppressed. Except for one fact: *James Wildman's pistol had been left with purpose in St. Lawrence churchyard.* Edward might dismiss that fact; but I clung to it as a drowning man will to the length of rope that might save him.

I drew another piece of foolscap towards me, thrust my pen into the ink, and wrote, *Why destroy James Wildman?*

He was an amiable young man; his temper was invariably cool; tho' handsome enough for a country neighbourhood, he had not incited the young men of his acquaintance to violent envy either through the mastery of sport or success in affairs of the heart; in short, James Beckford Wildman was far too unobjectionable for a pointed hatred.

I wrote: *Personal emnity or jealousy—springing from events or passions unknown to me?* If I considered of Julian Thane in this, I may be pardoned—neither of James's sisters should be likely to kill Fiske merely to throw blame upon her brother. Besides, I could not see either the complaisant Charlotte or the scornful Louisa venturing out-of-doors in the dead of night.

I wrote: *The fatal whist-party, and the nature of the betting three years since?* It was possible that some quarrel among the cardplayers, embroiling James, had revived with Fiske's return—but how had any of them known of Fiske's return, before discovering his body Thursday morning?

I wrote: *Financial expectations?*

James was, after all, the heir of his house—and stood to come into twenty thousand a year! It was a fortune great enough to figure even in London. He had no brothers; how should the elder Mr. Wildman's fortune be left, and who should benefit, should his heir predecease him—by hanging? The elder Mr. Wildman had a brother, one Thomas, whose sons were respectable young men of easy fortune; but the idea that either should have been upon the Pilgrim's Way at dead of night, in order to murder Curzon Fiske and destroy his cousin's prospects, seemed too improbable a notion to pursue. They should inherit their own father's wealth in time; and as it was fully as substantial as our Mr. Wildman's, deriving from the same family holdings in Jamaica, I could not find in James's cousins the slightest reason to incriminate and supplant him.

I sighed, and set down my pen. My thoughts were in a sad tangle. I required a greater knowledge of the Wildman family—and James in particular—than a few intimate dinners, balls, or the exchange of visits could provide. Had Edward stayed his magisterial hand, I might have paid a visit to Chilham Castle on the morrow, and forced a tête-à-tête with James himself—but the awkwardness attendant upon such a visit *now,* ensured that I should meet with a united silence. I could learn nothing in that quarter. And so I must apply to others.

It was only as sleep overcame me that I recollected two sources of intelligence should be furnished me on the morrow. Sir Davie Myrrh's solicitor should arrive in Canterbury; and Jupiter Finch-Hatton in our drawing-room. Of the two, I placed greater hope in Jupiter—for tho' I regarded his under-standing as less than powerful, he was not the sort to suppress his opinions when offered the slightest opportunity of declaring them. I should undertake to cultivate the young man tomorrow—if a lady so burdened in years could hope to engage his attention for a quarter-hour together.

I was awakened briefly, not long after midnight, by the sound of my brother's carriage returning to Godmersham. I did not go down to ask him how Adelaide MacCallister liked her new quarters in Canterbury gaol.

CHAPTER TWENTY

History of an Entanglement

Situations like that, today or tomorrow,
Let children turn too ripe too soon, and bolder. . . .

GEOFFREY CHAUCER, "THE PHYSICIAN'S TALE"

MONDAY, 25 OCTOBER 1813

"IS IT TRUE, AUNT JANE? HAS FATHER UNDERTAKEN THE hideous step of arresting Mrs. MacCallister for the murder of her first husband?"

Father, not Papa. Fanny was looking indignant, which lends considerable animation to her countenance, and by any stranger's judgement should be called a fine figure of a girl this morning, as she sat in the breakfast-parlour in her figured rose lawn, with her cheeks flushed and her grey eyes sparkling dangerously.

I had caught her in the act of pouring out coffee, as I entered the room; and saw that Jupiter Finch-Hatton was already lounging at his leisure opposite her, having arrived at Godmersham with a promptness unusual in him. That he had brought the intelligence of Mrs. MacCallister's arrest I little doubted; the young man came to us from Chilham Castle, after all. It was Godmersham's position halfway between Chilham and Finch-Hatton's home at Eastwell, that recommended us to him at present—tho' I suspect the prospect of bidding Young Edward farewell, and engaging in some last days of shooting before Fanny's brothers departed for Oxford, was an added inducement. Jupiter is the sort of man who progresses from one idle amusement to another, week after week, and thereby constructs of his pleasures a sort of life. Whether in his estimation Fanny figured as chief attraction or mere addition to Godmersham's charms, I could not tell. His provocative gaze, a complex of insolence and invitation, lingered on her countenance—then travelled, with some absorption, to her bodice. It was swelling with outrage at the moment.

"You had better tax your father with that question, my dear," I said. "I was not present on the occasion."

"But you knew that it was toward!"

"Indeed." I raised the lid of a silver dish set out on the sideboard, and inspected some kidneys, not without a shudder. The next dish held a species of small roasted bird, possibly ortolans, possibly snared by my nephews. To my infinite relief, the third dish held nothing more offensive than boiled quail's eggs. "Why do you suppose I could not stomach dinner last evening? But I should dearly like a cup of that coffee, Fanny. And some of that toast."

"How can you be so insensible, Aunt?" Fanny cried, as she set down the coffee pot with more decision than grace. "Only consider of the distress to Mrs. MacCallister, and all her relations. Her mother, and her brother." She hesitated a little over the idea of Julian Thane, and cast a sidelong glance at Jupiter. "Good God—consider the feelings of her husband, the gallant Captain! I wonder that he or Mr. Thane did not call my father out, for the insult visited upon Adelaide!"

"I assume they have more wisdom, and less heat, than you

do, Fanny. One does not challenge the Law to a duel—duels being entirely illegal in England at present."

"You cannot believe her *guilty*, Aunt? No, no!—Father has merely fallen into the gravest error. It springs, no doubt, from the limitations of his sex," she added thoughtfully. "For you and I will agree that no lady could shoot a man to whom she was once united in Holy Matrimony. It must be impossible! However one regards it—impossible!"

"Don't know about that," Jupiter drawled. "Known any number of ladies who were devilish fine shots, Fanny. And the gun was to hand, after all. Poor James is beside himself, 'course. Keeps saying he ought to have kept his pistols under lock and key! But I ask you! What possible use should they be to him then? Couldn't have thought that any passing rum'un would borrow the gun to settle a grudge. Stands to reason! Man's a gentleman, in his own home! I'll tell you what it is, Fanny. Dashed impudence. Not to say bad *ton*. Ought to use one's own pistol to shoot a feller."

"Exactly so." I settled myself at the breakfast table between the two of them, and availed myself of the rack of toast. "That is precisely the point I wished to canvass with you, Mr. Finch-Hatton—and I am thankful you saved me the trouble of introducing it! For I am persuaded that you are so well acquainted with James Wildman, that you must have an opinion on the subject. Why should any person employ James's gun in a murder, and then leave it behind to incriminate that unfortunate young man?"

"See him hanged, 'course," he returned with unexpected shrewdness.

I met his idle blue gaze, and detected a spark of interest in its depths. I began to wonder if the seductive Jupiter effected eternal boredom *not* because he was hopelessly dull, but because he found the bucolic environs of Kent a challenge unequal to his wits.

Fanny's eyes widened. "Incriminate *James*? Whatever do you mean, Mr. Finch-Hatton?"

"Do try," I urged, "to be a little less *ingenuous,* Fanny. I know that innocence is all the fashion in girls of your stamp—but it is a grave impediment to securing an intelligent partner in life! Obviously the murderer hoped to see James Wildman hanged. Else he—or she—should not have left the young man's pistol where the constable must be sure to find it. I am in complete agreement with Mr. Finch-Hatton. But knowing Mr. Wildman so little as I do, I cannot apprehend *why*."

Jupiter leaned back in his chair, so that the front legs of the spindly little article lifted several perilous inches from the carpet. His hands were thrust into his breeches pockets, and his eyes glinted lazily. "Needle-witted, ain't you, ma'am?"

"Flatterer." I took a draught of coffee; it was scalding, but I suppressed the impulse to choke. "If you know of any reason why Adelaide MacCallister should hate her cousin enough to attempt to kill two birds with one lead ball, I wish you may tell us, Mr. Finch-Hatton."

"Adelaide? Lord—when she and James have been smelling of April and May for years together?" The chair legs met the floor with a decisive crash. "Grew up in each other's pockets, y'know, Mrs. Thane being the sort to hang on Old Wildman's sleeve once her loose-screw of a husband stuck his spoon in the wall. Never had two groats to rub together. Mrs. Thane used to leave Addie at the Castle for months at a time, being determined to spend her blunt on young Thane's education. Hoped James would take Addie off her hands. That's why she turned Tartar when the girl eloped with Fiske."

I glanced at Fanny. "I had not realised Adelaide formed a part of the Castle household in her youth."

Fanny shrugged. "She may have visited Kent from time to time—and that, for protracted periods—but it is not as tho' the Wildmans *adopted* her. It is possible, however, that I was in ignorance of the extent of her ties to the family. Recollect that Adelaide is four years older than I, and among children, that is a considerable span. When I was but thirteen, and still in the schoolroom, Adelaide was married."

Of course; tho' neighbours, Fanny and Adelaide should never have been playmates. The fact of the former's being the eldest child of a gentleman's household, and the latter but a poor relation of another's, should have widened the gulf between them.

"Did Mr. Wildman form an attachment for his cousin, do you think?" I demanded of Jupiter.

"Should say he had! Always stiled himself Addie's devoted slave, long before Curzon Fiske bamboozled her in Bath. Thought he assumed he'd marry her, myself. Girl had other ideas. Regarded James as another brother. Could have knocked him over with a feather when she ran off with that scaly fellow. But James was only eighteen at the time—calf love, y'know—and I was sure he'd come about, provided Addie stayed on the Continent as she was meant to. But it didn't serve. Three years later the Fiskes were back in Kent, and cutting quite a dash. Met them everywhere. Devilish bad for James, poor fellow. Didn't like the cut of Fiske's jib. Thought him a rum customer. And he was right, of course—Fiske ran straight into Dun Territory in the end, and had to flee the Kingdom. The Wildmans stood by Addie, 'course, and saw her set right with her mamma. Tho' why she'd *want* to be—" he added reflectively, "when that Friday-faced woman never has a kind word for her—"

"And once Mr. Wildman knew Fiske to be in India—did he pursue his cousin?" I enquired bluntly.

Jupiter leaned across the table and lowered his voice. "Truth be told, he urged Adelaide to sue for divorce! Fearful scandal at the Castle—Old Mr. Wildman dead set against it, and none too eager to see his son hitched to an Adventuress, either. But it all came to nothing—Mrs. Thane wouldn't hear of divorce. James was at a stand. Addie, too. Seemed likely to dwindle into a grass widow, at an age when most girls were dreaming of their bride-clothes."

"The news of Mr. Fiske's demise must have sprung upon the entire family as an act of Providence."

"You've got that right and tight," Jupiter agreed. "Never knew a man so transported as James, when he learnt Fiske was dead!"

"And yet, he did not succeed in securing the lady's hand," I mused.

"Mourning," Jupiter confided owlishly. "Adelaide put on blacks for a year, of course, and shunned Society. Should have thought James would secure the girl's affections, all the same—she saw rather a lot of him—but the fellow's too dashed respectful by half, my opinion. Treats Addie as tho' she were a goddess. Too reverent, in short. Lacks address."

"I think James's delicacy is entirely admirable!" Fanny flashed. "He is not the sort of harum-scarum Corinthian so much the rage at present."

"Corinthians would never have him, Fanny!" Jupiter protested. "Doesn't box, doesn't fence, and he crowds his leaders when he drives four-in-hand! Friend of mine—but there it is! Poor fellow was entirely cast in the shade by Captain MacCallister, who knew the right way to go about the business with Adelaide, for all he's nothing like Curzon Fiske. Well, I mean to say! Hero of the Peninsula! Devilish fine fellow! So of course James retired from the field. Put a cheerful phiz on events once the engagement was announced. Urged his papa to stand the ready for the wedding ball, and planned the best bits himself. Well—couldn't expect his mamma to lift a finger! Never does! And those sisters of his, with their noses out of joint—complaining to any who'd listen that it was *too bad* Addie should be married twice, when they've never had so much as an offer between them! James did it all." Finch-Hatton nodded significantly. "Those lobster patties, brought down Express from Gunter's in London? *James.* Threw himself into making Adelaide happy. S'all he's ever wanted, in fact—Adelaide to be happy. Should imagine the poor fellow's blue-devilled at the turn in events—Adelaide being borne off to gaol! That's why I came away so early this morning—don't mind saying the tone of the Castle is dashed awkward at present."

Fanny was staring at Jupiter with something like awe. I suppose she had never heard him put so many words together without pausing for breath.

"Mr. Wildman's feelings, and his conduct in the face of bitterest disappointment, may be said to do him credit," I observed. "I wonder that Adelaide did not return his regard."

Jupiter managed one of his lazy smiles. "My opinion? Found the whole Chilham set-out too *tame,* after the madcap life she'd lived with Fiske. Always was a bit of a romp, Addie. Loved travel. Loved adventure. Thought she'd find more of both following the drum. Romantickal notions about the Captain; saw him as a hero. Poor James couldn't hold a candle to that."

"She sounds the very last person to borrow Wildman's pistol," I mused.

Jupiter shook his head regretfully. "Can't agree with you *there,* ma'am. Never said Addie wouldn't *use* the pistol. She's pluck to the backbone—and if she thought it best to shoot Curzon Fiske, daresay she'd steel herself to do it! Just don't think she'd be careless enough to *leave* James's pistol behind her. No desire to hang her cousin. Dashed sorry to see him in the box at the inquest, from all I can make out. Made her fair blue-devilled. But she's no coward, Addie. She'd admit to murder rather than see James hang. Forced to conclude, therefore, that it wasn't she who left the pistol in plain sight for the constables to find. Certain she'd have said so, straight out, if she had."

I was on the point of posing yet again the obvious question, the one that had inspired all my interest in breakfast-parlour conversation—*Who, then, wished James Wildman to hang?*—when the sound of a gentleman's approaching stride arrested all our attention. It should undoubtedly prove to be Mr. George Moore, come to bid his young friend welcome, and to regale himself in stony silence among the ortolans and kidneys. My heart sank. I might never be so fortunate as to fix Jupiter Finch-Hatton's interest so entirely in coming days.

But it was not Mr. Moore who appeared in the breakfast-parlour doorway.

"Morning, Hatton," Edward said with a careless nod. "Morning, Fanny—Jane. I hope you both slept well."

"I should not have managed a wink, Father, had I known what you were about at the Castle last evening!" she returned with asperity. "To arrest Mrs. MacCallister! Every feeling revolts!"

"Do not enact me a Cheltenham tragedy, I beg," he said brusquely. "If you've quite finished, perhaps you would be so good as to take Finch-Hatton for a turn in the shrubbery; it is no day for shooting, being likely to come on to rain."

"I am to be occupied with Mrs. Driver for most of the morning, taking an inventory of the linen."

"Do not be tiresome, Fanny! I wish to be private with your aunt!"

"Oh, very well," she said irritably, and tossed her napkin on the table.

Jupiter regarded me with amusement. "Doesn't like me above half, our Fanny. Daresay it's because I'm a dashed *Corinthian*. Your servant, ma'am." And with a bow of remarkable elegance, he ushered my graceless niece towards the back garden.

"You managed that very ill, Edward," I observed as I rose from the table. "Fanny is no Lizzy or Marianne, to submit in silence to your tyranny. I begin to think the power of the magistracy has gone to your head."

"I have only just heard that one Mr. Burbage, solicitor to Sir Davie Myrrh, is arrived in Canterbury, Jane. I intend to meet with him this morning, in the presence of his client. Would you do me the honour of accompanying me?"

CHAPTER TWENTY-ONE

A Visit to Canterbury

"Brother," he said, "do you really want me to tell?
I am a devil, and the place I live in is hell."

GEOFFREY CHAUCER, "THE FRIAR'S TALE"

25 OCTOBER 1813, CONT.

TO MY DISMAY, WE WERE JOINED IN THE CARRIAGE DRIVE to Canterbury by the entire Moore family, not excepting Young George, whom his mother adjured anxiously not to be sick from the lurching of the carriage. Edward took one look at the lad's face as his coachman sprang the horses, and called out to the fellow to halt.

"I am persuaded George should vastly prefer to ride on the box with Sallow," he suggested, and overrode Harriot's anxiety for her son's safety by jumping out to lift the boy up himself.

"It is never any use to tell the Infantry *not* to be sick," he advised his sister-in-law, "and in fact, might be regarded as a positive inducement to cast up their accounts! Fresh air is all the lad requires. He shall do splendidly now."

"I was never rendered ill from carriage-travel as a youth," Mr. Moore observed austerely, "tho' I was forever going about with my father, on matters of Ecclesiastical importance. I cannot account for Young George's lamentable weakness. I fear he lacks resolution. The influence of his mother's family, no doubt. We must hope he acquires strength of character in time."

The fond parent then buried his nose in his book—how anyone can read amidst the swaying of a carriage!—and ignored his companions for the length of the eight miles to Canterbury.

I was curious to learn how so ardent a champion of Adelaide MacCallister's welfare must regard the latest episode in her career; and indeed, had surmised that Mr. Moore accompanied my brother to Canterbury from a desire to plead Mrs. MacCallister's case. But in this I was evidently mistaken. Mr. Moore knew of the arrest; but he claimed to have inserted himself into Edward's carriage merely from a desire of visiting a tailor, and having his hair cut—and professed a keenness to have Young George's locks shorn as well. Harriot intended to do a little shopping while at liberty from her husband—visiting solely those Canterbury establishments that offered credit, no doubt.

"I wonder you may support the prospect of entering a gaol, Jane," she said with a delicious shudder. "I am sure I should swoon at the scenes then unfolded before my eyes!"

"I suspect I shall be obliged to enter only the Chief Warden's room," I returned calmly, "which is likely to offer a good fire and a clean floor—which is all that I regard."

"But do not you intend to visit Mrs. MacCallister?" Harriot's looks were puzzled; she could not conceive another purpose for bearing Edward company.

"Jane indulges me, Harriot," my brother interjected, "and

should not be present at all but for my urgent request. I am to meet with a distinctly odd fellow, who comes into this affair in ways I profess to understand not at all—and as I value my sister's wits above all others', I could hardly spare her presence at the interview."

"Indeed," poor Harriot murmured, no more enlightened than she had been before Edward spoke. But her husband lifted his eyes from his book.

"You refer, I take it, to the delusional seaman?"

"I refer to Sir Davie Myrrh."

"—As he stiles himself!"

"—As his solicitor assures me he has every claim to be addressed," Edward returned with remarkable calm. "He will undoubtedly prove to be an eccentric, George, but I greatly hope he will *not* prove delusional. I believe he may hold the key to this entire affair."

"Then I wonder you took so rash a step as to arrest Mrs. MacCallister," Mr. Moore muttered. I detected considerable rage, barely suppressed, in his tone; and was confirmed in my original conjecture regarding the clergyman. He might talk of haircuts, and affect indifference before his wife and child, but his whole mind was concentrated upon that tragic figure immured in a cell. If Edward went to Canterbury, there, too, should be George Moore, as surely as a moth sought the flame.

I gave Harriot a swift glance, but she appeared insensible to the subtleties of her husband's purpose. Perhaps it was safest, taken all in all, to cultivate ignorance.

"I arrested Mrs. MacCallister, my dear George, because I had no choice," Edward said gently. "And because I hoped, perhaps, to lull the *true* killer into a false sense of complacency."

I stared at my brother in sharp surprise—and should have pressed a further question, but that the coachman was drawing rein, and the carriage pulling to a halt. We had achieved Westgate, Canterbury—where the gaol is housed.[1]

WESTGATE IS THE LAST OF THE GREAT MEDIEVAL PORTALS to the walled city. All the others—dating perhaps from Thomas à Becket's time—have been demolished, as proving too great an impediment to coach travel. If Westgate remains, it is due in no little part to the gatehouse's employment as the city gaol; for tho' a large prison has been built on Canterbury's outskirts, in Longport, it is for the internment of those already convicted and sentenced—whereas Westgate houses those not yet brought up before the Assizes. It is a dour old place suggestive of the Tudors, sitting at the point where St. Dunstan's Street becomes St. Peter's.

"If you should find yourself at liberty in an hour, Jane," Harriot confided as we stepped down from Edward's coach, "I shall be waiting in Moffett's Confectionary. We might pay a call upon old Mrs. Milles, you know. She is a zany, to be sure—but there is no one like her for possessing all the latest gossip. She should give us a *minute history* of Mrs. Scudamore's reconciliation, I daresay."

Mrs. Scudamore is the wife of Edward's apothecary and physician, who lately scandalised the neighbourhood by deserting her husband; her return to the domestic fold has only served to further outrage her neighbours, who preferred to sincerely pity Mr. Scudamore each time he called with a draught for their ailing children. Such episodes are of consuming interest to Harriot, however much her husband may

[1] Jane describes this trip to Canterbury in a subsequent letter to her sister Cassandra (Letter 94, dated Tuesday, October 26, 1813), but makes no mention of entering the gaol with Edward. She discloses a second visit to Canterbury gaol in Letter 95, dated November 3, 1813. —*Editor's note.*

deplore them; I suspected she hoped to profit from Mr. Moore's interval with his barber, by wheedling the whole out of old Mrs. Milles.

Such a visit might serve, at least, to fill my letter to Cassandra; for of the latest murder I had told her not a syllable. Her conviction that I deliberately cultivated the macabre was growing with each passing year, and I had no wish to confirm her prejudice.

"I shall find you if I am able, Harriot," I said, and turned to where Edward waited, in the shadows beneath the ancient gate.

A CONSTABLE STOOD GUARD BY THE HEAVY OAK DOOR; AND when its bolts were drawn back, and the portal thrust open, the passage was discovered to be flagged in stone. Oil lamps hung on great hooks set into the wall, and lent a flaring light to the low-ceilinged way, which had no windows; it was narrow enough that we were forced to step in single-file, Edward preceding me. The flickering light of the lanthorns threw his figure in grotesque relief upon the walls; my own bonnet, with its stiff poke, appeared as a sort of silhouetted coal scuttle, bobbing in his wake.

We were led, as I had suspected, to the Chief Warden's room—and if my hopes for the cleanliness of the floor were dashed, my expectation of a fire in the grate was not. The atmosphere of the place being both damp and mouldy, I positioned myself near the warmth as unobtrusively as I might, while Edward performed the necessary introductions.

"Warden Stoke—this is my sister, Miss Austen, who has been kind enough to lend me her company."

"Pleasure, ma'am," the fellow returned, tho' without evidencing much of that sentiment. He stared at me pugnaciously from under beetling black brows, his dark eyes fairly snapping. "I hope you don't think to make a Fashionable

Tour, such as the Great are in the habit of doing up at Lunnon; we're no Newgate here, for the entertainment of them as think gaol is a mischief and a lark! We want none of your Penal Reformers, neither, being accustomed to go our own road and no complaint from any as bear hearing. There's precious little accommodation for gentlefolk in Westgate, saving Your Honour, and none at all for fine ladies; but it is not for me to question the Magistrate, ha! ha!, the questions being all on the other side, seemingly."

"We wish to speak with Sir Davie Myrrh," Edward said, as tho' this peroration had gone unheard and unheeded. "His solicitor—one Burbage, I believe—is lately arrived from Temple Bar?"

"He is that, and awaiting Your Honour's pleasure," Stoke returned. "I've only to send word to the Little Inn, and he'll step round in two shakes of a lamb's tail."

"Then do so."

The warden scraped a bow, and striding to his door, bellowed to one unseen, "Hie, there—you lummox Jack! Stir your shanks and fetch the Lunnon man for His Honour!"

I caught a glimpse of a wizened urchin in nankeen breeches scuttling along the stone passage, his pointed face set in a grimace; then Stoke heaved-to the door.

"My sister's brat," he said bitterly. "Seven-months' child, and a trifle touched in his upper works."

There being no possible reply, Edward and I turned our attention to the fire. It was smoking badly; and I began to wish that we might have conducted our interview with Sir Davie's solicitor in the comfort of the Little Inn's private parlour, with a trifling nuncheon laid out upon the board. But that would be to play into the solicitor's hands—it was not *his* relation of events that we preferred, but his client's. As Sir Davie could not go to the Little Inn, the Little Inn must come to Sir Davie.

At length our impatience was rewarded with the clang of

the outer door's bolts being once more thrown back, and a light tread audible upon the passage flags, and Mr. Burbage was revealed—as a tall and respectable figure in a driving cape and beaver hat. As I curtseyed to the fellow at Edward's introduction, I suffered the tantalising impression that I had *seen* Mr. Burbage before—but could not summon the particulars of time or place.

"You wish to interview my client, Mr. Knight?" the solicitor enquired pleasantly. "I must warn you that the conversation is sure to be protracted, and to span the globe, Sir Davie being little disposed to concision in his affairs. He is a raconteur of considerable power, and has long defied even his friends' attempts to curtail his speech."

"A wonder, then, that he has remained silent the better part of two days," Edward returned.

Mr. Burbage smiled engagingly. "I said that Sir Davie dearly loved a good story; I did not say that he was a fool. Naturally, having been placed in a cell, he preferred to hold his counsel until his Counsel should have arrived."

"Then let us waste no more of Sir Davie's time."

A nod for the chief warden, and a massive iron ring of keys appeared; with a grunt, Stoke made for the door and Edward followed. I trotted in his wake, while Mr. Burbage brought up the rear; we were led deeper into the Westgate premises, which, tho' not vast, so nearly resembled a warren of tunnels that I might have fancied myself in the dungeons of the Tower. Heavy doors with metal gratings set into their centres at chest-height, and then again below, at the threshold—presumably for the delivery of meals—lined the passages; and occasionally a visage would loom at one of these, unshaven and clothed in shadow, only the glittering eyes throwing back the lanthorn-light. It was, I reflected, an experience such as heroines of horrid novels should relish; and with quickening heart I absorbed the wretched atmosphere, as another lady might the candlelit glow of Almack's Assembly. What fodder for prose was this!

At length Stoke halted before a cell like any other, and fitted one of his numerous keys to the lock. "Prisoner, stand back from the door!" he bellowed, and I suppose the violence of his timbre was enough to cause most intimates of Westgate to quail. But when the portal swung inwards, we observed Sir Davie Myrrh reclining at his leisure upon a hard wooden shelf that served as a bed, his arms behind his head and his gaze fixed upon the ceiling.

"Appeared at last, have you, Burbage?" he demanded languidly—for all the world as tho' he received the solicitor in the anteroom of White's or Watier's. Try as I might, I could not reconcile the baronet's appearance—for he still sported the tar-stained breeches, the ragged beard, and the neckerchief of a navvy—with his cultivated speech.

"Get up, you dog," Stoke snarled; and for the first time, Mr. Burbage turned his eye upon him.

"Have a care, Warden," he said in an icy tone. "There is no call for insolence or ill-treatment of the baronet."

Again, I suffered the conviction that I had met Burbage somewhere before; but upon what occasion?

"That will do, Stoke," Edward said. "Leave young Jack to wait in the passage; we shall inform him when our conversation is done."

"*Conversation,* is it?" Stoke leered. "Seems to me as how a knave's only got to ape the Quality to win the indulgence of the Law. But it's not for me—"

"No. It is *not* for you to question the Magistrate," Edward agreed firmly. "But you might bring several chairs—or even stools—to this cell, Stoke. Do you imagine that my sister wishes to stand for the length of the interview?"

The warden cast a jaundiced glance in my direction. I smiled upon him beatifically.

"Hie, you lummox!" he called into the passage.

Three chairs were brought, one at a time, by the struggling urchin Jack. The warden glared around at all of us, then inclined his head with grudging deference to Edward, and turned on his heel.

As the door was locked with a metallic groan, I experienced a positive thrill of apprehension. It was as tho' I had become a character of Mrs. Radcliffe's, and must expect to find a skeleton behind every veil.

CHAPTER TWENTY-TWO

The Seaman's Story

He'd been in every harbor, no matter where,
From Gottland to the Cape of Finisterre. . . .

GEOFFREY CHAUCER, "GENERAL PROLOGUE"

25 OCTOBER 1813, CONT.

"WELL, THIS IS A DEGREE OF COMFORT UNLOOKED-FOR," Sir Davie observed with an air of gratification as we took our seats. "Unfortunate that I haven't any Port to send round, or ratafia for the lady. You are remiss, Burbage—quite remiss—you have made no introductions—but perhaps you are not in possession of the lady's name, never having expected to be honoured by her presence this morning."

"I am Miss Austen," I told him, "Mr. Knight's sister. We shared a bench at the inquest."

It seemed to me that Mr. Burbage started a little at my words; but Sir Davie was already assessing my countenance shrewdly.

"That affair was not very edifying, alas—too much of the curious truth was, as I suspect, deliberately left out, Miss

Austen. Forgive me for speaking frankly, Mr. Knight; I do not presume to infringe upon your province, or criticise one whose motives I suspect are pure. I may address you as Mr. Knight, I hope? 'Your Honour' seems unduly grave."

"Murder is invariably so," Edward observed. "If you are done with your pleasantries, Sir Davie, I have a few questions I should like to put to you."

The seaman opened his eyes a little. "Ought one *ever* to be done with pleasantries, my dear sir? How else, pray, is the savage world to be civilised?"

"You are, I presume, Sir Davie Myrrh?"

The seaman's eyes rolled towards his solicitor. "*Surely* you have vouched for my identity, Burbage?"

"Mr. Knight asks purely as a matter of form, sir. I would suggest you answer the Magistrate's question fully and frankly."

"And, Mr. Burbage," my brother added, "if you would be so good as to note down Sir Davie's statement? I may supply you with pencil and paper for the purpose."

These items being handed from one man to the other, with every appearance of mutual respect and understanding, Sir Davie Myrrh sighed. "Very well. I shall give it to you direct as the Baronetage would have it: Myrrh of Kildane Hall. Davie Ambrose Myrrh, born December 8, 1760, married May 15, 1784, Anne, daughter of Sylvester, Fifth Viscount Havisham of Pembroke, in the county of Warwickshire; by which lady (deceased 1785) he had issue, a stillborn son."

He turned his satiric gaze upon myself. "I could entertain you, madam, with a further recitation of my family's glorious history; its resistance under Cromwell, and exertions of loyalty towards Charles the Second; its elevation from mere knighthood to the baronetage; the demonstration, with each succeeding generation, of increasing attention to Duty and the Crown, ending—rather ignobly—with myself, the tenth baronet, who, tho' achieving the venerable age of three-and-fifty with health and humour unimpaired, has nonetheless lost wife, child, fortune, and even Kildane Hall. Should you like to learn how I managed it?"

"Not at present," Edward interposed firmly, before I could answer *Yes, very much.* "What we principally wish to know is how you came to be standing at the front entrance of Chilham Castle on the evening of the twentieth of October inst., presenting a silken pouch to one Adelaide Fiske MacCallister."

"Ah," Sir Davie murmured, "but to apprehend how I came to be there, Mr. Knight, you ought to know a little of my history. For no man springs newly-formed into a given day or moment—be it night or morning, October or April, Chilham or Timbuktu. If I am to explain how I came to have a gift for Mrs. Fiske—or did you call her something else?—you must first know how I fell under obligation to her husband. I do not refer, of course, to this person MacCallister. *He* has no place in the tale at all. I refer to Curzon Fiske, an excellent fellow now sadly laid into an early grave, who was so obliging as to save my life in Ceylon some eighteen months since."

Edward gave a slight sigh of satisfaction. "I suspected you were acquainted with Fiske. It was *he* who gave you the tamarind seeds, of course?"

"Not so swiftly, I beg! You leap to the story's close without a care for the intriguing coincidence of events! Burbage," Sir Davie exclaimed as he jumped from his hard wooden bed and began to stroll like another Kemble about the theatre of his cell, "you *must* make the Magistrate understand that he can never hope to penetrate this affair without a thorough knowledge of the peril in which Fiske and I moved, some years ago! If he persists in seeing merely a dead wastrel on the Pilgrim's Way, when he might rather know the final, agonising loss of a daring man's hope, as his blood trickles into the unforgiving earth, Mr. Knight cannot pretend to grasp the subtleties of man's existence—or, at the very least, this shocking affair!"

"Sir Davie," Mr. Burbage said, "as your solicitor it is my duty to urge you, most earnestly, to answer the questions Mr. Knight may put to you, as succinctly and swiftly as possible. To do aught else is to try the patience of a gentleman whose time is taken up with numerous affairs."

"*Burbage,*" Sir Davie uttered mournfully. "I had thought better of you. I had thought you a man of romance, and spirit."

Edward glanced enquiringly at me; I nodded ever so slightly.

"Very well," my brother said. "You may tell us, briefly, how you came to know Curzon Fiske."

"Ah," Sir Davie breathed as tho' released into a happy dream, "now *there* is a tale worth telling! But first perhaps I should just mention how I came to be in Ceylon at all—having spent the better part of my life on the *other* side of the world, rather as Columbus did, in attempting to reach the Subcontinent. I speak, of course, of Jamaica. My father, the ninth baronet, being a practical rather than a snobbish fellow, had sunk our fortunes into sugar—and did so handsomely from the trade, that I was sent out to the West Indies as a lad of but sixteen, to sit at the feet of the plantation overseer and learn the substance of the business. But it was not to be—for once upon the high seas I discovered a passion for ships that has never left me to this day! Tho' embarking as a supercargo—a passenger, you should call it—on a merchant vessel bound for the tropics, I soon begged to learn the duties of a true sailor; and being a likely lad enough, for all I was the heir to a baronetcy, I was allowed to have my way. I donned the garb of a common seaman, and earned my bread before the mast, so that my Creole friends did not know me when at last I disembarked in Freetown, and were obliged to take a brown and hale young man to their bosom, who appeared more like a plantation slave in their eyes than the English gentleman they had been led to expect!"

"All very interesting, I am sure," Edward broke in, "but your youth cannot have any bearing on your present incarceration. Pray honour us with the facts of your acquaintance with Fiske, and your reasons for appearing at the Castle on the night of your friend's murder."

If Edward expected the word *murder* to arrest Sir Davie's reminiscent flight, he was to be disappointed.

"All in good time, my dear sir, all in good time."

As Sir Davie launched into a further account of his experience of the islands—his passion for the tropics—his sad love affair with a Creole girl of passable birth but little fortune—the unfeeling nature of his father's overseer—a falling out with the fellow over the course of his apprenticeship—Sir Davie's determination to take to the sea once more—his flight, by night, to a merchant ship weighing anchor with the tide in Freetown Harbour—the years of travel that succeeded: rounding the Cape; his first sight of Alta California; assays in the Arctic; his first glimpse of Macao—and at last, when he was three-and-twenty years old, and had been absent from England some seven years, the news, received two months after the fact by letter delivered by H.M.S. *Laconia*, of his father's death, and his own accession to the baronetcy.

"I made for home immediately, of course, by constant exchange of ships, arriving some seven weeks after the receipt of the letter and posting as swiftly as I could to Kildane. A few days sufficed to put me in possession of the facts of my existence; I claimed a comfortable fortune, a house of the first stare, and an easy footing among the Great. My father's steward—now my own—displayed excellent management of

Kildane's affairs, but impressed upon me my duty to marry. I looked about the Marriage Mart once the Season was launched, and was so fortunate as to engage the affections of a reasonably-dowered and not ill-favoured female, the afore-mentioned Mary, with whom I lived barely a twelvemonth before she died in childbirth, and my son with her."

"I thought you said her name was Anne," I objected, frowning slightly.

"Anne? Mary? Elizabeth? They are all much of a much-ness, are they not? But perhaps you are right. Undoubtedly my late wife's name was Anne."

"You have my deepest sympathy," Edward said, less drily than Sir Davie's caprice should have urged; for he, too, had lost a wife in childbirth.

But Sir Davie waved an airy hand. "I underwent a curious change as Anne's dust was interred in the Kildane vault. I may almost describe it as a *liberation,* my dear sir. It was as tho', having fulfilled all the duties expected of my caste, I might now throw off convention in favour of adventure. A week had not elapsed before I found myself in Southampton, searching out a likely East Indiaman, and had embarked once more on the roving life that exactly suited me. Kildane I left in the steward's care, and for years the arrangement answered nobly. I might draw upon funds lodged at various locales— Malta, Halifax, Macao—with only infrequent halts in my travel at home. And so decades wore away in swift succes-sion! The American colonies revolted; the French King lost his head; armies moved about the globe; Napoleon rose to conquer the world, and fell to ruin on the Cossacks' steppes—and all the while I lived a sybarite's life: collecting stories and memories, enemies and friends, adventure and near-mortal escapes! If I had but leisure and inclination, I might pen a memoir that should set the Fashionable World *ablaze,* with a rage for seafaring exploration!"

"It was."

"I should think you will have every fortune-seeker in three ounties bent upon exhuming his remains," the baronet said ly.

"Good God!" Edward rose precipitately from his chair nd began to turn about the small confines of the cell. "Impossible! The corpse was disrobed, and washed, before bur-. Some one of the goodwives who performed the service ust undoubtedly have felt the weight of such a fortune, in king charge of the clothing!"

"Perhaps the wench robbed him, then," the baronet re-rned. "Who can say?"

"Sir Davie." My brother confronted the baronet. "I can no ger waste precious time in canvassing your reminiscence. y have the goodness to explain when you landed in En-nd with Fiske, and how you came to have that pouch of narind seeds in your possession."

"The tamarind exerted a powerful fascination upon e's mind," Sir Davie murmured dreamily. "He found the t to be only tolerable—there are any number of exotic ts native to the Indies that produce a more pleasing com-tible—but the tamarind figured as a potent symbol in e's philosophy. The seed, you know, may lie dormant for s in the absence of rain; and yet, when once refreshed by sweet elixir of water, will send out green shoots with a ur and a will. Fiske saw in this the constant renewal of , the resurgence of life . . . and the *enduring nature of* regardless of neglect or the appearance of ruin."

Adelaide," I said. Of course.

recisely. She seems to have been no mere Anne or Mary. ng fled Ceylon without detection—having secured a for-in gold within his coat—having in the person of myself, nd whose loyalty sprang from the obligations of grati-and who should never betray him—Fiske determined to

"No doubt," Edward said. "And if your present confinement in gaol cannot spur inclination, it shall at least provide opportunity. I will furnish pen and paper should you require it."

"You are very good, sir," Mr. Burbage said, with a quirk of his lips, "and your patience defies belief. Sir Davie, if you might turn at last to your acquaintance with Mr. Curzon Fiske—"

"Ah! Poor Curzon!" Sir Davie mourned. He gave up strolling and settled down upon his wooden bed. "Was there ever a fellow possessed of more engaging address? Or fewer morals? Have you noted, during the course of your life, Mr. Knight, how often the two coincide?"

"You met him, I collect, in Ceylon."

"There you would be out," the seaman returned with un-ruffled calm. "We met in Bangalore, in the midst of a decid-edly heated dispute between the local maharajah and the Honourable East India Company. Shots were exchanged. Heads rolled. A particular fort, as I recall, was beseiged. Fiske and I encountered one another when the subsequent looting had reached a fevered pitch, and both of us attempted to se-cure the same cask of jewels. Fiske sought the pistol thrust into his belt, but I was before him—and contrived to render him insensible with a blow to the head."

Edward, at this juncture, rubbed in desperation at his tem-ples.

"And the jewels?" I enquired.

"Proved to be nothing more than a lady's collection of valueless baubles," Sir Davie concluded sadly. "At which dis-covery, I tossed them over my shoulder for the next benighted fool to covet, and did my best to drag Fiske out of the melee. It seemed the least I could do for a fellow Englishman. By the time he came to himself, we were beyond the fortress walls and I was able to apologise most civilly for the trouble I had caused. In return, he generously invited me to join him on an expedition to Ceylon—in which legitimate business he had been engaged by the Company, before the regrettable affair at Bangalore had diverted him.”

“But I thought you said *he* saved *your* life,” my brother interjected, bewildered.

“And so he did! —A good two years since, perhaps less, when malaria swept through the lowlands, he saw me carried, by mule-drawn pallet, into the more salubrious air of the tea plantations. These are found amidst the Ceylonese hills, you know, and at that altitude, the mortal humours are dispersed, and the fever’s hold gradually abates. There is a hill-station there, frequented by Portuguese monks, who are adept at treating the illness; they offer a sort of tonic, steeped from bark, that is most effective. Certainly, my dear Mr. Knight, I should have died in the lowlands but for Fiske’s intervention.”

“Two years, perhaps less,” Edward mused. “Fiske’s people received word of his death not long after—by an epidemic fever in Ceylon. How came that error to be made?”

The baronet shrugged. “Having some little knowledge of Fiske’s character—his secretive mind, his deft manipulation of apparent facts—I should imagine he *wished* to be dead. A very little effort might serve. The dropping of some papers, of a private nature, on a suitable-looking corpse—and the thing is done, my dear sir! Particularly in so harum-scarum a locale as Ceylon.”

“But why?” Edward demanded, in some perplexity.

“I gather that the name of *Fiske* had become a burden to him. Some little difficulty, over the borrowing of Company funds—lamentably impossible to repay . . .”

“And yet, he saw fit to return to England?”

“His plans were not then fixed, his chief object being to depart Ceylon without further detection—or pursuit. As he had

so kindly deferred his flight to see me carried into lands, I felt it incumbent upon me to demonstrate measure of civility—and begged to accompany him should eventually quit the place. A month later, w fully recovered, we made by sea for Goa, a Portu ton on the western coast of the Subcontinent. T very kindly pressed upon us letters of introductio passage. Ah! The ladies of Goa! Such sublimity o softness of skin! And such an art in their fingers! your pardon, Miss Austen.”

“Not at all,” I said politely.

“None of this gets us any nearer Chilham Cast observed, with a jaundiced eye for Mr. Burbage.

“Sir Davie,” the solicitor prodded, “the hour i If you would be so good—”

“Yes, yes,” the baronet said with an irritable hand. “We spent a delightful interval in Goa, Fis an entrepot of trading, you know, and Fiske exchange a quantity of rubies he had collected Burma, I believe, but the expedition was before tance with him—for a considerable sum of g had sewn into his coat. It was thus he carried hi to England, and one presumes—to Canterbury

“His coat,” Edward repeated, in a tone of “But—”

“You did not consider of the lining of his co enquired with an air of melancholy. “It is among those who spend a lifetime without ve the shores of England; I daresay you expected in Hoare’s bank, and have buried the poor fortune! Once word has got out—through no I need hardly state—you will be forced t around the grave in St. Mary’s churchyard poor Fiske was interred, I believe?”

take ship for England's shores, and try what felicity the renewal of his attentions to his estranged wife might bring."

"When was this?" Edward demanded harshly.

"Some three months ago. The voyage home from India is a tedious trial, even without the occasional alarums of shipboard struggle, our Indiaman being subject to the intermittent French salvo. More than once I was myself obliged to man the twelve-pounders in the bow, your merchant seamen being nothing so adept as the hearties of the Royal Navy. But, however, we were fortunate to arrive unscathed; and in London, parted company for an interval, so that Fiske might discover his wife's present whereabouts, and send her a line to prepare her for the unexpected joy of his arrival."

"He wrote to Adelaide?" I broke in.

"Should not *you* have done the same, after an interval of three years?"

I exchanged a swift glance with my brother. Here was another instance of Adelaide's prevarication; she had insisted she believed Fiske to be *dead*. She had prepared for her wedding, however, in the apparent knowledge that it was bigamous. My heart sank.

"But are you certain such a letter reached her? How did Mr. Fiske divine where she was?" I pressed.

"I am afraid that is owing to me," Mr. Burbage supplied. "Mr. Fiske called upon me some five weeks ago, at the advice of Sir Davie, whose solicitor I have been for a period of years, tho' heretofore our acquaintance has been largely conducted through a protracted correspondence, much interrupted by the vagaries of distance and occasional disaster. Having acquainted me with the particulars of his history, Mr. Fiske retired to a respectable inn not far from the Thames riverfront, while I endeavoured to learn what I could of his wife and her family, the Thanes. Mr. Fiske was able to supply me with the direction of their country seat, whence I repaired; and through circumspect enquiries in the villages surrounding Wold Hall, swiftly learnt that Mrs. Fiske, having been informed of her husband's death and having undergone a lengthy period of mourning, was upon the point of a highly-advantageous marriage. I returned to London, and imparted these particulars to Mr. Fiske."

"And how did he receive the intelligence?" Edward asked.

"With sorrow and chagrin. His exact words, I believe, were: *Hoisted by my own petard, Burbage.* He was fully alive to the irony that events which had once urged his apparent decease, had now told against him—in allowing his wife to proceed, in all innocence, with the next chapter of her life."

"But he *did* write to her," I persisted. It seemed so material a point, I required to be convinced.

"So I believe. It was in that letter he advised Mrs. Fiske that he could not walk abroad under his true name without fear of prosecution for debt—and that she should look for the delivery of a peculiar token, as notice of his coming."

"The tamarind seeds," I said.

"Precisely," the solicitor replied.

Oddly, it was the face of Julian Thane that rose most forcibly in my mind at that moment—the dark, elegant countenance animated with sudden violence, as he wheeled upon his sister in the drawing-room at Chilham Castle, the day after the discovery of the corpse. *Fiske sends you his calling card,* he had said, in outrage that she had not told him of the silken pouch's delivery; and I guessed, sharply, that he, too, had known of Fiske's survival; that Thane as well as his sister had read that ominous letter, and awaited the return of one thought to be dead. Had all the Thanes propelled Andrew MacCallister down the aisle of St. Mary's in reckless disregard for the proprieties? And what had they hoped to gain, from such stubborn indifference to the truth?

The truth need never have been known, a voice whispered within, *if they had managed to kill Fiske sooner.*

I sank back against my hard wooden chair, a sensation of dread curling in my stomach. Despite every mark against them, I had learnt to like the Thanes too much.

"Sir Davie," my brother said in a weary voice—having revolved, no doubt, every dark thought that had spun in my own mind—"pray tell me, at last, how you came to be at Chilham Wednesday night?"

"Nothing simpler," the old seaman replied. "Burbage learnt of the wedding, and where and when it was to be. Fiske saw that his wife meant to brave it out—she never so much as acknowledged his letter, nor attempted to meet with him, tho' he sent her his direction in London. He determined to give her a shock, therefore, on her wedding night. But he preferred not to test the memories of all those at Chilham, by descending in the flesh upon the wedding-party. He still owed too much to his creditors in England to be entirely comfortable with full exposure. And there was some other matter—an old scandal he refused to disclose—an affair of honour that prevented him from entering Kent with precisely that measure of easiness he should have desired. And so he went as a common labourer, and I as the seaman I have always been, and we agreed that I should deliver the tamarind seeds, being unknown to the lady. I was to wait for Mrs. Fiske's reply; Fiske had enclosed a small slip of paper in the pouch, informing her she was to seek me in the back garden, on the lower terrace, once all the household was abed."

"I did not glimpse that paper," I said regretfully. "When the pouch was opened, I saw only a spill of seeds."

"And if she had not appeared?" Edward demanded.

Sir Davie shrugged. "Fiske should probably have given it up as a bad business—and commenced to blackmail the lady. She had certainly left herself open to such an action, however deplorable; and Fiske regarded her in no very amiable light. The desire to punish her for indifference was hard upon him. Yes, I believe I may say that Mrs. Fiske—Mrs. *MacCallister*, if you will—should not have enjoyed a moment's peace from that night forward. Poor mite."

"And she met you in the back garden?" Edward's tone was very hard; I guessed that considerable emotion roiled in his breast. Pity for Adelaide—or disgust for Fiske—I could not say.

"She sent her maid. The unfortunate child was frightened out of her wits at the commission, and the sight of me did nothing to support her courage. She thrust at me a knot of paper, and ran as fast as her legs might carry her back to the safety of the Wildman keep." The baronet smiled reminiscently, displaying very bad teeth indeed.

"And what did you then?"

Sir Davie's gaze lifted to my brother's. "I walked directly into the village of Chilham, where Fiske awaited me at the publick house; gave him the missive from his lady-love, and put myself to sleep on a straw pallet in the stables. One of the stable boys will no doubt remember me, for I disturbed him upon my entrance."

"Which was at what hour?"

"Perhaps midnight. I cannot precisely say. The wedding revels were still in full force at the Castle when I left."

And so Adelaide had communicated with Sir Davie well before the interview between Captain MacCallister and his batman, and the subsequent departure of the two men with their roll of banknotes intended to buy Fiske's silence. It was a wonder all three did not collide upon the path over the Downs in the dead of night, coming or going.

"And when you awoke?" Edward prompted Sir Davie.

"I proceeded to walk towards Canterbury, by easy stages, and was so fortunate as to be taken up by a grocer's dray a few miles out of Chilham. Fiske and I had agreed to meet at the Little Inn, when once his business should be concluded— but he never came there. Only his corpse appeared, on the Friday, with the coroner behind it."

"So it did," my brother said. He paused a moment, his eyes bent on the stone floor of the cell, his expression abstracted. "You have been exceedingly helpful, Sir Davie. I am in your debt."

"In that case, Your Honour," Mr. Burbage said, "might my client be set at liberty?"

Edward hesitated, and glanced at me. "I should like him to sign the statement you have recorded, and agree to give evidence, once Mrs. MacCallister is brought up before the Assizes."

"When are the Quarter Sessions to be held?" Sir Davie demanded, as tho' much put out. "I am bound on an expedition to the Galápagos in January!"

"I believe we shall not require too much of your time," Edward assured him. "If you will be so good as to leave your direction with Mr. Burbage, so that we might inform you of the occasion—"

And so the baronet was released, to the evident displeasure of the warden Mr. Stoke; and the baronet at least seemed to find the occasion a source of joy. For my brother and me, however, the outcome of our interview in Canterbury gaol was hardly happy. I dreaded to consider of the scenes that must be played in coming days.

CHAPTER TWENTY-THREE

The Clean-Shaven Liar

"You've got to be careful, Solomon once said:
'Don't open your door to every man who asks.'"

GEOFFREY CHAUCER, "THE COOK'S PROLOGUE"

25 OCTOBER 1813, CONT.

"WELL, JANE," MY BROTHER SAID AS WE PAUSED UNDER the arch of Westgate gaol, "what do you make of this tangled web?"

"Little good," I replied. "Sir Davie's account must weave a hempen rope for the unfortunate Adelaide. Did she deny it all, when you charged her last evening?"

"She admitted that the hand on the fragment of paper discovered in Fiske's coat was indeed her own. Still, she declared she never ventured out to meet the fellow that night—despite setting the assignation."

"I suppose that is not *entirely* improbable."

"Jane! Will you never be done defending the lady? Tho' she lies, and lies, and lies again?"

I lifted a troubled gaze to Edward's own. "I cannot find

any credible reason for Adelaide to leave James Wildman's gun behind her. Until you may supply one, I shall persist in believing that it was *not* her hand that took Fiske's life."

"Her mother would be gratified by your loyalty," he offered abruptly. "She informed me, with considerable hauteur, that she had intercepted her daughter on the point of setting out for her midnight confrontation near St. Lawrence churchyard, and forcibly locked Adelaide into her bedroom—where, later still, the Captain avers he found his wife. Upon his return from his *own* nocturnal jaunt, one presumes."

"You do not credit Mrs. Thane?"

He shrugged eloquently.

"Was this her attempt, do you think, to restore Adelaide's dignity before Captain MacCallister?"

"It may have been," my brother conceded, his brows knitted, "for I never saw a gentleman more shocked than he; the Captain was deprived of speech for several minutes, once he apprehended that his wife had deceived him—in this clandestine communication, as in so much else. The little matter of her then being taken up for murder was but an incidental blow. For one as deeply in love as MacCallister, each successive day brings its own measure of wretchedness."

"Will he stand by her, do you think?"

"He has that sort of courage. But it will be an ugly business, Jane. I cannot believe she will escape hanging. I must go to her, now, and put before her the matter of Fiske's letter, posted in London. It may be that she will deny ever having received it—or, once she apprehends we know of the full extent of her falsity, she may give way entirely and confess."

"If she does," I said, "I shall be profoundly surprised."

"You do not wish to accompany me?"

I shook my head, a reprehensible coward. "I am pledged to Harriot, who is kicking her heels at Moffett's Confectionary. We are to call upon old Mrs. Milles—Harriot desires it."

"I shall collect you from the lady's front door in an hour, then," my brother commanded, and turned back inside the gaol.

I STOOD UNDECIDED AN INSTANT, ENQUIRING IN MY OWN mind whether I ought not to see Adelaide MacCallister—whether the face of a friend, and a female at that, should not be infinitely cheering amidst the misery of such a place. Before I had taken a step in either direction, however, the great oak door of the gaol swung open once more, and expelled the solicitor, Mr. Burbage.

He lifted his hat at the sight of me, and bowed. "Miss Austen. It was a pleasure to meet you. I hope Sir Davie did not unduly weary—or appall—you with his reminiscences?"

"Not at all, sir. His stories were extremely entertaining—and I may say, enlightening. Is he gratified to have won his freedom?"

"I daresay. Sir Davie has been in far tighter spots than Canterbury gaol, as no doubt you have surmised."

"Have you been acquainted with the baronet long?"

"Some years," he replied. "It is my pleasure to serve so notable an eccentric; Sir Davie makes a decided change from the usual Wills and Marriage Settlements."

"I suppose you must often support him in tight spots, as you put it—for I recollect, now, where I have seen you before," I declared, with sudden comprehension. "You attended Saturday's inquest, did you not?"

"The inquest?" A look of puzzlement came over Mr. Burbage's countenance, and he seemed to take a half-step backwards. "You would refer to the inquest on Mr. Curzon Fiske's death?"

"Indeed. You entered the publick room at almost the same moment as Sir Davie—tho' you did not appear to notice one another. Having made room for Sir Davie on my bench, I had occasion to observe you standing against the wall. But you had whiskers, then, did you not? And are now clean-shaven? I presume that is why I did not recognise you when first we were introduced in the gaol. The light in the cell was exceedingly poor."

Mr. Burbage's frown deepened. "I regret that I have not set foot in Canterbury, during the whole course of my life, until this morning, Miss Austen; nor have I ever sported whiskers! I must assure you that you are mistaken."

My lips parted in surprize, for the solicitor was raising his beaver in a chilly gesture of farewell. I coloured, and managed, "I beg your pardon, sir."

"Not at all," he replied, and walked swiftly away.

I gazed after him some moments. Absent the confusion of whiskers—merely observing Mr. Burbage from the rear as he strode down St. Peter's Street—I was more than ever convinced I was correct. The figure, frame, profile—all declared the stranger of respectable appearance, who had taken up a position to the rear of the publick room. I was *not* mistaken in Mr. Burbage; but for reasons best known to himself, the solicitor preferred to utter a falsehood rather than admit he had been in Canterbury the day before yesterday. I must mention the matter to Edward—Edward, who had waited full *two days* for the arrival of Sir Davie's solicitor from London, when it appeared the fellow was already established in the neighbourhood.

And why had he seen fit to rid himself of his beard, if not to defy detection?

I had an idea my brother would regard the subterfuge with as much outrage as I.

I WILL NOT WASTE INK AND PAPER ON THE BANALITY OF MY subsequent hour with Harriot and Mrs. Milles; an account of that visit, and the good lady's effort to tell us, *in three words,* of the famous Scudamore Reconciliation, is reserved for Cassandra's amusement.[1] I returned to Godmersham with all our party, Harriot regaling her husband with the burden of our visit; her son, too sleepy to concern himself with being carriage-sick; and Mr. Moore contenting himself with a single question for Edward: "Is that foul-looking sea dog truly the baronet he claims?"

Of Edward's interview with Mrs. MacCallister I asked nothing; his countenance was troubled and careworn, and I forebore to tax him further. Once we had achieved the comfort of home, however, and I had accorded my brother an hour of contemplation in the sanctity of his book room—heard Harriot impart the high notes of the morning to Fanny, and yet again to Miss Clewes—and fortified myself with tea and cold meat by the fire in the library—I screwed myself to the sticking point and scratched at Edward's door.

"Come!" he commanded.

His expression, if anything, had darkened. He was fiddling with a silver letter-opener he kept upon his desk—a gift from Elizabeth, long ago—and did not raise his eyes to mine. "I must thank you, Jane, for your measure of self-control the length of the carriage ride home. I had no wish to canvass this dreadful business before the Moores. You desire to know what Adelaide MacCallister said, when questioned about her receipt of Fiske's letter?"

"If you desire to tell me."

"That her mother regarded it in the nature of a hoax. A brazen attempt to frighten Adelaide, on the part of some stranger who had known her first husband, and meant to unsettle her. Mrs. Thane advised her to burn the thing, and think no more about it."

"But the hand, Edward! Surely she recognised Fiske's writing as his own!"

---

[1] See Letter 94, dated Tuesday, October 26, 1813, in *Jane Austen's Letters*, Deirdre Le Faye, editor, Oxford University Press, 1995. —*Editor's note.*

"Mrs. Thane suggested there was just that degree of variation in the script that Adelaide was the victim of imposture."

"Mrs. Thane has a great deal to answer for."

At last my brother's gaze lifted to meet mine. "No more than any mother might. She is naturally alive to the terror of the scaffold—and wishes to save her daughter's neck."

"Was Mrs. Thane present at the interview?"

"She was not. I had the recital from Adelaide herself. Young Thane and MacCallister had been to Canterbury gaol, but Mrs. Thane has no stomach for the place."

"An unamiable woman," I remarked.

"And her counsel did not help to save Mrs. MacCallister. Indeed, the lack of frankness on the part of *all* that family has done her a decided disservice! Every word the principals have spoken in this affair, from first to last, appears a tissue of lies, Jane! I cannot endure it!"

My brother rose abruptly from his chair and moved to beat savagely at the fire with a battered pair of tongs. A shower of sparks ascended into the chimney; it was as tho' both our thoughts rose with them, into the darkening air.

"If you would speak of imposture, and a tissue of lies," I said, "I have an oddity to share."

I told him of Mr. Burbage—with whiskers, and without—of the solicitor's steady insistence that I was in error, regarding his presence at the inquest, and his studied disregard for his client Sir Davie, when that gentleman fled the proceeding with most of Canterbury on his heels. Edward heard me out, a frown gathering on his brow.

"But are you certain, Jane?"

"As sure as I am of my own name."

"But it is incomprehensible! In every way—incomprehensible! Why should Sir Davie and Burbage pretend that the latter must be summoned from London, and the former await his arrival to speak—"

"—when we saw, only this morning, that Sir Davie does

nothing else but chatter like a magpie! It is not as tho' Burbage forestalled any incriminating detail—we might have heard that lengthy history of the baronet's career days since, for all the solicitor's objection. No, Edward—I must believe that they observed the inquest as apparent strangers, with the object of learning what they could of Fiske's murder—and once Sir Davie was identified, took to his heels, and ended in gaol, were forced to concoct a credible tale between them."

"You believe Burbage is not what he seems?"

"I believe both men demand further scrutiny. We have only Burbage's word for it, after all, that Sir Davie is who he claims to be—and if *Burbage* cannot be entirely trusted . . ."

"Then neither can Sir Davie's account."

"—Which has served, in no small measure, to indict Adelaide MacCallister."

My brother groaned, and swept his hands over his face. He stared unseeing at the shattered logs in the hearth, and then deliberately replaced the tongs on their hook. "I shall have to post up to London tomorrow and learn what I may of our circumspect solicitor," he said. "There is nothing else for it. Do you wish to accompany me, Jane?"

I shook my head. "My time might be more usefully employed."

"—keeping an eagle-eye on Fanny and all her young swains?"

"Discovering, if I may, why *someone* chose James Wildman's gun to kill Curzon Fiske."

CHAPTER TWENTY-FOUR

An Affair of Honour

These are fruits from the cursèd pair of dice—
Swearing, anger, cheating, and homicide.

GEOFFREY CHAUCER, "THE PARDON PEDDLER'S TALE"

TUESDAY, 26 OCTOBER 1813

EDWARD WAS GONE BEFORE FIRST LIGHT, POSTING TOWARDS London in his travelling-coach. He intends to put up this evening in Henry's rooms, over the bank in Henrietta Street, where our brother has lived in bachelor splendour since the sad event of last spring.[1] Edward hopes to be returned by the morrow, as his sons depart for Oxford Thursday and the Moores—God be praised!—are also to take themselves off that morning; but if his business in London does not prosper and he finds himself delayed, he has begged Young Edward and George to put off their plan of travel until Fri-

---

[1] Jane refers to the death of Henry Austen's wife, Eliza de Feuillide, on April 25, 1813. An account of the weeks following Eliza's death may be found in *Jane and the Madness of Lord Byron* (Bantam, 2010). —*Editor's note.*

day. I noticed that he forebore to press Mr. Moore to do the same.

The young gentlemen are used enough to the claims of business in their father's life to make this present freak—as I am sure they regard it—nothing out of the common way; and as the shooting continues fine, and Jupiter Finch-Hatton is available at any hour to play at billiards, or make another at cards, or to ride out with them on one of their gallops, they appear resigned to passing the remainder of the week at God-mersham, with tolerable composure.

Miss Clewes was agog to know what could possibly draw Mr. Knight to London, such a little while after our passage through the Metropolis on our way from Chawton this past September; and not all the conjectures the governess and Har-riot could suggest between them, sufficed to settle the matter. Harriot was a little put out that no warning of the trip had been given, that she might have charged Edward with myriad commissions in Town—to be achieved, no doubt, *on credit*—but Fanny preserved a noble indifference to her father's schemes, sipping her tea with composure in the breakfast-parlour and enquiring of me only, with a sardonic look, if *I* intended any secret errands throughout the course of the morning.

I replied in good conscience that I had nothing greater in view than a vigourous climb up into the Downs, if she wished to accompany me; and at Jupiter's happening to overlisten our conversation, it was presently agreed that we should stay only to don our bonnets and pelisses, before setting out for our walk with Mr. Finch-Hatton as escort. To my relief, Har-riot declared herself fatigued after her errand in Canterbury the previous day, and preferred to bear Miss Clewes company in the nursery-wing, sorting Young George's small-clothes for laundering in preparation for the journey home. I intended to profit by my interlude with Mr. Finch-Hatton; and while I should not hesitate to put questions before Fanny, Harriot should have been a decided impediment to frank and easy conversation, as it was chiefly regarding *her husband* I wished to query Jupiter. I had not forgot George Moore's presence at the interesting whist-party, on the night of Curzon Fiske's flight from England; nor his dispute with Mr. Stephen Lushington, MP, at our own dining table; nor the matter of packets of gold, despatched to unknown points on the Subcontinent. For a man already in the habit of hiding so much, a mere murder seemed an incidental addition.

Jupiter whistled for one of the dogs—a spaniel of George's called Frisk—and swung a stylish ebony stick in his gloved hand; he was the picture of an elegant Bond Street Stroller, complete to a shade, for all he went in breeches and top boots. One look at his gold locks tucked beneath his curly-brimmed beaver, one glance from his bold blue eyes, one thought of the earldom that might eventually be his—and I grasped quite fully why even Fanny could not be entirely indifferent to him.

"Are you quite certain you wish to attempt the path along the Downs, Aunt?" Fanny enquired, with a doubtful look at the clouds gathering above the hills.

"I am afraid no other way will serve, my dear. It must be the Downs or nothing."

She looked at me sidelong. "And do you intend to walk all the way to Chilham Castle?"

"Not if I discover what I hope to find, before we reach it," I returned calmly.

"Lord! Are we hunting for clews, then?" Jupiter chortled. "It makes a dashed good change from billiards, I assure you. Only tell me what you seek, ma'am, and I shall train my full attention on the ground!"

"I am hoping the dog may nose out something for us," I said as Frisk's waving brush disappeared into the undergrowth at one side of the path. "A piece of cloth, perhaps, torn from a cloak; a few strands of horsehair pulled from a passing mount."

"But surely any idle walker might leave such things behind him, Aunt," Fanny said in puzzlement, "without them being *decidedly* a token of Fiske's murderer."

She is hardly lacking in sense, our Fanny; but I adopted an airy tone.

"To be sure, my dear. But it is equally possible we may discover something *decisive*."

"Such as . . . another pistol, tossed into the bracken, that does *not* belong to James Wildman at all," Jupiter suggested.

I studied his indolent countenance, so deceptive in its blandness. So the pistol had been troubling Mr. Finch-Hatton too. Perhaps our conversation in the breakfast-parlour yesterday had given him to think.

The pleasure gardens behind the house gave way to a walled kitchen garden, which amply supplied the Godmersham table three-quarters of the year; and I might have lingered there on a different morning, to indulge a few melancholy thoughts on the relentless march of Time, amidst the leafless espaliered fruit trees. This morning, however, mindful of the impending rain—is there any season so wet as Autumn in Kent?—I trod purposefully forward, Fanny keeping pace beside me, with Mr. Finch-Hatton at her elbow. He whistled a little tunelessly under his breath as he strode along, slashing at the dead grasses with his ebony stick.

"I have been considering of James Wildman's pistol," I mused as the ground began its gradual ascent and our pleasant saunter became an uphill toil. Below us, Edward's sheep dotted the grass like so much cloud come to ground. "If we are agreed—as I believe we must be—that Adelaide MacCallister is the last person who should have wished to incriminate her cousin, we must endeavour to put our heads together, Mr. Finch-Hatton, and discover who *did*. You know the gentleman far better than I, or even Fanny—what is your opinion on the subject? Does Mr. Wildman attract enemies, as a jam-pot attracts bees?"

"James?" Jupiter replied incredulously. "Attract *enemies*? I should say not! *James,* who was never an Out-and-Outer, nor Top-'o-the-Trees, much less a Rake-shame or a Loose Screw! No, no—he's far too good *ton* for anyone to come the ugly with James!"

"In other words—if I apprehend your cant correctly—Mr. Wildman's character and way of life are far too unobjection- able to excite either the envy or the hatred that a nonpareil of Fashion, or a reprehensible scoundrel, should certainly in- spire."

"That's it," Jupiter said gratefully. "Hasn't an enemy in the world, our James."

"And yet, someone deliberately left his pistol at a scene of murder. How is it that a man without enemies is positioned so neatly for the scaffold, Mr. Finch-Hatton?"

Fanny snorted, an indecorous sound that might have been a swallowed giggle. Tho' she was the sort who spoke most often only when she was spoken to—particularly among gen- tlemen, whom she had been trained foolishly to regard as leaders to be followed, rather than small boys to be led—she *did* appreciate a deft exchange of views, and the occasional triumph of her aunt.

"Does leave one in a coil, don't it?" Jupiter agreed affably. "Nasty, slippery articles, facts."

"I believe the coil might be cut, however, did we consider of the relations between Curzon Fiske and James Wildman," I suggested. "Mr. Wildman insists he was in happy ignorance of Fiske's survival, when that unfortunate man found his way to Chilham last Wednesday; and as Fiske was unknown in England for fully three years—we must cast our minds back to that fatal night, when James Wildman admits to having last seen Fiske: The night the gentleman was forced to flee the Kingdom. There was a game of whist played that evening, I believe? For odiously high stakes? And you were present, were you not, Mr. Finch-Hatton?"

Jupiter stopped short on the path. He studied me through narrowed eyes. "I was," he said tersely, "but if you may tell me how you got wind of such a devilish affair, I'd be much obliged to you, ma'am. I should like to have it out with the bounder who saw fit to share what should never have reached a lady's ears!"

"It was Fanny who told me of it," I replied.

"Aunt Jane!" Fanny cried in outrage.

"Do not attempt to deny it! We must disabuse Mr. Finch-Hatton of his misapprehension, my dear—that the whist game is in some wise a closely-guarded secret—for if *you* know of it, Fanny, we may be assured that most of Kent does, as well."

"Damme," Jupiter muttered, and lopped a thistle from its stalk with a single murderous stroke of his cane.

As we laboured up the pitch of the Downs, and the weak Autumn light was gradually blotted out by cloud, I succeeded in dragging intelligence most unwillingly from Jupiter's disapproving mind. To relate the essentials of what he termed "a dashed smoky business" to two unmarried ladies obviously offended his notions of decorum. The discovery that he actually *possessed* such nice sensibilities so raised Jupiter in Fanny's estimation, that by the end of his recital the two were conversing quite animatedly.

"We were all at Chilham Castle for a visit that November, one of James's sisters—never can tell one from the other—being on the point of *coming out,* and the Wildmans thinking to show her off round Kent before the London Season began, just to see how the chit took. Neither of 'em ever *did* take, come to that," Jupiter added thoughtfully, "but can't blame James's mamma for trying! I mean to say—two such anti-dotes on her hands, and the eldest of 'em past praying for! In any event, there was a dress party. —Believe *you* were indis-posed, Miss Fanny. Accounts for you not being one of the party."

"All the children had scarlet fever," my niece murmured, "and naturally I could not carry contagion into Louisa's coming-out party."

"We'd just dined—twenty couple or so, m'mother and sis-ter and m'father in attendance, along with the Moores and the Plumptres and I know not who else—"

"Mr. Lushington and his wife, perhaps?" I prompted.

"Aye," Jupiter said darkly, "and that chit of theirs, Mary-Ann, who's forever setting her cap at James, for all she's not yet fifteen."

"Is she, indeed?" Fanny enquired with interest. "I had thought her still in the schoolroom!"

"Ought to have been, that night—what Lushington was thinking, bringing a child no more than twelve to dinner, I should have liked to have asked him—but that's neither here nor there." Jupiter stabbed his stick into the soft earth with every step. "As I say, we were coming out of the dining par-lour, intending to get up a bit of a dance—you know the sort of thing, Fanny, most informal and dashed tedious, my opin-ion, but nothing for it—girl's coming-out party, after all—when there was a great pounding at the front door, and the peal of the bell, and that quiz they keep for a butler at Chilham—"

"Twitch."

"—the very one!—threw open the front door. There was Fiske and little Adelaide, looking as tho' she might faint at our feet, and practically stumbling to get inside. 'Oh, cousin!' she cried to James's papa, 'the bailiffs are at the door, and we are lost, and if you are not kind to us, cousin, I do not know what we shall do!' Never seen a lady so torn with anxiety as Adelaide was that night—and her increasing, worse luck."

"Increasing?" I repeated, quite startled. "I had not an idea of it. No one has mentioned a child."

"Lost it," Jupiter said significantly, with a tentative eye towards Fanny. "Miscarried, soon as Fiske took off without a word to anyone the next day. Kept the matter quite close at Chilham, it being but another tragedy in Mrs. Fiske's life."

"I see. Mr. Wildman took them in, of course?"

"Sent Adelaide straight upstairs with his wife, and shut Fiske into the library with a bottle of his best claret. Probably hopeful the damned fellow would drink himself senseless and leave the party in peace. Wildman urged us into the ball-room—you've seen it yourself, Miss Austen, so no need to re-cite the particulars—and we made a poor show of dancing, but the talk that flew round the couples was like nothing on earth. Any number decided to depart quite early, and made their excuses to James's mamma, once she appeared back downstairs. It was a sad end to their chit's coming out, and I daresay the girl holds it against Adelaide to this day."

"But you remained."

Jupiter shrugged. "Been invited to stay. Traps all unpacked in the best bedrooms. M'mother and father yawning their heads off, sister determined to seek her bed. I repaired to the library with James and Plumptre and a few others, and we found Fiske in a feverish state—the wine having done its work. Another man would have been snoring on the floor, but not Fiske. He was game for anything. Demanded we play whist, for pound points. James tried to reason with him—we were all aware the fellow's pockets were entirely to let, and he had no business playing on tick when the blunt to settle his

debts should undoubtedly come from Old Wildman's purse—
but Fiske would have none of it. Jeered at James, and called
him *a stripling too callow to play a man's game*. Well, must
tell you that Plumptre and I fired up at such Turkish treatment! James was no more a stripling than ourselves—well,
perhaps Plumptre *was* full young to be laying down his quarterly allowance in such a cause, being then not above eighteen; but he knew what it meant to stand buff for James, and
sat down at the whist table he did."

Now Jupiter was coming to it. I slowed my footsteps as we
achieved a plateau in the Downs, a slight shelf in the contin-
ual rise, and paused to survey the view. Edward's is a splendid fall of country, the house situated in a valley between two
hills, and the Stour winding below; it was difficult to believe
that so frightful an event as murder could occur amidst such
peace.

"Mr. Moore and Mr. Lushington sat down as well, I collect?"

"Not to play, whist being a game for four hands—but the
prosy old parson and the gabster from Parliament thought to
keep a stern eye on the doings—it being plain as a pikestaff
Fiske meant to pluck us all! I mean to say—fellow'd been a
Master Sharp for years, ran gaming hells on the Continent,
stood to reason he took us for a bunch of flats! He meant to
fuzz the cards, I daresay, and clear out of England plumper in
the pocket than he'd arrived at Chilham that night!"

"And did he?"

Jupiter shrugged. "Curiously enough, Fiske was badly
dipped by the time he broached his third bottle. James and
Plumptre and I decided between us to take our winnings, and
politely toddle off to bed—but Fiske would have none of it.
Demanded another round. Meant to win his own back, I
gather, tho' as he'd nothing to pledge, it was hard to see how
he meant to come about. James was fool enough to mention

the point—in the most circumspect way, 'course—but Fiske told him to go to the Devil. And then the fellow dealt us a leveller—"

"A *what*?" Fanny demanded with knitted brows.

"That is boxing cant, my dear," I informed her. "It signifies a stunning blow."

"Up to every rig, ain't you, Miss Austen? Nothing a fellow can't say to *you*. Friend Curzon floored us, to be frank," Jupiter affirmed. "Having not a feather to fly with—Fiske tossed his *wife* into the pot, and invited any who was man enough, to play for her."

CHAPTER TWENTY-FIVE

Deadly Stakes

*Why should I refrain from telling your
Misfortune, you who climbed so very high?*

GEOFFREY CHAUCER, "THE MONK'S TALE"

26 OCTOBER 1813, CONT.

"YOU CANNOT BE IN EARNEST," FANNY PROTESTED. THE exertion of our uphill climb had brought a becoming flush to her cheeks; but her colour was heightened, I thought, from indignation.

"'Fraid I am," Jupiter replied cheerfully. "Told you the fellow was dashed loose in the haft."

"Staking his wife," I repeated, "as tho' she were no more than a . . . a . . ."

"—Bit of muslin he wished to cast off. In the family way, too. Shockingly bad *ton*! Wouldn't touch the betting, myself."

"But others did not share your compunction, Mr. Finch-Hatton?"

"James did," he allowed. "Threatened to call Fiske out,

for offering his cousin such an insult! Plumptre and I had to talk James down, naturally—can't challenge a man who's three-parts bosky to a duel! Stands to reason. Not in his right mind. Can't be held accountable for what he says. Besides, James was Fiske's host. Can't go shooting one's guests whenever they put a foot wrong, what? Very bad *ton*. There was a good deal of it to go around, that night."

"Lord!" Fanny exclaimed in strong disgust. She began to plod forward like a foot-soldier, her shawl wrapped tight around her; I guessed her romantickal notions of gentlemen and chivalry were suffering a reverse.

"And then?"

Jupiter kept his gaze fixed upon the uneven ground. "Plumptre took James into a corner while I told Fiske he'd had his jest—much better to go to bed before he found himself at Point Non-Plus. But he wouldn't listen to me; drunk as a wheelbarrow, of course. Kept demanding of any who'd listen, *What am I bid for as fine a baggage as ever strutted the boards of Covent Garden?* Naturally, that stuck in Moore's craw. Nursed a *tendre* for Adelaide since I don't know when. Never seen the prosy parson look so enflamed! He pulled out his purse and tossed it into the centre of the table, and called Fiske's bluff."

"George Moore played a hand of whist for Curzon Fiske's wife?" I whispered.

"Loo, actually—whist being out of the question, as there were only three players by that time. James, Plumptre, and I would have none of it; James was all for fetching his papa and breaking up the party entirely, but Fiske locked the library door and pocketed the key."

"And the third player?" I queried.

"Lushington consented to sit at the table. Think he only meant to keep an eye on the other two, myself—no sort of personal interest in Adelaide. Thought the affair should get out of hand, no doubt, and the two men be at each other's throats once tempers flew high. Devil was in it, he was right!"

"I cannot conceive of George Moore being so easily drawn!" I exclaimed. "Nor *gambling* for another man's wife! His own should have been sleeping upstairs, I collect?"

"Understand," Jupiter said as he halted earnestly on the path, "no desire to slander the prosy parson! No interest in canvassing his morals! Moore's a right one, however dreary his conversation. Fiske simply tried the poor fellow too high. I should judge Moore hated Fiske with a passion. Cut him out once with Adelaide, then had the deuced effrontery to treat her like a doxy. Moore meant to teach Fiske a lesson— and play the Knight Errant with Fiske's wife."

"And the result?" I demanded grimly.

Even Fanny had halted in her march, and was listening now.

"Suspect Fiske fuzzed the cards. Well—stands to reason! Pile of silver on the table; pregnant wife asleep in her bed; the whole world to lose, and everything to gain! Not the sort to stop at Greeking methods, when his life depended on it!"[1]

"He won," I said.

"Cleaned Moore and Lushington out. First time Fiske's luck had turned, that night—and we've all seen the same. A man may throw good money after bad, round upon round, and stake his last groat—only to have his fortune come home again. Looked like that was the way with Fiske!"

"Until Lushington accused him of cheating," I murmured.

Jupiter cast me a sapient eye. "Heard about that, did you?"

"Mr. Lushington was so indiscreet as to refer to the matter at dinner a few days ago," Fanny said in a small voice. "Uncle

---

[1] "Fuzzing the cards" and "Greeking methods" were cant euphemisms for cheating. —*Editor's note.*

Moore was exceedingly angry, tho' Mr. Lushington attempted to pass it off as a jest."

"Little enough of laughter in the whole business," Jupiter declared. "Made me dashed uneasy, I can tell you. Fiske went silent, and looked sick; Moore was in a white rage, and ready to draw the fellow's cork; and our MP demanded to lift Fiske's coat-sleeves. I have an idea Lushington thought to find certain cards hidden there. Fiske refused; took up his winnings, and declared he was bound for bed."

"A cool customer," I observed.

"Only that James would not let him go. He demanded that Fiske answer the MP's accusation. We urged him to stow it, of course—but James declared it was a matter of honour; and that he would not see his friends cheated by a blackguard in his father's house."

"I do admire James Wildman," Fanny cried passionately.

I raised my brows at her. "There are occasions, my dear, when the most noble of impulses ought to be suppressed, for the sake of general security. And Fiske's reply?"

"—Challenged poor James to a meeting at dawn."

"Ah," I murmured. "Naturally, Mr. Wildman could not *then* draw back, without being accused of cowardice."

"Plumptre and I were to stand as Seconds. Nobody could be induced to act for Fiske, of course, until Lushington quite unwillingly consented to do so. Dashed rum set-out, when the fellow one's cheated at cards is forced to serve as one's Second!"

"And George Moore?"

"Was in a finer rage than I have ever witnessed, that day to this. He told James to make sure he got his man, and that he would undertake to bury Fiske with full Church rites—at a crossroads where the souls of thieves and suicides wander. Then he demanded the key to the library door."

Jupiter shuddered theatrically. "I hope never to see another face like Fiske's, when he gave that key to Moore! There was contempt and triumph in it—as tho' he knew he had the prosy parson in his power. *Covetous, aren't we, George?* he said, and, *You've not seen the last of me, my lecherous priest.* Moore knocked him down."

"You astonish me!"

"Astonished us all! Never thought the parson was so handy with his fives! By the time Fiske got up—as I say, he was three-parts drunk, and none too steady on his feet—Moore was gone. We settled the business of the meeting between us—there's a bit of meadow down near the Stour, on Godmersham land, where a man might measure twenty paces—and Lushington undertook to wake Fiske at dawn, if Plumptre and I should bring James up to scratch."

"—Which I assume, being men of honour, you did."

"Only that when we met in the Great Hall the following morning," Jupiter concluded with an air of apology, "six o'clock it must have been, and dark as Hades—we discovered Lushington was alone."

"Fiske had fled."

"Crept out of the Castle in the wee hours with his ill-gotten gains to frank his passage. Left Adelaide behind, and a passel of debts, and Old Mr. Wildman to settle the whole. We four, standing foolishly in the hall, agreed that no word of the sordid affair should ever pass our lips; and we took it as gospel that George Moore would not willingly divulge the part he played."

"Aunt Harriot should certainly be made miserable by it," Fanny murmured. "What brutes men are!"

I might have told Fanny to hush—poor Jupiter had done his best in a difficult episode, and his frankness argued for praise rather than censure—but my mind was too preoccupied. Mr. Finch-Hatton's story had supplied any number of people with motives for murdering Curzon Fiske. Moore had hated, and been cheated, by him and—if, as I suspected, the packets of gold sent quarterly to India were intended to buy Fiske's silence regarding the shameful card game—had been blackmailed for years by him.

James Wildman might creditably be suspected of a mortal desire for vengeance.

But it was Adelaide MacCallister whose beautiful face rose most forcibly in my mind. What woman, made sport of and abandoned as she had been—losing her child, indeed, in her misery—should not wish to put a bullet through Fiske's heart?

I had hoped Finch-Hatton might loosen the knot around Adelaide's neck; but it seemed his account had only tightened it. Why, why, employ James Wildman's gun?

A few drops of rain wetted my cheek; and with a strong sense of perplexity and depression, I suggested we turn back. But neither Fanny nor Jupiter was attending. They were listening to something else—the high, excited bark of a spaniel some way ahead on the trail.

"Frisk," Fanny said. "I believe he has found something, Aunt Jane!"

CHAPTER TWENTY-SIX

The Coppice

"To meet with Death, turn up this crooked way,
For there in that grove I left him, by my faith,
Under a tree, and there he intends to stay."

GEOFFREY CHAUCER, "THE PARDON PEDDLER'S TALE"

26 OCTOBER 1813, CONT.

I HAD NOT TRULY EXPECTED FRISK TO DISCOVER ANYTHING of note on the trail over the Downs—too many days had passed since the murder, and there had been rain in the interval. But as Fanny, Jupiter Finch-Hatton, and I hastened forward—Jupiter striding ahead of us—I saw that a horseman was endeavouring to control his high-spirited mount, as the spaniel jumped and barked about the animal's knees. A second glance at the dexterous rider, and I knew him for Mr. Julian Thane.

"Frisk!" Fanny called out in agitation. "Oh, if only the foolish dog is not to be kicked in the head! My brother shall never forgive me if any harm comes to him!"

But as we hastened on, coming within ten yards of the jibbing horse, Frisk suddenly turned tail and darted back into the long grass that covered the Downs, making with the decided purpose of a bird-dog on point, towards a thin coppice that rose from the hillside.

"By Jove, he *has* found something," Jupiter declared. He seized the bridle of Thane's horse, and the plunging beast quieted. "Fresh as paint, ain't he? Been eating his head off in the stables, I collect?"

"Kindly take your hand from my rein," Thane said through gritted teeth. "The day I fail to control my horse is the day I cease to ride."

Jupiter stepped back a pace and cocked an eye at Thane's stormy visage. "Apologies. No desire to offend, assure you."

Thane ignored these words and dismounted in a single, elegant movement. "Miss Knight," he said, doffing his high-crowned beaver; "Miss Austen. Your servant, ma'am."

I dropped the gentleman a curtsey, too aware that but for my interference his sister might even now be at liberty; he ought to have given me the cut direct, and cantered past our party without so much as a glance. Instead, he stood with his reins gripped tightly in one gloved hand, the other stroking the neck of his horse—a fine, black colt whose looks were as smouldering as his master's. Thane kept his earnest gaze fixed on Fanny's blushing countenance; Jupiter might have been so much thin air.

"I was making my way towards Godmersham," he said with a bow, "with the intent of begging Miss Knight to ride with me. There is not a seat in Kent to rival hers, and no fence she will not attempt."

"You flatter me, sir," Fanny returned with a dimple. "My brothers would have it I am both cow-handed and faint of heart!"

"Then they are too severe upon you. What does any brother know of a sister, after all? She is an uncharted country, dark as Africa." Thane's words were careless; but I caught the bitterness behind them. A greater intimacy with Canterbury gaol had not been good for him. "Do you continue your walk, or may I escort you home—and hope for the favor of a gallop?"

"Hardly needs escort," Jupiter murmured, in his most indolent manner; then he glanced irritably towards the coppice, where Frisk was baying loudly enough to wake the dead. "What *does* that deuced dog mean by sending up such a racket? All the birds in the Kingdom will be flown by now! Must have a word with Young Edward about it—dog's no use at all for sport!"

"Frisk!" Fanny cried impatiently, and gathering up her skirts, plunged into the tangled grass.

"Miss Knight!" Thane called out, in sudden concern, and glanced from his restive horse to Jupiter, who grinned.

"Escort, is it?" he drawled derisively, and set off after Fanny.

"She stands in no danger from Frisk, Mr. Thane," I assured him.

But he was not attending to me. His black brows were drawn down in a manner that put me forcibly in mind of Lord Byron; and his intent gaze was fixed on the coppice, where the sudden clatter of wings revealed a flock of crows, rising into the air. Another moment, and Fanny came pelting back to us, her hand holding down her bonnet and her pallor dreadful.

"It is a girl, Aunt!" she panted. "*Dead.* There were birds—tearing at her eyes—"

And my poor Fanny burst into tears.

SHE WAS NO MORE THAN SEVENTEEN, I JUDGED, WHEN AT last I stood over the sad bundle of bones and cloth that lay beneath the shade of the coppice. I had comforted Fanny briskly, then persuaded her to hold Thane's horse, so that he and I might lend our aid to Mr. Finch-Hatton; Jupiter was standing a little aside, now, a lounger no longer, and from the cast of his countenance I suspected he felt sick.

I was faint enough myself, and spots swam continually before my vision, as tho' I might swoon at any instant. The strong, animal stench of butchered flesh rose to my nostrils, and there was a singing in my ears—as if a scream, suppressed, rang shrilly through my disordered brain. I closed my eyes an instant to steady myself; and then, with a shuddering breath, opened them again and forced myself to see.

The girl's throat had been cut; the blood that had gushed from the great wound was long since congealed in dark gobbets all about her, and the birds—as Fanny had said—had been at their work. She had been seized from behind, I suspected, and had sunk down onto her knees before falling face-forward into the grass; her arms were flung out as tho' to embrace the earth that should soon enough enfold her, and her head—so nearly severed from her body—lay at an awkward angle, one eye socket to the sky. A brown-haired, healthy girl with a skin still tanned from summer, in the simple homespun dress of the serving class.

"Martha," Julian Thane said hoarsely, and fell on his knees at her side, his hand reaching out to touch the huddled figure's shoulder. "Good God, how shall I tell her mother?"

"You know this child?" I asked.

"Should think he does!" Jupiter turned from where he had been gazing unseeing over the valley and Godmersham, his lazy blue eyes suddenly sharp and focused.

"She is my sister's maid," Thane explained. "She came with Adelaide for this wedding, from Wold Hall—where her mother is our housekeeper, and has been since my father's time." Thane passed one hand gently over the girl's snarled hair, then shuddered profoundly. "Horrible! That any could do this—poor Mrs. Kean—this will kill her, I know it! Oh, God—that we had never come into Kent!"

He buried his face in his hands, and something like a sob escaped him.

"What were you doing here, Thane?" Jupiter demanded suddenly. "When we came upon you, just now, with the dog run mad and your horse plunging? Aye, and what is that blood on your glove?"

Thane stared wildly at him, then glanced down at his hands. In sudden horror, he leapt back from the body and began to tear at the glove, pulling it from his fingers with one shaking hand, then bent to wipe it frantically in the grass.

"Mr. Thane!" I cried.

But the sound of retching was my only answer; Thane was on his knees, overcome with sickness.

Furiously, Jupiter strode forward. "Where is the knife? *Where is the knife*, you rogue?"

"Mr. Finch-Hatton," I protested, stepping between them. "The girl was killed hours ago—it is nothing to do with Mr. Thane, I am sure! The blood came onto his glove merely because he touched her. I beg of you—do not be so hasty! There is much that we must do, and quickly."

The rage died out of Jupiter's face, and he stepped back a pace. Thane was still bent double, breathing heavily, but he managed to croak out, "Do not excite yourself, Miss Austen. Do you not know we are *all* murderers now? It is the Thane disease. My sister has taken it, and the Lord only knows who shall next succumb. I must be a monster myself."

"Pray strive for calm," I urged him. "We have need of you, and your horse."

He rose unsteadily to his feet. "You wish me to carry the dreadful intelligence to Mr. Knight?"

Too late, I recollected that Edward was far from home.

"It had better be Chilham," I said. "Explain to Mr. Wildman what we have found, and beg him to send for Dr. Bredloe. Then ask that a male servant be sent to stand guard with me over the body, until the coroner should be arrived; and when Dr. Bredloe appears, bring him immediately to me."

"I should be happy to remain with you, Miss Austen," Jupiter said.

"No, no—you are to bear Fanny home as soon as may be. Go quickly, Mr. Finch-Hatton! She is probably swooning as we speak! And pray—do something with that dog!"

Jupiter whistled; and Frisk, instantly recognising the command and decision of a Master, opened his jaws in a canine grin and loped obediently to Mr. Finch-Hatton's side. Jupiter grasped the spaniel's collar, nodded at me, and without a word for Thane made off immediately towards the path where Fanny had braced herself to hold the mettlesome horse—her heels dug into the dirt and both hands straining at the reins. Thane collected himself enough to join them and take charge of his mount; Jupiter touched Fanny lightly on the shoulder, and after an inaudible exchange of words, she cast a doubtful glance in my direction, and turned away.

Thane threw himself onto the back of his horse, wheeled, and made off for Chilham Castle as tho' all the hounds of Hell were at his heels.

I gave one convulsive look at the pitiful figure behind me. Then I wrapped my arms about my chest in a vain attempt to warm myself, and began to pace briskly back and forth some yards from the scene of carnage, as vigourous proof against the rain that at last had begun to fall.

CHAPTER TWENTY-SEVEN

Pretty Maids All in a Row

"And knowing this is what we old men fear:
Our only way to ripen, now, is weary
Decay."

GEOFFREY CHAUCER, "THE STEWARD'S PROLOGUE"

26 OCTOBER 1813, CONT.

"A DREADFUL BUSINESS," BREDLOE OBSERVED AS HIS FIN-gers sketched a thoughtful arc over the dead girl's great wound. "The principal artery is severed, of course, with a sin-gle cut. Whoever effected her death acted without the slight-est hesitation. A brutal will has been at work here. Poor child! And you found her, Miss Austen, just as she lies?"

"We did not think it wise to shift her in any way, before you had surveyed the ground."

I said *we,* because Jupiter Finch-Hatton had very kindly re-turned up the toilsome slope of the Downs to bear me com-pany after seeing Fanny safely restored to Harriot, who, however silly in most things, might be relied upon to comfort and coddle her niece once the horrid tale had been told. Mr.

Finch-Hatton had saddled a horse for this second jaunt—advisable at the time, perhaps, but requiring him now to walk the animal up and down the path lest its limbs stiffen in the chill rain. He had not, therefore, been of much use to me as a companion; but I honoured his chivalrous sentiment all the same.

Hunched some distance from the body, which justly horrified him, was the manservant sent out as guard from Chilham. He had arrived some moments before Mr. Finch-Hatton, but other than a laconic tug of his forelock, had vouchsafed not a word. He looked positively wretched in the rain.

Of Julian Thane there was no sign; he was required at Chilham, perhaps, to support the household.

The coroner flicked me a shrewd glance. "Mr. Knight is from home, I collect?"

"He is in London, sir—upon business that could not be delayed. I expect him returned no later than Thursday, and if fortune is kind, so soon as tomorrow evening."

"Blast," Bredloe said with forceful efficiency. "I should have valued his eyes."

"You may employ mine, sir."

He studied me. "Indeed. So I might. What have you discerned, Miss Austen, that I should hear?"

"I believe you carry a pocket watch, Dr. Bredloe?"

"I do."

"And what hour does it tell?"

He frowned at me, but dutifully pulled his watch and chain from his waistcoat pocket. "Half-past two."

"The messenger from Chilham Castle reached you when?"

"It wanted twenty minutes, I think, before the hour of one o'clock."

"And you were then at home. Let us say, therefore, that the messenger set out from the Castle at noon, perhaps, and our discovery of the body occurred some fifteen minutes prior to that hour—a quarter to noon."

"And you have been standing in all this wet for so long a period, Miss Austen?" The physician started to his feet—he had been kneeling by the body. "You shall catch your death of cold! Why has that fool of a Bond Street Lounger not offered you his coat?"

"Because he requires it himself," I replied. "I have endeavoured to keep my blood flowing with the constant pursuit of exercise. My point, Dr. Bredloe, is that before this rain commenced, and at our discovery of the corpse nearly three hours ago, the blood you see everywhere about you was thoroughly congealed; suggesting that the girl met her death well before the dog alerted us to her presence."

"Rigour has not yet begun to set in," the coroner murmured, "and since an interval of some eight hours is usual for its onset, I may judge that the poor child met her death no sooner than seven o'clock this morning. As you so correctly point out, Miss Austen, death can have occurred *no later* than—we may surmise—*eleven* o'clock, to allow for the congealing of the blood. Excellently done! That fixes the period to a nicety!"

"A full four hours," I said dubiously, "during which, any number of individuals might have been abroad on the Downs."

Bredloe glanced around, took in the roaming Jupiter, and shook his head. "It is a lonely spot, on a lonely path. Did you observe nothing else, Miss Austen, in your pursuit of exercise?"

"I did," I answered, with an effort at suppressing the chattering of my teeth, which—now that I was brought to a standstill by the doctor's questions—threatened to o'erwhelm me. "A person stood some time in the soft ground within the coppice, before a second person—Martha, I suspect—

approached the place; two sets of footprints are evident, if you should wish to view them."

Without a word Bredloe followed me the slight distance further into the shelter of the lopped trunks and leafless branches. Perhaps two yards from Martha's position, the prints were just discernible: half a booted foot, and the faint impression of another, in the moist leaf-mould. Opposed to them were a second person's prints: smaller in form, and less deeply embedded—the marks of a lighter figure, no doubt a girl of seventeen. So much one might distinguish, before the two sets of prints merged closer to the body.

Bredloe hunched over the impressions. "Impossible to discern whether this was a man or a woman. The two shifted about a trifle, as they talked. And then *this* person—" he indicated the more delicate prints—"turned away, as tho' to depart."

"At which instant the other sprang *forward*, and struck her down."

The coroner lifted his eyes from the ground. "Indeed. She knew her murderer—she approached and lingered long enough to speak with him—and was under no apprehension of danger when she bade him farewell."

My teeth were chattering in earnest now. "W-why lure a suh-suh-serving-girl to her d-death in such a p-place?" I mused. "Why k-kill her at all?"

Bredloe drew a flask of brandy from his pocket and pulled the cork. "Take this, Miss Austen—I insist."

The draught trailed its flame down my throat. I coughed and sputtered. "Th-thank you."

Without ceremony, the doctor removed his heavy black frock coat—the symbol of his profession—and cast it over my shoulders. "You'll do for a few moments; but I must insist you make for home as soon as may be. That fellow—" he indicated Jupiter—"may take you up before him."

I, to ride pillion before the most dashing blade in Kent! How Fanny and her friends should make sport of us both, behind their hands!

But I said only, "You did not hear my question, I think. Why lure this child to her death? What possible reason can there have been to kill her?"

The coroner's eyes narrowed. "Does she belong to Chilham?"

"Not at all! She is Mrs. MacCallister's personal maid, and merely visits the Castle in that capacity. Her home is Wold Hall, in Leicestershire."

"But her killer is presumably of this neighbourhood— quite possibly of the Castle itself. Our enquiries must begin there. Your brother will agree, Miss Austen, I am sure of it— but as such interrogations belong to his province, and not my own, I shall more fruitfully pursue a nearer duty. You there, sirrah!" he called to the manservant. "Pray carry my compliments to Mr. Wildman, and request a driver and dray, with all possible speed. We must convey this poor soul to the Castle. Do you return with the dray, mind, so that the direction is clear."

"Very good, sir," the manservant muttered, and set off with little enthusiasm for his errand.

"You mean to keep her at Chilham?" I enquired.

"Until such time as your brother has returned—I do. Her coffin might lie at St. Mary's, if Mr. Tylden will allow it; and we might even hold the inquest at the publick house in the village. The unfortunate girl must be returned to her people at Wold Hall, seemingly—and to send her first to Canterbury for the purpose of empanelling a jury seems unduly irksome."

Bredloe placed a hand on my elbow and turned me gently away from the fiendish wreck of what had been Martha. "May I say that you are remarkable, Miss Austen, for your *sang-froid*; any other lady of my acquaintance should have been overpowered by such a sight, and swooned dead away. I am grateful I was not required to attend to *two* bodies at my arrival."

I considered of the dizziness and swimming mind with which I had met the corpse's discovery; how I had blenched, and felt my gorge rise at the rank scent of blood. "I know not whether I should thank you for a compliment, Dr. Bredloe, or protest an insult! Do you regard me as *more* or *less* of a woman, as a consequence of my composure?"

He smiled—a strange sight in that creased and cynical old face—and saved his words for Jupiter.

"Mr. Finch-Hatton! Pray conduct Miss Austen with all possible speed to Godmersham!"

I drew off Bredloe's frock coat and presented it with my thanks; he protested, but I remained firm—God alone knew how long he should be required to stand in such weather, and he had long since left off being a young man. Then I was lifted onto Jupiter's horse and borne swiftly in his strong young arms towards the comforts of home.

I INDULGED MY NEED FOR SUCH COMFORTS PERHAPS LONGER than was strictly necessary. A steaming bath in my own chambers, supplied by cans of boiling water carried up by Edward's manservant; the combing out of my hair, and the drying of it by the roaring blaze Mrs. Driver had caused to be kindled in the Yellow Room's hearth; the restorative warmth of a glass of wine and a plate of macaroons, sent up from the kitchens; and an interval of rest, laid down on my bed in my dressing gown, when at last the shuddering of my body had eased. I should be fortunate to escape an inflammation of the lungs; I expected no less.

I dressed for dinner, however, and descended to the library, where Fanny and Harriot had assembled with the addition of Miss Clewes to round out our numbers. The gentlemen—

Young Edward, my nephew George, Mr. Finch-Hatton, and Mr. Moore—had been playing at billiards in the adjoining room; but at my entrance it appeared the game was concluded, and they soon joined us, in full-blown argument as to the merits of cross-breeding hunters for stamina and speed. I underwent a strong sensation of relief; the idea of Jupiter and Moore closeted together, with nothing to discuss but the events of the morning, must unnerve me; I should not like George Moore to know of all that Mr. Finch-Hatton had imparted regarding the dangerous game of cards at Chilham three years since.

"Miss Austen," the clergyman said with a bow, "I hope I find you recovered from the exertions of your walk. May I say that I could have wished you to have gone in the *opposite* direction to the Downs this morning! There was nothing so gruesome by the meadows near the Stour; you should have got your fresh air without all the agitation of discovery."

"Were you along the Stour this morning, sir?" I enquired.

"I was." He gave me a thin smile, his gaze remarkably steady. "The example of these young fellows so far persuaded me to shake off the lassitude of age, and take out a gun."

"A gun, Mr. Moore! And were you so happy as to bag anything, sir?"

"Not a single bird or rabbit!" he declared with an attempt at cheerful disregard. "But the exercise was beneficial. So lost in the beauty of my autumnal surroundings was I, that I may have been gone as much as several hours! —And only considered turning for the house once hunger assailed me."

"Fancy!" Harriot cried to Miss Clewes. "Mr. Moore, forgetful of his nuncheon!"

"I should have thought the rain would dissuade even the most ardent of sportsmen," I observed.

He inclined his head. "Happily, it commenced to fall only after I had achieved the gun room. I am not so much of a hearty as your nephews, I confess!"

He moved on to his wife, and engaged her in low conversation; Harriot was looking harassed and pale, as tho' the atmosphere of the house—or the prevalence of murder—had begun to tell upon her nerves. Curious, that Mr. Moore should be so eager to impart to me the vagaries of his morning; he had never elected to share such intelligence before. It was rather his habit to preserve a frigid personal distance, than to chatter about the mundanities of the day. I thought him rather too earnest in establishing his presence at the extreme opposite locale from Martha's resting place, high on the Downs. He had certainly been absent from the house, however, throughout the period at issue.

Why should George Moore summon a serving-girl from Chilham Castle and do her to death, Jane? a voice within me argued. *There can be no possible relation between them.* Or none, at least, of which I knew.

And this was a truth that applied to every person within ten miles' reach of the Castle. I knew nothing at all of Martha Kean, much less of those who might have come within her orbit during her stay in Kent. There was the entire class of persons serving below-stairs, at both Chilham and Godmersham, who might have formed an attachment to the girl; the folk of Chilham village with whom she came into contact; and above-stairs, there was Julian Thane. Captain Andrew MacCallister. Even Jupiter Finch-Hatton, who had been staying at the Castle some days before coming to us at Godmersham.

But why should any determine to kill Adelaide MacCallister's personal maid? —Because of something the girl had *seen*? Or *suspected*? I had heard mention of her only once: when Sir Davie Myrrh received a note from Martha in the back garden, on the night of Curzon Fiske's murder. He had professed to exchange barely two words with the girl—she had fled from him in fear.

I wished, suddenly, for my brother Edward. No one else was aware of the maid's rôle in that wedding-night drama— not even the coroner, Dr. Bredloe. There had been insufficient time to apprise him of our late interview with the nautical baronet.

"All right and tight, Miss Austen?" Jupiter Finch-Hatton stood before me, proffering a glass of sherry. I took it grate-fully; I could feel the weight of the inevitable head-cold gath-ering unpleasantly behind my eyes, and there is nothing like a little wine, after all, for helping one to bear it.

"I meant to thank you, Mr. Finch-Hatton, for all you did today—your mere presence was a support and a comfort," I said. "But my lips were so frozen when at last we dismounted that I confess I could not speak!"

"Happy to oblige," he replied with his usual air of in-dolence, which I had begun to apprehend was in fact a foil for a young man's embarrassment. "Devilish business, all the same. Don't like Thane's part in it. What was he doing there, I mean to say? Not ten yards from the girl's body? If we hadn't taken that dog out, might never have known she was there! Might have lain for months, in fact! And Thane, spot on the scene!"

He fingered his cravat, which was tied to a perfection, and glanced at me sidelong from his lazy blue eyes. "Must see it yourself, ma'am. You're dashed needle-witted. Said it be-fore!"

Needle-witted. It was a phrase that might have come from my old friend Lord Harold's lips—had he been twenty years younger. I smiled to myself and turned my glass in the fire-light, thoughtfully studying the shift in the wine's colour. "You have been some days at Chilham, I think—both before the wedding and after. Did you ever happen to notice the girl Martha there?"

"Shouldn't have, in the usual way—lady's maids being

not quite in my line," Jupiter replied. "Known my mother's Dresser for donkey's years, of course—devilish high in the instep, and jealous as a cat. Been with her la'ship longer than I've been alive. But that's neither here nor there. Noticed this Martha because *Thane* was forever cornering the girl in passages and side-rooms. Sort of thing he does—daresay you've noticed it yourself. Fellow comes the rake over anything in skirts."

"Really, Mr. Finch-Hatton," I replied mildly. "You strike terror in a maiden's heart."

Jupiter looked discomfited. "Don't hold with it myself. Daresay Thane only does it from boredom. I mean to say— fellow must be blue as megrim up at the Castle! Sister taken up for murder! Nobody to speak with except that mother of his, who'd freeze the blood of the hottest hellborn babe—and nothing much to entertain in poor James's sisters. But all the same—doesn't do to meddle with the servants. Not good *ton.*"

"Should you have called the affair a persecution on Thane's part," I asked thoughtfully, "or a mutual dalliance?"

Jupiter rubbed his nose thoughtfully. "The two tended to part company whenever I hove into view, so I've no way of judging. What went on when the whole house was abed, I shouldn't like to conjecture. Shabby thing if I did—no real proof Thane's a bad'un—and besides, girl's dead. *De mortuis,* and all that."

"Was Captain MacCallister aware of Thane's interest in that quarter?"

"The Captain doesn't chuse to meddle with Thane," Jupiter said succinctly. "Ask me, he meant to get his fair lady away from the household as soon as possible, and leave the dirty dishes behind. Trouble is, plan went awry. Fair lady's in gaol. Captain's up to his neck in dirty dishes."

I sighed and glanced at Fanny. "Is Julian Thane *truly* a dirty dish?"

Jupiter smiled crookedly, his countenance suffused with a shrewd self-knowledge. "Don't like the fellow above half, ma'am. Too dashing for his own good, and cuts me out with your niece whenever he sees the chance. So take anything I chuse to say with a grain of salt. Must wonder, all the same, why we came up with him this morning near that coppice."

"The girl had been killed hours before," I reminded him, gently.

"Know it. What I mean to say is: Looks like he'd been intending to meet her there."

I thought of the young man on the plunging black horse, halted on the path by the coppice, and the dog yapping at his feet. When we came up with him, he had been eager to turn us back—and ready with his tale of a visit to Fanny. I had wondered how Thane could contemplate such an errand—however charming he found my niece—when it was Fanny's people who had placed his sister in gaol.

"Reckon the coppice was a habit of theirs," Jupiter said wisely. "Stands to reason somebody besides Thane and Martha knew of it, too—and made use of the place for his own ends."

I stared at him, my mind working. Jupiter might actually have seized on the truth. "You mean—"

He nodded. "Girl went happily enough to her death. Thought it was *Thane* she was going to meet."

CHAPTER TWENTY-EIGHT

Ghosts

"We cannot kick our heels, or make much fuss,
But emotions never fade, and that's the truth."

GEOFFREY CHAUCER, "THE STEWARD'S PROLOGUE"

THURSDAY, 28 OCTOBER 1813

As predicted, I passed a wretched night, the cold in my head coming on with force. By Wednesday morning, I was discovered by the housemaid in so feverish a state that Fanny was roused, and was made anxious enough to summon Susannah Sackree, the Knight family's ancient nurse. Sackree hovered by my bedside in awful silence—awful for a loquacious old woman who stands not an inch over four feet, and is easily as wide—and pronounced me at death's door.

"That Mr. Scudamore did ought to be sent for, miss," she told Fanny, "but it's doubtful as he'll be able to do much for our Miss Jane, but ease the end."

I might have burst out in laughter had my head ached less, and had I been less mindful (even on the verge of delirium) of Fanny's history. A girl who has witnessed her own mother pass inexplicably from hearty good health to the coldness of a shroud, in the interval between dinner and bed, is never again to be remiss in summoning the apothecary. Indeed, the unfortunate Mr. Scudamore—reconciled or not to his scandalous wife—was rejected immediately in favour of a true physician, and a groom despatched with Miss Knight's compliments, to summon Dr. Bredloe from his breakfast-parlour at Farnham.

By noon that much-tried man had pulled up in his gig and mounted the grand staircase at Godmersham, to be received by me in all the splendour of yellow walls and damask hangings, sneezing pitifully beneath my best lace cap.

"Foolish," he said succinctly. "Very foolish, Miss Austen. You ought to have left that wretched girl to the manservant and been snug at home hours before you were. I shall be obliged to cup you, ma'am."

"After all the blood-letting we have witnessed?" I protested feebly. But Bredloe would not be gainsaid—a basin and razor were produced, his frock coat discarded, and my vein opened.

I *detest* being bled.

To divert my mind from the distasteful business, I studied the view from my window—indifferent, it being another day of rain—and interrogated Bredloe.

"You succeeded in carrying Martha to Chilham?"

"She lies even now in the publick house in the village."

"And the inquest is to be held—?"

"Tomorrow at noon, in the same place."

"Must Fanny attend? It was she who discovered the body."

"I cannot like to see Miss Knight in such a place," Bredloe objected brusquely. "A distressful scene, for a young lady. And *you* are far too ill to give evidence, Miss Austen. Your statement will suffice. I have required Mr. Julian Thane to attend, however, as he was in some wise the girl's master—and present at the body's discovery."

Her master. Such a curious word.

"I could wish your brother were here, Miss Austen—but to delay the business is inadvisable, given the state of the corpse, and the fact that it must still travel some miles to Wold Hall for interment."

The faint smell of blood dripping into the basin at my bed-side, coupled with fever, conjured a fiendish image of the dead girl in my mind; I closed my eyes tightly and shuddered.

"Do not excite yourself with conjecture, Miss Austen. It can do you no good. Your pulse is tumultuous."

"You intend to bring in a verdict of murder, I suppose?"

"—By Persons Unknown. There is nothing else to be done. The naming of the culprit I shall leave to Mr. Knight."

At length, when I lay slack upon my pillows and attempted only with difficulty to keep my eyes open, the doctor pro-nounced himself satisfied, and ordered Sackree to set about composing a paregoric draught, which disgusting mixture I was required to drink down under Bredloe's eye.

"You will sleep now," he said confidently, "and provided there is no putrid sore throat, or inflammation of the lung, I think you will go on very well."

Sackree snorted, her hands on her hips. The doctor cast her a jaundiced eye. "A little white wine whey in an hour, Nurse, and perhaps some restorative mutton broth."

"Arrowroot jelly," Sackree pronounced with finality, "and a hot mustard bath to the feet."

"Not until after she has slept," Bredloe returned, "and that, some hours." He donned his frock coat and bowed.

"Sir," I called hoarsely as he reached the door, "pray find out Mr. Finch-Hatton before you leave this house."

"Finch-Hatton? —The Exquisite who made himself useful yesterday, in parading his horse about the Downs?"

I smiled weakly. "He is not unintelligent, I assure you. You might speak with him before your inquest. Jupiter—that is to say, Mr. Finch-Hatton—believes Martha and Julian Thane were in the habit of trysting in that coppice."

"Thane, who is Mrs. MacCallister's brother?"

I refused to waste energy on redundancies. "Were I you, Doctor, I should learn who *else* at Chilham suspected the affair—and what use they made of the intelligence."

Bredloe stared at me some moments, his entire countenance alive with interest. Then he nodded once, and quitted the room.

I was most unwell the remainder of Wednesday, the blood-letting having done little to cool my feverish head; and tho' Fanny appeared to exclaim and sympathise, I would not have her sitting up with a sick aunt when Mr. Finch-Hatton was eager for diversion downstairs, and my nephews were about the business of packing for Oxford, and the Moores were expending their final hours under Godmersham's roof as tho' determined to wring from it the last full measure of enjoyment.

And so my care was consigned to the redoubtable Sackree, who relished the task enough to continually disturb me by plumping my pillows, and building up the fire or shielding me from its heat as the occasion required, muttering "Death's Door" to herself all the while. When the long afternoon had passed and my white wine whey was all drunk up, I alarmed her by rejecting the mutton broth entirely, and requesting that the curtains be drawn against the early autumn dark. "Failing, poor lamb," she muttered, and enquired if I had any final words for the Master, as the pore gennulman was certain to miss the Crisis that awaited me this night. I told her firmly that I should speak to the Master myself when he returned on the morrow—at which she shook her head dolefully, and asked whether I did not wish my Last Thoughts to be writ down for all my relations, and if Miss Fanny weren't the best body to effect the Sacred Duty? At this I lost all patience with the creature, and suggested that she return to the schoolroom—where Master George Moore was undoubtedly in need of her caresses as he prepared to quit Godmersham on the morrow. Sackree is so attached to this place, that she feels a depth of horror for those obliged to part from it, and all her warm sympathy was exerted towards the child. She cast a doubtful eye at the clock, and another at my bed. I closed my eyes firmly and emitted a snore.

I MUST HAVE DROPPED OFF IN EARNEST, BECAUSE THE NEXT thing I knew the rattle of carriage wheels broke through my slumber and brought me bolt upright in bed.

The fire was gone out, the Yellow Room was chill, and a grey luminosity at the edge of the draperies suggested night was giving way to a feeble dawn. Whatever Bredloe had put in his paregoric draught—or however much blood he had taken—his physick had done its work: I had slept nearly twelve hours round the clock. My fever had broken—and my brother was come home.

I slipped from beneath the covers and reached for the dressing gown draped over a chair. My entire frame ached, and my head remained heavy, but my thoughts were clear at last. I steadied myself against the chair a moment, then crept across the cold floor to the door and opened it a crack. Edward was banging on his own portal as if to wake the dead; the bolts were thrown, and all the servants still asleep.

I made my way down the stairs and reached the Great Hall just as Johncock, Edward's butler, staggered across it in his nightshirt, a single candle raised high. I sank down on the stairs, huddled my gown about me, and watched him set down his light to throw back the heavy bolts.

My brother strode into the house, tossing his hat and

gloves on the central table. He looked tired, cross, and every day his six-and-forty years.

"Good morning, Johncock."

"Good morning, sir. Trust your journey was comfortable, sir?"

"Tolerable enough. It is over, in any case."

I rose from the stairs, the white stuff of my gown as ghostly as a shade's in the dimness of the hall. Edward started, and stepped backwards, as my form fluttered upwards; his hand lifted involuntarily to his eyes, as tho' he could not believe the evidence of his senses. An expression of mingled yearning and horror o'erspread his countenance like nothing I had seen before.

"Good God, what is it?" I cried—and the dreadful look vanished.

"Jane," he said with effort. "I thought—that is to say—" He swallowed convulsively. "I did not think to see you there."

Johncock was staring hard at his master, as tho' Edward had thrown off a fit. The candle wavered in his hand, spilling hot wax on the polished marble floor.

Comprehension swept over me. In the half-light, with exhaustion hard upon him, my brother had thought he glimpsed a shade in earnest—that the spirit of his lost, beloved Elizabeth had awaited his return on the stairs. I knew, then, that despite the passage of five years he still looked for her everywhere—that he *expected* to glimpse her one day, flitting through Bentigh's allée, or lingering behind one of the temple's columns. Perhaps he *had* seen his Lizzy at Godmersham before this, haunting his footsteps. Who was I to say? But my heart twisted within me, and a painful knot formed in my throat. Edward, who possessed *so much*—his wealth and good fortune were the envy of all his brothers—yet lacked the one thing necessary to his happiness.

"We did not expect you so soon." I stepped woodenly to

the floor. My voice sounded queer in my own ears—heavy and forced, as it seemed sometimes when I cajoled my mother out of her sullens. "The boys *will* be pleased you are come back in time to bid them farewell."

"I have much to tell you." Edward pressed his fingers against his eyes. "But first I must sleep. Will you breakfast with me, Jane—let us say, at eight o'clock?"

"There is an inquest at noon," I told him, "in the village of Chilham. I think it would be as well if you were there."

CHAPTER TWENTY-NINE

The Plantation Steward's Boy

The young man's appearance seemed sound, to a casual eye,
But deep in his heart lay the arrow of which he might die. . . .

GEOFFREY CHAUCER, "THE LANDOWNER'S TALE"

28 OCTOBER 1813, CONT.

"YOUR ERRAND IN LONDON PROSPERED?" I ENQUIRED AS
I poured Edward a cup of coffee. It was now half-past eight,
and we had met again in the grey light of the breakfast-
parlour while the rest of the household still slumbered.
Edward had stayed to hear my tale of the maid's death,
frowning over Fanny's discovery of the corpse; listened to an
account of Bredloe's conclusions, and Finch-Hatton's conjectures; then repaired to his bedchamber to snatch a few hours'
sleep. I spent the interval in refreshing my appearance, donning a suitable gown for day wear, and writing down the previous account in my journal; by seven, I was longing for
coffee, and heard the movements of the servants below-stairs
with considerable relief.

"If by *prospered* you would suggest that I know more at

present than I did when I quitted Kent two days ago—then indeed, Jane, my errand prospered. But I fear it is in a manner that is likely to cost me much effort, time, and reputation."

My brother tossed off these words with such suppressed savagery that I was astounded, the coffee pot dangling from my hand.

"I have set free the one man I ought to have kept caged," he said, "and have already despatched orders that Sir Davie Myrrh, and that scoundrel he chuses to call his solicitor, be clapped in irons by any who chance to espy them."

"Not truly!" I cried. "I was correct, then, in believing I had seen Mr. Burbage before—at the inquest into Fiske's death?"

"Yes, Jane, he undoubtedly attended the inquest. Tho' as I have not seen the fellow again to speak to, I have not been able to wring a confession from him on that point."

I set down the coffee pot. "Pray speak plainly, Edward."

"Very well—I shall leave off being clever, and attempt to be patient. I shall start at the beginning, and tell you the whole."

And so, as my brother consumed a beefsteak and I dipped a few fingers of toast into my coffee—I heard a round tale.

Edward had begun his London odyssey with a visit to India House, where the name of Sir Davie Myrrh was not unknown. He was able to corroborate much of the seaman's phantastickal stories, and learnt that he had indeed been glimpsed in Ceylon last year, but had been little heard from of late; it was believed the baronet was voyaging in the West Indies at present. For further intelligence, Edward was directed to the chambers of Sir Davie's solicitors—Mssrs. Reeve and Bobbit, of Lincoln's Inn.

"*Not* Burbage at all," I supplied. "How curious!"

"—Tho' Mr. Reeve was familiar with Burbage's name and history," Edward continued. "The solicitor had no notion

Burbage was passing himself off as Sir Davie's man, nor that his client had been languishing in Canterbury gaol, and was most distressed to think that Sir Davie found no use for the talents of Reeve and Bobbit in such a pass. He apprehended why, of course, once I described the circumstances of our interview. Sir Davie, so Mr. Reeve confessed, lives in the grip of a singular obsession—and it was *that* which brought him to Canterbury, rather than any plan of Curzon Fiske's. Fiske was merely a convenient tool to a greater end—tho' the unfortunate rogue had no idea of it."

"What sort of obsession?"

Edward pushed aside his plate with a sigh. "Do you recollect Sir Davie saying that he once possessed estates in Jamaica—sugar plantations, naturally—as well as Kildane Hall in England?"

"I recollect he referred to them, but—"

"—he swaddled both in a fine-woven cloth of reminiscence and adventure that diverted our attention from the essential point. Sir Davie, in his years of wandering the globe, managed to lose Kildane Hall and all his family's hard-won fortune."

"Was he a gamester, like Curzon Fiske?"

"I should say rather that he was careless—and too trusting of other men, who took advantage of his complaisance. The firm of Reeve and Bobbit has acted in the baronetcy's interest for generations—Reeve himself knew Sir Davie's father well—and he maintains that Kildane's revenues were exhausted by a combination of poor management on the part of its steward, in whose hands Sir Davie left the business of the estate, and the greed of that same man—who absconded to the Americas with thousands of pounds in estate income. During Sir Davie's protracted absence, Reeve undertook to write to him, earnestly representing in what poor case Kildane stood—and was answered after some months by Sir

Davie's demand that he *mortgage* Kildane, and forward the funds thus received to *Jamaica,* where Sir Davie's plantations stood in urgent need of support. This Reeve did—tho' with a heavy heart, for he did not like to see a noble English place made to support a failing concern half a world away. However, it was done—and a bare eighteen months later Reeve was informed that the Jamaican plantation had failed, the land was to be sold, and that Kildane must be made over to its lien-holders in payment on the debt. You may imagine how powerless the solicitor felt, Jane."

"It is a wreck of considerable proportions," I agreed. "But how came this about? I had understood there was a fortune to be made in sugar!"

"That is because you are familiar with Old Mr. Wildman," Edward said with the first sign of satisfaction I had heard in his voice, "who has prospered in the Jamaican trade—and curiously enough, it is upon Wildman that the tale turns."

"Is Mr. Wildman acquainted with Sir Davie Myrrh?"

"Not at all, to my knowledge," Edward replied, "but he knows his late Jamaican plantation too well. It was Wildman who drove Sir Davie to ruin in those parts, so Mr. Reeve assures me, through a concerted effort at competition—and some ruthless methods no gentleman should have stooped to employ. There was a mysterious fire in a sugar mill, I collect, that brought production to a standstill, and a revolt among the slaves that wreaked havoc with the baronet's harvest. Wildman was then the chief steward of the famous Quebec Estate—the largest plantation in Jamaica, four times the size of Sir Davie's holdings, with four times the number of slaves required to work it. It was the Quebec Estate, Jane, which Wildman eventually bought from Mr. William Beckford; and it is the Quebec Estate that afforded our neighbour the wealth to purchase Chilham Castle, some decades ago, when he determined to return to England with his Creole bride."

"What has all this to do with Curzon Fiske—or Mr. Burbage, if it comes to that?"

"Burbage is the son of Sir Davie Myrrh's late plantation steward. He grew up in Jamaica, and was happy there—until his father shot himself, when the baronet was ruined. The lad was left with no home, no prospects, and nowhere to turn—except to Sir Davie."

"And both men blame Mr. Wildman for their misfortunes?" I said, with growing comprehension.

"As Reeve vowed—it is an obsession with Sir Davie to see himself revenged upon the family at Chilham Castle."

We were both silent an instant, as Edward's words lingered in the air. "But why Curzon Fiske?" I demanded. "What possible rôle had he to play?"

"That of victim, of course."

"I do not understand."

Edward leaned across the table with all the intimacy of a conspirator. "Fiske, you will recall, met up with Sir Davie Myrrh in Bangalore, and spent a number of idle months with the baronet in Ceylon. I suspect that the two canvassed their grievances a good deal during the period—and discovered a mutual object of hatred in Old Mr. Wildman of Chilham Castle. The one saw him as a ruthless despoiler of wealth, and the other as the enemy of his marital hopes."

I seized my brother's arm. "I had almost forgot! Jupiter told me the whole of that final evening three years since, when Fiske gambled his last—and put up his wife as stake! Our own George Moore nearly *won Adelaide at cards,* Edward—but that Mr. Lushington would have it Fiske cheated!"

"What in God's name are you speaking of, Jane?"

"The story will keep, my dear, until such time as you may turn your attention to it. But you were saying that Fiske had every reason to hate Old Wildman—pray continue."

"I think it probable that Fiske and Sir Davie saw their paths aligned. They quitted Ceylon with the intention of repairing to Canterbury—Fiske, in an effort to regain his wife, and the baronet, with the object of being avenged. It was Fiske's misfortune that he did not perceive *he* was to be the agent of Sir Davie's satisfaction. Burbage, however, was fully alive to it."

"Edward, are you suggesting that Sir Davie *killed* Fiske, and Burbage helped him to do it?"

"I can think of nothing more probable! One of them—I presume Sir Davie, as it was he who pretends to have stood in the back garden awaiting the message from Adelaide's maid—stole young James Wildman's pistol from the gun room while all the wedding guests were occupied at the ball; he may then have passed it to Burbage, along with the intelligence that Fiske would be waiting near St. Lawrence Church; and the thing was done."

"Fiske was murdered and poor James's gun left in the churchyard," I murmured. "Yes, I do see. They thought there could be nothing more natural, in the eyes of a suspicious Law, than for a *Wildman* to rid the world of Curzon Fiske on the night of his wife's bigamous marriage—only think of the scandal Fiske's timely death should avert! To burden James with the guilt is revenge, indeed; did Sir Davie succeed in bringing Old Mr. Wildman's beloved heir to the scaffold, he should visit upon Chilham Castle such a manifold tragedy! It is in every way diabolical!"

"You have stated my frame of the case in a nutshell," my brother concluded.

I glanced at him curiously. "But what of Martha, lying cold in the Chilham publick house?"

He shrugged. "Perhaps she saw Sir Davie steal the gun—or hand it to Burbage. And when Fiske was found, she began to talk."

"It *seems* quite apt," I said uneasily. "And yet—"

"And yet, we have not a single shred of evidence, from beginning to end. Not a particle of proof. We have helped the very men we suspect, to walk out of their cell; and wished them godspeed on their voyage to the Galápagos. I swear I could put a gun to my *own head,* Jane, when I consider of it!"

"What has been done, to recover them?"

"When I quitted the chambers of Reeve and Bobbit, I went to the Bow Street Runners—they are given to meeting at the Bear, a publick house in Covent Garden—"

"—not two steps from Henry's lodgings in Henrietta Street," I finished. "I am well aware. The Runners are even now in pursuit of Sir Davie Myrrh?"

"Their first object must be the principal ports. I am in no wise convinced that the Galápagos is truly the baronet's destination; the offering may have been a blind, intended to throw us off the scent. I have urged the Runners to search the Channel ports, as well as those giving on to the North Sea."

"I understand the Baltic is lovely this time of year. And now?"

"I must attend an inquest." Edward rose. "You are looking hagged, Jane, and decidedly unwell. You have taken a cold in the head, from an injudicious gallivanting about the country. Pray lie down upon your bed this morning, like a dutiful aunt."

"And miss the opportunity of speeding George Moore and all his family from the house?" I shook my head in disdain. "They have only to vanish down the sweep, Edward, with Harriot's brave handkerchief fluttering, for me to require Fanny to instantly harness her Rowan. I intend to pay a call upon Chilham Castle while you are at the village publick house—and she must drive me."

My brother's eyes narrowed. "You will not betray a word of my conjectures?"

"Not a syllable! I merely wish to know how dear Mrs. Wildman bears the protracted blessing of Mrs. Thane's continued presence. I have been sadly neglecting my duty; I have been tardy in paying my calls. And you know Jupiter is to leave us once your boys have gone to Oxford. Fanny will be wanting a diversion for her spirits. She shall sadly miss his company; he is the most engaging fellow."

"You might drop a hint in Thane's ear that his sister is very soon likely to be freed," Edward said doubtfully, "but do not allow that young buck to be waltzing with Fanny, pray!"

And so he left me.

I sat a while longer over my coffee and toast, revolving all that Edward had told me. If I indulged a very different set of conjectures than the Magistrate's, in my brother's absence, I am sure he shall be the first to forgive me.

CHAPTER THIRTY

A Convenient Indisposition

How can men, you say, defend the wall
Of a castle so assailed; it is bound to fall.

GEOFFREY CHAUCER, "THE WIFE OF BATH'S PROLOGUE"

28 OCTOBER 1813, CONT.

IN THE END, OF COURSE, IT WAS PAST NOON BEFORE GEN-tle Rowan was harnessed and Fanny at leisure to drive me to the Wildmans', for the morning was spent in bidding farewell to Young Edward and George, and all their sundry belongings, which were strapped to Edward's travelling-coach for the first leg of their journey by post to Oxford. They are to bait at Lenham, and spend a night in London, before journeying into Oxfordshire. Young Edward elected to ride his favourite hunter behind the coach, leaving his younger brother to the splendid isolation of its interior—or what *should* be splendid isolation, once the Moore family quits it. Mr. and Mrs. Moore elected to have a *saving* in their post charges, by travelling as far as Lenham at Edward's expence, and with his exasperated sons; from there, they shall have to fend for themselves in achieving their own home at Wrotham. But I have hopes of Harriot's greater comfort in future: in all the flurry of strapping bandboxes to the rear of the coach, and shifting my nephews' things so as to have their own nearer to hand, Harriot found a moment to embrace me, and whisper in confidence her thanks for my encouragement and understanding.

"And only reflect, Jane! Mr. Moore assures me that he perceives no *further need* for charitable works in the Indies—and our gold is to remain *quite our own*, henceforth!"

I tucked away this morsel of intelligence, as further confirmation of my suspicions—that Curzon Fiske had steadily blackmailed his old school friend George Moore, in return for silence on a delicate subject: that the late Archbishop's son had gambled at cards, for the stake of another man's wife.

My brother Edward had sufficient time only to offer his guests a distracted farewell, clasp his younger son to his bosom, and take his elder's hand, before being gone on horseback in the direction of Chilham.

"Ought to take leave myself," Mr. Finch-Hatton said doubtfully as he gazed at Fanny; and tho' the young man has risen much in my esteem, and I should not tire of learning more of him, I could not in good conscience encourage him to linger. He should look both too particular with regard to Fanny, and too diffident in declaring himself—and I cannot believe him *ready* to declare himself in a manner calculated to make my niece happy. There is too little of the ardent lover, and too much of the boy, still raging in the man of five-and-twenty.

Of her own feelings on the subject, Fanny betrayed nothing—unless one may interpret an air of distracted impatience, as evidence of her desire for her visitor to be gone. She is the female least susceptible in the entire neighbourhood to

Jupiter's charms, which cannot argue for his suit's prospering. I find, as these weeks of my visit to Godmersham wear away, that I cannot penetrate Fanny's heart at all—have no notion, indeed, of *which* qualities in a gentleman she most prizes—but should argue in favour of the quiet probity and sound understanding of John Plumptre succeeding, where Jupiter's casual presumption cannot.

—Or should have said so, before the advent of the dangerous Julian Thane. I fear Fanny has noted his inattention since that final encounter over the body of the maid—and that her spirits, so ready to soar at a clandestine note or unexpected posy, a stolen gallop of a Sunday afternoon—are sadly fallen in the absence of Thane's tributes. I wish it were otherwise; I cannot like a fellow who dallies with his servants; and tho' I have only Jupiter's suspicions in the case, I must suspect Mr. Thane's too-ready address and persistent proximity to danger. He seems the sort of reckless young man who was born to be hanged—a rueful encomium, when applied to a rogue one half-admires, but terrifyingly apt in the present instance. I could wave him heartily from the neighbourhood, for the sake of Fanny's tranquility; time alone shall restore her to peace.

Jupiter, in the end, took himself off with a langourous bow. Once this last of our male companions was sped down the sweep, I afforded Fanny an interval to attend to household matters. There were all the orders to be given to Mrs. Driver and Johncock, regarding the airing of beds and the inventory of the stores, the neat dinner she wished for and the number of places to be laid—no more than Fanny, Edward, and myself, unless our peace is to be entirely cut up by the unexpected arrival of some one of the Knights' acquaintance. Muttering a quick prayer against such a tedious event, I ascended the stairs to put on my carriage dress whilst Fanny should be occupied. The cold in my head raged unabated, and as I surveyed my countenance in the gilt mirror that adorned one wall of the Yellow Room, I saw with resignation that I should present a wilted appearance at Chilham, with reddened nose and streaming eyes, the very picture of spinsterly decrepitude.

It was full one o'clock before we were tooling along the road at last.

"How glad I am for this airing!" Fanny exclaimed as she snapped the reins over Rowan's back. "You cannot conceive, Aunt, how tied to Godmersham I am when the house is full of visitors—my very rambles through the gardens are constrained, from a fear of neglecting some duty. I should feel myself delightfully at liberty now, were it not that a certain dread must accompany this visit. Circumstances are so awkward."

"Meaning," I said delicately, "that tho' you are disinclined to encounter Mrs. Thane, in view of the gaoling of her daughter, you look forward to meeting once more with her son, and testing how adversity has tried his admiration of your excellent looks?"

"Aunt Jane!" Fanny cried; and her ready colour rose in her cheeks. I left her to pursue the subject, if she chose; she elected to hone her attention on managing her horse's ribbons. I had other concerns to occupy my mind as we bowled towards Chilham, and left her in peace.

Tho' I had as yet said nothing to my brother Edward, I detected a fatal flaw in the net he had spun for his killers of preference, Sir Davie Myrrh and Mr. Burbage—namely, that they could not be presumed to both *flee* the Kingdom by way of the nearest port, and *linger* in the neighbourhood to murder the unfortunate maid Martha. To entertain such conflicting purposes, as Edward plainly did, was to force the crimes to fit his interesting solution. I admired the entire fabric of Sir Davie's history—the motives for revenge it argued—the indignation of the unfortunate Mr. Burbage, at his father's ruin and demise—the very natural impulses that must bring both men into collusion with the late Curzon Fiske, and indeed, to Canterbury, where the final scene of Fiske's long pilgrimage was played. To destroy Old Wildman by employing his son's pistol, in the hope of placing James on the scaffold, should have been a stroke of genius only Lucifer might fully enjoy. Edward's theory was neat; it was ingenious; it was seductive in the extreme. But my doubts lingered. They swirled about the dead figure of Martha. I found my brother's confidence in Sir Davie's guilt, arising as it had in total ignorance of this second murder, to be lacking. Perhaps Edward should reconsider, once he looked upon Martha's cold form.

"You are very silent, Aunt," Fanny observed as she took the left turning in the northern road towards Chilham and its castle.

"I am considering of motive," I replied, "which must be a consuming subject for any woman. Our hearts so often work in subtle ways, towards complex ends, that the placidity of our outward appearance will invariably mislead the observer."

Fanny glanced at me sidelong. "Is this meant for me, Aunt?"

"I think rather of that unfortunate creature in Canterbury gaol—whose heart remains obscure, perhaps even to those who love her best. I should wish you to study *all* the ladies of Chilham, Fanny, while we pay our call. I should dearly value your opinion."

"And what will you be about, Aunt?"

"I shall study the men," I replied, and subsided into silence for the remainder of the journey.

WE WERE MET IN THE GREAT HALL BY THE BUTLER TWITCH. His countenance was grave, and he wore a black riband tied about his arm—in respect of the maid Martha, no doubt. I murmured a few words of condolence as I drew off my bonnet, and he inclined his head.

"I believe you discovered her, ma'am?"

"Miss Knight saw her first—but I was of the walking party, as was Mr. Finch-Hatton."

"—And you met Mr. Thane, as was riding in the direction of Godmersham." Twitch's gaze fixed on my own; he was no fool, and would not wish to appear to gossip, but neither was he insensible to the murderous construction that might be placed upon the presence of that young gentleman so near a corpse. "Mr. Thane is not at home, being obliged to attend the crowner's panel, but my mistress shall be happy to receive you, I am sure. If you will follow me, ma'am—"

"What do you mean, sirrah, by making free with my son's private concerns?" a harsh voice demanded. "You ought to be horsewhipped. And if you were in my employ, that is *exactly* how you should be served. I should place the whip in my son's hands, and have the satisfaction of seeing him exact revenge himself. Insolent scum!"

It was Mrs. Thane, of course, poised on the stairs descending to the Great Hall. Her eyes blazed in her haggard face, and her hands gripped the baluster so fiercely that the frail bones showed through the mottled skin. She appeared to have aged several years in the days since her daughter's arrest; and she made no pretence of noticing Fanny or me, as we stood beside the butler. In the fog of her present torment, we must be invisible.

Or perhaps we were merely beneath her notice.

The butler did not reply—indeed, he did not even spare Mrs. Thane a look—but led us in stately fashion towards the gallery. "Mrs. Wildman will receive you in the drawing-room," he intoned.

"Thank you, Twitch," I managed unsteadily, aware of the crazed figure to my back. Even Fanny hurried a little in her pace, so as not to be left hindmost. We both of us dreaded to be the next object of attack; Mrs. Thane's vituperation could chill the blood.

"Poor creature," Fanny murmured low; "she has undoubtedly suffered in recent days! To see her daughter publickly shamed—to fear the worst of the scaffold—one cannot be amazed at her agony. It is a wonder she is capable of quitting her bed!"

"She doesn't care *that* for Miss Addie." Twitch angrily snapped his fingers, to our considerable surprize. "There's only room enough in that shrivelled heart for Mr. Julian—he's sun and moon both to Mrs. Thane, aye, and Prince of Wold Hall into the bargain! Much joy may that young devil bring her!"

Fanny raised her brows in wonder, but there was no time for conjecture or comment; we had achieved the drawing-room, and from the comfort of her sopha Mrs. Wildman was lifting a languid hand in greeting.

"Such palpitations as you must have suffered! I wonder you did not swoon! Was there a great deal of gore spread all about?"

"Mother!" Charlotte cried reprovingly.

Any plan I might have harboured, of surveying the gentlemen of Chilham on their home ground, was defeated at the start. The men of the house—Old Mr. Wildman, his son James, Captain MacCallister, and Julian Thane—were gone to the inquest in the village two miles distant. As Dr. Bredloe had convened his panel at noon, however, and the hour was now half-past one, we might reasonably expect to see the men soon returned; it was for this reason, no doubt, that Mrs. Thane had remained fixed on the staircase in the Great Hall, in hopes of greeting her son. It was for Fanny and me to entertain the ladies of Chilham during the tedious interval; we might have been delivered to their avid questioning expressly for that purpose; and the mistress of the Castle, at least, was determined to milk every drop of excitement from our threadbare phrases.

"Poor Miss Knight! How you must have felt it!" Mrs. Wildman exclaimed with ready sympathy.

"But she had Jupiter to support her," Louisa observed with a sidelong glance, "and I am sure there can be nothing so romantickal as for a lady to find herself in such an interesting situation, with *such* a gentleman!"

"I declare I should swoon regardless, merely for the pleasure of having Mr. Finch-Hatton catch me!" Charlotte added with a tinkle of laughter, as tho' the small matter of a seventeen-year-old girl with a severed throat was not worth consideration. "Is Jupiter yet at Godmersham, Fanny?"

"He departed for Eastwell this morning," my niece answered. "My brothers having quitted the house for Oxford, there was nothing to keep Mr. Finch-Hatton longer."

"Such modesty," Louisa murmured, with a look for her sister that spoke volumes to my jaundiced eye. The Wildman girls were disposed to see in Fanny a rival. On account of Finch-Hatton, who had been staying at the Castle nearly a week before coming to us—or Julian Thane?

"And what do you think of this shocking business of Adelaide's?" Mrs. Wildman said in a half-whisper, leaning towards me from her couch as tho' to shield the ears of the younger girls. "I should not be saying so, when Mr. Knight is our magistrate, and our dearest neighbour these many years—but I confess I believe he must be mistaken! That our Addie should take James's pistol and shoot her husband— impossible! But Mr. Knight will not believe her! And now this second distressing death—"

I might have seized the opportunity to assure Mrs. Wildman that her cousin should soon be released; I might have pressed her on the interesting question of *which* among her acquaintance might rejoice in seeing her son James accused of murder; but as I parted my lips to speak, I sneezed.

It was a small sound, discreetly suppressed, but fell upon Mrs. Wildman's ears as a thunderclap. She surveyed my reddened eyes and nose with keen attention, and started upright as I sneezed again.

"Miss Austen! You are unwell!"

"I was some hours exposed to the rain," I muttered from behind a square of linen, "the day of Martha's discovery."

"But of course! You should not be raised from your bed!"

I sighed lugubriously, and closed my eyes as tho' deprived of all strength. "I was most unwell yesterday, to be sure, but I could not consider of *myself* when so much trouble has descended upon this household, ma'am. I insisted that dear Fanny convey me to you as soon as I felt restored enough to rise, for I should never wish to be backwards in any attention to so close a neighbour of my brother's. I confess, however, that I feel most unwell. Perhaps the drive has proved a danger."

"You must certainly lie down in one of my bedchambers, Miss Austen, and if you feel equal to it—have a mustard bath to the feet."

With an energy unexpected in so indolent a creature, Mrs. Wildman hastened to pull the drawing-room bell, and at the ready appearance of a footman, required him to summon her housekeeper.

This excellent woman being already about the task of providing refreshment for the party in the drawing-room, in the form of pears from the Castle's own garden, a Stilton cheese, and various sweetmeats, the footman did not have far to look—and in a little while I found myself conveyed by Mrs. Twitch (for she was the butler's wife) to a comfortable bedchamber. There was no sign of the baleful Mrs. Thane on the stairs; perhaps she had given up her vigil, and retired to her rooms. I had an idea of her being lodged in a suite in the Castle's tower: a remote fastness, where she might prowl by midnight and fret over the fates of her children. None of Chilham's intimates seemed disposed to seek out her company—nor she, theirs.

I took off my pelisse and bonnet while Mrs. Twitch kindled a fire.

"Indisposed are you, ma'am?"

"A dreadful cold, taken while I waited for the doctor at the scene of the maidservant's murder," I said with calm precision.

Mrs. Twitch stared at me penetratingly. "You could not have took ill in better cause, if I may be so bold—for a sweeter girl never lived than Martha Kean, and how the Lord saw fit to serve her as he did—cut down like a lamb to the butcher—" She broke off, and stabbed viciously at the fire, which needed no encouragement to burn.

"How well did you know her?"

"Not so as to say *well*—she only come to us with Miss Addie, near a month ago. Mrs. MacCallister, I *should* say. But she was a taking little thing, and a day was as good as a month for knowing Martha. Not for her the high-in-the-instep airs of a lady's maid—*which* she was, *and* learning to be a Dresser. No task was too mean for her to undertake, for she'd grown up in service. Saw the lot of us as in some wise family. 'Can I carry the linen for you, Mrs. Twitch?' she'd say, and whisk it out of my hands before I could so much as answer; and was nothing but kindness to Scullery Nan, what hasn't enough wits for a baby, tho' she's full forty year old."

"Did the other maids befriend her?"

Mrs. Twitch sniffed. "Not they. *Jealous*. All four of 'em are Kentish born and bred, ma'am, and don't take easy to foreigners. Talked scandalous about Martha, they did, as having aims above her station—which'll be due to the letters, no doubt."

"Letters?" I had a sudden swift thought of Sir Davie Myrrh, summoning the girl to her lonely death with a missive sent by post. Edward's conjectures might prove correct after all.

"Aye. Martha knew her letters," Mrs. Twitch said simply. "Martha could read. *And* write. That's a rare talent below-stairs, let me tell you. Fair turned the other girls' noses, the way she was always tucking a bit of paper in her pocket."

Good Lord. A maidservant who could read. I had been thinking Martha was brought to the Downs in expectation of meeting Julian Thane—an assignation established in a whis-per, by a turning in the stairs. But a summons in a note might have been left her by anyone.

"I understand Martha belonged to Wold Hall. The Thanes must be terribly distressed."

"*He* is," Mrs. Twitch replied succinctly, "Martha having been a playmate of Miss Addie and Mr. Julian when a child, as will happen on a great estate—which is why Miss Addie chose to take the girl with her, as lady's maid, when she left to marry the Captain. Mr. Julian rode into Canterbury yester-day to break the news to his sister; and that Miss Addie should be forced to shoulder another grief is more than the good Lord ought to allow! But if *Mrs.* Thane turned a hair at Martha's loss I'd be fair amazed. *That* care-for-nobody!"

"She cares for her son, I gather."

"Near enough as to fall down and worship him," Mrs. Twitch returned with obvious contempt. "Aye, and in the teeth of his dislike—for it's my belief Mr. Julian can't abide sight nor sound of his mother. Never forgiven her, if you ask me, for her Turkish treatment of Miss Addie when she run off with Mr. Fiske. Thought to make a great match for her daughter, Mrs. Thane did—on account of the fortune she wanted, to save Wold Hall. Ready to sell Miss Addie to the highest bidder, she was. No wonder the poor mite fled across the Channel with the first rakehell that offered. I'll send up the mustard bath directly, ma'am."

The housekeeper curtseyed and pulled closed the bed-chamber door.

I had no great wish to plunge my feet into a steaming kettle of nostril-curling bath, but it seemed a small price to pay for verisimilitude. Feigning illness had won me the wisdom of Mrs. Twitch; and in the murder of a maid, one could do far worse than interrogate the housekeeper.

CHAPTER THIRTY-ONE

The Maid's Clutches

"I place your soul in his hands, my little child,
Obliged by your mother's sins, so soon to die."

GEOFFREY CHAUCER, "THE CLERIC'S TALE"

28 OCTOBER 1813, CONT.

I WAITED UNTIL THE MUSTARD BATH APPEARED IN THE hands of an upper housemaid, and allowed the girl to fuss over me, and arrange my skirts that I might set my feet in the steaming water without staining the fabric of my best—I may say my *only*—carriage gown before I attempted further researches. This particular maid I judged to be in her twenties, plain-featured and without the slightest suggestion of frivolity about her person; she wore no armband, and her visage did not bear the marks of weeping.

"I am sorry to cause so much trouble," I attempted. "I was so stupid as to stand in the rain some hours, a few days since, and caught cold as a result."

The maid's glance shifted towards me, then glided away; but her lips compressed. She was not the sort to be tempted by an oblique approach; I should be forced to confront her headlong.

"Were you at all acquainted with the unfortunate girl who met her death on the Downs?" I persisted.

"That Martha?" The maid shrugged. "I shared my room with her; but as for being *acquainted,* I don't hold with encouraging foreigners. She was no Kentishwoman. Of Leicestershire stock, was Martha—and terrible free in their ways, such folk be."

"In their ways?" I repeated as tho' perplexed. "What do you mean?"

A shuttered look came over the maid's face. "Don't mean nothing at'all, ma'am. Is the water hot enough for your liking?"

"It is very well, thank you. By free, would you suggest that Martha was *friendly*?"

"Aye, and to all the world—both above and below. No proper sense of place, had Martha—and look what it got her."

"You believe that she was murdered by a friend—and one not of her station?"

"No *friend* would cut a girl's throat," the housemaid returned drily. "If you've nothing further, ma'am, I'm wanted downstairs."

"Of course—thank you. You have been very kind. And I don't even know your name."

"Susan, ma'am." She bobbed a curtsey, her face wooden.

"Susan," I repeated brightly, and reached for the reticule dangling from my wrist. I pressed a shilling into her palm; she thanked me with a nod; and the door closed behind her.

I waited until the sound of brisk footsteps on drugget had died away. Then, pulling my dripping feet from the mustard bath, I hurriedly donned my stockings and boots.

THE SERVANTS' QUARTERS AT CHILHAM WERE IN THE SEC-ond attic two flights above. I chose to travel as silently as I might by the back service stair, and met no one at that hour, the staff being employed in meeting the wants and demands of the Wildman family and their guests. The stairs wound first past the main attic level, where the old day and night nurseries were housed, and the schoolrooms, where governesses had once attempted to teach Louisa and Charlotte to read Italian; but all were silent now, with the stale sensibility of disused rooms, and I did not chuse to linger.

A greater sense of life animated the servants' level, tho' no creature stirred. The ceiling was lower here, and numerous doorways gave onto the narrow passage, which curved with the hexagonal shape of the Castle. Light came only dimly through slits of windows intended to affect a medieval stile. I guessed that just the female staff were lodged in this aerie; in observation of the proprieties, the men would be housed below-stairs, near the kitchens and offices. Mr. and Mrs. Twitch, being senior staff and a married couple, probably merited a suite of rooms in that part of the house. It should not be too difficult, therefore, to discover the bedchamber Susan and Martha had shared. It should be the only one with a stripped cot and bare shelf on one side of the room.

What was it I hoped to discover, two days after the murder—two days that ought to have afforded anybody with a guilty conscience and mortal purpose time enough to ransack the maid's room? A scrap of paper, perhaps. A journal. If Martha could write, who knew what damning facts she might have set down? The girl had been murdered for a reason—and it must be because of something she *knew*, regarding the death of Curzon Fiske.

But I was fated never to find the maid's room. As I moved noiselessly around a curve in the hexagonal passage, a sinister figure loomed—silhouetted against the faint light seeping through the Castle's false battlements. Tall, thin, and severely coiffed, with a profile as handsome as an eagle's, and just as merciless. Mrs. Thane.

"What do you think you are doing here?" she demanded harshly, as I came to an abrupt halt.

"I might ask the same of you—were I so presumptuous."

She was standing, I observed, near one of the doors, which was firmly closed. On the point of exiting—or entering?

"My maid did not answer my bell," she said austerely. "So I came in search of her. What possible reason can you profess, Miss Austen, for invading these quarters?"

"The gentlemen are returned from the village, Mrs. Thane. I thought you must certainly wish to know."

It was a commendable lie; and it succeeded in its object. For the woman brushed past me imperiously in a rustle of silk, without vouchsafing another word.

To my surprise and secret gratification—few liars are so lucky as to be shielded by Fate in a cloak of seeming honesty—the gentlemen *had* returned from the inquest. Or rather, three of the gentlemen had returned. Julian Thane was not among them.

The absence was immediately perceived by his mother at her entrance into the drawing-room. She halted abruptly, and following too close behind, I nearly trod upon her heel.

"Where is he? Where is my son?"

Captain MacCallister turned from some activity among the decanters and crossed to Mrs. Thane, a glass of brandy in his hand. "Pray be seated, ma'am, and try a little of this cordial."

"I do not wish for brandy!" she exclaimed imperiously. "Where is Julian?"

"He has been taken up by Mr. Knight," said Old Mr. Wildman quietly from his position by the fire, "for the murder of Martha Kean. I am sorry for it."

A cry broke from the woman, and she wavered where she stood. I stepped forward to support her, but the Captain was before me, and led her towards a chair. She shook him off, however, with an expression of contempt, and remained upright, her blazing eyes fixed on poor Fanny's face. "Mr. Knight is the greatest fool! Julian—*murder* that girl? Calumny! Nonsense! An outrage! Her throat was cut; and had my son wished to kill her, his pistol should have sufficed. I am sure I do not know a keener shot than Julian."

The indifferent practicality of her words was such as must astonish. I observed Mr. Wildman close his eyes briefly in forbearance; his wife pressed a handkerchief to her lips in mute horror.

Fanny rose. There was a queer look of shock on her countenance that was painful to behold. "We have trespassed too long on your privacy. We must take our leave."

James Wildman moved towards her, one hand outstretched appealingly. "Pray do not regard it, Fanny; your father has done only what duty required, and cannot be blamed for having acted in a manner I am sure he found most distasteful. I expect it was the very *last* outcome he expected, to this morning's events. But the proofs against my cousin were such that Bredloe's panel could hardly ignore them. It was they who forced the Magistrate's hand, in bringing in a verdict of murder against Thane."

"What *proofs*?" Mrs. Thane demanded harshly. "What *possible proofs* could those unlettered men of the village weigh?"

James Wildman turned and regarded her steadily. "When Bredloe examined the maid's body yesterday at the publick house, he discovered a button of Julian's—for you may be sure that Julian identified it, it bore his vowels and was torn from his shooting coat of drab—clutched in the girl's fingers. She must have fought him as she died, and lying as she did, with her hands beneath her, the thing went undiscovered at the scene."

"Anyone might have worn that coat!" Mrs. Thane declared. "I am sure I have seen it lying discarded in the gun room any number of times in recent weeks."

"Indeed, ma'am," James rejoined mildly. "But there was also the note, written in Julian's hand—to which he swore."

"What note?"

For the first time, Mrs. Thane's voice quavered. Her countenance paled.

"A brief missive, establishing a time and place of meeting—*Six o'clock, by the lone coppice*. Bredloe found it in the maid's apron pocket. He conjectures that it was to retrieve the note—which my cousin may have forgot in the heat of violence—that Julian rode back up to the Downs later that morning. He was so misfortunate as to encounter the Godmersham party—and all was discovered."

"That *jade*!" Mrs. Thane ejaculated. Her countenance was now twisted with a terrifying fury, and her hands worked like a demon's. "That meddlesome, designing, *whorish* girl—raised in the bosom of Wold, and bent upon its destruction! I should have throttled her in her cradle, by all that's holy!"

"Ma'am!" Captain MacCallister cried, in a tone of shock. "The maid is dead!"

"Aye, and good riddance to her. I thought to send her away with Adelaide, and be free of her wiles forever—I thought to preserve my son's future happiness—but he *would* come with us, as must be natural for the wedding, and nothing I could do or say was sufficient to guard him against her. Serpent! Succubus of the Devil!"

"Succubus," Charlotte repeated in a hollow tone. "What in Heaven's name can you mean, Cousin?"

Mrs. Thane's eyes narrowed. "She was carrying his child, you little fool! A fine thing for Mr. Thane of Wold Hall—to be saddled with a serving-girl's bastard!"

CHAPTER THIRTY-TWO

Where There's a Will

"Let God on high drive me insane, and dead,
If I'm not good and true as any wife wed. . . ."

GEOFFREY CHAUCER, "THE WIFE OF BATH'S TALE"

28 OCTOBER 1813, CONT.

~

AS FANNY AND I TOOLED FOR HOME BEHIND A ROWAN longing to be once more in his stall, we espied a horseman galloping towards us along the Canterbury road—a rider revealed in a few moments as none other than the reviled Magistrate.

"Papa!" Fanny cried. "How *glad* I am to see you!"

"You have been to Chilham?" he enquired, reining in his mount. "You will have learnt the news?"

"Indeed—and most distressing we found it," I said.

"I am even now on my way to consult with Mr. Wildman. Do not wait dinner for my return, Fanny—you and your aunt might enjoy a comfortable coze by the fire in the absence of visitors. I shall take a cold collation once I am at home."

A comfortable coze. With a girl of twenty whose most romantickal notions had been brutally overthrown. My heart sank.

"Papa!"

Edward checked his horse and glanced down at his daughter. Her gloved hands were working at Rowan's reins. "Is it *certain*? There can be no mistake?"

Edward's lips compressed at the desperate entreaty in her voice. "I am sorry, Fanny. Thane denies it all—but the evidence is black against him. We must allow the Assizes to weigh the case; we must allow Justice to run its course."

"Do you not ask yourself," I interjected as my brother's horse danced impatience beneath him, "why any man should be fool enough to commit a *second* murder in the very teeth of your investigation? —A murder, moreover, done from personal motives that may be entirely unconnected to the Curzon Fiske case?"

"I imagine he did not *intend* to kill the girl. It was an act no doubt committed in a fit of passion."

"Nonsense! Nobody lures a maid to that lonely coppice with the note found in her pocket, and slits her neck with a knife he then prudently carries away—without *premeditation*. But to plan a murder, when the neighbouring magistrate has *already* incarcerated one's sister, is utter madness! I cannot believe Thane fool enough to do it."

"What would you say, Jane?" Edward demanded wearily. "Do not speak in riddles, pray."

I sighed. There is so much that must be explained to men. "Merely that had Thane *wished* to end the life of his mistress and bastard child, he might have done so at any time— preferably a month from now, in another locale entirely, when he was no longer so blatantly beneath your scrutiny. In short, the evidence may be black against him—but the evidence does not make sense."

"Am I then to ignore the button and note—both Thane's— that were found on Martha's person?"

I shrugged as Edward's horse tossed its head and neighed.

"Martha's killer clearly wore Thane's drab shooting coat. But Thane himself was *not* wearing it when Fanny and I met with him on the Downs."

"That is true!" Fanny cried eagerly. "He wore his black coat and leather breeches, with top boots—I particularly remarked the white cuff, so like that which Mr. Beau Brummell is supposed to wear. I thought it excessively dashing."

"The gush of blood from a slit throat should seriously stain the white tops of those boots," I murmured, "but perhaps Thane exchanged his murderous attire in the interval between killing the girl and returning to search her pockets some hours later. One imagines, however, that his bloodied clothes—including the interesting coat of drab—should then have been found in his bedchamber. Do you not *see*, Edward, that anyone at the Castle might have taken Thane's shooting coat from the gun room, as Thane's mother told us only an hour since? And disposed of it when the deed was done? As for the note—I have it on the authority of the Chilham housekeeper that Martha was forever tucking letters into her apron pocket. Thane might have pressed that summons upon her at any time—it might indeed refer to an altogether different meeting, some days past. There was no date on the paper, I collect?"

"There was not." Edward gazed at me with an arrested expression. "Must you always complicate matters, Jane, with questions that are entirely unanswerable?"

"Two people have died, Edward, and died in pain and violence. I should like the proper person to hang for it."

He frowned. "You are persuaded the murders were done by the same hand. Whose, then? Sir Davie Myrrh's? Burbage's? Explain, if you may, how either man should have come by the shooting coat of drab. Neither has been seen in the neighbourhood of Chilham, much less the Castle's gun room, of late."

"Have you had *any* word of them?"

"Burbage was taken this morning in Deal," Edward said

abruptly, "attempting to hire a private vessel for the crossing to France. He should be conveyed to Canterbury gaol by nightfall. Sir Davie, I regret, is still at large."

"Then you may pursue your researches yet a few hours," I assured him affably. "We have delayed you already too long, with our vexing questions. May I suggest, Edward—when you speak to Old Wildman—that you enquire most narrowly into the terms of his Will, and the disposition of his estate, in the sad event of his death?"

"Naturally the whole shall go to his son," he retorted impatiently.

"I meant, rather, in *default* of heirs male."

My brother stared at me, brows knit, then wheeled his horse towards Chilham without another word.

WE WERE NOT VERY GAY THAT EVENING, I CONFESS, DEspite the luxury of a house emptied of visitors and sporting-mad young gentlemen. We invited Miss Clewes to make a third at table, and toyed with the excellent fowl presented by Cook; in my lowered health and Fanny's lowered spirits, the cream soup was more to our liking. Miss Clewes shared her stories of the little girls, and the morning spent in the schoolroom, and the droll thing that Marianne had said, and how she had been obliged to deny Marianne her custard in consequence; but neither Fanny nor I were properly attending. Before the governess, who knew nothing of the day's events, we could not speak of murder or Julian Thane; but Miss Clewes's prattle allowed each of us to pursue our own unsettling thoughts: Fanny's, on the subtleties of handsome young men, about whose true proclivities no gently-reared female could presume to know anything; and I, on the hidden and deadly purposes of the human heart. We were so much abstracted that we did not devour above a fraction of the delicacies set before us, I am sure; but I comforted myself, and dosed the cold threatening to o'erwhelm my head, with Edward's delicious claret. I shall be sadly spoilt by the time I return home, and disdain the fruits of Cassandra's stillroom as not worth drinking.

"And is your papa expected this evening, Miss Knight?" Miss Clewes enquired brightly. "If you mean to wait up for him, I shall be happy to fetch my work-box, and sit with you a little in the drawing-room. Only I must first assure myself that the young ones are comfortable in the night-nursery. They will be wanting their warm milk."

Fanny coloured slightly, and looked down at her hands. "I fear that I have the head-ache, Miss Clewes. I should like to retire early. And my aunt is *most* unwell."

"Of *course* you have the head-ache!" Miss Clewes said archly. "For Mr. Finch-Hatton has left us, has he not? And it is a wonder that even little Lizzy is not drooping apace! How dull we shall be this week, to be sure, until *some other* of your beaux, Miss Knight, appear to cheer our solitude!"

The colour in Fanny's cheeks deepened. "I have no beaux, Miss Clewes, and indeed I can find little to enjoy in the society of young men," she retorted crisply. "There is a want of . . . of . . . *openness,* and much of calculated deceit, in the general run of that sex. Goodnight."

Miss Clewes looked bewildered, and curtseyed her *adieux;* I pressed her hand and shook my head warningly. Then I caught up to Fanny as she ascended the stairs with more haste than grace.

"Take care, my dear," I murmured as I kissed her cheek. "That was a speech that smacked strongly of disappointment. You should not wish to expose yourself to the ridicule of the world, for ruined hopes."

———

WHETHER FANNY FOUND SLEEP READILY ENOUGH, OR TOSSED
and turned on her unhappy bed, I was determined to wait for
Edward—and having built up my fire, and exchanged my carriage dress for a warm wrapper, I sat at the writing desk in the
Yellow Room and recorded the day's events in this journal.
The clock in the Great Hall had not long chimed the quarter-
hour past nine, when I was rewarded by the sound of approaching hooves; Edward, gone round to the stables. He
would gain the house in a few moments' time by the back
way, and no doubt summon Johncock to require his supper;
and if I knew my brother at all, he would take it in his book
room, rather than the awful majesty of the empty dining parlour.

I waited until the clock had chimed the half-hour, then
opened my door as noiselessly as possible. A glance along the
corridor revealed Fanny's white face, peeping from the doorway of her own bedchamber; she, too, was clad in a dressing
gown and slippers, and looked absurdly youthful beneath her
night cap. She hesitated an instant, then stepped into the passage and joined me, the candle she held trembling slightly in
her hand. "You intend to speak to Papa? May I come with
you?"

I might have spared her one sleepless night out of two, by
shielding her a little longer from the evils of the world; but
she was twenty, after all, and could hardly be urged back to
bed, like a child recovering from nightmare.

"Of course. I told you I valued your opinion."

We found the Magistrate devouring a plate of cold fowl
and cheese, washed down with a tankard of ale. The fire in
the book room was blazing, and he had lit several branches of
candles, as tho' he intended to work long into the night. But
there were no papers or books before him; the work, I collected, should be done entirely in his brain.

"Jane. Fanny. You ought both of you to be in bed."

"Pshaw," I returned briskly. "It is not yet ten o'clock." But the weariness in Edward's voice reminded me that he had been travelling on the London road until nearly dawn, and what little sleep he had snatched before our shared breakfast—days ago, it seemed—had long since been spent in hard riding between Chilham, Canterbury, and home.

"I am relieved to know that you were not met with pikes and broadswords at the Castle; and that they have let you go again, without demanding an exchange of hostages."

His lips quirked at this sally; but his expression of sadness did not materially change. "The family were kindness itself, and treated me with a forbearance I ought not to expect, having gaoled two of their members within the week. It was all I could do to refuse to dine with them—the mere thought was as a mouthful of ashes to me! To accept the hospitality of one of my oldest friends, when I feel myself to be the merest scrub! It was damned awkward, Jane, I do not mind saying— damned awkward, and I hope I shall never again be forced to a similar exertion of duty, however long I may live!"

"Poor Papa." Fanny perched on the edge of his desk, hope warring with anxiety in her countenance. "Did you speak to Mr. Wildman, sir? Did you learn anything to the purpose?"

"I learnt a good deal." Edward's eyes narrowed as he took his last bite of fowl, and washed it down with a draught of ale. "But nothing I learnt can hope to lighten Thane's case. If anything, it merely confirms it."

Fanny paled. "How is this?"

He gazed at her levelly. "Your aunt asked a pertinent question, my child. The one question, indeed, likely to tie Curzon Fiske's murder to that of the maid. In default of heirs male, Mr. Wildman's estate goes *not*, as I might have expected, to his brother's sons—but entirely to his young cousin, Julian Thane. Wildman told me he thought it only just to provide for Thane in the eventuality his son James predeceased him, because his nephews will richly inherit from his brother, who is an even warmer man than Wildman himself. He confided, moreover, that Wold Hall was grossly encumbered with mortgages in Thane's father's time, and cannot possibly provide the kind of income that expensive young buck requires. With his pockets entirely to let, Thane was unlikely to prove acceptable to any heiress, either—not even to our own Miss Knight, the principal young lady in the neighbourhood. The added knowledge that his mistress, Martha, was soon to present the world with a pledge of her affection, should have blasted his marriage prospects entirely."

Fanny looked about wildly, searching for reason in my countenance she could not discover in her father's. "You cannot mean to blame *me,* and any . . . interest . . . Mr. Thane might have shewn me, for the murder of that unfortunate maid?"

"Fanny! No, no, child—do not think it!" The distress in Edward's countenance was painful. "You can have nothing to do with so sordid a business!"

"But I *have* to do with it," she said tremblingly. "I encouraged Mr. Thane's attentions. Indeed, I was gratified by them. Whatever his faults—whatever his *crimes* may prove to be—he will remain in my memory as the most . . . *engaging* gentleman I have ever known."

"Dear God," Edward said.

Fanny's chin rose. "I cannot believe him capable of murder, Father. And I do not see why Mr. Wildman's Will has anything to say to the purpose! He is *not* in default of heirs male. James is perfectly well!"

"But James only narrowly escaped," I reminded her gently. "Some *one* tried to tie a noose around young Wildman's neck—by leaving his pistol near Curzon Fiske's body. Had James hanged for it, Julian Thane might expect no less than a castle—and twenty thousand a year!"

❧ CHAPTER THIRTY-THREE ❧

There's a Way

"Lo, what tricks and deceiving subtleties
Women can use! They're always busy as bees,
Buzzing and humming tales for men to believe,
And up and down, around the truth they weave. . . ."

GEOFFREY CHAUCER, "EPILOGUE TO THE MERCHANT'S TALE"

FRIDAY, 29 OCTOBER 1813

FANNY TOOK BREAKFAST ON A TRAY IN HER ROOM THIS morning, and I confess I was inclined to imitate her example, for the sleep I might have trusted to cure my tiresome cold proved elusive last night. My mind was too busy weaving and discarding theories of murder, tho' all my cherished notions had proved useless thus far. I had never met Old Mr. Wildman's nephews—they live, I believe, in London, on the fruits of the sugar trade. One is a Colonel of Hussars, or some such; the particulars do not signify. But I had taken a powerful fancy to the unknown Colonel. My intimacy with the entire Wildman family is so limited, indeed, by my infrequent journeying into Kent, that I could not be *expected* to know any real truth of them—and certainly not in what manner Old

Wildman's Will had been drawn. There is a decided fascination to the notion of the Absent Heir: the unseen hand wielding both gun butt and knife. He ought ideally to have been an expensive young man, who held his uncle's life cheap, and might be expected to remove the obstacle of his cousin James with a ruthless and cunning efficiency. I confess I had cast the Colonel—whose name, I think, is Thomas—in the rôle of chief conspirator; for a soldier, you know, will generally have a high tolerance for bloodshed, and might be depended upon for a steady shot on a night of limited moon. He might just as well have killed Curzon Fiske, and left his cousin James to swing for it.[1] The little matter of his having not the slightest reason to murder Martha Kean, I had conveniently set to one side.

It was not to be, however; Edward had blasted all my hopes of the Absent Heir with the stunning news that *Julian Thane* was the very same; and I was sick with disappointment, for Fanny's sake as much as for the ruin of my interesting ideas.

I drank the coffee the maid had brought and got out of bed, therefore, to dress myself with neatness and propriety, as befit a lady of dubious health who was determined to pay a call at Canterbury gaol.

I found my brother on the point of setting out for the town. He did not look as tho' he wished for company, but I gave him no opportunity of refusing mine.

"You can have little to say to Burbage," he observed. "It is to meet with that scoundrel that I am bound for Canterbury gaol."

---

[1] Colonel Thomas Wildman, though unacquainted with Jane Austen, would intersect the life of one of her contemporaries and fellow writers, when he purchased Newstead Abbey—ancestral home of George Gordon, Lord Byron—in 1818, for the considerable sum of £94,500. Wildman was a friend of Byron's dating from their schooldays at Harrow. —*Editor's note.*

"I have nothing at all to say to Mr. Burbage," I agreed, "other than that I prefer his countenance free of whiskers. I would speak, rather, with Adelaide MacCallister—and might profitably do so while you are closeted with the spurious solicitor. Surely you intend to release Mrs. MacCallister, now that her brother is to be held in both murders? I might convey the intelligence."

Edward looked uneasy. "I ought to do so, I know," he said at length. "But my fingers have been burnt once, Jane, in freeing Sir Davie Myrrh—had I *then* been less merciful, a deal of worry and trouble should have been saved. Mrs. MacCallister, returned to her family, might be a comfort to her mother; and that must weigh heavily with me. I am a magistrate, indeed—but I am first a father. You see how I am torn."

"Mrs. Thane sets no value on her daughter at all," I returned with asperity. "Her son is everything to her, and leaves no room for rival interest."

"Indeed? Who chuses to tell you so?"

"Twitch and his good wife, who have been observing the family forever. Recollect that Adelaide was practically raised at Chilham; her mother had no use for the girl until she turned out a beauty—and then, the excellent lady's attack upon the Marriage Mart was entirely in the cause of her *son's* prospects. She hoped Adelaide might make a brilliant match, and use her husband's fortune to save Wold Hall from the lien-holders' clutches."

"That is hardly a scheme designed to foster affection between a sister and brother," Edward mused. "The one's happiness to be sacrificed to the other's security—they might justly be forgiven for hating each other."

"And yet, their mutual cordiality appears complete. I should say rather they are united in their disdain for their mother."

"Unnatural family." Edward shuddered. "You may condole with Adelaide if you wish, Jane; but I do not envy you the task."

THE WARDEN'S DOGSBODY, YOUNG JACK, LED ME CRING-ingly to the women's quarters in the gaol, where a creature I took to be his mother, from the intimate abuse she bestowed upon him so cordially, surveyed me from head to toe.

"MacCallister?" she repeated. "Aye, we've got her, right enough—but her 'usband's with her now, and I doubt as you'll be welcome."

Feeling absurdly out of place, I proffered the woman my card. "Pray convey this to Captain and Mrs. MacCallister with my compliments. I will await an answer."

She was a massive and stone-faced creature in her middle years, with a plain cap pulled low over greasy locks of inde-terminate colour—and took the card frowningly between her fingertips. Such an one might refuse my commission for the sheer pleasure of disobliging me. With a grunt, however, she sorted among the keys that dangled from her chatelaine, and having found the one she required, made her heavy way down the corridor, slippers loosely slapping the stone flags. I was reminded by the sound of a cavalcade of dead fish. I lin-gered some moments, the boy Jack staring at me fearfully but unblinkingly.

"How old are you, Jack?"

"Dunno."

"Is that woman your mother?"

"Dunno."

I was half-listening for the slapping notice of the woman's return, and was startled nearly out of my wits when a cordial voice said, "Miss Austen. How kind of you to come."

Captain MacCallister—his honest, plain face and thatch of red hair, looming from the shadows of the passage. "If you will allow me to conduct you—Adelaide is at liberty now."

"How has she taken this dreadful news?"

"She refuses to believe her brother culpable," he said simply. "She is positive the truth will out, with time. It is the quality one so admires in Adelaide—her loyalty! She has a courage that is beyond everything!"

I was gratified to know that the Captain's ardour was undimmed by the hideous events that had attended his nuptials. "A quality you share, then, Captain—for certainly your faith in your wife has never failed."

It was difficult to see much of the countenance beside me in the torchlit corridor, but I thought MacCallister's expression changed. There was regret in his visage; and bitterness, too. "I ought to have saved her *this*. I ought to have prevented it—if only by taking the blame myself! But it could not be done—by the time I understood the danger in which she stood, the Law already had her in its grip. Any professions of mine should *then* have been dismissed, as a husband's too-willing sacrifice."

"Pray, do not berate yourself. I believe—I am almost certain—that all representations against Mrs. MacCallister's innocence are done away with. Indeed, I am convinced she shall be very soon at liberty."

He glanced at me then. "You have not understood, I fear. Adelaide shall never be free, so long as her brother's life is at issue."

I could offer the wretched man no answer; but thankfully, the prison door was nigh, and the Wardress poised to open it. The Captain bowed, and I passed before him within.

Adelaide MacCallister was standing composedly in a narrow shaft of sunlight afforded by a slit in Westgate Tower's walls. I was recalled suddenly to the high, narrow windows that lined the servants' quarters at Chilham Castle—and to her mother's austere figure, silhouetted in the passage. There could be nothing in sharper contrast to Mrs. Thane's harsh aspect than Adelaide's dark beauty; but the air of self-command was the same.

My maid did not answer my bell, she had said. *So I came in search of her.*

"Mrs. MacCallister." I dropped a curtsey. "I must offer my gratitude at your willingness to receive me. I should not have been surprized to find myself turned away, as being among your greatest enemies."

"Not at all," she said gravely. "Should you care to sit down? There is only one chair, but I am perfectly willing to stand. Indeed, I am obliged to sit so much that I grow restless—and pace and pace like a caged tiger. Pray sit, Miss Austen—if the mistress of such a shabby establishment may be allowed to protest, I *insist* you accept my meagre hospitality."

I sat, conscious of the interesting couple's eyes fixed upon me in perfect politeness, awaiting whatever I should chuse to tell them, without anxiety or fury. "I ought to say how distressed I am—how distressed my entire family is become, indeed, at the turn of events at Chilham—the arrest of your brother—but such words must fall hollowly upon your ears, when spoken by the Magistrate's sister."

"I am persuaded Mr. Knight is as mistaken in my brother's guilt, ma'am, as he has been in mine." Adelaide's eyes kindled swiftly, but as swiftly the blaze died. "I accept your good wishes in the spirit they are offered. I bear you no ill will. If that is all the burden of your visit, however—to free yourself of anxiety, in offering condolences for the fate that has overtaken my brother and me—I must ask you to accept my thanks, Miss Austen, and be gone." She swayed slightly as she stood. "You are very good—but I fear my nerves are not equal—"

Captain MacCallister supported her with his strong arm, and I rose immediately from my chair. "I will leave you in an instant, Mrs. MacCallister, if you will be so good as to answer one question."

"What is that?"

"Where does your mother's personal maid sleep, while your family is in residence at Chilham Castle?"

Adelaide stared at me in bewilderment. "Her maid? My mother employs none, Miss Austen. Our income did not permit of such luxuries. We shared the services of Martha Kean, until—" She paused, recovering herself. "Mamma was to be forced to an alteration, indeed, once the Captain and I should be married and gone—as we intended to be, a week since."

They had shared Martha's services. The thought reverberated in my head with all the force of a clanging bell. Mrs. Thane had lied, when I discovered her in the servants' quarters—because her purpose there had been to search the dead maid's room, as I myself had intended.

"Where, oh where, is my brother?" I cried, and turned to the cell door in a fever of anxiety.

"Miss Austen, are you unwell?" the Captain demanded.

"It is imperative I speak to Mr. Knight without delay!"

"You there," MacCallister called, in a voice accustomed to command. "Unlock this door at once! Miss Austen—is it possible you might save her?" he added in an undertone.

"Unquestionably. But at a cost," I warned. "I may not stay— Pray support your wife, Captain."

"God bless you," he said, as the door closed behind me.

I never felt less worthy of his words.

WE DROVE AS FAST AS TWO HORSES WHIPPED TO FROTHING-point could pull us—direct from Canterbury to Chilham, no more than half an hour on the road, at the spanking pace Edward set. Twitch was standing before the Castle door as the curricle drew up; I did not stay for Edward's assistance, but jumped down as he did.

"Your master," Edward said in a rush to the butler. "Where is he to be found?"

"In the north tower, sir," Twitch replied.

Edward was already bolting up the grand stairs, taking two at a time. I followed with as much haste as my carriage dress allowed.

CHAPTER THIRTY-FOUR

The Lady in the Tower

"Four glowing coals are all old age possesses:
Boasting, lying, anger, and greed."

GEOFFREY CHAUCER, "THE STEWARD'S PROLOGUE"

29 OCTOBER 1813, CONT.

"GOOD GOD, MAN! MUST YOU ALWAYS APPEAR WHEN YOU are *least* wanted?"

Edward drew up in dismay, his feet rooted to the floor. Old Mr. Wildman stood before a heavy oak door. His sparse white hair was in disarray, his broad face suffused with choler, and his aspect so entirely wild, as to suggest a profound disturbance of mind and temper. I had never heard him speak with such acerbity to my brother.

"I had very nearly got her to unbar the door—which she will *never* do, now you are come!" he concluded.

"You would speak of Mrs. Thane?" My voice held no little urgency. "She has secured the bolt on her chamber—she is immured within?"

"She took to her bed as soon as you were gone yesterday

e'en, and has not emerged since." Old Wildman glanced at Edward with less heat in his aspect. "I confess that I fear for her mind. This latest blow—young Julian's charge of murder—has overset her reason entirely. I know not *what* she might do in her despair . . . some dreadful violence . . ."

Behind him, as tho' animated by a spectral presence, the massive oak door swung slowly inward. A chill autumn draught, as from an opened window, swirled into the passage. I felt a finger of fear travel up my spine, and stepped impulsively forward.

"Augusta?" Old Wildman called out.

I halted in the doorway, the two men at my back.

Mrs. Thane was standing barefooted on the stone sill of the tower's great window, the leaded casements flung wide to the elements. Her grey hair was unbound and fell nearly to her ankles; she wore a linen shift, which billowed and sank like a sail in the October wind. She did not turn her head to acknowledge her audience, tho' it must have been she who admitted us, before mounting to her precarious perch.

"I am glad you are come, Mr. *Magistrate,*" she spat with bitter contempt, "that you might witness the ruin of a once-great house! *Your* hand—your overweening arrogance, your meddling in what does not belong to you—has brought misery on me and mine! But I will have my vengeance! I *curse* you, Edward Knight! May all your family be haunted by the trouble you have caused, and end, *every one,* in an early grave!"

The colour drained from my brother's face, and his lips parted as tho' to protest. But it was I who stepped forward, however tentatively, into that wind-swept room, and halted with a word the woman who might have dashed herself to the carriage sweep three storeys below.

"Fiddle," I said calmly.

Augusta Thane turned her basilisk stare upon me with an

expression of hatred so profound I felt my heart quail within me. But I took another step forward. Neither Edward nor Old Wildman dared to move, it seemed.

"Every note of tragedy has been struck by yourself, has it not, Mrs. Thane?"

"What do you know of tragedy?" she retorted, her words as venomous as her aspect.

"Enough." Another small step into the room, nearer to her position. "And I apprehend even more of the ways of murderers. How they may betray themselves by the smallest mistake. You do not possess a maid, I think, as you suggested yesterday when we met in the attic passage? —Or perhaps I should say, *No maid living*. For you cut Martha Kean's throat in the coppice, did you not, having first lured her to the place with a note penned in your son's hand?"

A groan fell from the lips of Old Wildman, but the woman who held all our gaze did not regard it; she smiled glitteringly at me, instead.

"Aye, I slit the wench's throat—and was glad to do it! In *that* I preserved the reputation of my son, at least. That she should presume to bear his child!"

"*His* hand alone should secure the girl's trust and her eager vigil in the coppice," I mused. "I imagine it was your discovery of such a note—tossed in a corner of a room or mislaid upon a table, and establishing an assignation between Mr. Julian Thane and Martha Kean—that first apprised you of their clandestine entanglement. Did you keep the slip of paper by you to *confront* Julian with your knowledge?"

"I soon found a better use," she retorted bitingly. "I never thought the idiot girl would keep the note in her pocket—I assumed she would toss it on the fire."

"Unfortunate," I agreed. "Indeed, when I consider of your every choice in the affair, you might almost have intended to hang your son."

"Never!" she cried out. "Vicious jade—my son is *all in all* to me . . . a more princely being was never born . . ."

These last words trailed off in a keening sob, and she crouched low as tho' in anguish, hugging her arms about her knees, grizzled locks trailing about her face. Her form rocked precariously on the sill. I felt rather than saw Edward start forward, as tho' to intervene, but I held up one hand. She had not told us enough—and any approach *now* might send her flying into air.

"Really?" I said wonderingly. "Why, then, did you wear your son's drab shooting coat when you murdered Martha, if not to see him hang?"

"So that the girl should take no alarum as I approached!" She spoke so rapidly, her words might almost have been gibberish. "Can you not have an idea of the beauty of it, clever Jane? I, tall as I am, striding towards the wench, the folds of the coat hiding the knife in my gloved hand—and she *flung herself into my arms to die*! Martha wanted Death. Oh, yes—she wanted Death as wantonly as a lover. Until, of course, the knife was at her throat—she turned to flee, but I had her in my grasp, I pulled back her hair and did the thing in seconds. Killing, you know, is a paltry business."

Old Wildman had sunk down into a straight-backed chair that sat near the door; I risked a glance, and saw that his head was in his hands. He should be of little use; but Edward still stood beside me. I resumed my study of the raving figure in the window.

"But as Martha struggled," I observed with as much calm as I could command, "her fingers tore at your coat, securing a loose button. And you never noticed. That was fatal to Julian, was it not? I imagine you felt some horror when you learned of your mistake. Taken in company with the incriminating note you failed to secure—it was in search of *that* you took the risk of visiting Martha's bedchamber yesterday—you may congratulate yourself, Mrs. Thane, on having thoroughly botched the business. And secured a noose around your son's neck."

"You are a *vile* creature," she whispered.

"It seems the only just return for your earlier efforts," I added serenely, "to hang young James Wildman."

"*What?*" Old Wildman sat up, his hands clenched upon his knees. "What do you say of my son, Miss Austen? What has Augusta done to James? I will be told!"

"—Only borrowed his duelling pistol to despatch Curzon Fiske." It was my brother who spoke this time, in an aside to his neighbour. "Your James stood between Julian Thane and an inheritance Mrs. Thane was determined her son must have—*your fortune*, old friend."

Spots of mottled colour stood out on Old Wildman's cheeks. His eyes sparked dangerously. "Do you mean to say that you crept out by night and *shot* poor Curzon Fiske? Good God, ma'am! To what possible end?"

"I discovered Martha in her meeting with the seaman in the back garden," Mrs. Thane said in that same rapid, maddened accent. "Adelaide had sent her. Martha was frightened. She was always afraid of *me*—and I made her divulge the whole—where Fiske meant to wait, and with what hopes. I saw how he might be used. I took James's pistol from the gun room, and when the thing was done, I left it in the churchyard. One death, after all, might bring about another."

"Or several," Edward observed. "What unnatural mother, Mrs. Thane, should willingly send *her daughter* to gaol, for a murder she did not commit, and say not *one word* to preserve that child's life and reputation?" He turned away in disgust.

"Adelaide is *nothing* to Julian!" Augusta Thane cried. "She proved as much when she disdained my counsel, and threw herself away on Curzon Fiske! Aye, might they *both* die and be damned, for the insult they served me! A thousand such should be ample sacrifice for my son!"

"And young James Wildman, as well?" I murmured.

"Good lord," Old Wildman muttered. "Of *course*. I see it now. Would that I had cut my tongue out, before I said aught of my intentions! It was too vast a temptation for you, Augusta. I never dreamt, you know, that anything would ever *happen* to James, and make Julian my heir—simply meant it as a kindness to you, and a mark of my concern for all your family. What a fool I've been!"

"Julian *deserves* your fortune!" Mrs. Thane flashed. "He was born to it. Anyone who saw my son and yours, standing side-by-side, should immediately know which *ought* to be the other's master! Julian, so noble, so elegant in every aspect, his mind informed and his manners the equal of the Great—to be . . . *usurped in his degree,* by a cousin with nothing more to recommend him than an amiable air and the fortunate accident of *birth*!"

"Augusta," Old Wildman said warningly. "Don't say what you'll regret. Come down from that window like a sensible woman, now."

A sensible woman? I glanced at Edward, appalled.

And at that moment, Augusta Thane began to laugh.

It was a hideous and chilling peal of merriment, all the more terrible for being utterly free of hysterics. I would swear that Mrs. Thane was not mad, but as sane as I am—and that it was the Devil she saw, advancing across the room in the form of my brother, to lift her down from the window.

As the thought entered my mind in one blazing instant, she stepped forward into air, her gaze fixed upon the sky—and still laughing, was gone.

CHAPTER THIRTY-FIVE

Exit Dancing

". . . *be pleased*
That neither of you lies dead or about to be seized
And imprisoned. Thus we'll reach the end of this road."

GEOFFREY CHAUCER, "THE KNIGHT'S TALE"

THURSDAY, 11 NOVEMBER 1813

AND SO I AM COME AT LAST TO THE CLOSE OF MY TWO months at Godmersham, and my interesting sojourn among the rich and contented folk of Kent—who have provided unexpected matter for study, and enlivened with their prevarications and poses the essential folly of my fictitious Emma. I have found occasion, during the relative peace of the past fortnight (which encompassed only one concert, one bout of unexpected houseguests, an intimate dinner for fourteen at Chilham Castle, and a *third* expedition to Canterbury gaol in the Magistrate's company), to turn once more to that bewitching creature of my own invention—who, tho' full twenty years of age and the mistress of her father's establishment, is utterly unlike my own dear Fanny. Emma is happy and vain, secure and carefree, bossy and endearing; while Fanny—Fanny, I fear, has been crossed in love, and in a manner likely to blight her future for some time to come. She is less cheerful, less active, less given to sudden quirks of humour—and more melancholy in her looks when she believes herself unobserved. In short, she recalls to mind another girl of twenty, whose first attachment proved to be less than she had dreamt—myself, in the aftermath of my beloved Tom Lefroy's abandonment.

If I might have spared Fanny this pain—! I, who know too well the black despair of disappointed hopes—! But I should then have spared her Life, in all its desperate striving; and I would not have Fanny miss a particle of real feeling that comes in her way. She will be a better woman, I daresay, for having endured the heartbreak of Julian Thane.

He left the country with his sister and her husband the morning after our final dinner at Chilham, which—tho' awkward enough—served as a useful coda to the unhappy events that had bound the two households. No mention was made of the hateful woman whose desperate last act of self-murder, had at least been accompanied by a full letter of confession, signed and dated in her hand. In this, Augusta Thane succeeded in saving both her children—not merely with the sacrifice of her neck, but in the explicit details of each mortal act she had accomplished: the shooting of Curzon Fiske on the side-path near St. Lawrence churchyard, and the brutal slaughter of Martha Kean. Her account was at once so thorough, and so entirely without remorse, as to convince any reader of its veracity, and clear all suspicion of *others* from the Magistrate's and coroner's minds. The happy release of Mrs. MacCallister that very evening, at which I assisted, was the sole episode on which my brother Edward might congratulate himself; and the earnest hand he offered both the lady and her husband, and the manner in which he *then* expressed all his joy in Adelaide's deliverance, may be taken as evidence of his previous misery at the progress of the affair.

And so the folk of Godmersham had accepted Old Mr. Wildman's invitation to dine, as a gesture of thanks and expiation; we had gone to Chilham, and canvassed the hopeful future of the MacCallisters—their expected travels in Cornwall; their brother's decision to join them on their wedding-journey; the Captain's hopes of his duties on the Marquis of Wellington's staff; the likelihood of Buonaparte's defeat, now that the French were crippled from their exploits in Russia. Fanny endeavoured throughout the whole, to appear as tho' she had not a care in the world, and knew nothing of the true history of poor Martha Kean. Julian Thane, for his part, was sombre and grave. He was much given to staring earnestly at my niece with his smouldering dark eyes; but she was at pains never to be alone with him—from a kind of cowardice, I imagine, at what might have been said. Fanny has learnt caution, at an age when I should have wished her to study romance—and I cannot help but be sorry for it.

This evening, however, she seems determined to forget her troubles—and is even now under my eye, dancing the waltz with Mr. Finch-Hatton at the final Canterbury ball of the Autumn Season. They make a striking pair as they circle the floor, Fanny glowing in her cream-coloured silk, and Jupiter every inch the Bond Street Beau—his golden locks brushed in fashionable disorder, his silk knee-breeches fine enough for Almack's. Fanny will never have Jupiter for a husband, I am sure—but he will serve to increase her consequence at such affairs, and silence the chatter of the Impertinent. I do not fear of *his* heart suffering in the pursuit—or at least, of his betraying it. Jupiter shall lounge to the very end, and no doubt set a Fashion among his intimates.

"You are looking very well tonight, Miss Austen," observed Mr. Tylden, as he bowed and offered me a glass of lemonade. "I do admire that wine-coloured silk—as I must have told you on a previous occasion."

I smiled my thanks at the clergyman. For a simple man, Mr. Tylden has performed his duty nobly—in having twice married the same couple without reproach, and having buried in rapid succession the lady's first husband, *and* her mother. Mrs. Thane's rites were unattended, I fear, and her coffin placed in unconsecrated ground—but of this, *too little* cannot be said.

"You are to leave us, I apprehend?" Mr. Tylden enquired.

"I go to my brother Henry's, in London, on the Monday," I replied.

"Then we must hope to see you often again in Kent," he said. "I wonder—may I have the honour of this dance?"

My gaze was on Edward—who was standing alone, supporting one wall of the Canterbury Assembly Rooms, that perpetual lost look upon his face; and my heart went out to him. So many distinguished ladies circling the floor, with an eye to his handsome countenance and distinguished bearing—so many glittering neighbours who wished him happy—and Edward remained enthralled to his enchanting ghost. Like Fanny, he did not love readily, or give up his heart without a fight. But as I studied my brother, he caught my eye, and his melancholy softened a little.

I turned to Mr. Tylden.

"You are very kind. But perhaps we may defer the pleasure until I am next in Kent? I am promised to my brother for this dance."

I made my way through the breathless whirl of the ballroom and raised my glass to Edward's. It was only lemonade, after all—but it would serve.

"To the future," I said.

He studied my countenance. "After all you have seen in recent weeks, of the folly and bitterness of mankind, you still cherish hopes of *the future*, Jane?"

"I do." I searched for Fanny's face among the waltzing couples; she was more animated in Jupiter's company this evening than I had observed her in days. "For what else do we live, Edward—but our hopes of joy to come?"

ACKNOWLEDGMENTS

Since 1995, the Jane Austen Mystery series has been shaped and sustained by the genius of one person—Kate Burke Miciak, Editorial Director of Bantam Books. Kate was the first to recognize the possibilities of *Jane and the Unpleasantness at Scargrave Manor,* and her support for the series over the subsequent sixteen years and eleven novels has been unflagging. Janeites everywhere owe her a debt of gratitude; mine is one I can never repay.

Editors Caitlin Alexander and Randall Klein have patiently lent their expertise to this author through numerous books, with a control of temper that would have astounded our Jane.

Susan Corcoran—an enthusiastic Janeite if ever there was one—promoted the series in its early years, then handed the baton to Sharon Propson and Lisa Barnes, crack publicists who constantly found ingenious ways to win readers' attention.

Borrowing Jane's voice and idiom is a tricky business, particularly for an American born two centuries too late, and without Kelly Chian's deft supervision of copyedits—and her staff's ability to catch every one of my egregious errors—these books would not have withstood the rigorous test of the critics' eye. Thank you for saving me from myself.

Finally, Bantam's art department spearheaded the commission of some pretty glorious cover art. Knowing Jane's delight in frivolous dress, I'm sure she approves.

Stephanie Barron
Denver, Colorado
May 2011

ABOUT THE AUTHOR

STEPHANIE BARRON is the author of the standalone historical suspense novels *A Flaw in the Blood* and *The White Garden,* as well as the Jane Austen mystery series. As Francine Mathews, she is the author of several novels of espionage, including *The Alibi Club.* She lives in Denver, Colorado.